WHEN THE DEAD ARE RAZED

SAMUEL MARTIN

When the Dead are Razed

~ A Novel ~

WHEN THE DEAD ARE RAZED
A Novel

Slant Books
P.O. Box 60295
Seattle, WA 98160

www.slantbooks.com

HARDCOVER ISBN: 978-1-63982-067-2
PAPERBACK ISBN: 978-1-63982-066-5
EBOOK ISBN: 978-1-63982-068-9

Cataloguing-in-Publication data:

Names: Martin, Samuel

Title: When the dead are razed. / Samuel Martin.

Description: Seattle, WA: Slant Books, 2021.

Identifiers: ISBN 978-1-63982-067-2 (hardcover) |ISBN 978-1-63982-066-5 (paperback) | ISBN 978-1-63982-068-9 (ebook)

Subjects: LCSH: Thriller — Suspense. | Murder — Newfoundland and Labrador — Fiction. | Canadian fiction (English) — 21st century.

Classification: PR9199.4.M3627 W44 2021. (paperback) | PR9199.4.M3627 W44 2021. (ebook)

10/13/21

For Liam, Micah, Charlotte, and Emberly.

There will be times when it feels like the world has turned on you
and all you will want to do is lock yourself away from it.
In those times, do everything you can to stay open.
Be brave. Love deeply.

~ 1 ~

ONE TEQUILA, TWO TEQUILA, three tequila, floor.
The dance floor.

More mosh pit, really. The Skuzzcuts thrashing their instruments on stage, ear-bleedingly loud and record-cut tight—beer splashing everywhere. Not a bad place to hide.

Teffy shoulders into the hair-tossing crowd, boyfriend Ger in tow. It's Ger she's trying to hide, though he doesn't know it yet. And what would he do if he did? Order another round and start trashing himself defiant? Say, "Give me the number, Tefs, and I'll tell the fucker where he can meet me!" Like this is the Old West or something.

She knows she can wear him down to halfway reasonable if she keeps him on the tequila and moshing all night. Hungover and wore out is the only way to approach this sort of conversation with him, really. Only way to tell him that Troy Hopper—his ex-boss and St. John's most notorious meth king—is out of Her Majesty's Penitentiary on early release and creep-texting her on her work phone.

Ger must know Troy is out. That shouldn't come as a shock.

No, it's Troy texting that'll tick him off.

Ger bumps up against her and she pulls him in with her hand in his back pocket. Wonders what exactly Hopper is trying to start now that he's out. The rank dealer just served six years for arson and possession-with-the-intent-to-distribute. Far cry from the murder charge Ger pressed for, but so things go. She's seen enough of the courts to know that.

Ger leans in—to kiss her, she thinks—but says he's going for more shots, and she yells, "Go on then!" and shoves him off, the double kick drums frothing the crowd wild as the Skuzzcuts break into the next song.

Ger disappears toward the bar and Teffy starts head-banging, whipping her red hair wet as she works up to the pace of her Wing Chun sessions.

Martial arts have made moshes strange comforts rather than panic-attacks-in-the-making. It's a relief to know she can separate a guy's shoulder if need be. Loosens the knots in her neck as she jumps against the floor's stick, shirt slick as she throws herself at the singer's spit:

> *Bring it on! come on come on!*
> *Bring it on! come on come on!*
> *Bring it on—you fuck—come on!*

And she does, telling herself to channel it—channel the fear. Fight to make something of it. Like she used to when she'd wedge herself between the local gang of stump-faced homophobes and her best friend Fin. Him the chopping block for blunt jokes about his sexuality, being the only openly gay kid in Placentia at the time. And what did he get for being himself? Hatchet-jobbed by zit-lipped morons.

By his own dad.

The bruises on his throat why he started wearing those fancy neck scarves. "A bit of personal flourish," he said. "To keep people from asking the wrong questions." And to piss his dad off at the same time. Save some trouble, make some trouble, they'd say—and seeing those bruises, the way Fin winced when she touched his sides, made her want to make some trouble for his old man. "You know what your dad deserves?" she said.

She falters now, drops the beat. Lost a second in that recollection of Fin with blood on his hands. In his father's stage. He locks eyes with her. Wide eyes. Screaming eyes. And she stumbles in the crowded bar. The knife still buried in his dad's chest. Second degree murder charge. Steady *thud thud thud*. Three years in custody. For the blood on the floor. And the bruises? What about them? Deep-bass heartbeat—double kick drum—her pulse jacked and Fin's dad limp at their feet. Last kick of his leg. Sirens screaming like a soloed guitar.

"Go on!" Fin yells. "Go on!"

Strobing cherries. Dancefloor lights.

"Go on!" someone yells.

But it's not Fin. She's knocked some guy on the dance floor and he's telling her to get lost. "Go on!" he yells, thinking her a drunken mess, red hair pasted to her sweaty face.

She elbows past him and presses deeper into the throng, away from the angry prick—the memory of Fin dragging after her like a net. They trucked him off to Her Majesty's here in *Sin* John's. And she followed him. Studied journalism at the university so she could visit him every week. But she never managed to make a single visit. And why was that? Not one visit in his three years before being paroled. And now he's out in Corner Brook. Eight hours away and on the other side of the island—the other side of the goddamned world, for all she's seen him.

To start over, he wrote in a parting email.

Bouncing, she sees Ger through the pasty-faced crowd, down by the bar and chatting it up—six shots by his splayed hands. He tosses one back, then another. Tattooed arms gesturing. Inked sleeves she's come to love. Like she used to love getting drunk with Fin by the old military base in Argentia, spread-eagled on a cracked runway leading nowhere. Heads together and sharing an iPod. Listening to grunge-hop. Like the band harshing the crowd now. Fin's face tequila-hot and happy, the familiar bottle rolling empty between them.

To curb her drinking since, she's turned to martial arts as a kind of therapy. Calculated power shots against everyone that would ever make a sacred heart like Fin feel small. *Never again,* she thinks, thrashing herself livid on the dance floor—slamming the door shut on that bloody night. "Never again!" she screams into the music, the whole time running—running in her mind—running like her whole world is on fire.

> *Bring it on! come on come on!*
> *Bring it on! come on come on!*
> *Bring it on*

An arm tightens around her, rough hand squeezing her chest and a hot body presses into her, belt buckle thrust into her backside. She stomps down on the foot behind her, hears a sharp "Fuck!" in her ear, and the arm around her chest loosens enough for her to elbow-crack the jaw of the guy holding her. He staggers back a step, grabs her shirt's neckline, and yanks—and she hacks down on his arm as she pivots and punches his throat with her other hand.

She's loose of him now, tight space between them. Chest-punches him twice and sees his winded shock. Then his fist hammers down and she blocks the clumsy blow. Grabs his shirt, yanks sharply, and kicks sideways through his bent kneecap.

He drops. Eyes empty shot glasses.

She steps back.

The music scratches out and every eye turns on her. Including the two bouncers she knows—Tim and Kevin—who are dragging the guy to his feet now and asking her what the hell happened. Then Ger is back from the bar and in six snapped seconds they're outside, Kevin phoning an ambulance while Tim holds the groper upright. Tim nods them on down the street—"Better get going," he says—and the guy in his arms starts yelling: "That's her! That's the bitch that broke my fuckin knee!"

And she hears Tim tell the guy to shut-up.

"You fuckin slipped, man."

The rest of the night is dance after dance, bar after bar—hip-hop to Irish rock to pop chart country line dancing with a Bud Light in each hand for balance. Yee-haw! Either go full on or go home, Ger says on nights like these. So they go for it, as you would, thumping through to the wee hours in the back room of a closed-down bar owned by somebody Ger knows—Ger leaning into those gathered around the table, telling the story of her kicking that guy's ass. Telling it over and over again. His thin face more beautiful the more he talks—the more she drinks.

There's something special between them.

Fucked-up, sure, but . . . special, right?

They're finally turned out of the bar at 5 a.m.—a new day cracking—and they begin the long climb to their place on Merrymeeting, over the hill in Rabbittown.

"Could call Vinney," Ger says as they cross Duckworth.

"You gotta walk it off, Stuckless. Come on."

She slings her arm into Ger's, preferring the wind-sucking climb ahead to the manky back of Vinnie Coles's cab. The cab is bad enough but it's more Vinnie himself. Vinnie has been Ger's buddy since childhood, but as far as Teffy is concerned he's a shit dad to his kid, and his business isn't one she wants to support. Hence the call to Gulliver's at the start of the night.

The two of them press on and climb steep streets and staircases, staggering against each other until they're about ready to collapse on Carter's Hill. Sucking wind, Ger nods to the alley they often use as a breath-catcher. An alley he's shown her before, with a dumpster they hop to springboard onto a low roof.

"Steady on," she says and grabs his hand and pulls him up onto a higher roof from which they can see all of St. John's and straight through the Narrows to the Atlantic beyond.

They settle down. Second time up here in less than a month. But it's warmer this time: both of them beat-out. Ger lays back on the shingles, his boots crossed just shy of the eave, and Teffy fixes on the rising sun. Tequila makes her mildly apocalyptic on the best of days. But this morning—her tipsy on the edge of this rooftop—it's all blood and fire, the whole sky smoldering. Sun rising in deep, wet fog like God's own burning face—a mammoth sea urchin's writhing underbelly, bright rays spiking a bloody crown of thorns. Blindingly bright and rising now. Up . . . up out of the deep—and it's humid out.

Jesus, it's hot already. "Gonna be a rare choker today," Ger mutters. And she takes in their hilltop view of the port town crowded around the harbor's tabletop, rowhouses leaning into each other like friends in love after a dumpster-night's binge.

"Never seen steam rise off roofs like that," she says.

"Like what?" he says, his eyes still closed.

"Like the whole shabby city is on fire."

"Wouldn't be the first time, would it?"

"Or the last," she says. "Wrath of God when the whole place goes up again."

"Poof," he says. "Like that fister you dropped on the dance floor, hey?"

"He shouldn't have groped me," she says.

"Sure he realizes that now."

"Do you think I actually broke his knee?"

He whistles off a long belch. "Looked broke."

She nudges his knee with her red shoe, and he takes a hand from behind his head and fumbles for one of her belt loops. Tries to pull her down but finds it easier to pull himself into a sitting position. *Eyes like piss holes in a snowbank*, she thinks as he squints against the early morning light. He closes his eyes and wobbles close to the edge and she catches him. Says, "Sit back a bit, will you?" And he lies back down on the damp shingles.

"You any further on that artist story?" he says.

"Her name is Ellie Strickland."

"So the story's done?"

She sighs. "For a story like this, it takes time. To build trust."

"Thought this Ellie Strickland was building the trust and you were just getting a scoop on her." He hiccups and flutters his eyes. "Is your artist missus not shacked up with Markus O'Shea?" He winces and swallows heartburn. "Big enviro-tourist guy?"

"I knows who Markus O'Shea is," she says.

"So what's the story?"

"There is no story."

"There's always a story," he says. "If you dig for it."

She eyeballs Ger, flat-out on his back, and remembers shagging him a few weeks ago. Up here on this very roof. A joyful, slow, sunrise fuck and naught but frostbit knees for regret. That and Ger's shingle-scraped ass.

Poor boy.

"What'll happen," Ger mutters, "if the glammy literals—"

"Liberals you mean?"

He burps. "What if Markus O'Shea turns out to be none better than that orange jizztrumpet south of the border?"

"A world on fire," she says—and it feels it today.

A taxi climbs Carter's Hill next to them and she sees the car's rust-rimmed pink and wonders if it's Vinney's ride. It's a Skimpy cab at any rate, Troy Hopper's old company. Unless he kept control of it when they shut him away in Her Majesty's by the lake.

Ger makes a snoring sound and she says, "You awake?" nudging his boot.

"Only if you wants to climb aboard, missus."

"Should be gettin down, shouldn't we?"

He peers beyond his boots and sniffs at the glaring sun. Closes his eyes against it. Five more minutes, that means. She hugs her knees, hoping the heat today will burn off the chill she's been feeling since that text from her friend at the courthouse.

She looks at Ger, sprawled out like he hasn't a care in the world. Like the world for him will go on regardless. "Did you ever bring Teresa up here?" she asks. Ger's dead girlfriend, for some reason, has been crowding her thoughts since breaking that guy's knee. By all accounts Teresa was as feisty as Teffy—*and more,* Teffy thinks, *if Ger's stories are halfway true.*

He says, "Are you thinking about her 'cause Troy's out?"

So he knows. "Well?"

He crosses his arms, eyes still closed—thinking what, she can't tell. Teresa is Ger's lockbox, though. Whenever she comes up, he clamps down.

Latch and click—and we're done now.

Probably still has a thing for her, she thinks. *And why not?* They grew up together. Teresa: the childhood friend-turned-girlfriend. Taught Ger how to siphon gas into tin cans they'd blow up on empty streets. Like this one. He's told her how Teresa used to bum smokes from old fellas at the corner store with this wink and nod. Fourteen years old and she could make you cough up what you didn't have. Caught Troy Hopper's eye, anyhow, and the old sleeveen offered her a job. Her and Ger both. Weed and pills at first, then E. Then heavier shit. Her sampling, then snatching and short-changing. "Strung-out stupidity," Ger said.

And it was Ger that found her overdosed in an alley. With belt-burns around her neck. Seven years ago that was. And that's when he flipped.

Sold Troy out for a plea bargain and a chance to jump free of the drag-net lifestyle drowning him.

Teffy job-shadowed the reporter who covered the trial—her first post-college gig—and after Troy's sentencing, Ger asked her out. Out of the gray and with this swagger she liked. Confident—God, he was cocky—but quiet too, and brooding. Like Fin.

"Is it another bottle of wine, you want?" Ger asks.

"Don't be a dick," she says.

Three years into their relationship, she'd put it to him: asked if she was the rebound girl after Teresa. But Ger didn't say, did he? Only bought her a top shelf bottle of wine with a note taped to the label. *To another 3 years*, it said.

"'Cause I can get you another bottle," he says.

"Are you not worried?"

He squints at her. "Troy's not stupid."

"But he *is* out."

"And?"

"You testified against him."

He shrugs. "Didn't get nearly what he deserved."

She looks away from him, from the thought of his head smashed-in and blood trickling down the shingles here. *Drip, drip, drip.* "But does he think you deserve something in kind?"

"I'm in the public eye now," Ger says. "And so is Troy. If he wants to get back to business, he'll keep a low profile. It's all about the payoff for him. He'll keep to himself."

Will he though? She wants to say this, but doesn't. Squeezes her phone instead, and thinks of the texts she got yesterday.

You must be Ger's new thing. Tell him I said hi.

Who is this? she shot back.

But all she got was a winky face.

So when the Skimpy cab ghosted slowly past their house last night, she figured it was Hopper and pulled Ger out from under his laptop, nudged her knee between his legs and said coyly, "Take me dancing, will you?" The downtown like a table to hide under. He'd have jumped her then, she could tell. But she piled him into a Gulliver's Cab and they headed out to hear the Skuzzcuts—the new local grunge-hop group Ger's into.

Out all night, as they do from time to time, and this their sober-up stop before the last hill home. And what'll she find at home? A note in the mail slot? A smashed window maybe? Troy Hopper at their kitchen table?

Hopper never struck her as subtle. More an old school fuck-you kind of dealer. Run straight at you till you swerved or hit him head on. Then what? What would it look like to run headlong at Troy Hopper? Call him out and see if he. . . .

What? See if he what?

She hasn't mentioned the texts to Ger, but thinks Troy likely got her number off *The Miscreant* website—the online news rag she and Ger started after he'd served his brief sentence. But why her? Both their numbers are posted to the site, so why her number and not Ger's? Especially if Troy is after some kind of revenge. It's the fear of revenge that's got her on edge. But what can he really do? *Couldn't you just corner him?* she thinks. *Ask some hard questions. Take a proper run at him: a little fuck-you-too-buddy.* It's not hope exactly, but next door to it. A slight lift. Buzzing in her gut. Daring. Maybe there'll be something more besides.

Won't know if she doesn't get close.

She can do that, she tells herself. Dropped that fucker last night and him twice her size. What's he to an old rustfart like Troy? No, Hopper should be easy enough to handle. Especially if he's as toothless now as Ger claims. Only one way to get that story, though. Run straight at him. Don't back down. Don't blink—*come on, you fuck, come on.*

She finds the winky face and sends a message back:

Ger wants to talk. Tonight.

She looks straight at the blazing sun then—long enough she can still see its burning orb when she shuts her eyes. Sees that same sunspot all the way home, slugging against the tequila she threw back before leaving the bar—sun shocking now and hot enough to split the rocks.

~ 2 ~

BARELY A BREATH OF WIND as they approach their place on Merrymeeting. No drifting chip bags or rolling cans in the gutters, which is strange for this town. Teffy checks her phone and sees a message from Ellie Strickland.

Do you have time to meet today?

"Maybe after lunch?" she speaks-to-text and sends.

Ger pats his pockets for keys. "Who's after lunch?"

"The artist." She looks past him to the house, searching for signs of break-in. Their place looks . . . shitty. But otherwise unmolested. Chipped paint on the clapboard, cinderblock stoop, and that red Folger's can by the door, half filled with Dougie's spent butts.

No apparent break-in, but she still starts when Ger steps up to the door and makes to twist the knob. She grabs his arm and he glances back at her. "What?" She points at the Folger's tin—at the wisp of smoke rising from it. "Dougie must've come by," he says.

"Try the door," she mouths. "But quiet."

He does and says, "It's locked . . . still."

She takes a deep breath and glances again at the front window. Not broken or jimmied. The door is still locked. That's good. It's all good. Troy's not here and that's not his smoke in the can. Stop thinking on it.

But why would Dougie be by this early? He's never up before noon.

"So," Ger says, "can we go in now?"

She blinks. Just business as usual. No drug lord lying in wait. Deep breath. "You gonna call Larry back about the LSPU line-up this month?"

"I'm gonna sleep off a hangover," he says, "*then* I'll call Larry. And you?" He turns the key in the lock. "What are you gonna do?" The door swings in and . . . *nothing.*

She breathes deep. "Think I'll spend some time editing Ellie's memoir."

"Your artist lady?"

"Yeah," she says, and they walk into the house. Ger heads to the kitchen and Teffy follows and leans against the counter, not minding the look of Ger's ass in those jeans as he reaches for a glass in the cupboard. He runs the tap cool, swigs a glassful, then grabs a fork from the drawer and goes hunting in their half-empty fridge for something salty. Comes out with a pickle on his fork and a chunk of cheese in hand, torn right off the block.

"Could've used a knife," she says as he gnaws at the cheese.

"Is the memoir any good?"

"Haven't really got into it yet." She turns to the living room and jumps. "Jesus, Dougie!" she yells at the figure sprawled on the couch. "How did you get in here?"

"Through your bedroom window," Dougie says, the crotch of his sweatpants stretched between splayed knees—ball cap cockeyed on his head.

"You crawled through our bedroom window?" She flicks on the lights—and Dougie pulls a hand out of his pants to shield his squinting eyes.

"What?" he says. "Your door was locked."

She grabs a book off the coffee table and wings it at Dougie, clipping the hand he holds up to shield his face. "The fuck?" he yells, rubbing his nose.

"A locked door's not an invite to go through our bedroom window." She grabs another book off the end table and heaves it at him.

Dougie scrambles to his feet. "You're fuckin nuts!"

"You went through my drawers, didn't you?" She reaches for another book but finds an empty wine glass.

"Easy now!" and he's smirking. Doing that *calm down* gesture with his hands. She hates when guys do that. "Don't worry," he says, "I put the cock ring back under the *Kama Sutra*."

The wine glass explodes on the wall by his head.

"Geez!" he shrieks. "It was a joke, okay!"

Ger hands her a hefty hardback and she heaves it at Dougie's face, but he blocks the blow with his wrist. "Christ!" he yells. "You broke my fuckin hand!"

"Why'd you break into our house?" she says.

And Dougie looks from her face to Ger's to the books in both their hands. "Alright! Fuck. I just thought it was safer in here than out in the fuckin street with Troy Hopper cruising by in his fuckin cab, alright!"

"You saw Troy?" Ger's eyes narrow.

"Casing your place, man. He gave me the cock-and-boom and I booked it."

Teffy looks at Ger. "The cock-and-boom?"

"The finger pistol," Ger says, blowing faux smoke off his fingertip.

"So," Teffy says, less than impressed, "he pointed his *finger* at you and you ran?"

"It's fuckin Troy Hopper!"

"You didn't know he was out?" says Ger.

"What do you mean 'out'? Since when did he get parole?"

"Early release."

"And *you're* not worried?" Dougie cradles his wrist. "If he's after anyone it's *you*, man. You owe him six years—you, Critch, and Moffet. Dad too!"

"If he wants to find me I'll be here. Writing his obituary."

Teffy smiles at that—flush of pride in her cheeks—but she wonders what Ger is actually willing to do to make good on that threat.

"All I know," says Dougie, "is he saw me. But he was looking for you."

Ger squints. "How do you know he was looking for me?"

"'Cause he said to say hi."

"Hi?"

"Yeah, hi."

Like the text, she thinks. *Intimidation tactics? Or full-on threat?*

"If you testify to that," Ger says, "then I can have him charged with harassment. Violating the terms of his release."

"I don't know if you fuckin heard what I said, yo." Dougie looks from Ger to Teffy and back to Ger. "This is Troy fucking Hopper. I'm not saying *anything* to *anyone*, let alone a cop or a fuckin lawyer. You know what my dad would do to me? No way!"

"I can still quote you as saying you saw him case my place," says Ger.

"So you're gonna write this up?" Teffy says and sees Ger's neck muscles tense.

"Tonight," Ger breathes. "Right now I'm gonna sleep."

"Can you *please* just keep my name out of it?" Dougie pleads. "Please."

"If he's reading us online," Teffy says, thinking of that winky face text and how Troy likely got her number, "then he knows you've already been talking."

Dougie's face pales. "You mean that shit you put online for the group home story?"

They both nod, and Dougie looks like he's gonna be sick. He pulls out his phone and stumbles past them, dialing a number.

"Dougie," she calls after him.

But he gives her the finger and elbows out the front door, phone to his ear now. "Dad!" he barks. "Can you pick me up on Merrymeeting? Yes, it's fuckin urgent!" Then he storms off down the street. She's about to close the door when Vinnie pulls up in his pink cab.

He rolls down his window and says, "You seen Dougie?"

She points him on down the street, and Vinnie is about to pull out but she says, "He's upset because Troy Hopper is out."

"Hopper's out is he?"

"Yeah," Teffy says. "And he told Dougie to pass a message on to Ger."

Vinnie leans out his window a bit. "What kind of message?"

"He said to say hi."

"Hi?"

"Yeah."

Vinnie shakes his head. Says, "Fuckin kid."

"He's scared for you and Ger," she says. "And your buddies."

"My buddies?"

"Critch and Moffet."

"He's a paranoid little prick," Vinnie says—and Teffy hates the way he talks about his son, even if she sometimes feels the same way about Dougie. She's never heard Vinnie say a good word about his kid. Not even when Dougie has run some errand for him. And Vinnie's errands are usually just south of legal, according to Dougie. "If the kid asks you for money," Vinnie says, "tell him it had better be to pay off what he owes me." He spits out his window and pulls out, heads down the street after his son.

Teffy pulls the door shut and turns to Ger. "You're seriously gonna write up that Troy's harassing you?"

"If he's gonna push, I'm gonna push back."

"But shouldn't you—"

"What? Let him get away with it?"

"Get away with it?" she says. "Are we talking him taking a run at you or is this Teresa again?" She sees him fight the eye roll. "That's it, isn't it? It's her you're thinking of right now."

"As opposed to you bringing her up earlier?"

"Fighting him won't bring her back, Ger."

He takes a step at her sudden and she meets him. Eye to eye. For a second she's back in that fish stage with Fin, his dad dead on the wooden floor: "Just go," he says. "Go on!"

Ger blinks. So mad his hands are shaking. And she wants to slap or maybe hug him, hold those hands still or push him away. Hug him like he's helpless. She doesn't know what she wants in that shivering moment, but wonders if he would feel this for her.

"I'll fight him," Ger says.

"If you're using *The Miscreant*," she says, "you gotta get more on him."

"Oh?"

"If you jab back now, he knows he spooked you. It's as much a mental game as anything. You know that from the trial."

He takes a deep breath, steps back, and sags against the wall. "I just. . . ."

"You just gotta prove that he's into *something*. Something he can be put away for. For more than six years."

He looks at her as if to say: Like what?

"Whatever it is," she says, "we'll find it, and we'll break that story. Together." She dips her head to catch his eye. "That's why we got into this, didn't we? You and me? This online paper? To tell the stories not getting told. To give people without a voice some say in the world." He looks away, and she touches his face. Feels him press his chin into her palm. A quiver—like he might cry. "We might even give *her* a voice one day." *Teresa.* "We just can't let Hopper rattle us." And she knows in that instant that she'll do whatever it takes to put Troy away again. Put him away or put him down, she doesn't care. She'll do it.

For Ger and for Teresa—for herself.

She'll write that story.

Her phone buzzes and she pulls it out to see the message from that unknown number: *I'll send a cab.* She quick-texts an *ok*.

"Who's that?" Ger says on his way to the couch.

"Just mother," she lies.

Ger flops on the couch and rests an arm over his eyes, his fingers brushing lightly the strings of his electric guitar. "Tell her to come over for Sunday dinner," he mutters. "And remind her to bring the dinner if she wants something edible."

"Thanks," she says, sarcasm thick as the bacon grease in their cast iron pan.

"We're neither of us cooks, missus."

"The burned soup?"

"Seriously, how do you burn soup?"

"Just sleep," she says.

"You're good at other things," he murmurs, drifting off—and she pulls the curtain to look at the sunlit street—a rarity in this town. She checks the weather app on her phone, though, and sees, with some dark satisfaction, that offshore clouds will be scudding in by midday. She clicks back to what she believes is Hopper's text: *I'll send a cab.* Good. Though she has no idea what she's going to say to him when he shows up here.

Her phone buzzes in her hand and she looks to see another message from Ellie Strickland. *Can you maybe meet now? At the gallery?*

~ 3 ~

ELLIE'S GALLERY IS A CONVERTED warehouse downtown. Two stories with studio spaces on the first floor and the main show space upstairs, accessible by a narrow set of stairs and a rickety old lift. Teffy takes the lift, fishing her phone from her satchel to see if there's a message. But there's nothing. Not from Ger. And not from that unknown number. Just a reminder to pay her cellphone bill, which she forwards to Ger as the lift clatters to a rough stop.

She half expects the lift's floor to give way as she *screaks* open the metal gate and gasps at the slack-jawed whale leaping toward her.

A ghost fish, she sees—suspended from the ceiling's exposed pipes.

"I was gonna crotchet the whole hide," Ellie Strickland says from across the room. "But do you know how expensive yarn is?" The older woman smiles, short gray hair gel-spiked, face stark as the cinderblock room.

Teffy runs a hand over the rough greenish-blue wool, past the ragged edge to the molded chicken wire that gives the whale its lifelike shape.

"I likes it half finished." This from another woman blowing on a cup of hot tea. Light-wisped steam tickles the woman's chin, and Ellie introduces her as Marjorie Petty.

"And this," Ellie says to Marjorie, "is the Teffy Byrne I was telling you about."

Teffy walks the length of the breeching whale to shake Marjorie's tattooed hand, and says to Ellie, "This is quite a departure from the last show." She spies a great wad of netting balled-up inside the beast's belly. The kind of net her father used on his boat before he took the linesman job with Newfoundland Power in '92, just before they closed the cod fishery.

"They'll say I still have an old-time whale fetish." Ellie runs a hand over the spiny tips of her gelled hair. "There's this one guy calls me Old Sculpin online."

"Is the whale to scale?" Teffy asks.

"Had to quarter-size it to fit."

"Quarter-sized?" Teffy takes in the length of the creature and whistles. "You've measured a live one, have you?"

Ellie takes a deep breath. "You've read the book on it, sure. *Lured to Slaughter* by Ken Barry. About killing the whale down by St. Mark's. I mention it in the memoir."

"Which is next on my to-do list," Teffy says quickly. She skips a glance over Ellie's crossed arms, faint liver spots starting on the woman's strong hands. "Is this a replica of the St. Mark's whale then?" She's sifting story ideas now. Pictures Ellie at sixteen or so, with a rifle drawn up to her cheek. "Were you one of the shooters?" she asks.

Ellie waves off the question. "The original thought was to patchwork the hide out of traditional fabric-based crafts. Full-on traditional. Crocheting, like I said, but also rug-hooking and quilting. Patterns particular to St. Mark's."

Marjorie laughs and says, "Tell her what that one maid said up to the quilting circle last time you dropped in."

Ellie smiles. "Ethel Pike, you mean. She's one of a handful of women down home making quilts for this project. When I was there last, to the church where they makes the quilts, I comes in and hears Ethel and the others in the balcony, chewing about this and that. Then Ethel up and says, 'There's a reason I built my outhouse over the cliff edge, mind. Shakes like a bridal bed in storm, but I'll tell this: a good wind does what a good man can't!'"

Teffy snorts, thinking it something her Nan would say to get a laugh. "So this is a community project? A St. Mark's thing?"

"That's how it started," Ellie says. "But it's grown beyond that initial concept. Which is what I wanted to tell you about. You've heard of Marjorie's not-for-profit?"

Teffy looks blankly at Marjorie, then to Ellie.

"It's called NEXT," Marjorie says.

"For women involved in the sex trade?" Teffy tries to read the tattoos on Marjorie's hands now. Work-hardened, she thinks, but what work? *Does it matter?* She's heard of NEXT and of Marjorie, of course, but she's not been able to get a face-to-face with the woman. Until now, apparently. She looks Marjorie in the eye. "Were you . . . ?"

"Trafficked." The woman nods. "By my boyfriend no less."

"It's often an intimate," Ellie says.

"Partner, boyfriend, spouse," says Marjorie. "Take your pick. Ellie here says you won't spin this to be a fallen woman piece, though. Is that right?"

"That's right," Teffy says.

"What kind of stories you usually cover?"

"Working class riffs," Teffy says. "Some inside scoops on street kids and organized protests. That shooting at the Sobeys on Kenmount a while back. Plus coverage of the local arts scene—plays, concerts, book reviews, and the like."

Marjorie nods. *Unimpressed*, Teffy thinks—and Ellie says, "She also did a group home exposé a month back." That raises Marjorie's eyebrows. The group home story had been the kind of investigative journalism Teffy longs to do fulltime. Interviewed some kids that used to be Troy's runners for that one—some from The Brow, Ger's old neighborhood—and Dougie, who's turned out to be quite the little skid-shit. Thanks to Vinnie. Marjorie looks out the gallery's harbor-side windows, and Teffy asks about the boyfriend: "The one that got you into it."

"He said it was this game we'd play," Marjorie says. "With other couples at first. Wife-swap kinda stuff. You know. Then it was just guys awhile . . . long string of guys. Some wife-away weekenders in the Pearl. Outcalls in CBS. Those were the better paying gigs, for the most part. Not that I saw much of the money. Mostly it was just lonely johns in hotel rooms or half-decent apartments."

"Half decent?"

Marjorie laughs. "You have to have some serious cash to afford what I can do."

"What you can do?" Teffy says. "So you're . . . still into it?"

Marjorie sighs. "I'm not trying to save people from sex work," she says. "I *am* a sex worker. Not everyone in the trade likes the term, by the way, but it's what I do, so I sees no shame in it."

"But your work now, how's it different from before?"

"For starters, I'm in charge of my business now. I puts up my own ad and I takes it down when I want. I'm clean and sober too. And, most importantly, I don't do anything I don't want to do. That's the control that was taken from me. Now I have it back."

"So NEXT, what is it—what do you do?"

"What I'm after doing with NEXT is advocating for our human rights. We deserve to be safe. And we deserve to be treated as human beings."

"She's even got the Anglican Archdiocese onboard," Ellie says.

Marjorie smiles. "The Anglicans gave us our new offices."

"Are the Catholics a harder crowd?" Teffy asks.

"They are," Marjorie says. "But there's still more love from them than the evangelicals."

"Well, I can only speak as a lapsed Catholic," Teffy says, "but the story I got growing up was that people in your line of work are either immoral or victims. And even if you are a victim, that's still your fault. What are folks not seeing?"

"Well, for one," Marjorie says, "there's less kink than you'd think in the work itself. I imagine my life is infinitely more interesting in a preacher's head than it is in real life. Bottom line: it's work and I have bills, same as everyone else. But what people might not get is just how buzzed you can get off it."

"Buzzed?" says Teffy.

"Buzzed," Marjorie says. "Feeling in control. Powerful even. You remembers that—being in control—long after you've lost it. Like I did. 3 a.m. fights dragged out onto the street. Sheer bloody screaming and telling that cop to go fuck himself 'cause you're not going with *him*. And you're sure as hell not going back inside." She fires a look at Teffy, candid light in her eyes. "When they handcuffs you in back of the cruiser, though—high as a kite and crying big black tears—all you wants is that feeling again—being in control. Being the one calling the shots. When you're good, and halfway sober—in control—you can get the johns to do what *you* want. Not the other way 'round."

"So your organization . . . ?" Teffy plays out the question, fishing.

"As I said, NEXT advocates for the human rights of sex workers. A main thing we do is provide support for folks like me, help them regain control of their own lives. On their terms. That's the whole point. No guilt, no moralizing—no nunnish bullshit. Just putting them back in the driver's seat of their own life. Setting them up to write their own next chapter, whether inside the trade or outside it. And if it's inside the trade, we work to make the conditions safer. One of the things I'm working on now is trying to get the constabulary onboard with sensitivity training—hopefully start changing the ways cops see and treat us."

Teffy nods at Ellie. "And you have this one's ear now. How do the arts figure into this?" She presses the whale's flank and sees the tail swish.

Marjorie and Ellie share a look, but it's Ellie who speaks. "Marjorie is set on changing the conversation about people in the sex trade. Getting people to see the human side of it."

"The girls's stories, you mean?"

"It's not just women, but yes."

Teffy nods at the room-sized leviathan. "And the whale figures how?"

"Shooting the whale," Ellie says, "was seen as *my* community's shame back in the day. Never mind it was a freak storm surge made the water deep enough for the thing to get trapped. And never mind there was no way to free her before she suffocated."

"It was a female then?"

"And pregnant."

"Sure you got slaughtered by the activists."

"We did," she says. "My ex took the brunt of it. But, to be honest—and no one's ever really wanted to say this—shooting her was a mercy. A bit of fun, sure. I'll admit that. If you've ever fired a gun you know."

"Oh, I know," says Teffy, recalling target practice with her Nan up on the barrens. *Tick tocking* old bean cans off a stump with a .30–30 lever action.

Ellie nods at her. Says, "Shooting the thing was an act of kindness. Period. After that Ken Barry fella called in the media, though, that national gaze—all them mainland cameras and reporters—*they* made it shameful. Spun it as some sort of sadism. Bloodthirsty baymen, they called us. Savages."

"It's not too far off the shame foisted on us," Marjorie chimes in, "anytime a news camera zooms in and wants to talk about *Sin* John's 'prostitution problem.'"

Teffy kicks gently at a pile of odds and ends piled on the floor under the great swimming fish: old clothes mostly, sheets of paper—and a journal, she sees. The journal—a dollar store lock-and-key thing—slides off a pair of tangled fishnets. "And these are . . . ?"

"I brought those over today from my office," Marjorie says. "Mementos from some of the folks contributing to the show. And some from folks I've known over the years." She stares out the window at the storm clouds over the Southside Hills. "Some of them long gone now."

The gallery door opens and closes below them. Someone walks to the elevator, soft-soled shoes scuffing concrete, and the lift rattles down to the first floor. Ellie's phone dings with an incoming text. She checks it and says, "That's my ride coming up."

Teffy picks up the journal. "And this?"

"From a girl found strangled." Marjorie drops the information like a clattering wrench. Teffy blinks. A floor below them, the lift gate squawks open and shut and the elevator shudders to the second floor.

"Strangled, you said?"

"Six, almost seven years ago now." The lift clanks to a halt and a clean-shaven man in a slick gray suit pulls open the gate. Ellie waves to the guy but Marjorie ignores him to finish what she was saying. "The girl was new into it from what I could tell. Supporting a habit, I think. But she said she had stuff she wanted to tell someone. Someone she could trust."

The suited man slides an arm around Ellie and kisses her cheek—and Teffy thinks, *So, this is the famous Markus O'Shea.*

Marjorie nods at the journal in Teffy's hand. "The girl said she wrote it out—what she wanted to tell me. In there."

Teffy flips open the journal, noting the way O'Shea raises his eyebrows and seems to be trying to read the journal upside-down. Nosy beggar. He flashes her a quick smile when she catches his eye. "A mystery journal, is it?" he says jokingly.

"I guess," she says. But there's no actual writing in it. Or very little. Teffy flips again through the book. Only a few pages filled and those with stick fig-ures in various poses cartwheeling across the page. Some with hands. Some without.

"It's some sort of code," Marjorie says. "Key's gone with the girl, though. Dead before she could pass it on." She turns to Ellie and nods at O'Shea. "And who's this fella?"

Ellie taps the man's arm. "This is Markus," she says. "We grew up togeth-er. Opposite sides of the bay, mind." O'Shea smiles, teeth whalebone white.

"I seem to have dropped in at the juiciest part," he says.

"We were just talking about Marjorie's role in the show," says Ellie. "And Teffy here was asking after some of the artifacts we're gonna include."

"Like the journal?" he says.

"The journal's key to the show." Ellie nods at the book in Teffy's hands. "The girl had a story she didn't get to tell."

Teffy can't help thinking of Teresa, Ger's dead girlfriend. She sifts quickly through the trial-related details surrounding Teresa's death: the gaps no evidence seemed to fill. She scans a line of stickmen in the journal and stops on one. Handless. Like others on the page.

But in a pose she's seen before.

On Ger's left hip.

A tattooed stickman standing on its head. Cockeyed, she's thought more than once, kissing her way past it. Like the figure is about to lose its balance.

Marjorie voice brings Teffy back into the room. "So we're featuring the journal to acknowledge that fact. That silence." They're quiet a moment, the only sound in the building the *tick tick tick* of the baseboard heaters coming on.

O'Shea clears his throat.

"Are you on your way home?" Ellie says to him, and he nods. "Well we're just finishing up," she says. His phone buzzes in his suit jacket. "Want me to meet you outside?"

O'Shea checks his phone and glances at the journal in Teffy's hands. "I can wait," he says and slides the phone back in his pocket. "No worries."

Teffy turns to Marjorie. "How did you know this girl?"

"They find me," Marjorie says. "'Cause I'm out there and actually listen to them. 'Cause I knows the world they're in and am willing to talk about it."

"Talk about what?" O'Shea asks.

"The sex trade," she says.

He swallows a smirk.

"See that!" Marjorie points at his blinking face. "You're embarrassed. And I don't mean to drag you into this, love, 'cause I don't know ya from Judah." Teffy watches O'Shea's neck redden against his white shirt. Ellie squeezes his hand. "But embarrassment," Marjorie says, "embarrassment keeps people quiet. And keeping quiet's a stranglehold on moving forward, on changing things. Fuck the shame game, I say. I'm not playing. Folks in the trade know that too, and that's why they trust me with their stories."

"Takes time to build that trust, though." Ellie squeezes O'Shea's hand again, and Teffy sees Marjorie nod. "Hence the show," Ellie says. "It's all about owning your shame, or others's shame foisted on you, and it's about undoing it. Turning the stories people tell about you back on themselves."

Teffy waves the journal. "And nobody's been able to decode this?"

"Can't parse it," says Marjorie.

"Can I see it?" O'Shea says. Teffy balks until she gets a nod from Marjorie, then hands over the book. O'Shea flips through it. Stops here and there. Tilts the book to follow the tumbling stickmen, then shrugs and hands it back. "Not much to go on, is it?"

"No," says Marjorie.

Teffy wants Ger to see it, though. She wants to know about that stick-man tattoo on his hip. But she doesn't dare pinch a dead girl's journal in front of these two women. Or the likes of Big-Money Markus O'Shea.

She wonders who this girl was, though, and why she used a code.

"So you'll cover the story?" Ellie says.

Teffy looks from Ellie to Marjorie. Sees O'Shea shift. "So, you want me to tell *both* of your stories?" The women nod. "The art show *and* the NEXT angle?" She glances at the journal of dancing stick figures, then to the two older women nodding their heads—O'Shea looking away toward the old elevator. "Yes," they say, trusting as good Catholics at a strict sister's say-so. "And killing the whale too?"

"All of it," Ellie says. "Fish it all up."

Marjorie nods. "Silence serves no one."

"We should be going," O'Shea says to Ellie.

"Maybe we could get these ladies lunch at your new restaurant, Mark." Ellie turns to Teffy and Marjorie. "It's pretty high end for St. John's. But all locally sourced and eco-friendly."

"I can't," Teffy says and drops the journal on the pile of knick-knacks. "Late night last night and a nap's calling me hard."

"And I got another meeting," says Marjorie.

"Then I'll lock us out," Ellie says. "Since I've started talking about the show online some people have started trolling me. Making threats. Posting old clips about us killing the whale. One with my face circled."

"And holding a gun," says Markus.

Ellie sniffs. "They seem to have forgot *you* were there too."

O'Shea shrugs and offers his arm. "Irish luck," he says—and Ellie mumbles something about "your friggin Irish luck" before taking his arm and dragging him toward the lift. Marjorie shakes her head and falls in behind the couple. Says to Teffy, "You coming?"

Teffy motions Marjorie on as she unwraps a stick of gum from a pack in her satchel. She rolls the wrapper into a tight ball. Then dips casually to snatch the dead girl's journal and slips it into her satchel as O'Shea rattles back the old lift gate. Teffy catches them up and sidles in-between the two women—two women trusting her with their stories.

O'Shea reaches for the *down* switch but Ellie beats him to it.

It's a jolting drop, and on her way out the door, Teffy stuffs her gum wrapper in the main door's striker plate. She'll return the journal later tonight. Or early tomorrow. And in the meantime she'll show it to Ger, scan a copy, and meet-up with Troy Hopper. If indeed that's who's behind the unknown number and those creepy texts. She presses a hand to the journal inside her bag, and prays it's nothing, feeling a wave of nausea hit her. *The after effects of last night*, she thinks, swallowing the bile in her throat. But the notion that the journal *is* in fact something sticks to her like the smell of Fin's father's fishing stage—another nauseating wave—the taste of blood in her teeth as she wrestled Fin away from his dad's dead body.

She says to Ellie, "Will you be back in the gallery in the next few days?" wanting to make sure she has the journal back in place by then.

"I'm picking up my niece," Ellie says. "Niece-in-law, I guess. Day after tomorrow in Port aux Basques."

O'Shea rolls his eyes, and Teffy wonders what that's about—thankful, though, that she's got a couple of extra days now to return the journal if the gum wrapper gets dislodged or picked loose. God forbid one of those online trolls Ellie mentioned gets it in their head to trash the place. *Not likely*, she thinks. If there's one thing she knows about online trolls, it's that ninety-eight percent of them are cowards. Sure, they may snark and spit venom online, but they do it from their scroungey little screen-lit holes. Half of them hitched to their mothers's wi-fi signals. She thinks of all the verbal sewage she's waded through running this online news site with Ger, and the thought hits her that maybe, just maybe, the creepy texter is one of her many Twitter trolls. Maybe it's not Troy Hopper at all. Maybe she's losing sleep over nothing.

"Is your niece coming to see icebergs?" she says to Ellie.

"She's actually bringing her mother's ashes back to St. Mark's."

"And what's Daryl think about that?" O'Shea mutters.

"Daryl can stuff it," she says.

"And Daryl is . . .?"

"The girl's uncle," Ellie says. "Anyhow, I'll be in St. Mark's a couple of days after that. Might be back to town by the weekend though. Should we meet up then?"

"I'll text you the once," says Teffy, and she heads off on her scooter, mind full of stickmen dancing around Ger's tattoo.

~ 4 ~

SHE KICKS PAST BISHOP FEILD Elementary and sees a raft of girls the other side of the street. Wonders how many might one day find themselves with a past like Marjorie's—raped or trafficked by people they know and trust.

There are stats on such things. Graphs online.

Punchy Ted Talks.

She's past them now—the girls—gliding *clickety-click clickety-click* when her phone screams in her pocket. She stumbles, the scooter clatters to the ground, and she whips out the device—the phone wailing like an actual infant. Ger's number flashing on the display. She ends the call. Smothers the baby's scream. Looks to see if anyone's taken notice, then dials Ger.

When he picks up, she says, "You'd better fix this fuckin ringtone, Stuckless!"

He laughs and hangs up. Two seconds later the baby's scream vibrates her wrist bones and she recognizes the infant wail from the end track to the Skuzzcuts's new album. Some experimental shit, Ger had said. Like that Norwegian band that recorded patients in a psychiatric ward wailing at night. She clicks off the phone.

If he's heavy into that Skuzzcut slag that means he's at home working on a personal project, close to the bone. She knows his moods and what he's into by his choice of music. Death Metal for arts and culture features. Grunge for street punk pieces. And Glam Metal for politics—"What?" he says. "It's all big hair, fake shlongs, and shazam, isn't it?"

Local bands he saves for personal stories, which means he's buzzing on Troy. And if he's thinking on Troy, that means Teresa is there too, in his mind's back alley, dropping a smoking butt into a tin of siphoned fuel.

She flicks the scooter back underfoot and pushes off. Pictures Ger in their backroom, having a laugh at her expense. Then calling up another mate to see what news there is now that Hopper's out. She buzzes under John the Baptist's white-stone arms, raised in religious triumph over the reprobate streets below, and she tilts right onto Bonaventure, then left on Merrymeeting and home out of it.

She finds Ger bouncing rhythmically on her gray exercise ball in their backroom, just as she'd thought. His eyes fixed on his laptop, finger scrolling the screen down through Hopper-related hits. "How's the whale lady?" he says, not taking his eyes off his screen, knowing she's scan-reading over his shoulder.

"It's gonna be quite the show," she says. "More complex than her debut."

"Deeper than a winter's piss hole then?"

"As an art critic, you're a real prick, you know that?"

He shrugs. "So it's good—the art show?"

She can't find the words to describe Ellie's show, its connection to Marjorie and the journal in her satchel—to the long-buried memories of Fin turned loose by last night's tequila binge. She nods at Ger's screen. "See you're into something slightly more useful than frigging around with my phone."

"You should use something other than your birthday for a password."

"Is it gonna scream when everyone calls me, or just you?"

"Just me," he says and cracks a faux innocent grin.

"So I'll know when to expect a headache."

He straightens and stops bouncing on the exercise ball. Looks at her slyly. "That's the shit you talk when you wants me tied to the bed post, missus."

"At least you can read a hint now you've slept off the hangover." She flicks his forehead and he winces. "Lucky me."

Squinting, he takes in her frizzy red hair—the *come-on-then* cock to her head. She knows him, knows every inked inch. "Come on then," she says on her way to the bedroom.

"I'm halfway there," he snaps, close to heel.

"Try for more than five minutes, will you?"

He laughs. "I'm a writer, maid. Not a runner."

She turns and hitches his belt. Pulls him close. Last night's funk and fresh air on him. Faint salt of cigarettes too. He hasn't smoked since moving in with her and she wonders if it's a hungover whim or if he bummed one off Dougie. God knows she likes a few puffs after a night-long session. That's why she keeps a pack in her satchel.

His breath's hot on her neck now, hands fevering up under her shirt as she fiddles for his buckle. His jeans drop belt-weighted to his ankles and she reaches for the stickman tattoo on his hip. Digs her fingers into it as Ger goes to step out of his jeans, but he trips and knocks her back on the bed. She laughs, both of them in breathy stitches as she struggles off the satchel and lets it slip from the bed—the journal *thunking* the floor.

Six minutes later, he falls off her, his one foot still stuck in the limp jeans he drags across her knees. "You didn't even get them off?" she says. "Seriously?"

"Duty first," he mumbles—and she shucks the cuff from his heel with her socked toes. Pulls a sheet over herself and reaches down for the satchel, for the half-spent pack of cigarettes inside. She darts a smoke before fishing again for her lighter. Knocks against the journal and draws it out.

"What've you got there?" he says—and she shifts back to her pillow. Rests the journal on her stomach and pinches the unlit smoke from between her lips. Ger lifts his elbow to spy the book's plastic lock. "Who gave you the diary?"

She lifts and closes the front cover with her thumb. "Kinda pinched it."

"From the whale lady?"

"From her friend."

"Is it juicy?" he says.

"It's coded."

"That why you snagged it?"

When she doesn't answer Ger drops his arm from his eyes and sits up. She watches him take the journal from her and flip through it. He stops on the odd page, stares a while, then moves on. And she has the strangest feeling he's reading it, though she sees no change to his face. Expressionless as a sea urchin's bleached shell.

She says, "I saw the stick figures and remembered this." She slides the cover away from his tattooed hip. "The girl who wrote it died seven years ago. And I couldn't help wondering if it was . . . her."

"Teresa?"

She looks from the tattoo to Ger's face. "That's why I wanted to show you," she says. "I had to ask you."

"Ask me what?"

"About these figures. The tattoo. Did you and Teresa . . . ?"

"It's just some ink," he says. He takes a shaky breath and she half expects tears but it's a shiver that passes through him. "She was always doodling in some book," he says. "But this. . . ." He tosses the journal on his nightstand.

"I should return it then." And she wonders if the gallery's door is still held open by that balled-up gum wrapper.

He swings his legs over the far side of the bed and reaches for his jeans. "You gonna do that today yet?"

"Later tonight."

He stands to shimmy into his pants. Pulls them up over the tattoo. "Let me snap some pics first," he says. "Maybe I can figure something out." And he grabs the journal from the nightstand. He's halfway to the bedroom door when she says his name.

He turns to her. Blinks.

"I just thought it was coincidental," she says. "That's all. And because I know what she meant to you. If it is her journal, maybe you don't want to know what she wrote in there. You said she was messed up at the end."

He weighs the journal in his hand. "It's alright," he says.

"Is it though?"

He runs his free hand through his hair and looks to his computer desk in the room across the hall. "Troy creeping the place has got me on edge. That's all."

She smiles. "That why you were smoking?"

He looks at the unlit cigarette pinched between her fingers. "Did you smell them on me or do I look guilty?"

"Your face looks like a spanked ass."

"Is that why you're so fond of it?" he says.

"Your face or your ass?"

"My finer side."

"Go on," she says, and he does. Off to the backroom and his computer. Across the hall she can hear his cellphone clicking, and she knows he's taking snaps of each page. Maybe something will come of it. Maybe there's some note in there about Troy. Something incriminating, please God. Something that'll lock the limp prick back up.

She reaches back into her satchel for her lighter and feels her phone vibrating in the bag. Pulls it out and sees a text from that unknown number: *On my way.*

She types, *I'm here,* and sends.

A second later her phone dings.

Be ready, it says.

~ 5 ~

S HE KNEELS ON THE COUCH by the street-facing window in their front room, satchel slung across her chest and the journal tucked inside. She peers through their curtains, then checks her phone. Clicks on the Dropbox she shares with Ger for *Miscreant* stories. A new file has been added. She opens it to find a slideshow of the journal's pages. The dancing stickmen smaller on her phone, somehow less significant than she'd thought them earlier.

She's not sure why but she emails a copy of the file to herself.

A reminder, maybe. To return the journal after this little joyride with Troy. Or whoever it is. She looks out the window again then tries to read one of the novels she chucked at Dougie earlier, but none of the story sticks. An hour passes and still no Troy. She's flipped twenty odd pages in that time and couldn't tell you what's happened.

Ger's got the Skuzzcuts thrashing in the back room on repeat, so loud that when she presses a palm to the damp window she can feel it shiver. She stares at the window, her face more and more visible in the glass as the world darkens. "Coming on duckish," her Nan would say. A shadowless gloom thick with the threat of rain.

She's about to go put the kettle on when she spies a Skimpy cab parked up the street by the bus stop. Lights off. Tailpipe smoking. Rain on the windshield and the wipers lazily swiping side-to-side. She watches a sec, thinking it must've just pulled up. Then her phone lights with Troy's number.

Ride's here.

And she looks down the hall to their room. Imagines Ger on his exercise ball, messaging anyone willing to talk, anyone who might still have some finger on Troy's pulse in this city.

You do your thing, she thinks, seeing the cab's lights flick on and off. *I'll do mine.* And she jumps from the couch, kicks into her red Converse shoes, and shoulders into a jacket. Flicks the hood over her tangled hair—thankful, as she opens the door, that the rain broke the day's stupid, hair-frizzing heat.

The driving wet she can handle.

"Not made of salt, are you?" her mother would say. She runs across the street to the cab, flings open the rear door, and clamps herself inside, seeing first the fat lady jiggling on the dash. Then the guy in the sports jacket next to her, checking her out through round-rimmed glasses.

"Thought you were *sending* a cab," she snaps. "Not coming yourself. Isn't that a no-no for a newly released felon: stalking the guy who put you away—harassing his girlfriend?"

Troy Hopper pushes his glasses up his sharp nose. Sniffs and says, "So you're Teffy Byrne." If she didn't know him, hadn't seen him in court, she'd think him an academic. An athletic one. Gray-haired prof or vice president. Put-together businessman. Composed. Fit and well-clipped. And with an air of entitlement, like the too strong smell of Old Spice in the cab. Sphincter tight as a snare drum. Fin used to say such things of such people. Always got something on the go.

"I knows who *you* are too," she says after a bit.

"You do, do you?" and he pulls a cigarette from a pack, tamps it on the box. Then lights it and breathes deep, letting smoke seep out his nose. He looks her up and down. "Did Stuckless ever tell you that you look a lot like his dead girlfriend?"

Don't rise to that bait, she tells herself. "Why do you want to talk to Ger?"

"Why are *you* here asking and not Stuckless?"

"You texted me."

"A legal buffer, let's say."

"What? So you're not making direct contact?"

"Not *my* fault if he initiates a meeting after I message you on a publicly displayed, professional number."

"Pretty sure that'd be considered bullshit in a court of law."

"Toffee," he takes another long drag, "you don't mind if I call you Toffee, do you?"

"It's your cab."

"Sweet name for a sweet personality."

"What do you want?" she says.

And he smiles, blowing smoke out his nose. Sizing her up. Then he taps the driver's shaved head, knocking ash on the guy's neck. The guy doesn't flinch, though, just looks at Troy in the rear-view mirror. "A little excursion around the bay for the lady here, Mitt."

"I'm just here for a story," she says. "For our news site."

"Oh, I'll give you a story," he says.

And Mitt flicks on the lights, speeds up the wipers, and pulls out onto Merrymeeting, headed toward Bonaventure and the Basilica. She can feel Troy tallying her, like she's a stack of receipts in need of summing up. And she wants to look the other way or tell him to pull over. But instead she looks him straight in his calculating eye.

He nods at the scuba mask on the seat between them. Nudges it so the mouth piece pokes her thigh. "Are you a water person, Toffee?"

"I grew up around the bay, if that's what you mean."

"Which bay?"

Nice try, sicko. "You dive, do you? Dry suit?"

He taps a knuckle on his window as they pass the Rooms Museum. "Your parents have done a nice job with that new house on the water," he says.

She slowly bites the inside of her lip to keep her face still, expressionless. Don't react. Don't give him anything. He said, "On the water," but how many Newfoundlanders don't live on the water?

"Propane heat too." Troy makes a tutting sound with his tongue. "Must be doing alright, your dad, isn't he?"

He is, she thinks. His post-fishery career in hydro finally paying off now he's north of sixty-five and retired. Mom wanted propane in the new house so she could have a gas-range.

But how . . . ?

"Shame if something caught those tanks. Could blow the side of the house off."

She remembers that raft of photographic evidence from the trial. A whole file smacked down by Ger's lawyers to pin half a dozen high profile arsons on this psycho. Letter bombs. One resulting in a punk kid's death. One of Troy's runners.

Troy nudges the snorkel into her hip—twice and again. Face board-meeting straight. *Pervert*, she thinks, and glares at him. *He's just trying to get you, that's all.*

They're rounding the harbor now, Mitt driving along the base of the Southside Hills, along the fishing wharves there, boats bobbing on the rain-bubbled water.

Eventually Troy says, "Stuckless didn't want to meet, did he?"

"Doesn't even know you messaged," she says.

"So . . . *you* wanted this to be a private rendezvous?" He chuckles, like a teacher might at a student's mistaken notion. "Should I ask Mitt to pull over and step out?"

If he pulls over she's gonna roll out the door and run. But Mitt keeps driving. And Troy keeps staring. "Looks like you wants to ask me a question," she says.

"Do you know how much Stuckless cost me?"

"He doesn't work for you anymore."

"A debt's a debt, Toffee."

"So, start up the old business."

He smiles grimly. "In my business, when you get knocked out of the game, you might have to kill a few people to get back in." He glances at her phone in her hands. "You gonna record that or do you think I'm just bullshitting you?"

"I'll remember," she says.

"Maybe that's something we have in common," he says. "Long memories."

The cab turns slow and heads back along the hills, Troy staring at her the whole time. As if she's not there looking back at him. As if he can do what he wants with her . . . once he figures out what that is.

He goes on studying her freely—her trying to read his unreadable face—till they turn up the hill toward Shea Heights. "You been to The Brow?" he says at last, looking out his window as they climb past the community center. And she has, for that group home story, but she's not telling him that—not letting on that boys in the community were willing to talk. To rat him out. Mostly because they knew Ger.

"What's to see?" she says.

"All of St. John's, Toffee." And Mitt turns them into a lot, front windshield facing the town below—the dark mirror of her sunrise view this morning. That jeezly sun, she remembers, rising christlike out of the water. She sees the brightly colored jellybean houses she'd looked down on earlier, made bleak now by the rain and dark. A few lights blinking. Wipers slashing rain as the view wobbles and clears, washes and clears.

"It wasn't raining that night, was it, Mitt?" A grunt from the front seat. "Mitt here shoved us off. Nobody around to notice the body under the tarp." He's watching her face—she bites the inside of her cheek. "An old associate," he says. "Friend of Ger's, actually. From the old days. We had this falling out, see. Same as me and Stuckless. This guy cost me money too. Money I still owe, 'cause it's all business," he says. "Your boy and this guy cost me a lot. And as I said: when you get knocked out of this business, sometimes you have to kill some people to get back in. That's just the way it is."

"Just business?"

He laughs and nudges the snorkel into her leg again. "I took this guy—"

"What was his name?" she says.

And he asks, "Is this for your story?" seemingly amused by her question.

"What was the guy's name? Say his name."

"It's alright, Toffee," he soothes. "Nobody'll miss him. Except maybe Ger." Troy pulls a phone out of his pocket, swipes it open, and pulls up the recent calls. "Seems Stuckless tried calling him tonight, in fact. Three or four times. Wonder why that was?"

"I wouldn't know," she whispers, thinking of Ger running through his contacts, trying to find some new dirt on Troy—the Skuzzcuts blasting dust off the lampshades. "Why do you have this guy's phone?" she says.

"He wanted me to have it."

"Did he really?"

Troy clicks the camera icon and pulls up a pic, the phone turned so she can't quite see the screen, but she sees the cell is in a waterproof case. "He wanted me to take this last shot. For Stuckless." And he turns the phone's display toward her. An underwater pic of a naked man, lantern-lit and flailing in dark water, ankle-roped to a sack of rocks—his scream a cloud of bubbles.

"You want to go for a swim, Toffee?"

She tries not to blink. Tries to stare unfeelingly. Like him. But she can't. This guy—this guy in the photo—was Ger's friend. But which one? Connor Moffet or Ben Critch?

One of them, she thinks. *One of them is gone now.* She closes her eyes so tight she sees snow. Hears Troy light another cigarette. Opens her eyes to the smoky, washed-out cityscape, rain hammering the rooftops. *This was a mistake, girl. Getting in this cab was a mistake.* Troy pockets the phone. Then leans over, his face a hand from hers.

"When was that?" she whispers. "Two days ago?"

"Yesterday," he says. "Do you want the boat number?"

"Was it nearby?"

He laughs. "They won't find him." His breath hot on her face.

This psycho killed one of Ger's friends *yesterday*. And he's a hand's breadth from her now. So close she can't see his lips, only the skin around his eyes spiking squint lines, as if from staring too long at the fluorescent lights of a lockdown cell. Thinking. Scheming. He blows smoke in her face and she closes her eyes and coughs. As she squints to look at him, he flicks ash down the front of her shirt and she punches his throat.

Sees his eyes widen. But with . . . what?

Delight?

He sits back, rubbing his neck. Swallows and says, "I like you, Toffee." Swallows again. "Stuckless doesn't have your"—he coughs—"audacity. You know that? Which makes me wonder why you're with a skid like him."

She doesn't say anything, trying to swallow the fear she feels clawing out her mouth like a crazed ghost-child.

"It's 'cause you love him," Troy says. "Why else would you climb in my cab? Not just for one of your stories, was it?"

She swallows the scream. Tells herself to take control. What can he do to her, really? If she goes missing, the cops will be on him, sure.

Yeah, she thinks, *but you'll still have gone missing.*

"I want to know," she says, changing tacks, "if there's something I can do to get you off Ger's back." She blinks. "Something to pay his debt. Help you out."

"You want to know if there's something you can do?" he says—and she nods. "Did you hear that, Mitt?"

"I heard it," says Mitt.

"What do you suppose you could do to balance Ger's ledger with me?" He eyes her beltline. "Unless." He raises his eyes and winks at her.

"Do you need anything done?" she says.

"Toffee." He smirks. "What exactly are you asking me?"

"You're fresh out of Her Majesty's, right?"

He nods, takes another drag of his smoke. "Go on."

"And you're in the public eye now." That's what Ger said, his very words. "So," she says, "they'll be watching you closely—you and any . . . associates. Not me. What do you think?"

"You didn't like what I was thinking earlier."

"*I'm* off limits," she says

His eyes flash. "Are you?"

She pinpoints the neck artery she'll jab with the pen in her pocket if he comes at her. Right there. Click and jab. Simple as that. A blood geyser in the backseat—and what would Mitt do? No one would doubt it was self-defense. But can she get both of them?

Is it in you to do that?

"Toffee," Troy says, voice even. As if presenting her with a simple business pitch. "If you get down on your knees, right here in this cab, and swallow what I give you, then I won't bother you or your boyfriend again. That simple. A kind of grace, really."

"And Option B is?"

He smirks at that. "Option B," he says, "involves you crossing the island by bus and taking the Port aux Basques ferry to North Sydney."

"Nova Scotia?"

"I'll text you an address when you set sail."

"And *at* the address . . . ?"

"There'll be a package for you."

"A package?"

"You can put it in this," he says and pulls a big, gray ziplock bag from the pouch in the back of Mitt's chair—*O'Shea Shoreline Inc.* printed in black on the bag. "Believe it or not, these are so you can shit in the woods and carry it out with you. Leave it to the environmentalists."

"So . . . it's a package of . . . shit?"

"You're funny, Toffee."

She takes the gray bag from him and slides it into her satchel. "But you do want me to put the package in that ziplock, right?" He nods and re-lights his cigarette. "Then what?"

"You bring me the package."

She tries to read his face, his tell. But she's shit at poker, at reading straight faces—and the cigarette smoke is making her blink. Can he guess that she has no intention of fetching his package, whatever it is? "If I do this," she says, "will you leave Ger alone?"

"You mean *not* take him for his dive offshore? You're no fun, Toffee. All business and no throat punches now." He blows smoke in her face again. "Come on."

"If I get you this package, will that even things between you and Ger?"

"Even things?" he says. "How do you mean?"

"Will you leave us alone?"

"I'll tell you that, when I sees you've done it."

She looks at him, waiting for his next move—the next quip or intimidation tactic. He takes another draw, then nods at her door handle. "You're kicking me out?" she says. "Here?"

"Option B." He shrugs. "You want to stay in the car, it's Option A, and I'm fine with that, as you might well imagine. Six years is a long time. And"—he smiles—"if you're any good, I can offer you a job—one that'll pay more than your three-hit news rag."

She pulls the door handle and steps out, hearing Troy cluck his tongue behind her. "I like you, Toffee." He leans across the seat. "Here, let me show you one last thing before you go and write your story." Now that she's out of the cab, she's hesitant to lean back in. Would he drag her back into the cab by her hair?

"What do you want to show me?"

He spins his phone so she can see the screen. It's a live feed of their front porch on Merrymeeting. Dougie's cigarette tin by the cinderblock stoop. The cameraman's hand opens the front door, and Troy flicks up the volume on his phone so Teffy can hear the Skuzzcuts still grinding away. The phone's camera swings right into their front room, to the couch she sat on not an hour ago. Then left into the kitchen and down the hall.

Toward the back room.

Ger's room.

Troy drops the phone from her view. "I thought you might need a little incentive to make this trip," he says. "So Stuckless is gonna be my personal house guest till you get back from North Sydney with my package."

"But you thought it'd be Ger in the cab. Not me." She can barely get her voice above a whisper. "You had this planned?"

"Didn't know who it'd be, actually. But given your living situation, I figured if not you, then him. If not him, then you. Either of you will do as ransom for the other. I have preferences, sure. But I'm not picky."

She's scrambling now, trying to think fast—trying to hold it together. "And if I just text him to get out of the house?"

"My guys are already *in* the house." He looks at his phone again. "And . . . it's done." He pockets the phone. "And in a half hour, Stuckless's phone will be in my hand. Are you starting to see how this is all going to play out?"

"But," she swallows, "if I deliver. . . ."

He smiles now. "Did I say you have four days to deliver?"

"What?" She swallows. "I can't get there and back in four days."

"Best start running."

And he pulls the car door shut.

Mitt backs the cab away from the cliff-edge view, the car turns out of the lot, and she's left standing there in the rain. She wants to collapse or curse or kick something. Smash in a car window. But she just starts walking. Walking and searching her phone for a bus ticket first thing tomorrow.

She wanted a bloody story, and now she's got it. That and Ger's in a panel van headed to God knows where. What was she thinking getting in that cab? And what's Hopper making her fetch that he needs Ger as collateral?

She buys the bus ticket online and pockets the phone. Kicks gravel all the way down from The Brow and into town. She is soaked by the time she sees Mile One Stadium. Bone-drenched and steaming. The baby wails suddenly in her back pocket, and she rushes to answer it. But stops. "In a half hour, Ger's phone will be in my pocket," Troy had said. And how's she gonna turn this around on him? What if pinching Ger isn't just motivation for her, but payback for six years—what then?

She walks to the bank and takes five hundred dollars out of Ger's account. Enough to get her there and back again. She stares through her lank-haired reflection to the empty, wet street.

A half-drowned girl struggling to make shore.

~ 6 ~

SHE DIVES INTO THE RAIN and finds her way to Ellie Strickland's gallery. Pushes the door open easily—no alarm, thank God—and digs the gum wrapper out of the striker plate and pockets it. The door clicks shut behind her and she heads up the stairs to the gallery, avoiding the clank-and-grind of the rickety lift. She steps into the gallery, the only sounds her ragged breath and rain slashed against glass. Shadows blue the fishbowl room, cast from the faint glow of unseen harbor lights out the rain-pelted windows. The whale's tail seems to flick in the strange light and the whole room tilts nauseously toward her, making the humpback look as if it's diving deep from the outside storm, its maw wide to swallow her whole.

Just pick up the package, she tells herself, gulping against the sudden urge to vomit. *Call the cops on the way back across the island. Say Troy blackmailed you into playing delivery girl and abducted your boyfriend to force you.*

Yeah right, she thinks.

And when Troy sees the cops, he'll text whoever's holding Ger and then Ger gets buzz-sawed and buried in the concrete sub-floor of a McMansion in CBS or some other godforsaken suburb of St. John's.

What if Troy's asking her to carry something big? Big enough to warrant a manhunt, maybe. What if he sicks the cops on her, to give her the same experience Ger gave him?

Why do that, though, and give up what she'll be carrying?

Maybe he doesn't want her to make it.

Maybe that's the point.

She drops the journal in the very place from which she'd pinched it earlier—Ger's digital copy sitting unread in her inbox. But where's Ger? In some dark basement or shed, some warehouse in Portugal Cove. Tied and gagged. His phone in Troy's hand.

Her phone screams, and she thinks it must be Troy trying to call her—to prove his point. Set the hook. The child screams as if from inside her, and she feels sick to her stomach. Like she's going to puke. She's that guy in the underwater pic Troy flashed her. Chained and screaming bubbles. Screaming something no one will ever hear.

She clicks off the wailing ringtone, sets the phone on vibrate, and slumps against the wall, waiting for sunrise and that first bus across the island to Port aux Basques.

A window smashes on the first floor and she jumps.

Then someone starts kicking glass. Some heavy breathing that echoes in the empty cinderblock building. Footsteps, crunching glass. Coming toward the steps. She spins to find a place to hide and sees a spattered drop sheet thrown over a stack of paint cans. There's just enough room between the cans and wall for her to wedge herself.

Boots in the stairwell now.

She shimmies in behind the cans and flicks the drop sheet over her. The person who just broke in downstairs steps into the gallery, their glass-studded footsteps by Teffy's head.

She can hear them breathing.

Then a faint hissing sound, like her parents's gas range before the clicker ignites the blue flame. *Gas?* She can't smell anything except paint and turpentine. There's a long hiss, then it stops. Starts again, then stops. Can rattle. More hissing. Steps. Silence. Snipping sounds. Step. Snip. Step, step. Snip. The length of the room and headed for the harbor-side windows.

Teffy closes her eyes to the drop sheet. As if closing her eyes will sharpen her hearing. Something like a heavy wicker basket drops to the floor, and the snipping continues until another basket-like thing drops. *The whale.*

They're cutting down Ellie's whale.

Teffy hears whoever it is haul the mesh-wire monster across the room in a muttered "goddamn-this-fuckin-thing" racket. The elevator crankily ascends to the second floor and she peeks out from under the drop sheet's lip to see a guy in a black hoodie drag the whale's head into the lift's rickety metal box. Then the guy squeezes out and presses down on the lift and there's a godawful mangle of rusted gears and grinding metal, and the handcrafted humpback's bulk rises off the floor in a violent flail, as if suddenly shot. The splayed tail swipes side-to-side with sickening ferocity as the creature's head is crushed in the elevator shaft.

The lift *screaks* to a stop.

The tail swipes a last time across the room. Hooks the drop sheet covering Teffy and flicks it back like a cape off a magic trick. Teffy stiffens. Stays rabbit-still behind the paint cans, staring at the hooded man by the lift controls.

Please don't see me. Please don't see me.

He doesn't see her.

He's too in awe of the room he's trashed: the vandalized artwork and spray painted wall. She thinks he's about to head for the exit, next to her head, but he ducks under the whale's tail—two feet from her feet—and yanks loose the drop sheet ghost. Slips his backpack off to rifle through the piles of stuff Ellie and Marjorie had said belonged to the women in on the show.

Teffy can't see what but the guy stuffs handfuls of gear into the bag before zipping it shut. He turns on his heel, glass grinding in the tread of his boot, and *click-click-clicks* back to the stairs, slinging the backpack over his shoulder as he goes.

Teffy sees his work boots near her head—*Don't look down*, she thinks. *Don't look down*—a streak of red spray paint cut across the Kevlar-capped toes. She shuts her eyes and prays he doesn't see her on his way out of the room.

Prays he doesn't look left. She peeks.

He looks her way.

His eyes glint in his dark hood. Then she flings a paint can at his face. Hears him yell as she presses her hands flat to the ground—arms straight, legs like springs beneath her—and launches herself into the guy's soft gut. Drives him back into the stairwell.

He's got her shirt in one fist and her hair in the other, and he manages to kick off the landing wall and knock her backwards down the stairs. But she claws his belt and drags him down the stairs with her, both of them scrambling to keep their feet. She swings him around mid-fall and slams him into the cement wall at the bottom of the stairs.

The guy groans and Teffy knees his junk, and as he folds, she frees her hand from his belt and hammers both fists down on the back of his hooded head.

He crashes to his knees, grabs for her shoes, but she kicks him off and sprints for the door. Elbows through the door onto the rain-slick street and starts running toward George Street. She needs people. To be with people.

In a crowd. Safe.

She hears a yell behind her but doesn't look back. When she makes George Street she races up around the back corner of the Yellowbelly and into the alley by the Fat Cat. Three smokers passing a joint are like "Hey girl" as she bumps past them, sorrying her way into the bar and the ladies's room next to the stage. The band is playing Neil Young through thin wall and she squeezes into the farthest stall. Locks the door. Steps back. Damp toilet against the back of her legs. She steadies herself, a hand on either wall. Puts a heel on the toilet seat and steps up to sit on the tank so no one coming in will see her shoes.

Fuck, she thinks. *Just . . . fuck!*

And she pulls out her phone, hands shaking now. The whole thing plowing her down those gallery stairs again. The whole night. Troy's fuckin deal and that video of someone in their house, Ellie's gallery and that guy— *That fuckin guy! And they've got Ger*, she thinks. *They've got him and—*

Her phone buzzes in her hands and she nearly drops it in the toilet. Sees Ger's number. But it's not Ger, is it? It's Troy on Ger's phone.

And she closes her eyes and leans her wet hair against the wall. The wall. This grody stall. Here. It was here she'd dragged Ger one night. Right here. And he'd straddled the toilet, trying to do his bit but the band went on break and suddenly there was a wash of women in the room. People rattling the door and Ger trying to get off and her trying to bite her lip till she couldn't hold it anymore and laughed in his face. And he turned in a rage and went to barge out the stall door but she leapt on his back and he lost hold of his jeans and they fell around his ankles as he staggered through the half cut crowd with her on his back, hugging his neck and laughing into the alley. Toppled off him into the grimy snow. The snow on her bare arse like a stinging spank. Smoke in the air. Ger staring at her, three sheets gone and his dick a melting icicle. He grinned at her. The bouncers sounding off like distant gull-bangers on some fogged-in wharf, telling them to shag off already. That was ages ago and yesterday.

The phone stops buzzing in her hands and she squeezes it like it's Ger's hand. Thinks of the money in her pocket and the ticket on her phone. All the way to Port aux Basques.

Alone and for what?

Ellie, she thinks suddenly. Ellie had said she was headed that way. But when was that? When did she say she was picking up her niece?

She finds Ellie in her recents and taps the green phone icon.

Three rings and "Hello?" Ellie says. "Teffy?"

"I was at your gallery," Teffy says and bites her lip to keep from crying.

"At my gallery? Wh—"

"Your show's been vandalized."

"What?" Ellie snaps.

Teffy squeezes her eyes shut against the sudden tears. The mangled whale in mind. Its quilted hide shredded like a body washed up on sharp rocks. The body of that guy Troy showed her. That guy naked and screaming underwater. *Me*, she thinks. *That'll be me. Or Ger if I can't pull off what Troy's asked me to do.*

"Are you there now?" Ellie says. "Are you at the gallery?"

"No," Teffy says. "I'm at the Fat Cat. On George Street. I'm locked in a stall."

"You're locked in what?"

"Just come," she says. "Please."

~ 7 ~

ELLIE FINDS HER IN THE same stall, crouched on the back of that rust-scabbed toilet. And a little while later they meet the Constabulary at the gallery. Teffy's story, rehearsed while waiting for Ellie to pick her up, is that she saw the big display window broken and had stepped in to get the first-person scoop.

"Scoop?" the constable says to her.

"I'm a reporter," Teffy says.

The constable rolls her eyes, and Teffy goes on to say how she'd run into the vandal in the stairwell. How she'd managed to get away and run to the downtown, where she called Ellie. She doesn't mention the streak of red paint across the guy's work boot. Or that she'd been in the gallery before the guy got there, to drop off that coded journal.

But it turns out the journal was one of the items the thief stuffed into his bag before his stairway waltz with Teffy. When Ellie notes the missing journal to the constable, Teffy squeezes her phone in her pocket, wanting to tell Ellie she has a copy of the journal in her dropbox. But then she'd have to admit to having stolen and returned it. She'd have to explain that's why she was actually at the gallery—at least in part. One question will lead to another, sure. She's been privy to interrogation transcripts in her reporting, so she knows the way a cop's mind works these things into flow charts of cause and effect. And she sure as hell does not want the RNC inquiring into *her*.

If she tells them Ger is missing, she'll never see him again.

So she keeps quiet about the journal.

After the police are finished with their questions, Ellie ducks under the yellow tape, climbs the stairs back up to the gallery—Teffy in tow—and takes some careful pics of the damage with her iPhone. Seven shots of the whale mangled in the elevator shaft. When she finally pockets her phone, Teffy asks what she's going to do. Ellie gestures at the spray-painted wall. "Well, for one, I'm gonna leave *that* as it is. And underneath it I'm gonna hang blow-ups of the scene here."

"Why not erase it?" Teffy asks.

"What? Burn the evidence, you mean? Or bury it?"

Teffy shivers, chilled from her runs in the rain and sitting in that bathroom stall, the adrenaline-heat gone from her body. "If you burn it up," she says, "you can just start new."

"And make it look like I have something to hide?"

We all have something to hide, Teffy thinks.

"The dead will always find ways to speak," Ellie says—and Teffy imagines she's thinking of that dead girl's journal. "They'll hag-ride our dreams long after their ashes are scattered. Ghosts demand justice. There's no way forward without a common memory." Ellie stares a while at the word MUR-DERER gashed across the wall. "That's why the graffiti stays."

"To put ghosts to rest?"

"At least my own," Ellie says.

"I don't think your vandal meant to become part of the show."

"Then he shouldn't have been such a dick."

The line is familiar: from Ellie's memoir. From that passage in which she takes on that Ken Barry fella, father to this niece of hers and the guy who threw St. Mark's to the mainland sharks in his book on them killing the whale. *Lured to Slaughter*—the title apt to her own situation now. She looks at Ellie as the older woman scans the room a last time.

Not defeated. Just riled.

Ready for a fight.

They duck under the yellow tape on their way out, and Teffy finally asks the question she's been burning to ask since Ellie picked her up. "Are you still picking up your niece in Port aux Basques—at the ferry?"

"Her car broke down," Ellie says.

And Teffy blinks. "So you're—"

"Taking the ferry to North Sydney," Ellie says, "then driving south to this B & B she's at. In Truro, I think."

"Can I tag along?" Teffy says—and Ellie raises her eyebrows. "If I'm gonna tell this whole story, an extended interview would be great."

"You'll be with me a week," Ellie says. "I'm taking the niece back to St. Mark's. A week with me is a long time." There's a glint in her eye. "Just ask my ex-husband."

"I can clear my schedule," Teffy says. She should be able, she thinks, to pick up Troy's package in North Sydney while Ellie dips south to get her niece. Then hitch a ride back with them to Grand Falls-Windsor, and bus back to St. John's from there.

Ellie says, "I make no guarantees as to the quality of the conversation."

"I'll just be glad for the company," Teffy says, and she means it. She'll be glad of the company, even if it is sitting next to an artist she barely knows. An artist she's stolen from and lied to. *Put the thought away*, she tells herself. *And get your head around it.* She can do that. She will do that. Anything to keep her thoughts from the back of Troy's smoky cab and the reality of what she has to do and what's at stake.

"Four days," Troy had said. Two there, two back. *But carrying what?* She presses her hand against her satchel, against the folded gray ziplock inside.

~ 8 ~

FIRST THING TEFFY DOES WHEN she staggers off the ferry in North Sydney is Google Maps a Pharmasave north of the Terminal. Ellie had said she'd be back in the line-up in eight hours or so if there's no traffic between here and Truro. And while Teffy had registered what Ellie said, she was admittedly more focussed on not hurling on Ellie's hiking shoes.

It had been a rough crossing, and Teffy couldn't make out why. It's not like it was her first time on the water. She'd even done the long ferry to Argentia, after catching a concert in Halifax with Fin, and that on a big sea.

But this crossing had been a particular kind of nauseating hell. For one, she's never been that intimate with a public toilet before. Which is why she's keen to find the nearest pharmacy.

Twenty minutes after disembarking the ferry, she's staring at her rough reflection in a cosmetics mirror: face pasty, eyes bloodshot, and hair fit for a crow's nest.

She tries to smooth her rumpled clothes, then sniffs an armpit and breathes on her palm to check her breath, which makes it official: she smells like ass and her mouth's a lit roach from puking the whole way—heaving her lungs out in the ladies's room.

And that's strange, she thinks, finding her brand of deodorant and dropping it in her satchel with a travel-sized toothpaste and brush. *On the water your whole life and seasick now? What's with that?*

She grabs a scopolamine patch, for the voyage back to Newfoundland, and an oral thermometer to check if she's actually running a fever and not just seasick. If that's the case, the scopolamine patch will be useless. But at least she'll know. She's halfway to the cashier when she stops and stares at the pregnancy tests. *Stupid,* she thinks. *But ... possible?*

The rooftop shag? Or the time before?

Jesus, Ger . . . seriously?

She holds the test in her hands, wishing Ger was here. Wishing she hadn't just spent eight hours with her face in a high-seas toilet bowl. Wishing she wasn't in clothes that smelled of pit-sweat and cigarettes. Troy's second-hand smoke on her still and Ellie had the heat cranked all the way across the island.

She thinks to wait until she's back in town. Call Ger into the bathroom and show him the little pink plus sign. If there is one. But she's got to turn around here and board that boat in a few hours. Hook back up with Ellie and her niece. Play it cool. It'd be nice to know if she has a reason for being seasick, though, beyond being a wuss.

She drops the test in her bag, along with the other gear, and pays for it all upfront, then maps the address Troy texted her in Port aux Basques.

46 Peppett St., Unit 2.

As she follows her phone's voice through North Sydney, she texts Ellie the Peppett Street address. Says she's stopping in there before she heads back to the ferry. It's a text she normally would've sent to Ger.

But here we are. . . .

Twelve minutes walking, her phone tells her. And when she gets there and this lady opens the front door, the first thing she says is, "Can I use your can?"

"Who are you?" the woman says, closing the door behind herself.

Teffy looks at the number on the mailbox. "Is this Unit 2?"

"Ike is around back." The woman points down the side of the house. "Basement apartment." She sniffs and scowls at Teffy. "You can use *his* toilet."

"Thanks," she murmurs as she sidesteps the lady and heads around back. Knocks three sharp raps and dances a bit foot-to-foot, waiting on Ike to answer. She's about to knock again when this tall guy in torn jeans answers the door, sockless feet stuck in camouflage crocs.

"You look like an Ike," she says.

"I am Ike," he says. "Who're you?"

"Troy Hopper gave me this address."

He cracks the kind of pedderass grin she's seen too often downtown. "Ohhh," he says, and steps aside so she can see his skidrow apartment—stack of Bud Light boxes by the fridge, six black garbage bags full-to-bursting on the floor, and dishes gone septic in the sink. "Come in, come in."

"I need to use your toilet," she says, regretting the words as soon as she says them. She doesn't want to be using this shagger's toilet, but it's that or the alley beside the house.

Ike chuckles. "Can's down the hall. On the left."

"I'll grab that package when I'm done," she calls back, already wending her way around piles of junk in the hall, trying not to touch anything—her shoes sticky by the time she treads on the bathroom's linoleum. She closes the door and locks it. Test-turns the knob to see if it holds. It's wobbly in its socket. But locked. She turns and sees there's piss on the floor, black mildew in the shower, and pubic hairs worming the toilet seat.

So much for freshening up before the boat.

She pulls out the pregnancy test and thermometer, and eyes the toilet under the lone chin-high window. The bowl, cracked and dead-tooth brown, leaks across the floor into a soppy towel. A hover test, she decides, lodging the thermometer under her tongue and unbuttoning her jeans. She's about to squat when there's a sharp knock on the door.

She bites the thermometer and yells, "I'm on the can!" hoping he'll shag off. But he twists the knob and rattles it. "Just a second!" she snaps and pees quickly. Watches the knob rattle again and rise an inch in its socket. She pulls up her jeans quick, just as the door bangs open and Ike steps into the bathroom with her, clicking the door shut behind him.

She whips the thermometer out of her mouth. "I was on the can!" she yells, gripping the pregnancy test.

Ike runs his tongue over his grody teeth. "In the middle of something?"

"I did just fucking say that!"

And he smiles and steps closer, the backs of her legs to the damp toilet bowl and a mere foot between them now, Ike's bald head a few inches from the sagging ceiling panels. He takes a step and she steps up onto the toilet rim, her back to the window. Thinks of trying to dive through it—it's open a crack, air cool on her neck—but Ike would have her by the ankles before she could scramble free.

He'd drag her back in, then what?

She curses herself for being more stuck on that stupid pregnancy test and her bladder than on putting herself alone with a dealer. *What did you think would happen? Seriously! Did you think you'd just take a piss, get the package, and go?*

"This where you usually do business?" she says from her toilet bowl perch, trying to steady her voice—trying not to sound like she's in an utter fucking panic.

He moves closer, face to her chest, eyes where you'd expect, and the smells off him! Cigarette breath, sour chews, and varnish. Could be a boy from around the bay or an odd-jobbing townie needing a break. Desperate, sure, but more than that, she thinks. Willing to rough a girl up. Or worse.

"I can just take the package and go," she says.

He doesn't smile, doesn't blink. And she sees a plastic grocery bag in one hand and three knotted condoms in the other—the condoms filled with something sand-like and sagging from between the busted-up knuckles of his right hand.

"Are those the package?" she asks.

Ike shrugs and hands her one of the knotted condoms, and she weighs it in the hand holding the pregnancy test.

"What's this?" she says.

"Scat," he says.

"Heroin?"

The word sucks all the moisture out of her mouth.

Ike grabs a condom in each hand—the plastic bag dangling from a middle finger—and he bounces them on his palms. Smiles at the way they jiggle, and she can imagine what the blunt spliff is thinking. She sniffs the latex, wondering how much heroin Troy has arranged for her to carry. Said a package, the sly fuck, not . . . this. "Cherry?" she says.

"Heard it was your first time."

"Seriously?"

"What?"

"Flavored condoms?"

Ike takes the two scat-filled condoms and plastic bag in one hand and flicks a yellow-handled utility knife out of his pocket with the other. Thumbs the blade out two inches, cocks his head. And winks.

She tries to cram her Monday night Wing Chun and self-defence training into the tiny bathroom. What to do? What to do? Grab the pepper spray in her satchel that she always carries. But buddy has his eye on her satchel. She sniffs the condom again.

At least it's not pineapple.

She crouches down, squatting over the toilet bowl, and Ike tilts his head and grins. Thinking her submissive or scared. But she's getting under him is what she's doing. Getting low so she can use her leg strength, like she did with that guy in the gallery. Make her upper body a battering ram. Shoulder into him. She calculates a chin-crack if he comes at her sudden.

Launch her head into his face. She smiles.

And he smiles.

Sicko.

He steps closer—and she eyes the two condoms in his one hand, wondering what all is in the plastic bag. "I'm not swallowing them," she says.

"We'll see," he says.

And she almost slips off the toilet bowl. Opens her satchel—hands shaking, pegging the distance between them. Then she drops the condom she's holding into her bag.

Enough scat to stop a girl breathing, she thinks. Is this how it went down with Teresa? What was it they found in her system?

Ike gives Teffy another. Says, "You've done this before, eh?" and laughs. But she neither hears the laugh nor marks the words. Just watches the distance between them—between her and the window above her. Wondering if the window is big enough for her to get through if she can kick free of him. She drops the second condom into her satchel and Ike gives her a few laxatives out of the plastic bag, along with a suppository and a tube of Vaseline.

"Told you I'm not eating it," she says.

He hands over a baggy of baking powder too, "And some quinine," he says. "To cut it." She stuffs the gear in her satchel. Drops the pregnancy test in the water by the toilet but fists the thermometer tighter now, pointy end down. Like a blunt needle. She watches Ike's eyes to see if she can slip out her pepper spray—elbow through him and the door there. Make a dash down the street for the boat and Ellie's car.

But he's watching her close—closer now—knife twitching in his hand.

Likely coming down off shit he snorted after she came in. He'd need that, wouldn't he, the rough dog fister?

Ike pinches the third condom's knot and lets it bounce between their faces. Says, "*This* is the one you swallow."

She's gargoyled on the toilet, knees burning. "And if it breaks in my stomach—what happens then, hey? Have you thought about that?"

He shrugs. "Split-second hell-yeah before your heart explodes."

"Yeah?" she says. "Then what?"

"Gotta take out the trash today anyway."

She wants to yell in his face—scream him down—but remembers her self-defence training. De-escalate, de-escalate—diffuse. Steady on.

"Don't worry," he says. "You'll pass it." He flashes a yellowed meth-hook grin. "Eventually." He presses the knife blade just below her left ear. Tells her to open wide, and she feels the blade's bite.

No space between them now.

Steady thud in her ears.

"Swallow," he says and scrapes the blade an inch.

She grinds her teeth. Her whole body shaking and not a breath between them now. She opens her mouth, jaw tense. Marks the artery bulged between jaw and collar bone. Grips the thermometer tight, then grabs his knife hand quick and stabs the thermometer into his neck. Ike yells and shoves her onto the sink, cracking it off the wall. And he grabs a fistful of her hair, jerks her head to his chest—the thermometer jiggling in his neck—and presses the knife to her throat. "Open your goddamn mouth!" And she does, reaching for the thermometer but feeling the knife's bite. She swallows, opens wide— "Wider!" he hisses, and he shoves the condom to the back of her throat, gagging her.

But she swallows it.

He tightens his fist in her hair but she grabs his knife hand and smashes it off the broken sink. He drops the knife on the wet floor and right-hooks her, cracking her jaw, just as she presses a foot against the toilet and drives her shoulder into his guts, heaving him against the closed door—his one camouflaged crock skittering the knife against the toilet bolts.

Ike gurgles, tightens his grip on her hair, and yanks her head back as she twists her fist into his shirt, steering him around in the tiny room: her head craned back—hair ripping out of her scalp as she glimpses the knife by his crock.

She knees his junk—Ike squeals and lets go of her hair—and Teffy cracks her forehead against his jaw, releasing him. He staggers, spits a bloody tooth in her face and punches her in the chest, grabs both her ears—fistfuls of red hair—and thumb-gouges her eyes.

But she yanks her head loose and bites his wrist—scrap of flesh in her mouth—and he swears and slams her head against the wall: once—*fuckssakes!*—and again. *Jesus!*

She sees the yellow of the knife by her shoe—scrapes it back under her heel and he slams her head against the wall a third time. And she goes limp.

Thinks to stay still and reel him in.

Get that knife.

He pins her head to the wall with a scarred knee poked through shredded jeans—her face upturned, seeing him through half-slit eyes as he licks his cracked lip, sucks blood from his bit wrist, and plucks the thermometer from his neck.

She doesn't swallow or spit the skin in her mouth.

Just stays limp.

Dead to it.

Use his weight against him, she thinks, feeling for the knife.

"Like it rough, do you?" And the bastard grinds his knee against her ear, but she just hangs there, scraping fingers across damp linoleum. Feels the knife and grabs it.

But before she can slash it across Ike's leg, he grabs another fistful of her hair and drags her face to the piss-spattered toilet bowl.

"Fuckin Newfie," he says and thrusts her face into the shitter.

She holds her breath—water in her mouth, nose pressed against slimy porcelain. Flailing her arms as she stabs the knife blindly at the fucker behind her who is pressing her head deeper into the hole.

She screams, water bubbling her ears as she swipes the knife between her legs.

Catches something on him and slices back.

Ike lets go of her hair and she throws her head back, spits and gasps as she elbows him in the head—and again in the side—doubling him over.

He steadies himself, bloody hand smearing the wall. Face dead-skin white—other hand gripping between his legs, blood dripping off his knuckles.

He wobbles, barely able to stand—and she drops the knife in the toilet behind her. Spits and feels her ears burn as she grabs his fleshy lobes, his mouth a drooling O.

She leans in—face an inch from his ferreting eyes—then shoves him onto the toilet. Watery plunk and the guy's jeans slide down tattooed calves to his quivering boots.

"You . . . you. . . ."

His voice a half-boiled hiss.

She swings her satchel behind her. A tear slips down Ike's whiskered face and she turns to open the bathroom door, but Ike catches her satchel strap and yanks, and she panics and spins—half-lifting him off the toilet, his blood-slick thighs shaking as she hoofs him in the chest, hand thrust in her bag for her pepper spray.

He comes at her again, swiping the pepper spray out of her hand. It clinks across the floor and she kicks his left knee. He buckles and she boots him in the face, staggering him back onto the toilet bowl.

Ike vomits on his shaking knees and she shoulders through the door, breaking the flimsy latch, and books it down the junk-filled hall and out the apartment door. She runs down Peppett Street and some side alley in the direction of the ferry, or what she hopes is the direction of the ferry. But she doesn't know. She's just running now. Running with no time to check her phone to see if Ellie has messaged. Running blind. Flat-out till she sees a church spire and heads for it, driven by some old memory of hiding beneath the high altar of her church back home. With Fin. The both of them safe for a while—an hour, maybe two—as the cops searched the bay.

She tries the front doors of the church and finds them locked. Races alongside the sanctuary to the side door, turns the knob and swings inside, closing the door behind her, quiet as she can. She scans the aisles for some sign of priest or cleaner—old ladies fussing. But the sanctuary is empty, thank God. Tomblike. The only sound her thudding pulse.

She checks her phone. Sees she has six hours to Ellie's return.

Six fucking hours.

And all she can think to do in that instant is follow her young self beneath the high altar. Fin there with her. Both of them shivering. She'd tried not to think about him as Ellie drove past the exit for Corner Brook on their way to the ferry. But she *did* think of him—longed to see him as she longs to see him now. To have him hold her as he did that night. Please. That desire knife-sharp in her gut.

She twists under the solid oak table, holding herself tight as she begins to sob, crying into her knees and sick to her stomach now, nauseous—so sick she's gonna vomit. But there's a condom the size of a baby's fist in her stomach and she's scared it'll break if she brings it up. Crying so hard she's choking, gagging now, and she rolls onto her knees and heaves—heaves—coughing the condom into her shaking hands, bile dripping between her fingers, marking the carpet like great drops of blood.

She slips the slimy latex balloon into the gray ziplock Troy gave her. And she adds to it the other two sacks of heroin and the extra things Ike supplied. The suppository and Vaseline. The baking powder and quinine. And she zips it all together, wiping her eyes with the backs of her hands, trying to swallow the sickly sweet cherry-taste in her mouth.

She cowers back under the altar, satchel in her lap, not knowing how much heroin she's carrying now and who'll be coming after it. She knows she can't stay here forever.

She knows that. Knows she'll have to run.

But for now she curls into the tightest ball she can, able to see nothing save Christ's pierced feet and the flickering red glow of the chancel lamp.

~ 9 ~

SHE WAKES TO THE SOUND of vacuuming, and when she checks her phone she sees that the ferry started boarding ten minutes ago and that she has six missed texts from Ellie.

The last one asking: *Are you still here at the Peppett St. place?*

She texts Ellie in a panic saying she's on her way to the ferry and will meet her onboard. *Please don't have gone into that apartment*, she prays, rolling to her knees to peer under the altar and see an old man bend to press a purple vacuum under the front pew, cleaning his way toward the exit she came in by.

The vacuum clicks off. She hears a door suck open and swish shut. Then . . . nothing. She peeks out from under the altar and sees the vacuum standing in place like an old guard. But the man is gone—outside for a smoke, most likely.

She climbs out from her hiding place, opens the door, and bumps the old man's elbow, scattering cigarette ash on his cardigan.

"Who are you?" he says, flicking more ash off his cigarette with one hand and dusting his sweater with the other. "I didn't see you in there."

"Thought the priest might be in for confession," she says.

He looks at her skeptically. "Hours for that are posted on the sign out front," and he points the way with his smoke.

She smiles, pushes her satchel behind her, and says she'd love to chat— really—but she's late for the ferry. She starts for the street and he calls, "It's only a five minute walk," and she breaks into a flat-out run, chugging as her phone calmly dictates directions to the terminal.

She runs across the half-filled parking lot to the massive boat, not looking back: afraid to see Ike or the old man or anybody paying her mind or chasing her down. But she sees no one. Pulls the collar of her shirt up over her face, as if wiping sweat from her eyes. Flashes her ticket and lurches past the helmeted guard in his reflective vest.

She weaves between two over-packed minivans and takes a set of white steel stairs, her thigh vibrating suddenly as she reaches the uppermost deck. The ferry lists on the water and her leg buzzes again.

A check of the phone shows a call from that unknown number. Troy . . . but not calling on Ger's device. Why's that? She sends Ellie a text to say she's onboard. And Ellie texts back with the lounge that they're in. Teffy flicks back to Troy's missed call, even as she looks for a hatch to the open-air deck, not wanting some nosey bayman to overhear anything. Her phone zizzes in her hand again—Troy calling back—and her stomach sloshes with the movement of the city-sized ship.

Another eight-hour voyage, she thinks. *Brutal.*

Same as it was coming, and she remembers her scopolamine patch. The thermometer stuck in Ike's neck. The pregnancy test dropped in toilet water.

She pulls out the patch, hoping it's just that: that she's seasick and not feverish. Or pregnant. Or both. *Fucking hell. What if?*

Jesus, Ger.

She sticks the patch behind her ear and the phone wriggles in her fist. Troy again. She dodges past a little girl who casts her a strange look. Ducks through the open hatch and feels cold rain on her face. The phone goes off again, she answers—and Troy barks, "Toffee!"

"Yeah?" She turns her hunched shoulders to a guy who's just come out for a smoke.

"You not hear your phone?"

"Just trying to find a quiet place," she says.

"It's a phone call, not a séance."

She glances at the smoker and says casually to Troy, "So what's on the go?" like she's chatting up a friend.

"*You'd* better be on the fuckin go, Toffee. Know what I mean?" His voice crackles. "Did you make the boat?"

"On it."

"On making it?"

"On the boat," she says.

"With my package?" He sounds surprised.

She cups her hand to her mouth. "You told him to force-feed me that stuff!"

Troy tuts her childlike. "Either way you were gonna eat it, Toffee. There's only ever Option A with me." She hears a lighter spark. "Stuckless should've told you that."

She wants to detonate the phone pressed to the bastard's ear. Hears him breathing on his end. She waits . . . waits . . . waits . . . and finally he says, "Did Stuckless actually think I forgot it all inside Her Majesty's? That I forgot his ratting me out put me there?"

"Least you had a view of the lake," she says. "More'n most of us."

"Baygirl charm won't get you out of this one, Toffee."

Smell of Ike's breath, face in the shitter, air now iodine-sharp—all to try and what? What choice did she have but to pick up the package and try to keep Ger alive another day.

Troy says, "You still there, Toffee?"

"Is Ger alright?"

He laughs. "A debt is a debt. And it's Stuckless's time to pay up."

"How do you expect Ger to pay you back for six years? You earned those years, remember. And more. A kid died in a bombing tied back to you."

"The case fell apart, Toffee. That's why I got early release."

"Ger just wanted out," she says. "Can't you understand that?"

"He wanted to pin that squirrely cunt's death on me."

The smoker on deck with her shrugs and tosses her a burnt *hey-girl* glance, then saunters off down the deck. Once the guy is out of earshot, she says, "If it wasn't you, then who was it?"

She looks back across the water waiting on his reply. Sees the church spire and recalls the night Ger told her about his dealing, hands clasped and shaking. Things he'd done and never said. Bashed this one guy bloody and left him a wheezing mess. Waterboarded another in a bathtub because he owed Troy money and wouldn't tell Ger where he had it stashed. She hadn't thought him capable of such violence. But she knew her own thoughts. Her memory of Fin's dad dead between them.

"Toffee?" Troy says.

"I'm still here."

"I'm not what a writer like yourself might call benevolent. Stuckless owes me skin, and I want people alive so they can pay up. Blood makes no money."

The captain's voice crackles over the loudspeakers, announcing they're setting sail, and she feels the boat roll on the roughening waters, its engines churning them out to sea.

"Absolution," Troy says. "Like blood it makes no money. So I don't deal in it."

"Did you send someone to the gallery last night?" she asks.

Troy laughs and she wonders if that's a yes. She hadn't thought about the question, just blurted it out. Troy says, "Cunts like Stuckless don't just get to walk away, Toffee. Sure, he might for a while, might think he can rat out the boss and make a clean exit. But guys like me, we don't forget. We keep hard ledgers. We come back for what's ours."

She knows Troy isn't the kind to forget anything, let alone the likes of Ger putting him behind bars. "I have the stuff," she says, throat still burning from coughing up that condom.

"I know you do, Toffee. Know how I know?"

She grips the rail, thinks of flinging herself overboard into the churning gray sea. "Three bobs and you're sunk," her Nan would say.

"I knows you have the stuff," he says, "'cause I know you loves him. Why else would you have stormed out of your house and hopped in my cab? Why else would you have tried to push me around with your fuckin newspaper talk?"

She's still in his cab in her mind. "Feels like a big sea," she says and hears the lighter spark again on the other end. "Might mean getting in late."

"Toffee . . . you knows how much I like being on the water."

She feels the ferry heave as they churn out past the headland and veer north, the land disappearing in fog behind them, a lone lighthouse winking.

"Did I lose you, Toffee?"

"No," she says, recalling the snorkel and scuba mask, the picture of Ger's old friend drowning. The look on Troy's face that night, his non-answer about the gallery break-in. *He wants to drown you, girl. You and Ger both.* "I'm still here," she says and shuts her eyes. Says, "I'll make the drop," and opens her eyes, gutsick at the sudden thought of Troy's face when he told her his guys had already picked Ger up.

"When you deliver it, Toffee, I wants it cut, ready to sell. Got it?"

And he hangs up.

She lowers the phone and her stomach gurgles as she ducks inside the ferry's lounge, scouting for a place to sit. Eventually she finds a big empty chair and curls up in it, holding her satchel across her chest. Her phone buzzes again and she pulls it out to see a text from Ellie: *Where are you?*

She clicks off the phone. Clenches her shaking fists to still them. Tries to shake Ike from her mind as she touches the knife scrape on her neck: that thermometer jiggling just below his bulging jaw. She blinks and spits on her bloody knuckles. Wipes them on her red-snap shirt before shouldering back into the chair. She should text Ellie back, but she doesn't. Sees that same girl she glimpsed earlier poke her head around the bank of chairs.

"Mom," the girl calls over her shoulder, "there's two here!" And Teffy sees she means the two chairs next to her.

"I'm sorry," she says when the mother joins her daughter. "I'm saving these for two friends. They're just getting a few things from the car. Sorry."

The woman sniffs and walks off. The girl looks at her strange, and Teffy almost tells her to go on, but doesn't for some reason. Maybe it's that the girl's hair is as red as her own. Like Teresa's in those trial photos. Teffy holds her satchel to her chest. Smells puke and cherry syrup on her hands. Waits for the girl to leave, but the girl just stares at her.

"Better go find your mother," Teffy says after a while.

The girl's eyes narrow. Then she pulls her pink jacket sleeves over her fists and punches them free, making Teffy jump. "Pow! Pow pow! Pow!" she says, pumping her fists.

Teffy can feel her pulse in her eyeballs. The girl scared her. She tries to laugh, tries to get a hold of herself. Says, "And who're you pretending to be?"

"Thor," the girl says. "From *Avengers*."

"Why?"

"'Cause he smashes *everything*."

"And that's what you want to do?"

The girl shrugs. Looks at her funny. "What's the point of being a hero if you can't smash stuff?" The girl blinks, smiles again at Teffy, and then runs off in search of her mother.

Spit of your own tongue, she thinks, shuffling quickly through all she's smashed to this point. *No hero, though, are you? Just a baygirl everyone expects to slut-the-fuck-up and head home out of it. Everyone but Ger.*

She knows this from being with Ger: You can grow strong on one person's belief. Even a Brow-raised thug like him. Like when she first met him outside the courthouse. A former collector but with this white-hot desire for them both to somehow make it. Break free of their pasts. Together. Buck the system and become something.

Neither token townies nor lifers on skidrow.

Something of their own making.

She wonders what Ger will say when he finds out what she's done. What she's had to do already to make sure he sucks air another day. She wriggles deeper into her chair, feeling her stomach turn as the ferry churns through deepening swells. Feels herself slipping, so she curls up, pulls out her phone to see another three messages from Ellie.

The last asking where she is.

She messages back, and in a few minutes Ellie comes around the bank of chairs with her pink-haired niece, a woman of thirty or so in torn jeans, a *Jesus Is Queer* T-shirt, and tattooed sleeves delicately inked to her purple nail-polished hands.

"I'm Lisetta," the woman says kindly.

"My niece," Ellie says, darting her a strange look.

Teffy motions to the free chairs and Lisetta and Ellie slump into them, sounding as exhausted as Teffy feels. Lisetta puts her feet up on the wall in front of them, her backpack on her lap. Something shifts inside the bag and Teffy hears a clink. "Ellie tells me you're bringing your mother home to Newfoundland."

Lisetta says, "To St. Mark's, yeah," and looks over at Teffy. Raises an eyebrow. Ellie is busy digging in her purse, muttering about where the hell she put her ginger Gravol. "You have something on your face," Lisetta says, and touches her finger to her own left cheek to indicate where. "Yeah, there," she says when Teffy touches the spot.

A scab of dried paper comes off on her fingertips.

Toilet paper.

She stands shakily and goes to brush past them, saying, "I gotta use the washroom." But Lisetta grabs her arm and says, "Here," and thrusts her backpack into Teffy's hands. "There's shampoo in there."

"That's alright," Teffy says. "I can just—"

"You don't want to smell like pink soap for the next eight hours. Trust me. I'm a musician. I know these things."

Teffy looks at the bag in her hands. "Thank you," she says.

And Lisetta says, "No worries. I know what it's like to be stuck needing a sink shower after a show. And don't freak out about the urn inside." She nods at the bag. "Just bring Mother back in one piece." She winks at Teffy. "And tell me if she talks your ear off."

Ellie laughs. "Stefany could do that, now couldn't she?"

And Teffy hears them start into it as she walks toward the restroom, not sure what's freaking her out more: the human ash in Lisetta's bag or the heroin in her own.

~ 10 ~

T HERE'S A BUSTLE OF WOMEN in the restroom, and once Teffy gets her turn, she stays in her stall until the faucets stop running and the last pair of legs disappear. Finally, there's a lull as people settle in for the long voyage.

Teffy holds both her satchel and Lisetta's bag on her lap, wondering if Ellie ventured into Ike's apartment when her texts went unanswered. The old artist gave her a strange look back there, but said nothing.

Should be fine, should be fine. Except for the heroin in your satchel. What if you're pulled over and they finds it in your bag, what then?

She pulls loose the drawstrings on Lisetta's bag and peers inside. Sees the silver lid of the urn and slides it out of the black T-shirt it's wrapped in. A black-glass mason jar urn. She holds it in her left hand. Feels the weight of it.

Then she flips back the flap on her satchel and pulls out the gray ziplock with the condom-socked heroin inside.

She holds them both up, the jar of human ash only slightly heavier than the bag of hard drugs. *Okay,* she thinks. *Are you really gonna do this?*

A quick switch and the heroin would be ensconced in a funeral urn. And what cop would check that? If they did happen to test the ash in her bag, they'd find it to be human remains. My father's, she could say. And that would be fine until the RCMP check her story and find her dad alive and mystified as to why she said he was dead.

She'll have to work on that story. But the switch—the switch will work. She's sure of that. Hope like a hook in her jaw and she can't stop smiling.

Just do it, she tells herself.

Okay, okay.

So she spins the lid off the urn and sets it in Lisetta's bag. Then she peels open the O'Shea Shoreline ziplock and immediately smells cherry vomit.

Maybe just fill the urn with the quinine and baking powder? Would that be heavy enough?

Not by half, she thinks.

Inside the urn is a thick plastic bag that's been slit open. Lisetta has been into her mother's remains already. No telling now if it's been tampered with. But that's a good thing.

She slides the bag out and sees ash the color of beach sand. Which worries her because she has no idea what color the heroin is. She'd just assumed it would be white.

She holds up a knotted condom, and feels her throat phlegm-up. Remembers what it felt like to swallow the thing. The taste of fruity latex. Ike's fingers in her mouth. Sour chews on his breath. Yellow flash of that knife in her mind.

Her face in the toilet.

She pinches one of the condoms and sets it aside. Then opens the two-ply baggy of cut-powder, slips out the inner bag, and reaches for the thick plastic one containing the remains.

It's just ash, she keeps telling herself. *Just dust.*

But her hands quiver as she shakes the urn's contents into the spare baggie, the remains chalky as a cold fire pit. She holds her breath, trying not to get the granular bits on her fingers as she shakes the bag. The ash is fine as flour, save for the odd bone chunk.

Down to the dusty dregs now.

She flicks those loose then sets the heavy-duty bag back in her satchel and notices the printed label on it. But she doesn't read it, knowing what's written there.

She pinches a condom's knotted end and fishes out her pen. Clicks it against the artery in her neck. The mark she'd aimed for on Ike. Right there. She spins the pen on her thumb. Holds the condom over the empty ash-bag and carefully pokes a hole near the knot. She pulls the hole wider and sees— as the heroin pours out—that it's sandy and only a little darker than the ash.

She shakes out the condom into the urn's bag. First the one, then the other two. Holes carefully poked in each. The contents poured out like beach sand into her purse on that day she and Ger spent at Sandy Cove.

She opens the baggie of cut-powder and pours it in on top of the heroin, trying not to imagine what Fin would say to her if he saw what she was doing now. Him or Ger. She thinks of Ger and the unanswered calls from his phone. Wonders where he is and if he's still alive. *Just stay alive,* she tells him. *Do whatever you need to do, just stay alive.* Someone walks into the bathroom and pees in the stall next to her. She sits motionless and waits for them to be done. To leave. And it seems a long while after they've left before she allows herself to breathe again. She folds the plastic bag and shakes it to mix. And after she's given it a good toss, she holds it up to see it's lightened a little.

Looks sandier now. Almost like the cremated remains. Almost.

Quick look and you wouldn't be able to tell the difference.

She eases the thick plastic bag back into the urn and spins on the lid, then replaces the urn in Lisetta's backpack, wrapped again in its black T-shirt. She zips it all shut—clasp and click, and then she shoulders Lisetta's bag, opens the stall door, and decides to ask if Ellie found her Gravol or if she has anything else for an upset stomach.

She stops when her mirrored reflection halts to stare at her.

The scab of dried toilet paper on her face. Hair a mess and her skin so pale every freckle stands out like a fleck of dried blood. But she's smiling inside. This'll work. It'll work and she'll do the switch-back in Grand Falls and that'll be that. Safe passage from here to there and a step closer to closing the deal with Troy and getting Ger back.

She rests both her satchel and Lisetta's bag on the counter and uses Lisetta's travel shampoo to scrub her skin raw. Sees the scrape on her neck hidden by her jawline, barely noticeable with her hair down like this. A final check for blood spatter and she feels herself sway under the scopolamine's influence. Sleepy and longing for that chair as she looks in the mirror a last time, imagining Fin shaking his head. When she gets back to her chair, she drops the heroin in Lisetta's lap, casual as can be, recalling what she'd told Fin on that dark night long ago.

It had to be done. It had to be done.

~ 11 ~

I T'S DARK WHEN THEY REACH Port aux Basques and instead of braving the highway at night, Ellie opts for a cheap hotel. "Better than hitting a moose," she says—and Teffy agrees, the scopolamine still fogging her mind.

She needs a bed, a chance to reset. And the hotel they find online sounds alright. The Beacon, it's called. But when they pull up, Teffy sees that the 'e' on the neon sign is out, so it reads The Bacon. And it smells of old fry oil when they walk through the door. They get their room key from a woman named Joyce and drop their stuff off before finding their way to the bar, where Joyce said there was a makeshift party on the go.

Lisetta has brought her guitar because Joyce said, "We can always do with a bit of music, love." And when Joyce sees them all walk through the door she waves them over, a half-spent cigarette in hand, smoke tickling her rheumy eyes. "Now the party's doubled in size," she says, and introduces them to Skip and John.

Teffy says a friendly "hello" and Lisetta slings her bag under the table, the urn clinking against the table leg. Teffy eyes the bag, then asks if Joyce has any scissors.

"Behind the bar," Joyce says, waving a yellowed finger.

At the bar, Teffy looks back at the group circled around the table, drinking and smoking—Ellie teasing the two men like they're cousins or childhood friends—and she wishes Ger was here to draw her in, find them a place at the table—so she could tap her toe against that urn and relax.

John, the heavy-set guy serving drinks, says, "Sounds like buddy in 205's getting swung round by his ankles again."

John's friend Skip tips his ball cap, forehead bleached from the hat-line up.

Joyce wipes her eyes with the sleeve of her sweater, and John rubs the faded tattoo on his forearm—a Sacred Heart cinched in barbed wire. Shakes his head as he reaches into the cooler for a handful of ice that he dumps into a red cup before glugging in a swish of rum and cracking open a Coke.

Teffy looks down at her fanned fingers. After handling the heroin and ash she wants the nails cut back to the quick. *Leave no trace,* she thinks and snips a few, then turns to the small television behind the bar. Nips a few more and shifts to the next hand. *NTV News* flickers on the TV and a dark-haired woman addresses them, though the volume is too low to hear.

She nods at the screen. "Any big news?"

"Only that *Sin* John's is earning back its old nickname," Joyce says as she lights another cigarette. "I wouldn't go near the place myself."

"Why's that?" she says and clips her last nail.

"Well, my love, it's like this"—Joyce whirls her hand theatrically—"if ya wants the salt of the earth, you comes around the bay, don't you?"

Lisetta laughs at that. "You sound like my mother," she says—and Teffy sees the girl touch her toe to the bag under the table.

"Your mother a baygirl, is she?" Joyce says.

"From St. Mark's," Lisetta says, turning to Ellie. "We're gonna try to catch the ferry tomorrow." And Ellie nods at that, but John cuts in that they'd better be up before dawn—or earlier—if they wants to make tomorrow's ferry.

"Then we better get our drinking in now!" Ellie raises her cup and catches Teffy's eye as Joyce cackles, the proprietor's head warbling drunkenly.

Like Ger, Teffy thinks, *when he's half cut.*

"The bar still open?" she asks Joyce, though all she wants is tap water. But buying drinks will keep her in kicking distance of Lisetta's bag. And the heroin inside.

"Joyce is the founder of this illustrious party," John says.

And Joyce looks from Lisetta to Ellie to the nearly empty bottle of Lamb's. "Five bucks, three drinks!" She slaps the table. "Evening special, seeing as how we have live music." And she claps as Lisetta pulls out her guitar and starts tuning. "John will keep the cash," she says, "won't ya, John?" and John grins at Joyce as he pulls another forty out of the cooler, wipes it on his pant leg, and thumps it on the table as he cranks off the cap.

Teffy's hip buzzes and she slips it out to see Troy's number. Again. Must've got tired of trying to get through on Ger's phone. She blinks and watches the call drop in her hand.

"A round for everyone!" she blurts, tossing a twenty on the table. She waves her phone and says, "I gotta take this," praying it has something to do with Ger. Some hint he's alive. A muttered hello. Anything.

"I think it's her *boyfriend*," Lisetta sings, strumming her guitar—and Skip whistles as Teffy makes for the exit. She taps Troy's missed call in the hall, holding the phone to her ear. Wind shudders the front door, rain lashing the glass.

The phone clicks. "Saw you rang," she says.

"Just heard from Ike."

She heads for the rattling door, not wanting anyone in the party room to overhear. "Ike called you?"

"He's an associate, Toffee."

"A what?"

"An associate. And when an associate gets his balls knifed in his own home, that's bad for business."

"So is fucking the delivery girl!" she hisses.

"I don't think you understand my business, Toffee. And you—you fucked with my business today. When people fuck with my business, I fuck them with a crowbar."

"If you—"

"If I what, Toffee? Are you gonna tell me how things are gonna go down? Are you gonna threaten me?" His voice is eerily calm. Cold. "Or are you gonna get me my goods so I don't pull Stuckless's tongue out of the second mouth I intend to cut in his neck?"

"I was just—"

"You're gonna make the St. Mark's ferry morning after tomorrow. Did ya get that? The St. Mark's ferry."

"The St. Mark's ferry," she says, hoping that means he's not going to sic the cops on her. He's playing another game, though. But what? She thinks of the ride she's hitched with Ellie and Lisetta and the fact that Ellie's dating Markus O'Shea, and it is O'Shea's company name lettering the ziplock of human ash in her satchel.

So much mud and dirt, she can't think straight.

"Why St. Mark's?" she says.

"So you don't get blood on my nice clean townie streets."

She hears a Bic lit on the other end. The wind howls outside and the door bangs open and sucks shut. Joyce pokes her head out of the barroom down the hall.

"Someone come in?" the landlady calls.

Teffy slips a hand over her phone. "Just me."

Joyce waves her off and ducks back into the room, Troy breathing in her ear. "You better make the St. Mark's ferry, Toffee."

"And when I do?"

"Watch your texts."

The phone dies and the wind screams outside. She wants to punch a fist through glass—press some button and incinerate the cab Troy's likely sitting in right now.

She walks back toward the barroom, fishing in her pocket for another twenty. She needs a drink. She needs six. But can't stomach one.

Christ on a crutch.

~ 12 ~

TEFFY'S STOMACH GURGLES AS SHE sits up from her slump in the back seat. Sees its dark now and there's a coffee shop and pharmacy across the street in front of them. And a restaurant behind. They all slept in and were sluggish getting on the road this morning, Ellie and Lisetta having both nearly disappeared into the bottle of rum last night. But once hangovers had been treated with Ibuprofen and antacids, they'd driven into the afternoon and evening.

Teffy has slept through most of it, drugged with this scopolamine patch she picked up in Stephenville. She was asleep before Corner Brook, which is good, she thinks, because she might have asked Ellie to drive her to Fin's house. And then what?

What would she have said to him after all these years?

Waking now, she's thankful the conversation never happened because she'd have wound up spilling everything to Fin—every last detail and damn the fact that they haven't spoken in years. She'd tell him everything if she saw him.

The thought makes her nauseous and she's about to unbuckle, but a police cruiser pulls in beside them. And all she can do is blink.

Lisetta says that they're in Grand Falls to grab a burger.

"You hungry?" Ellie says.

"My stomach's still a bit off," she says, eyeing the cop.

Lisetta pulls a pack of Export A's out of her pocket, reaches back to grab her backpack, and glances at Teffy. "We can get you something."

"I'll be okay," she says, and hears the two front doors *thwack* shut. Lisetta and Ellie cross the wet pavement to the restaurant's entrance, Lisetta adjusting the bag of heroin on her shoulder and pointing back at the car with a lit cigarette.

Saying something about her, sure.

But what?

Teffy watches them in the mirror until they go inside. She'd said she wasn't hungry so she could stay in the car with the urn and switch back ash for heroin. But now the urn is gone and there's a cop next door, the windows fogging, pulse throbbing in her throat. She sinks lower in her seat and watches the constable in the car next door.

Wonders if Ike talked to anyone other than Troy. Did he give them a sketch? Or was there a camera she didn't see? Maybe buy some hair color at the pharmacy. Change her look and hitch a new ride. Or catch the bus back to St. John's after she makes the switch-back.

She swallows hard against a surge in her throat. Presses a hand to her belly and wonders again. *No, there's no way.*

But she's been pinballing the thought all day, in her waking moments, knocking it up against her worry for Ger and wondering what Fin would make of this mess. The pregnancy test dropped in Ike's bathroom. What would it have read? The pharmacy sign glares at her through the wet windshield. And the cop hasn't moved. But maybe he's not looking for her.

Just sort it! Hair down or up when you cross the street? It was up when she caught the ferry south. But it's down now.

She tousles it.

Ike must've talked to more than Troy. Or his DNA did. Blood all over that bathroom floor. She shivers. Savage what she did—but fuck him. Seriously: fuck him. She hears faint bass thumping and spies the cop's crewcut sharp against the blue of his computer. Just walk nonchalant across the street. That's it. Hair down and he won't look twice.

So she stands.

But a car door clicks—thumping loud bass into the parking lot—and she drops to the pavement. Sees Kevlar-capped boots two cars over. She stretches under Ellie's car, water seeping through her jeans, and she needs to pee now—*Fuckssakes, girl! You don't even have the stuff on you. What are you doing?*

She pulls her satchel closer to her side and glances past her own shoes to the restaurant door. Watches the cop's boots. Sees them shift.

Jangle of keys and a cellphone goes off.

"Constable Neary here," the cop says. "Yeah. Wait a sec." Then he gets back in the cruiser and closes the door, cutting the bass back to half volume. Nixes the music altogether. Teffy shuffles further under Ellie's car, dragging her satchel with her.

Gravelly asphalt scrapes her back, her face under the car's front passenger seat, the undercarriage is so rotted she can see the floor mat. She's breathing hard, thinking the cop should be moving on soon. Praying he moves on soon.

The concrete is cold on the back of her head, hair wet.

Christ.

Her leg vibrates and she pulls out her phone, presses it against the car's undercarriage, two inches from her face, and taps the touchscreen.

A new text from Ger's number, saying: *I'm headed out of town. Call me.* Why would Troy tell her he was going out of town?

She hits reply and turns the phone to get a fuller keypad, but cocks her thumbs when she hears another door open. Big black boots on the pavement again.

Hold your breath. The cop takes a step and stops. Keys jingle—two electronic hiccups—and a car horn barmps. Then her phone buzzes and the screen lights up. Kevlar toes turn and the constable crouches to see her prone in the muck under the car.

"Muffler trouble?" he asks.

She goes to say yes, but glances at the lit-up text. Sees it's Ger again and says, "It's my boyfriend."

"You hiding from him or looking for him?"

She reads the last text from Ger's number—*Why're you ignoring my calls?*—only half hearing the cop. She looks at the constable. Blinks, then nods. Her screen dims and goes dark.

"Saw the glow under the car," he says, "and thought: who'd put ride lights on an old junker? Gotta check this out!"

Her phone buzzes again and relights her face with another text from Ger. She glances back at the cop and kind of waves the phone at him.

Says, "It's him again."

"Well, I'll leave you to it," and he grunts to his feet and walks off toward the coffee shop. Teffy watches him go. Then scrambles out from under the car and her phone goes off again—this time a call from Ger's number. She answers and snaps, "What do you want!?"

"Excuse me?" But it's not Troy's voice—it's Ger.

She blinks. "How did you . . . how?"

"Are you okay?" he says,

"How did you escape—you've escaped, right?"

"Escaped from what? Tefs, seriously, are you okay?"

She can't think, can't put words to all the questions going off like gun-shots in her mind. "From Troy," she whispers. "How did you escape from Troy?" She heads across the street to the pharmacy—Lisetta's bag slung over her shoulder, phone in her free hand.

"Why would I be with Troy?" he says.

"Troy said he kidnapped you."

"You've been talking with Troy? When?" And before she can answer, he says, "Did you take five hundred dollars out of my account? Was that you?"

"You said it was *our* account."

"Yes, but five hundred bucks?"

She jingles through the front door, nods at the lady behind the register, and starts down the aisle looking for antacids or Tylenol—anything. She'd take anything right now. Ger's alive.

Ger. Is. Alive.

And he has no idea what she's talking about. About Troy or the kidnapping or anything. She fell for it. She fell for a dumb bluff and almost got raped in a dealer's grody apartment. And now she has human ash in her bag and an urn full heroin in some busker's bag, and—

"Fuck!" she yells.

"Fuck what?" Ger says.

She holds the phone away from her face and yells, "JUST FUCK, STUCKLESS! FUCK! FUCK! FUCK!" Then she looks up in one of those rounded corner mirrors to see the woman at the cash look her way. She takes a deep breath and presses the phone back to her ear.

"Tefs," Ger is saying, "honestly, where the fuck are you and why haven't you answered your phone? I've rung you like a dozen times. Even called your parents."

"You called my parents?"

"Yeah."

"And told them what?"

"That I hadn't heard from you."

"Well call them back," she snaps.

"And tell them what?"

"That I'm fine."

"You're fine, are you?"

"I don't want them to worry."

"And what about me!" he yells, and she winces away from the phone. "It's okay that *I've* been trying to get hold of you for two days and got nothing but your answering service?"

"I'm sorry," she says, and grabs a bottle of Tums on her way toward the feminine hygiene section, thinking: *This had better not be why I'm sick, Ger. 'Cause if it is and I was force-fed scat 'cause you pissed off your dealer—*

"You're breathing hard," he says.

"'Cause I'm walking fast."

She finds the display and grabs two. Then puts one back.

"So where are you?" he says.

"Around the bay, Ger. Geez. What's the big deal?"

"You took five hundred bucks," he says. "And you haven't answered your phone in two days. And in case you forgot, Hopper is out and looking for me! *And apparently you've been talking to him!* Jesus Christ, Teffy, all that makes for a very big fucking deal!"

She puts her stuff on the counter by the register, for the lady to scan, and digs in her pocket for cash, still holding the phone to her ear. "It's just—"

"Just what?"

She pays up, leaves the change on the counter, and clinks out the door, scanning the parking lot for that cop. No sign of him. "I thought Troy kidnapped you," she says.

"He's a Class-A Bullshitter, Tefs. Why would you believe him?"

She slips her stuff into her satchel. "He showed me a feed on his phone."

"A what?"

"A live feed on his phone. Someone was in our house, Ger. The night I met up with Troy. Someone was in the house. With you. I could hear your music playing."

"Vinnie dropped by," he says as she heads back across the street to the bar.

"I saw that feed," she says, "and I thought they had you. I thought that Troy had your phone. He said he had your phone."

"And that's why you weren't answering?"

"Yes," she says.

"What did he tell you to do?"

"I had to pick up something in—"

"Did you pick it up?"

She stops. "I hid it in some lady's funeral urn."

"In an urn?" he says. "Where's the urn now?"

"It belongs to Ellie Strickland's niece. It's her mother's urn. She has it now. I wanted to switch it back tonight with her mother's ashes but she took it into the restaurant, and there was this cop—"

"You have human ash in your bag?"

"It's better than the stuff Troy had me pick up."

"You need to get that stuff back," he says. "And don't tell me what it is. Not over the phone. I can guess, just don't say it. You need that on you so we can deal with Troy."

"Troy told me to catch the St. Mark's ferry tomorrow. If I tags along with Ellie and her niece maybe I can switch it back there."

"St. Mark's?" Ger says. "You'll be there tomorrow?"

"Ellie wants to be in the line-up tonight for the morning ferry."

"I'll meet you on the boat," he says—and a surge of relief washes through her. She moves on, across the parking lot to the restaurant, knotting her fingers in the satchel strap as she goes. "I'll head out tonight," Ger says. "And I'll meet you on the boat."

She presses through the restaurant door but stops halfway through, spying Ellie and Lisetta in a booth across the room from her.

"Are you still there?" Ger says.

"I'm here." She waves at Lisetta and Ellie gives her that strange look again as she cuts left to the ladies's room. Pushes through the swinging door and edges into a stall. "Have you made anything of that coded journal yet?"

"I think we can kill two birds with one shot in St. Mark's," he says.

She pops the button on her jeans and sits down

He says, "I might've scored us our biggest story yet." And he sounds excited about it. Like this is familiar territory for him. His old turf. Like he's forgotten she's carrying something for Troy—something he's guessed but won't let her say. Seriously, how is this his normal?

"That's great," she mutters, nestling her satchel between her feet and rifling through it to find the box she just bought—trying to hold her pee the whole time.

"You okay?" he says.

She rips open the box and tears off the plastic.

"What're you doing?"

Hold it steady . . . yeah . . . right there. "I'm just. . . ."

"Are you peeing?"

"Yes, Ger! I'm on the fuckin can alright!"

"You could've just said so."

"What's the story on St. Mark's?" she says. "It's not about O'Shea is it?"

He lowers his voice. "One of my old buddies gave me a tip about a smuggling operation."

Almost done . . . last bit. "Smuggling what though?"

"What I think *you're* carrying for Troy," he says—and she almost drops the phone. "That's right. Coming in off the boats and going through the fish plant."

"So you're gonna. . . ." She caps the test. "You're gonna what then?" She watches the little white circle begin to color. *Please God.*

"My buddy thinks Troy is heading up the operation," Ger says.

"What buddy?"

"He thinks Troy is trying to make a statement to his old suppliers and get back in business. Took a little . . . persuading, but I got a contact. On St. Mark's."

She stares at the test. "So. . . ."

"So if this ties back to Troy and what he has *you* carrying, this might be that story, Tefs—the big one! It might be the one to put Troy back where he belongs."

She squeezes the satchel between her shoes. She wants to throw-up—the taste of toilet water in her mouth, the memory of that fight with Ike, the human remains in the satchel between her shoes. Troy's deadline tick-tocking down.

"If I can tie him to the operation," Ger says, "that puts him back inside. We hand over the whole story to the Constabulary and RCMP and publish when they makes the arrest. Everyone will subscribe, baby—everyone! Think of our online presence then!"

"That's great, Ger. But what about what I have in my bag?"

"We'll figure it out," he says. She stifles a sob and he asks, "Are you okay?"

"So I'll meet you in St. Marks?" She wipes her cheek.

Staticky shuffle. "Just putting a few things in a bag now, then I'm on the road to you. I'll be there before the boat loads."

She stares at the test and thinks of the condom she swallowed. The condom she vomited in that church. Taste of puke and cherry latex. No rips in the latex, though—she checked on the boat when she made the switch.

But what if . . . ?

Ger says, "I'm almost ready to go," and she wants to tell him about Ike. About the break-in at Ellie's gallery too and the hell she's been through thinking he was tied-and-gagged in a basement somewhere, wondering if she'd ever see him again. She won't survive losing another person she loves. She wants to tell him that, but she can't—the words gone to ash on her tongue.

"I'm gonna make coffee," Ger says, "then I'm on the road."

She can't stomach his enthusiasm and can barely breathe as she drops her head, tears dripping off her chin—*What have you done, girl? You swallowed that shit and now what? Now what's gonna happen to the—*

"Are you there?" Ger says. "Baby . . . are you crying?"

She sniffs. "You're a real bastard, Stuckless. You know that?"

"Well, I know but—"

"You know what you're after doing?"

Silence—dead air on the line. Then, "What's going on?"

"Ger, you big dick. I'm pregnant."

~ 13 ~

BIRCH TREES WHIR BY in the dark.
Mist like sheets on her Nan's line. The Trans Canada Highway behind them now as they wend their way on this north road around
bays and inlets, by ramshackle old churches and saltbox houses—fishing
stages shunted out over the water.

Boats collared offshore.

Land and water Teffy knows. Shed parties she remembers and dozens
she doesn't. Scheming and stupid shit done by night, beach fires with Fin, an
empty bottle of tequila broken between them. Burnt mornings all hungover.
Sundays to Mass with Nan. Always. Regardless of her sandpaper eyes or the
rust on her tongue.

She looks out the window and knows this is not her shore, this string
of asphalt and blast rock. Not hers but . . . familiar. A familiar seascape made
strange now by what she carries—this heroin, these pinprick cells kicking to
live.

How long till the heart beats?

Ger asked her if she was going to keep it, and she hung up on him.

And he didn't call back, though he texted while she sat at the table with
Ellie and Lisetta after coming out of the restroom. Cold fries and ketchup.
Ellie acting weird. Uptight.

When did you find out? he wrote.

She has let that sit unanswered since Grand Falls.

An hour past now. She opens the coded journal on her phone. Just to
watch the stickmen dance. Remembers one of the notepad cartoons Fin
drew for her. Starting on the last sticky note, she could flip through the pad
and see a skeleton pluck two of its own rib bones and *rat-a-tat-tat* a march-
ing drum strapped to its spine. *You can strike up the march on your ragged*

little drum, Fin had muttered; and it wasn't until later that she realized he was singing Cohen's "Anthem," that sketched skeleton a crack in Fin's façade. A keyhole through which only she was allowed to look. The journal lights her face and she pictures these stick figures in one of Fin's notepad animations, the figure spinning around like the hand of a clock. *Tick tock tick tock.* 1, 2, 3, 4, 5, 6, 7, 8, 9, and she sees it is 9:58 p.m. on the car clock. *Past ten when we get there*, she thinks, wondering where on the road Ger might be at this point.

She writes, *Who's your St. Mark's contact?* and sends the message, not expecting a reply. She presses her forehead against the cool window, her backside wet still from scootching under the car. And she's sleepy. Sick to her stomach and sleepy. Her phone vibrates.

Ben Critch still has an in with Troy, Ger says.

She blinks. Ben Critch was the buddy Ger needed to persuade? Ben was one of the four who testified against Hopper. So it must not have been Ben in the underwater pic Troy flashed her. And not Vinnie because Dougie called him after leaving their place, asking for a ride. Connor Moffet then. Connor Moffet is dead. And no one knows but her.

Ben Critch, though—how did he keep an in with Troy through all the shit surrounding that bloody trial? That would be a trick and a half. Help put the boss away and keep your job when he gets out. Ballsy.

But Ben, as she remembers, was that kind of brazen sleveen.

She asks: *Was it Critch you had to persuade to get the St. M contact?*

The contact, Ger writes back, *part-times between fish plant and ferry.*

Okay. But if this contact is in on the deal, Teffy cannot fathom why they'd sell out the dealer paying them. Ger certainly has no money to buy info like that. So how did he get this contact's info from Critch? What kind of persuasion did that take?

She asks: *Did you offer to pay the lad?*

No . . . why?

Then why is he selling out the money?

She watches the ellipsis flicker then stop, flicker then stop.

Maybe he's not on the payroll?

Then how's he close enough to give you something useful?

Guess we'll find out when we get there ☺

You haven't left yet?

I just had to clean some stuff up. Headed out now!

She's about to ask what he had to clean, but Ellie asks, "Did you happen to see anything besides rust under the car?"

"Sorry?" Teffy says, snapping to.

"You said you were under the car, back in town."

"Yeah," she says.

"Said you heard a rattle."

"That's right."

"Did you see anything?" Ellie says again.

Teffy plays the pull string on Lisetta's bag nestled next to her now in the back seat. She thinks of the canned scat inside, the burnt bones in her own bag. That cop's red face when he asked after her boyfriend. "Nothing to cause a rattle," she says. "But Lisetta's feet might get wet if you drives through water."

Lisetta looks at her aunt in the driver's seat. "Seriously?"

"What?" Ellie shrugs. "It's an old car."

"Is there anything beneath this floor mat?"

"Sure. Whirring road."

"Doesn't the Canada Council pay artists like you?"

Ellie laughs. "Enough for a can of paint, a cardboard box, and a tooth-brush," she says. "But you only gets those if you say they're supplies."

"Things were different for Dad, I guess," Lisetta says.

"No offense," Ellie says, "but your dad can suck eggs."

"So you've said." Lisetta taps her passenger-side window. Takes a deep breath, then says, "I won't argue the fact that he was a self-righteous prick."

"At least he's dead so we can speak ill of him," Ellie says.

"I did love him, you know."

"We all did," Ellie says. "Which is why his betrayal still stings."

Lisetta looks sideways at her aunt, then out her own window again. "He thought he was doing the right thing," and Ellie snorts at that. "In writing the book, I mean: about the whale. He was trying to tell the truth, he said. That's what he always told me. Wasn't until he died that I started to hear the understory from Mom."

Ellie clucks her tongue, and Teffy sees the way she's gripping the wheel. "Thought he was telling the truth, did he?" The speedometer clicks five then ten above the speed limit, enough to rattle the car on this rough road. "A lie is given power when it's taken for truth," she says—and Teffy recognizes the line from Ellie's memoir, from the chapter in which she takes on Lisetta's dad and his book about St. Mark's and killing the whale.

She thinks of the hold Troy's lie had on her: what she did thinking it true that Ger had been abducted, what she's found herself capable of doing.

She wants to believe she and Ger will make it to the other side of this. That there will be another side to all this. Some land through this mauzy haze. *Just give me some sign*, she prays. *Some little hint this will all play out.*

A stickman spins like a clock hand in her head, the Jackson 5 singing *A, B, C, Easy as 1, 2, 3*, the jingly tune eerie in her head. And she wonders why the song has sprung to mind when her phone buzzes. A text from Troy: *My guy will message you on the morning ferry.*

She sends back a thumbs-up and stares at the back of Lisetta's pink head, wondering what the busker thought when she handed her back the bag on the ferry. She'd gripped the bag when Teffy passed it to her. Squeezed the urn inside. *Like it was a baby*, Teffy thought. *Like it was a baby and not your dead mother's ashes.* She blinks. *What you think are your dead mother's ashes.*

Teffy shakes her hand out, makes a fist and rests it like a hammer on her phone. Everything flashes red and blue of a sudden, her shadow sprawling over the console and slithering up the dash. A siren blips twice.

Ellie hisses, "Where'd he come from?" and flips on her blinker.

Teffy can see the cop's cherries in Lisetta's visor mirror—the girl's eyes wide at the twitch of the twirling lights. Teffy takes a deep breath to steady herself. Feels Ellie steer onto the gravel shoulder. This is it. They're gonna get searched for sure. But the cruiser zips past them—siren off now and the top lights too. Just the taillights blinking rat-like in the dark—winking, winking, then gone.

"What's your hurry?" Ellie says. "Geez."

Teffy slouches in her seat, trying to breathe as she taps her finger against the urn in the bag beside her. *Tick tock tick tock. . . .*

~ 14 ~

T EFFY WAKES TO A WOMAN in a bright orange raincoat knocking on Ellie's windshield. The woman knocks again and Ellie snorts from sleep, sees the woman, and lowers her window an inch.

"Cars are moving around you, Ellie," the woman says. "You wanna beat Daryl on this boat you'd better move."

"Okay okay." Ellie yawns, and the ferry worker backs away from the car to stop the next pickup from passing the Toyota. The worker gives Ellie the move-along signal with her other hand, and Ellie nods, starts the car, and rolls toward the boat.

Teffy takes a deep breath, her heart pounding. She can hear Lisetta's yawning over the sound of the metal ramp scraping the concrete wharf as the ferry rocks on rough water. Another ferry worker in the hull of the boat— zipped-up in blue coveralls and blinking through round, rimless glasses— motions for Ellie to nose her car in behind a rusted green minivan. The big blue half-ton that tried to pass her in the line-up pulls in behind her: the last vehicle to make it onboard before they crank up the ramp.

"Time to wake up." Ellie jostles her niece and Lisetta groans, reaches for her cigarettes and asks what the hell's going on.

"Where are we?"

"First in the lineup last night," Ellie says, "and just about missed the boat."

Teffy peers out her window, blinks to clear her blurry eyes, but she doesn't see Ger's car in the cluster of vehicles onboard. Did he not make it last night? Or was he too far back in the line-up? Surely he would've come knocking, she thinks, heart still pounding from the jolting wake-up call, the panic at almost missing the boat.

Jesus, girl—just stay awake.

She shakes her head, rubs a hand over her face as Lisetta steps out of the car to light a cigarette. Teffy takes a last look out the back window at the vehicles still lined up on the shore, then flings open her door, hitting the trucker who parked behind them.

"Sorry," she says, scrambling out of the car and casting a quick glance over the deck to see if she can spy Ger's rust-bucket Ford.

The trucker tips his Co-op cap and motions at Teffy with his cleft chin. Says, "Friend of Ellie's, are ya? Up from town."

She glances at Ellie who is staring straight out her windshield, shoulders stiff. "Ellie," the guy calls through the window, but Ellie refuses to look his way. So the guy knocks on the passenger's window and says, "I see even Markus can't get you out of this deathtrap."

Ellie turns to give the guy a hard glare, and he snorts.

"There's that dandelion look," he says, smirking as he squeezes past Teffy, and Teffy turns to see that Lisetta has gone around the front of the car and is fishing something out of the trunk now—her purse or bag, maybe.

A look in the back seat says the bag is gone. Lisetta slams the trunk and Teffy sees a big purple purse slung over her shoulder. But no bag? In the trunk, then. She's locked it in the trunk. But the car's unlocked. See there? Just flick the trunk-latch and make the switch.

Tickety-boo.

She hears bleating and steps back to see three goats tethered in the bed of the grumpy trucker's pickup.

"I hate goats." Lisetta swipes the cigarette from her mouth and blows smoke. Teffy steals a glance at the Toyota's trunk, the cracked reflector and the keyhole in its center.

And if the trunk latch doesn't work?

Then she'll go through the back seat.

More than one way to gut a fish.

Ellie pulls herself out of the driver's seat and stands there like she's just been slapped. "Coffee's up the stairs," she says and they all head for the upper deck and lounge, Teffy glancing behind her, hand on the phone in her pocket.

Waiting for that text from Troy's guy and thinking on Ger—wondering why he didn't make the boat. She looks over the rail and sees land slip by as they heave their way across the tickle, water rough and the boat small enough to feel it.

She tries calling Ger, but his inbox is full and the call drops.

~ 15 ~

TEFFY CLAWS A STYROFOAM CUP of creamy coffee scored from a machine in the corner of the lounge, globs of powdered cream floating on the surface. Ellie is stewing in the seat next to her, and Lisetta is staring longingly at Teffy's coffee. She asks if either of them wants anything, and Ellie asks her niece, "Can I bum a smoke off you?"

Lisetta hands over a cigarette and her lighter and Ellie makes for the door, nodding at two women watching her go. Lisetta checks her purse and pockets, patting away until she finally sighs and asks if Teffy has some coin for a coffee. Teffy slides a toonie across the table to Lisetta, who scrapes the coin into her fist and heads to the coffee machine. The two women who'd nodded to Ellie on her way outside are there now, one slipping in a packet of instant java, the other waiting for an electric kettle to boil. Both close enough Teffy can hear their nattering.

"How much is the tea?" Lisetta asks the woman waiting on the kettle.

"Kettle's mine, love," the woman says. "Can't stand that gut-rot Maisey's got on the go."

Maisey chortles. "She's some tea snob, this one. But Del will spot you a cup, hey Del?"

Del nods and pours boiling water into her own pink travel mug. "And you," she says to Lisetta, "you a tea drinker?"

"Tea was my mother's drink," Lisetta says.

"Your mother a Newfoundlander?" says Maisey.

"From St. Mark's."

"A St. Mark's girl!" Del's voice lilts with delight as she reaches for another cup and drops a tea bag into it. "Sure you might've said that before," she scolds, reaching the kettle. "A St. Mark's girl! She lives away now, does she?"

"We lived in Ontario," Lisetta says as she accepts the steaming cup.

"Lived?" Maisey says. "So your mother's passed on?"

Teffy slides a hand over the satchel in her lap, phone on the table next to her coffee.

"She was a Strickland," Lisetta says, and Del asks if her mother was related to Hilda or to Mattie, or were her people the South Shore Stricklands. "Must be Mattie's people if you knows Ellie there," and she nods at the door.

"My mom was Stefany," Lisetta says. "Ellie's my aunt."

Del puckers, pink mug to her lips. "Your mother's Stefany Strickland?"

Lisetta nods.

"That Ken Barry's wife?"

Lisetta says, "Yeah?"

"Ken Barry," Del spits. "He turned the whole friggin country against us, ya know, with that book of his. Jobs lost, fishery almost closed. Poor picture of Newfoundland and half of it pulled straight out of his arse. Did your dad ever tell ya that—that he made the most of it up? So much smoke over something he didn't know three ticks about."

Teffy watches Lisetta. Sees Del's eyebrows flick—Maisey sipping her drink. The three women stand silent, a kettle steaming between them.

Then Maisey asks if Lisetta is planning to see her uncles. "Mike will be glad to see ya," she says. "But I'd have Mike call Daryl, then maybe wait three or four days."

Teffy sees Del shift in her purple windbreaker. "That was Daryl's truck a few cars back of us, wasn't it?" Del says.

"Didn't think he'd got on," says Maisey.

Teffy looks up from her cup to see Del staring cold at Lisetta. "You wants to steer clear of Daryl," she says.

Lisetta nods—and Maisey asks her how long she's staying on St. Mark's. She says, "I want to sort a few things out."

"A word of advice." Del shoulders her bag and reaches for her mug on the counter. "Don't dredge up what's settled."

"I was just bringing Mother's ashes home."

"As well you should," says Maisey. "Now, if you'll excuse us." She takes Del's stiffened arm. "This one and me have a date with a deck of cards." Then she leads her friend around the corner and into the other lounge.

Lisetta returns to the table—shell-shocked and blinking still. Teffy is about to say something—some offhand quip to make the girl feel better: *Just the way things are. So don't worry it much.* She's about to say just that—for Lisetta and herself both.

But her phone starts buzzing.

~ 16 ~

SHE SCOOPS UP HER DEVICE so Lisetta doesn't see the text. Says she forgot something in the car and heads for the stairs, passing through the bow-facing lounge where she sees Del and Maisey with that grumpy trucker who seemed to know Ellie and asked if Teffy was from town.

She darts them a nod, then takes the stairs two at a time to the loading deck. Looks to the bow—over the hoods of trucks, cars, and SUVs—but sees no one.

Not a soul at the stern ramp either.

She texts: *I'm here, where are you?*

A ferry worker steps out from a stern-side stairwell on the far side of the boat. Pulls out a phone and thumbs something, then looks her way.

Her phone vibrates. The ferry guard stares at her. And she reads the text.

Give me a wave, it says.

She waves.

And the ferry worker heads her way, sloughing in his blue coveralls. She recognizes his round, rimless glasses—the guy who helped them park. Thick neck, she sees, and broad shoulders—lazy-ass swagger and bigger than her by eighty pounds.

But a bit of a doughboy, aren't you, buddy?

She rounds Ellie's car to meet him by the truck at the back of the ship, the goats staring at them slot-eyed from the bed of the truck.

She reads the tag on the lad's coveralls—*Jake*, it says.

And Jake nods at the goats. "Says he's gonna use them to make goat cheese."

"You knows the driver?" she says.

"Everybody knows Big D."

She asks if he's a bastard to everyone.

"Only if ya pisses him off," Jake says, one hand slung behind his back. "You have the stuff on ya?"

"Not on me," she says.

He drops his hand from behind his back—a thick chain swings from his fist—and he pushes his glasses up his nose with his other hand. "Hopper told me ya might punk out."

"Told you that, did he?"

"Told me to be ready."

She nods. "Hence the chain?"

"For securing motorcycles in rough weather."

"I'm not a Harley," she says, flirting the words to see if she can play him.

Jake stretches the chain between his fists. Says, "No . . . no, you're not," with that same look Ike gave her. She feels herself seizing. Takes a breath. Tries to quell the panic.

"Not afraid anyone'll see you?" she says.

"No cameras, and twenty minutes to the docking call."

She takes a step back toward Ellie's car.

"If you don't have it," he says, "then I'm supposed to box ya in that van." He motions with his chin to a blue Chevy. No rear windows, she sees. Jake flicks the chain once, and again—and she looks him in the eye. Wonders if his name is actually Jake and who might be running that van if this skid is loading and offloading vehicles.

Jake gives her a nod. "So it's the van then?"

"Not much choice, do I?"

"He said you're a smart one."

The lad grins, and she tries to read him. Thinks, *If he's killed anything it's elk or moose. And how many hundred rabbits snared and sliced open? Knows how to use a knife, this one. Could do anything. Especially if he has you chained up in the dark.*

She won't let that happen, though.

She can't let that happen.

Not like Ike. Not again.

She sizes him up. Invisible hands squeezing her skull. Someone kneeling on her chest, holding her face in water. The lad can't be more than nineteen or twenty. The kind of guy Troy *would* recruit—offer him oilfield money if he stays home and runs Troy's errands. Errands like boxing her up in a van and driving her where? To the broad back of nowhere and then what? She watches the chain flick in the kid's hands. Says, "I hid it," and takes a step back into Ellie's driver's side mirror.

Jake rattles the chain. "Where?"

She nods at Ellie's car.

"Then get it."

"The bag's in the back seat," she says.

Jake takes a step back and drops one end of the chain. Pushes his glasses up his nose and nods for her to retrieve the bag. "You knows Ellie, do ya?" She opens the door—buddy an arm's reach from her and a bear for height.

"See the salt beef didn't stunt you," she mutters, leaning into the backseat.

"What's that?" He swings the chain and grabs its other end. Says to hurry it up. Her knees and elbows are on the backseat now, arse out the door. She shoots him a look and sees him staring at her ass. Almost Ike-like. But blinking. Unsure of himself. Like he's not done this before. Good to know, good to know. She twists a fist in her satchel strap, trying to think how she'll use it as a weapon if need be.

No room to swing in here. She scans the backseat and floor for the bag. But it's not there. And she remembers Lisetta slamming shut the trunk.

"It's gone," she says.

"Gone?" says Jake.

Maybe she—

Jake yanks her feet, and she face-plants the seat. A buckle to the teeth and he's on her legs now, her swinging the satchel and yelling into seat fabric, trying to kick as the guy chain-wraps her ankles. She cranes back and grabs the collar of his coveralls, but he hops off her legs, cinches the chain tight, and twists an S-hook through the last links.

She flips to her back and kicks him in the ribs, thunking him against the next car so hard his rimless glasses slip to the end of his nose. Cocks her knees again but he flicks a knife from his pocket and slashes at her, nicking jeans and grazing her skin.

"Hey!" she yells—Jake ready to go at her again. "The trunk!" she snaps—and Jake thumbs his glasses back into place with his knife hand, one lens fogged. "The stuff's in the fuckin trunk!" she says.

He rubs his ribs, and she nods again at the trunk.

"Kick me again," he says.

"And what?" she says.

He waggles the knife.

"Am I supposed to be dead or alive in that van?"

He nudges her chained ankles. "Alive," he says, voice shaky—*Nervous,* she thinks. "Unless ya choose otherwise."

"You're not some narco hitman," she says. "Fuck, b'y, look at yourself."

He shrugs—and she can't tell if he'll club her or not. Can't tell if he's bluffing. Can't read his chubby face. She tries to focus. Tries to clear her head as she raises her hands like her Wing Chun instructor has taught her. *Self-defense, girl. Self-defense.*

"Stuff's in the trunk," she says again, and reaches for the latch on the backseat's shoulder. Clicks the latch and shuffles out the car door, stands and bounces to get her balance. Then reaches back inside the car and pulls the seatback down.

"Could just pop the trunk," Jake says.

"Feel free." She nods at the driver's door. "Please."

"Might be safer this way." He grins. "For me. Troy said you were a scrappy cunt."

"Do you even knows what cunt is?"

"I knows what cunt is," Jake says.

"So you've heard of the internet."

"Heard you knifed a guy there." He points the knife at his dick. "Troy says you sliced the guy's ballsack."

"He said that?"

"Yeah."

"He said 'ballsack'?"

Jake nods and knocks twice on his crotch with the knife—muffled *click-click.*

"You're wearing a cup?" she says.

He adjusts his grip on the knife and nods. "Old hockey gear."

"And the van?"

"Stuff goes in the van and you go on."

"Just like that, hey?" She shuffles her ankles and rattles the chain. "Do I get to keep the shackles?"

"They'll hardly miss a bit a chain."

Like nobody'd miss you, she thinks, darting Jakie-boy a last look before twisting her head and arms into the trunk, praying Lisetta actually stashed the urn there. *Please have been doing that when we set sail—please!*

Half inside the trunk, she cranes her neck and blinks, eyes adjusting to the dark. She fans her arms for the urn but only feels a deflated canvas backpack. With no urn inside. A sleeping bag next to it. There. And Lisetta's guitar case. She reaches over the guitar and feels a set of loosely coiled jumper cables and a windshield scraper.

Sharp tug on her ankles. "Hurry it up," Jake says.

Her throat throbs.

She's inside her own bloody coffin if he gets her in that van. A seam of light along the trunk's rim burns her eyes and she imagines the car being driven off the boat with her jammed in here. And right now that seems preferable to Jake having her by the boots.

Fuck, girl. You're gone. It's all gone.

Face it.

Nothing in the trunk—no urn or weapon. Nothing. Not a fucking thing! She thrashes her arm on the other side of the guitar case to see if she missed anything, screaming in her head and batting the jumper cables, nicking her knuckle on the windshield scraper.

The windshield scraper. She grabs its brushed end—tightens her grip. *Seriously?* Jake kicks her chained ankles. "Time's up."

"Got it," she yells.

And he hauls her out of the trunk.

~ 17 ~

HER HEAD COMES FREE of the crawlspace and she boots Jake into the next car. Glasses fly from his face but he stamps on her bound feet and slices at her, missing her belly by an inch.

She yanks the scraper out of the trunk, both hands clenched above the brush, and hacks aside another knife-swipe. She jabs at him and takes a swipe of her own. Slashes again with the scraper and Jake dodges the blow and steps back, surprised.

He grins. "A scraper—really?"

She jumps to her feet, wobbles a bit, and then bounces at him, swinging the scraper and forcing him back a step.

He says, "What the fuck?" and grabs at the scraper like it's a toy—but she *thwaps* his knuckles and swipes at his face, the scraper's edge gouging his cheek.

He takes a step back.

Touches his face.

Blood on his fingers, and she yells and jumps at him, but he dodges back by the three goats in the truck bed. She hops again. He takes a stab with the knife but she cracks the scraper over his wrist and sends the knife spinning under the pick-up. A goat lunges at him and he bolts for the stern-ramp.

Seeing him run, she whoops and bounces after him, wielding the scraper and hollering as he lunges behind the pick-up. She grabs the top of the tailgate to swing herself around, but a goat rams her knuckles and she lets go of the truck and falls, just as Jake axes another chain at her, sparks flashing off the truck hitch.

Jake swings the chain again and slashes down as Teffy raises the scraper with both hands. The chain wraps around the handle, and she twists the scraper and yanks Jake off balance. Boots him again and slams him into the tailgate.

He coughs and the goat butts the back of his head, sends him sprawling onto her—the scraper crossed between them like a bench-press bar on her chest, the second chain still wrapped around Jake's fist.

Jake spits in her eye and she bites his cheek. He screams and shoves the scraper's handle under her chin and leans on it. Her eyes bulge, bound feet quivering. But she gets her hands under the scraper and tries to bench the bar off her throat, heaving against Jake's bulk, but she can't budge him, the big shagger leaning hard on the scraper, crushing her windpipe.

Come on, you fuck! come on!

She wedges a shoulder under the bar and twists to her right, freeing one hand but the scraper slips, the bar pressed against her throat now, choking her.

Jake spits in her face again, and Teffy gropes blindly for the end of the second chain still wrapped around Jake's hand. Finds it. Wraps it around her own fist and clobbers Jake in the side of the head with it.

His grip slackens, and she rolls to the left and chain-punches him again, this time following through and looping the chain around his thick neck. She reefs on it and he croaks. Gets a knee under him and tries to stand and catch his breath. Teffy tightens her grip and pulls, using the guy's neck to heave herself out from under him and roll to her knees.

Jake gurgles and releases the scraper.

Blinks and boxes Teffy's ears.

She buckles, head ringing—body held upright by the fisted chain neck-tied to the kid. Then she yanks down and he bulls backwards, hauling her to her hitched-up feet. But as soon as she has her shoes under her, she launches into his gut and his elbow cracks the truck's taillight.

A goat butts him hard and sends him into her and he grabs her with both hands and throws her to the floor, crashes down on top of her—and Teffy sees him cock a bloody fist.

But Jake freezes, eyes fixed on something over Teffy's head.

"Easy," he says. "Easy now." He uncurls his fist and slowly raises his other hand. "That might be loaded."

"Oh, I can guarantee it's loaded," Ellie says—and Teffy cranes to see the artist with the walnut stock of .308 Winchester drawn up to her shoulder, the old woman staring coolly down the long, black barrel. "Jake Crawley," she says, chambering a round, "give me one good reason why I shouldn't shoot you in the fuckin hand."

Blood drips off Jake's chin. "This is not what it looks like, Ellie."

Ellie says, "Both of you stand up," and both of them stand shakily to their feet, sloughing off the chains. A goat bleats at them from the back of the truck.

Jake nods at the gun. "Is that Daryl's?"

Ellie doesn't answer, just waves them both to sit on the truck's back bumper. They sit. And she lowers the gun. "First," she says, glaring at Teffy. "What happened on Peppett Street?"

"Peppett Street?" Jake says.

"Shut-up, Jake."

Teffy stares at her. "I thought you—"

"What?" Ellie snaps. "What? That I waited outside for fifteen minutes then knocked and was told to go around back. Which I did. And the door's wide open. Garbage everywhere. And there's blood on the floor and you weren't answering texts. What was I to think?"

"Was he still there?" Teffy says.

"Who!?" Ellie yells. "Who was still there? Who did you go to see and why? What aren't you telling me?"

"So there was no one there?"

"No," Ellie says. "But there *was* blood all down the hallway and that fuckin toilet was slick with it." Jake turns to stare at Teffy, eyes big as boiled eggs. "Go ahead and ask her," Ellie says to Jake. "Ask her who wasn't there and why there was all that blood. Who were you supposed to meet on Peppett Street?" Ellie nods at Jake. "And what's this cheese-fed idiot got to do with you?"

"Ask *him*," Teffy says.

And Jake says, "I'm not saying anything."

"I wouldn't believe you if you did," Ellie says, not taking her eyes off Teffy. The captain's voice comes over the loudspeaker, announcing that they'll be landing in fifteen minutes and that people can begin to return to their vehicles. "You," she says to Jake, "you have a job to do." Then she squares Teffy with a fierce look. "And you—you and I are gonna finish this conversation. Later." She unchambers the round she'd loaded, safeties the .308, and tells Jake to get the hell out of her sight. "I knows where you live, Jake Crawley, and I'm not done with you."

"I can explain," Jake mutters.

"Trust me," Ellie says. "Everyone is gonna explain everything. Now get going." And Jake does so, grabbing his glasses and limping to retrieve his hard hat. Wiping blood from his face. "Come on," Ellie says to Teffy, and

Teffy follows the artist, who replaces the rifle in a combination-lock case under the back seat of the grumpy trucker's blue pickup.

"How do you know this guy?" Teffy says—but Ellie just nods at the Toyota.

"Get in," she says.

Teffy starts shaking as she buckles herself into the backseat, coming down off the adrenaline and glancing from Ellie's reflected stare in the rear-view mirror to the Chevy van Jake was supposed to have loaded her into. She keeps waiting on the driver to return to the van, but she hasn't seen anyone so far. She's gotta ID whoever it is, though. See who else is tied-up in this. So she keeps looking though she wants to shut down. Shut it all out. Go to sleep. Ellie's voice in her head asking what the hell happened on Peppett Street.

I was attacked.

And who's gonna believe that?

Lisetta opens the passenger side door and Teffy slides her bloody knuckles under her leg. Lisetta buckles and glances back at her, then at Ellie in the driver's seat. "Wasn't sure where you'd both gone off to," she says to them.

"It's a ferry," Ellie says quietly, trying to smile. "Couldn't have gone far."

Lisetta clicks her buckle and asks her aunt, "How was the smoke?"

"Lovely," Ellie says. "I may give up quitting."

Ellie looks at Teffy in the mirror, then asks Lisetta if she was up at the bow of the boat when they approached the island. "Or did you get talking to Maisey and Del again?"

"No, I was up front to watch the landing," Lisetta says.

The cars around them are starting, and Teffy looks over at the blue Chevy van to see exhaust whisping from its tailpipe.

And how did she miss the driver passing right in front of her?

Lisetta digs in her purse and pulls out the urn, then sets it sideways on the dash. "Wanted mother to see us coming into St. Mark's," she says—and Teffy can tell by Lisetta's voice that she's smiling.

"So you had her with you the whole time?" Teffy says.

"Been a long time since she's taken this boat," Ellie says, still staring at Teffy in the rear-view mirror. All Teffy wants to do is curl up and sleep. Get word to Ger somehow, wherever he is. He's not with Troy, she knows that much. And she kicks herself again for believing Troy's lie. For getting anywhere near Peppett Street and that heroin that's now tucked inside the funeral urn on the dash there. Fucking Troy. What's he gonna do now? Now that she's off-script and the kid he sent to collect her is empty handed?

She looks for Jake but doesn't see him anywhere on the quickly clearing deck. Will Troy care, though, about Jake fucking things up? And what's a kid like Jake need so bad in the first place that he'd take a job like that?

Buddy behind them barmps his horn. Flicks his lights—on off, on off—and Teffy realizes the windowless Chevy van is gone from the deck and that the green van in front of them is off board as well. Another barmp from the trucker and Ellie gasses it and the car clunks over the ramp, scraping the undercarriage and shifting Lisetta's floor mat.

"Easy!" Lisetta says, hitching her knees up to her chin.

Teffy finds a pen in her satchel and clicks it sharp, presses the tip to her throat—to that place she'd aimed for on Ike's neck. She presses the pen hard. Harder. One skin-puncturing jab and she'd be done and gone. And Troy Hopper could go to hell out of it. Her hand is shaking. Fuckin Troy and the driver of that Chevy. Some other islander, but who?

She presses two fingers to her throat and they come away ink-wet. A smeared scribble on that artery now: that artery that could cut her loose— her from Troy, and Troy from Ger.

Abort it all. Right here.

She thinks on it, but only hunches deeper into Ellie's backseat as the old woman drives on, following the lonely road through the center of the island, evergreens stunted and bent over bogs, log piles labelled with names and numbers—a buckshot sign for caribou crossing.

She pulls her bruised hand from under her leg. Sees Ellie eyeing her and shivers. Glances at Lisetta's pink hair, at the urn on the dash.

The black jar leering at her.

A horn blares behind them and she turns in the backseat to see the trucker riding their taillights. Buddy flicks his hand, motioning them to pull over and let him pass. But when Ellie doesn't move over, the trucker veers out and roars past the Toyota—his three goats tethered in the truck bed.

"Do you know where you're going?" Lisetta says.

"There's only one road," Ellie says. "And yes, I did grow up here."

"I know but—"

"Just hang tight," Ellie says, the truck getting smaller and smaller ahead of them. Ellie ticks the speedometer higher.

"Do you think you can drop me at Uncle Mike's?" Lisetta asks.

"He offer you a room in the old place?"

Lisetta nods, and Teffy can see that they're gaining on the truck now. "We've been emailing each other for the past few months," Lisetta says.

"Has he told Daryl you're coming?"

"He didn't say."

"Then he didn't do it."

"Is that a bad thing?"

Ellie glances sideways at her niece. "Did your mom tell you anything about Daryl?"

"Only that he's got a bit of a temper."

"Ha," Ellie says, a few lengths from the truck now. "Well that's a case of the pot calling the kettle black."

"Sounds like a real sweetheart," Teffy mutters, watching the speedometer and wondering if Lisetta's uncles will be distraction enough for her to make the switch-back when they get where they're going. She presses her hand to her belly, thinks of the baby there: of Ger in his car somewhere between St. John's and the St. Mark's ferry—*but where?*

The urn jostles on the dash.

"Your Uncle Daryl," Ellie says, "chased that whale around an inlet in his speedboat. Remember that from your Dad's book?" And Lisetta nods. "Drove the poor thing mad until she beached herself in like twelve feet of water. Then he got to the cove's clifftop and emptied a case of shells into her blowhole." Ellie shoots Teffy a look in the rear-view mirror, and all Teffy can think is how comfortable Ellie had seemed with that .308.

And how many shots did she fire?

The car lurches and Teffy eyes Ellie's speed. She tries to swallow but feels the bruise of Jake's weight on her throat. The speedometer ticks higher and the car shivers as it gains on that blue pick-up. "Is the speed limit just a suggestion?" Lisetta says.

They're only three car-lengths behind the pickup now and gaining on it. The curving road bends ahead into a straight stretch paved over bog lands and Ellie revs the Toyota, flicks on her blinker, and pulls out and passes the pickup.

"You still wanna be dropped at your Uncle Mike's?" she says to Lisetta—Teffy losing sight of the truck out the back window as they zip along. She feels Ellie ease off the gas going up a hill, and she turns to see the speedometer fall back a few notches.

"Sure," Lisetta says.

Teffy sees the sign for St. Mark's as they round a thickly treed corner. Another sign says that the speed limit is forty. And Ellie lets her foot off the gas and the car slows as the road straightens and dips down a hill into a sheltered cove surrounded by squat, boxy houses, sheds, and fishing stages. And one oddly tall, three-story gray house that looks to Teffy like an architectural tumor on the landscape.

Ellie pulls into a gravel driveway on the left, across the road from a red clapboard bungalow in need of a paint job, and parks behind a four-wheeler.

Teffy can feel her pulse in her skinned hand as she unbuckles, watching Lisetta ease out of the passenger's seat. Ellie climbs out too and a light comes on over the door. A man steps out, wearing an old Boston Bruins T-shirt, paint-spattered blue jeans, and camouflage crocks.

He walks to them, a bit bowlegged, and says to Ellie, "So this is Stefany's girl?" nodding at his niece.

Lisetta wipes her palms on the bum of her jeans. "Uncle Mike, I guess."

"In the flesh!" He grins and shakes her hand, clasping his other hand overtop.

"And that," Mike says, letting go of her hand as the truck they'd passed pulls in the driveway behind them, "that's your uncle Daryl."

"That's Daryl?" she says.

Ellie spits. "That's Daryl."

"Yup," Mike says. "Back from Gander with those goddamn goats."

~ 18 ~

TEFFY STAYS PUT in the backseat, hearing Lisetta's uncle Mike telling her uncle Daryl that she's come back to bury their sister's ashes. "She's come a long way," says Mike, hitching his jeans.

Daryl sniffs and says, "She should've called first."

"She's written *us* a couple of times," Ellie says, motioning to Mike and herself.

"Then you both should've told her the Catholic cemetery's closed, like the Anglican cemetery—not that the Anglicans would take a Catholic."

"It's not like that now," Ellie says. "Markus—"

Daryl spits and mumbles something Teffy doesn't catch through the closed window, so she opens it a crack. "The only one open is the community graveyard," Daryl is saying as he looks up the road to that ugly gray house.

Mike says, "The community graveyard is looked after by the council though."

Daryl shoots him a look. "And your point?"

"*You're* on the council," Ellie says.

"So?"

"So," says Mike, "put in a word for her."

"For a niece I've never seen?"

"For your sister, ya stunned arse."

Daryl says, "That'd be convenient, wouldn't it?" and crosses his arms, a slight grin deepening the wrinkles around his eyes.

"I don't see the problem," Ellie says.

"The problem," Daryl says, "is that the community graveyard's only open to *resident* islanders."

"You're head of council." Mike backhands the air between them. "You could do something. Explain the situation."

"And where's she now," Daryl says, "our dearly departed sister?"

"On the dash," Lisetta says, and points at the urn.

Daryl smirks. "Suits her."

"So will you explain things to council?" says Ellie.

"What I'll do"—Daryl glances from Ellie to Lisetta—"is make sure, *as head of the council*, that her plot request is denied."

Teffy rolls down her window all the way to better hear the argument over where to bury the urn full of Troy's heroin.

"She was your sister too!" Ellie yells. "She was your sister and she asked to be buried on St. Mark's!"

"Sister or no," says Daryl, "she was not an island resident."

"She was born on the same fuckin day as you," Mike says, "in the house behind me, la!"

"The by-law says a person requesting to be buried in the community graveyard must've been a resident islander at their time of death or have lived a majority of their life on the island." Daryl looks between his ex-wife and his brother. "And neither of those things applied to Stefany."

Ellie raises her eyebrows. "That's the first time in forty years you've used her name. Do I detect a crack in that shell of yours?"

"You," he says to Ellie, voice sharp but even, "you've already fucked off elsewhere, so feel free to do so again."

"This isn't about me," Ellie says. "This is about Stefany—your twin—wanting to be buried on St. Mark's."

"She might've been my sister," Daryl says, "but she *cannot* be buried on St. Mark's."

"That's bullshit and you knows it," Mike says.

"It's the by-law," Daryl says.

"It's bullshit!"

Daryl grins. "Is it?"

"It's been over forty years!"

"Exactly."

Teffy rolls up her window to muffle their voices. Checks her satchel and the seal on the ziplock, the urn on the dash burning in her mind as she tries to think what Lisetta might do with Troy's shipment if she's not allowed to bury her mother in one of the island's graveyards.

She's worried now she won't catch what Ellie or Mike suggest.

Something stunned, she thinks, listening to the squabble. She's heard Ger say he has no time for family fights, having no kin of his own. Aside from his dad. His dad who disappeared when Ger was in high school. Ger said he didn't even know his dad was dead till St. Clare's called and asked if he'd sign for the ashes. He's got no other family now, save Teffy. She touches her stomach as the conversation erodes outside her window—Mike and Ellie yelling and Daryl staying smugly quiet. Until finally the whole thing collapses with Mike telling Daryl, "Then fly the fuck out of it!"

Daryl tips his hat to them. Slowly saunters back his truck. Climbs in the cab. Revs his engine and roars out of the driveway in reverse.

Only to back into the yard across the road.

Through the rear window, Teffy sees him jump out of his truck and disappear inside his house. "Shag him," Mike says as Teffy opens her door. "He'll come round." She catches the look Ellie shoots her brother-in-law. "Eventually," he says.

Teffy steps out of the car and sees Mike eyeing her—her satchel, skinny jeans, and red shoes. "From town, are ya?" he says, and offers his hand. "Mike Strickland."

"Teffy Byrne," she says, shaking his hand. "And I'm from Placentia."

"Sort of like town," he laughs, and she goes to pull back her hand, but he holds it and says, "You in a fight?" inspecting her skinned knuckles.

"She's a writer," Ellie says. "A journalist."

Mike's eyes widen and he lets go of Teffy's hand. "Lots of stories down here, love."

"I'm sure," she says and scans the bay. "Just out of curiosity, is that gray monstrosity over there Markus O'Shea's house?"

"Ugly architectural ass-welt, isn't it?" Mike says.

"So it's O'Shea's?"

Ellie rolls her eyes.

"Built by his gang," Mike says, "but for Doug Crawley."

"Doug made his money in Alberta," Ellie says. "Took over his dad's crab boat when he came home." She nods at the house. "Doug's mom Del picked out the design. You remembers Del from the boat—Del and Maisey?"

Mike asks Teffy how she knows Markus O'Shea. "Is it through this one?" he asks, gesturing to Ellie.

"Teffy's doing a story on me," Ellie says, cutting Teffy a sharp look. "Or trying to. You've got a few irons in the fire, don't you?"

"If you're writing up Ellie," Mike says, "then you'll wind up touching on Markus. And I can tell you this: you knocks on the right doors around here and you'll get *lots* of opinions on Markus O'Shea."

"That's what I hear," Teffy says, returning Ellie's look. "I'm just not sure which the right doors might be."

"Seriously," Lisetta murmurs.

"We'll sort it out," says Mike. "But come into the house—all of you now—come into the house and I'll put the kettle on."

Lisetta grabs her mother's urn and hands it to her uncle Mike. And the old man cradles the jar—not knowing, Teffy thinks, that he's holding a pound of southern-born tar, cut and ready to sell. Scat forced inside her and chucked on a church floor.

~ 19 ~

MIKE'S HOUSE REMINDS TEFFY of her mother's place. Every room with its own crucifix. Saints's medals and prayer cards cluttering the living room windowsills. And a palm-frond cross above the front door.

Mike taps down the draft on the stove and waves them into his kitchen. Says not to take him for a religious nut or anything because of all the saints and so forth. "House used to be Mother's," he says.

"Does Maisy still bring you a bit of holy water?" Ellie asks.

"Every other week," he says. "When the priest is in town." Mike wags a finger at the old tuna dish bolted to the wall beneath a bronze cross. "Told her tap water will do but she has her own mind, that one."

"So this is where you all grew up?" Lisetta says. "Mom too?"

"It is," Mike says. "And it was to go to your mother, in fact. But after what happened, I guess mother changed her mind."

"After her letters went unanswered for so long," Ellie says.

"So then it went to you?"

"I was living away in Toronto," Mike says, "when mother called and told me. So I moved home, trained as a fisheries officer—"

"Daryl and I were what . . . five years married then?"

"If that," Mike says. "Anyhow, when Mother died I left it as she had it. In my mind, it's still her house."

Lisetta sets her bag on the kitchen table and Mike sets the urn next to it. Says he'll put the kettle on.

"Is there a place I can crash?" Teffy asks. "Didn't sleep too well in the car." She cracks her kinked neck and feels the bruising on her throat from the scraper.

Mike says, "Take the bedroom at the top of the stairs."

And she says, "Thanks," thinking she'll wait till they're all in bed tonight to make the switch-back. No one watches her go, save Ellie. And as she squeezes past the old artist, Ellie whispers, "I'll be by when you wakes up. To finish our chat about Peppett Street."

Teffy swallows and nods. Takes the stairs two at a time, pushing into the bedroom and flicking on the lamp. Above the bed's brass headboard hangs a picture of the Sacred Heart.

Like the one in Fin's old room.

She shivers in the room's chill, hears Lisetta talking with Ellie and her uncle at the kitchen table below. Keeps feeling as if she is in Fin's house, his bedroom where they'd spend rainy afternoons in the summer when school was out. The memory is choking, like a damp cloth pressed over her face. She flops on the bed and tries to breathe, tries to bring herself back into the room: to think of what she said to Ger on the phone in Grand Falls, how she broke the news of her surprise pregnancy and hasn't heard from Ger since. Save that brief texting exchange in the car before he left St. John's. Then nothing. Radio silence. And no sign of him on the ferry.

Right when I could've used you, Ger.

Mike and Ellie's voices drift through the uninsulated floor, clear as if she was sitting at the table with them.

Teffy tries to tune them out, and thinks about playing some music on her phone, but sees her battery is low. Then she hears Mike telling Lisetta that if she's okay with it, they can bury her mother's ashes somewhere else on the island.

"Someplace . . . unofficial," Ellie says.

Teffy sits up, springs squeaking beneath her.

"Somewhere that was special to her," says Mike.

Lisetta asks if she had any favorite spots—and Teffy strains to hear.

"Shanahan's Point maybe," Mike says, "or Biggoty's Bog. Copperfield's Cove might be a good spot too, out by the Blowing Hole. Father had a cabin a mile out from there, halfway to Cape Cove, and Stefany and mother used to go out to pick blueberries or bakeapples, depending."

"And there's Whalen's Pond," Ellie says. "It's not too far from Cove and Stefany always asked to go swimming there. Quite the berry picker, your mother was."

Mike laughs. "Only if there was a swim at the end of it, mind."

They go on like that for a while, working their way through a litany of place names Teffy will never remember let alone be able to find. She wants to panic, but she is too exhausted. "Bone-weary," Ger would say, massaging her with sharp thumbs before he flopped back on the couch and put his cold feet on her lap. "My turn," he'd say and she'd start at his feet and work up past his anklebones to his ticklish, tattooed hip.

She blinks.

Prays Ger is somewhere on the road or in line for a later ferry. Feels herself drop off. Catches herself falling again. Dropping. She doesn't know how she'll do it—the switch—

Or where.

But she has to get the heroin. Has to get the heroin before they wander off into the backcountry. Wander off and bury the urn in an unmarked hole.

"You have to get it back to Troy," Ger said.

But he didn't name it. Didn't name it but he knew. Knew what she's carrying. What she's having Lisetta carry. Lisetta. And Ellie. Ellie too. And how much does Ellie know? How much has she figured out?

How much will Teffy have to tell her?

She's worried about what happens next—catches herself falling off again—this heart beating steady in her ear. Steady. Steady now. Her head on Ger's chest. And she can feel wind through the window. Like his breath on her cheek. The pleasant weight of his arm on her, pressing her deep into the low-slung mattress.

~ 20 ~

SHE JOLTS AWAKE YELLING and whips the covers against the wall. A second ago, Jake had been riding her like an old hag, prying down on that scraper's bar. Choking her.

Spitting in her face.

Then the sleep paralysis broke. And now it's just her in the room. Christ on the wall there, holding out his Sacred Heart. The house quiet but for the wind knocking the window frames. That breath on her face. Ger's breath. She listens. A roundabout wind by the sounds of it. How did Fin say it? *Anything can happen in a roundabout wind.*

She touches her bruised throat, tries to swallow. Thinks this is how Fin must've felt every morning after his dad beat him around the kitchen and would end up putting him in a choke hold, telling him to man up—his dad bent on whiskey and angry as an infected cut.

In the bathroom she sees it's nearly noon. There are no messages on her phone and she flicks the child's scream back on so she'll hear if Ger tries to call her. To say why he didn't make the boat this morning.

Out the toilet-side window, she sees Ellie's car in the drive still and Daryl's goats grazing freely beside the house. Still not a sound. So she zips up and thinks it's now or never to make that switch and call Troy. Find out where she can drop this shit, then get a hold of Ger.

And what if Troy implicates her?

Just get it done, she thinks. *Don't get caught in his trap.*

She looks in the mirror over the sink and scrubs the pen mark on her neck. Sees how grimy her jeans are from Ike's bathroom and being under the car in Grand Falls, not to mention her row with Jake on the ferry.

She glances again in the mirror. Peers more closely, and spies flecks of blood on the shirt she's wearing. Jake's blood. Or Ike's. Both maybe. Hard to see in the weave of the red plaid. But still there if you look close enough.

Just wash your gear and get on with it.

If the house is still, now's the time to make that switch. She knows that. Providing Lisetta left the urn somewhere findable and Ellie's off to her quilting crowd at the church to get them re-stitching her whale's multicolored hide. Teffy grabs her satchel from her room, tears down the stairs to find the urn, and nearly screams when she sees Ellie at the kitchen table. Just sitting there. Silent. Eating a slice of burnt toast. Slurping hot tea.

And staring at her. Hard.

"Two bags a cup." Ellie lifts her mug. "Stiff enough to stand a spoon in. At least that's what Mike says."

"Mike made you tea?"

"Half hour ago," Ellie says, the urn by her elbow. "Just warmed it up in the microwave." She glances at the urn, then at Teffy. "Mike took Lisetta for a walk to show the girl some of her mother's old haunts." Ellie's eyes drift to the clock on the wall, then back to Teffy. "You sounded like a goat coming down those stairs."

"I saw the goats outside," Teffy says.

"You in a hurry to get somewhere?"

"Almost fell down the stairs."

"Gotta watch your step," Ellie says, wincing a sip from the hot mug. "Like some punk kid I know who had no clue what he was getting into with you." *Tick-tock* goes the clock on the wall, Ellie tapping the seconds on her mug. The old woman's eyes cool, like when she stared down the barrel of that .308. Teffy stares a sec at her charred toast.

"What you saw. . . ." she says.

"On the boat or in that basement apartment?"

Teffy stares at Ellie, willing herself not to glance sideways at the urn.

"I've trusted you with my story," Ellie says. "With the stories of women who've trusted me. Marjorie Petty. And everyone who's added to the show. That's a lot of trust."

"And I'm gonna honor that," Teffy says, her phone heavy in her pocket, knowing the copy of the coded journal—the stolen journal—is sitting open in her inbox.

"And what if I can't trust you?"

"Can't you?"

"You have blood on your shirt," Ellie says. And Teffy is about to say it must be Jake's, but Ellie cuts her off: "You've had blood on your shirt since North Sydney. And that apartment was slick with it." She sets her mug down by the urn. "What happened on Peppett Street?"

Teffy looks from Ellie's eyes to the haggard face of the saint on the prayer card pinned to the wall by the artist's head. John the Baptist holding his own head on a plate. The head gazing her way, as if saying, *Go on. Offer it up.* Johnny-boy there and the Mother of God over the stove. The old pope by the window and Ellie reading her pose like a model stripped bare. All eyes on her. A cloud of witnesses. And this calm in the room like confession.

Like having everything out there and known.

Tell her. She's gotta tell her. She needs someone in her corner until Ger shows up. Someone who might have her back—someone who might get it.

"I should wash this shirt," she says, beginning to unbutton it.

Ellie says, "Mike's got a wash basin in the mudroom there." And she nods toward the entrance they came in by. "So you're *not* gonna tell me what happened in North Sydney?"

Teffy pulls her satchel off and drops it in Ellie's lap. "I was blackmailed," she says. "Into picking up a pound of heroin." Ellie's eyes blaze. Teffy nods at the satchel, refusing to let her eyes slip sideways to the urn. "It's in the satchel," she lies.

"Blackmailed?" Ellie says. "And heroin—in this bag?"

Teffy shrugs off her filthy shirt. "They said they'd kidnapped my boyfriend. That if I wanted to see him again, I had to pick something up in North Sydney." She turns and heads to the back room, trusting she's set the hook. She doesn't turn to see but she's sure Ellie is still watching her fill the sink and soap the shirt, scrub raw knuckles against fabric.

When she risks a look, the satchel is still in Ellie's lap.

The urn by the old woman's elbow.

Teffy is just wringing out her shirt when the door bangs open behind her and she whips around, flicking water in Lisetta's face.

"The fuck?" Lisetta says, looking from Teffy in her bra to her aunt at the kitchen table. "Did I walk in on something?"

"Just laundry," Teffy says, wet shirt still dripping in her hands.

"With an audience, I see."

Ellie shrugs. Sets the satchel down by her foot—carefully, Teffy sees—then reaches for her mug of tea and takes a sip. Teffy says to Lisetta, "Heard you were out and about."

"With Uncle Mike, yeah."

Mike stomps in the back door then, sees Teffy shirtless and says, "Nice bra." And he's about to say something else, but Teffy asks if he has a dry shirt she can borrow.

"Sure," he says, gaze slipping off her collarbone, "I'll go get it," and he heads through the kitchen, past his sister, and up the stairs—Lisetta stealing a glance at Ellie and the urn.

"Mother didn't say anything, did she?" Lisetta asks jokingly.

"She hasn't told me everything. Yet."

"I'm sure she will!"

Teffy crosses her arms and shivers. She can hear Mike coming down the stairs. "Here's the shirt," he says as he pokes back in the mudroom and tosses Teffy a plaid button-up. Then he turns to Lisetta and asks what she thought of St. Mark's.

"People aren't afraid to stare, are they?"

Teffy hears Mike laugh as she shoulders into the shirt.

"It's the pink hair," Ellie calls from the other room.

"Thanks for this," Teffy says, doing the last button.

Mike takes in the way the shirt hangs on her. Stares a bit too long and Ellie says, "She's got a boyfriend, Mike."

Mike laughs, "Lucky bastard," and Lisetta asks if he's still up for boating out to the islands today.

"The islands?" Teffy says.

"There's an old fishing village out there," Mike says. "Used to be one of Stephany's favorite spots. Before the whale."

"So that's where you'll. . . ." Teffy almost fixes on the urn. "That's where you'll scatter her ashes?"

"Maybe," Lisetta shrugs and asks her uncle if he has any coffee.

"Instant," Ellie says, and smirks when her niece cringes.

"Maybe tea?"

Lisetta follows Mike back into the kitchen and leaves Teffy by the wash bin, shivering in her new shirt, the wet one still in hand.

"We should go if we're going," Mike says. "Tune up the motor and launch the punt. I'll be down to the stage when ya gets your tea."

Lisetta leans back into the mudroom. "Can *you* make the tea?"

"So I'm invited?" Teffy says.

"Why not?" Lisetta looks to her aunt, and Ellie rises from her chair. Toes the satchel by her foot. Taps the urn's silver top. And looks Teffy's way. "You should come," Ellie says. "We still got lots to talk about. For the show, I mean."

"A regular ol' boatload," Mike says, rubbing his hands together. "Hey, if you're making tea," he says to Teffy, "there's some tuna in the cupboard there. Think you could make up some sandwiches too?"

"Sure thing."

A few minutes later, Teffy waves them off, and Ellie goes too. That surprises Teffy. She'd thought the old artist would stay and grill her about the heroin. But no.

She must be saving that for the island.

But she's left the urn on the table.

Okay then. Now's the time.

Teffy watches the three of them walk down to Mike's stage, along a length of rock punched up through sod like a bone through torn skin. They duck into the darkened stage and she slams the door and turns to face the urn on the table.

~ 21 ~

SHE THUMPS THE SATCHEL on the table next to the urn. Double-checks her phone to make sure the baby-wail is on. Then unscrews the silver lid. Pulls at the plastic bag inside with one hand and reaches to unclasp the satchel with the other.

The bag is halfway out—the satchel flipped open—when someone walks through the back door. She jerks to see who it is and tips the urn, spilling heroin on the table, just as Markus O'Shea ducks into the kitchen.

She freezes, and he says, "You're not Mike," looking from her to the dust heap on the table top.

"I'm a reporter," she says, voice choked.

"From town right? The one covering Ellie's show?" She nods, and he looks at the spilled powder and tilts his head. "And what's this?"

"Human ash," she says, cool as she can, reaching to flip shut the satchel.

"Well," he smiles and scratches the back of his head. "I was expecting you to say whole-wheat flour. Human ashes, though? Wow."

"The name's here on the plastic," she says. "The black jar's the urn."

"Relative of yours?"

"Mike's sister."

"So you've been travelling with Ellie and her niece?"

"Yeah," she says.

"Getting the scoop on her?" He smiles at that. "She's kept me out of it I hope."

"Hasn't hardly mentioned you," she says, and watches him deflate a bit.

"Ah. So how long have you been on St. Mark's?"

"Came over on the morning ferry," she says. "And you?"

"I came over on the second boat."

"You didn't happen to see an old rustbucket Ford?" she asks. "Blue and barely holding together. Would've been a young guy driving—my age. Tattooed arms and neck."

"Not ringing any bells," Markus says. He glances around at the saints on the walls, at headless John the Baptist pinned in place. "Do you like St. Mark's so far?"

"Seems like a nice place."

"Ha," he says, humorless. "It's a hornet's nest you can't help kicking. That's why I'm in to see Mike, actually. Know where he's to?"

She nods at the window by the stove. "Launching his punt," she says. "Down with his niece and Ellie."

"And they left Stefany's ashes with you?" He gestures at the spilled urn.

She tries to swallow. "That's right."

"By the way, how's the story coming along?"

"The story?"

"On Ellie and her art show. Heard the gallery got sacked."

"Yes," she says, inhaling the word. "I was there actually."

"You were?"

"Ran into the vandal in the stairwell."

"Did you recognize him?"

"Only that he had red paint on his boot."

O'Shea scratches the back of his head and looks past her out the sea-facing window. "You said the rest of them are down to Mike's stage?"

"They're getting the punt ready to go out to the islands," she says.

"The Kid Brothers?" he says. "That'll be a trip. You staying here with Stefany?"

"I'm going with them, actually."

"Did Ellie tell you they shot the whale out there—Mike and Daryl and her?"

"She said *you* were there too."

"Hardly," he says, drawing on an imaginary reefer pinched between thumb and forefinger. "It was the sixties. What can I say?" He smiles, and nods at the spilled urn. "So what's the deal with Stefany there?"

"Lisetta, Mike's niece," she says, trying to think fast, "she asked me to fetch a ziplock of her mom's ashes."

"Is that right?"

"To scatter out on the islands."

"Well," he spins suddenly on his heel and flings open a couple of cupboards, "Mike should have some baggies up here now. Not supposed to scatter remains, legally speaking, but what's it matter out there, right? Here they are!" And he tosses her a box of ziplocks.

She has trouble slipping one free because her hands are shaking so bad, but when she does manage it, she fumbles to hold the bag open by the table's edge, trying to steady herself as she scoops spilled heroin—right in front of a local billionaire who thinks it's human ash.

Flaming Jesus, she thinks. *Steady on.*

Just bag it and say goodbye.

But O'Shea steps over and says, "Here, you hold the bag." And she does, and he's swiping cut heroin off the table with his bare hands—and quickly too. Three dusting swipes and he's done. The ziplock—a wee sandwich thing—is half full now.

Like a super-sized eightball in her cold hands.

O'Shea looks at his powder-dusted fingers, and she thinks he might smell or test it somehow. Lick a finger. Somehow see what's right there on his own hands. But he just dusts them off and heads to the sink. Scrubs with soap and asks her what kind of stories she usually covers: "You often do these downhome features—life around the bay kind of thing?"

"Not exactly," she says.

"You write for the *Telegram* then?"

"For an independent news site," she says. "*The Miscreant.*"

He dries his hands on his pants. "I've heard of it," he says. "Covered a couple of decent-size stories, haven't you? That shooting last year at the Sobeys on Kenmount. Any money in an independent operation like that?"

She shrugs. There isn't any money in it, but she's not going to tell that to Markus O'Shea. The shooting had been Ger's first big story after his insider's report on the scoop that put Troy away. Not much came of it, though—the shootout story. Nothing uncovered or disclosed by police. Just a flash in the local media pan. *Not like the one Ger's after now,* she thinks. Going after Troy again. A smack-down story. Literally. And she wonders if O'Shea knows anything about smuggling on St. Mark's, seeing as how he just hand-scooped three month's wages into a sandwich bag and washed a gram down the drain.

With stupidity like that, she thinks, *no wonder Troy gets away with murder.*

"If you want to talk to Mike," she says, "he's down by the water."

O'Shea nods again at the sea-facing window. "Rain's blowing in. And quick by the looks of it. You said Mike's at his stage?"

"That's what he told me." Rain starts to peck the windowpanes, and Teffy squeezes her wet shirt on the table. "Guess I won't be hanging this on the line." She shakes out the shirt—sees the stains scrubbed clean.

O'Shea says, "Daryl has a fire on next door. In the shed there. See if the old cuss will let you hang it by his stove."

The rain is coming down harder now, pelting like hail.

"And it looks like I lost my window," he says and opens the seaward door to see if it's as bad as it sounds. But when he does, a muddy goat barges in out the rain and shakes itself out. O'Shea goes to grab its horns but it butts at him and he dodges out of its way.

She looks at him. "Are *you* gonna tell Mike?"

"Do you think it might wander out on its own?"

"I'm not touching it," she says.

"I'll tell Mike," he says, and darts into the rain, cussing his way down the hill.

The goat blinks at her.

"Shoo!" she says and goes to backhand it, but it charges her and rams the table, and she just manages to catch the open urn before it hits the floor—a slight puff in her face that she tries not to breathe in. But the goat does.

Shakes its head.

Bleats.

Then rams a leg right off the table.

Teffy grabs her satchel mid-air and snags her wet shirt on the goat's horns, tearing it as she dodges a rear hoof and runs out the door into the rain, screwing on the lid as she goes—that small baggie of heroin clutched in her fist.

She slips in the mud by Daryl's shed but grabs the latch, steadies herself, and shoulders through the door just as the baby starts screaming in her pocket.

~ 22 ~

NO BABIES IN THE SHED!" Daryl yells when Teffy ducks through the door—phone wailing in her hand still—the old man sitting on a water-stained couch opposite the stove. A blast of heat hits her and the phone stops crying.

All still for a sec, save the wind.

"Door's open," he says, and clicks a duct-taped remote, changing the channel on the TV at the back of shed.

She glances at the ply-patched door swinging in the wind.

"I'm not heating all of St. Mark's," he says.

She waves the phone at him. "The baby is a ringtone."

"Whatever, just reef up on that knob."

He nods at the door, and she hauls it shut, cutting the wind to a cat's cry. Takes a step back and sees a line of Bud Lights on the lintel, a dartboard to her left, and to her right a scuffed wrestling figurine screw-nailed to the wall.

"You a wrestling fan?" she says.

"That's been there a while."

"Kind of feel like I should cross myself."

He snorts, and she relaxes a bit. "You religious?" he says.

"Catholic."

He huffs off the couch, knees cracking as he hobbles over to her. Pinches off his cap and tosses it on the wrestler's fists. Says, "It's just a hat hook," sweat beading on his forehead.

"Mind if I hang this shirt?" she says.

He shrugs and saunters over to the workbench in back, the bar fridge there, both of them glancing at a live shot of a blackened house on NTV. The news camera pans left and she sees the rowhouses and knows immediately it is St. John's. *A house fire*, she thinks, not registering the news captioning scrolling beneath the reporter.

"Rum or rye?" Daryl says.

"Rum," she says, as she hangs her wet shirt on a hook by the stove.

Daryl brings her a Rum and Pepsi in an old mug, big chunk of ice in it—*Iceberg ice*, she thinks, like her dad serves up in his shed. Fishes the bergy bits himself when he visits a buddy in Bonavista and brings back three coolers full. She looks at the mug. "You a Bruins fan?"

"Long-time Leafs fanatic."

"Somebody get you this as a prank then?"

"It's Mike's," he says. "Always been contrary, that one."

She eases into an old kitchen chair, missing two of its five back spindles. Green rope strung from backrest to bum-groove to give it more support. An awkward rigging but comfortable. She sets the urn beside her and slips the baggie into her satchel on her lap, with Lisetta's mother's remains. Looks for a toilet but sees none.

She's about to ask where the outhouse is, but Daryl says, "I was gonna break that thing up for kindling"—motioning to her chair—"but I gots a thing for salvaging useless shit . . . like the fishing industry here." He flops onto the couch. "If you falls on your arse, just blame me. Everyone else does."

Someone sounds sorry for himself, she thinks, trying to picture Ellie with Daryl here, but can't quite make the artist fit in a room like this, a world away from her hip downtown gallery.

"That drink," Daryl nods at her cup, "was a million years in the making."

She looks at him and figures him to be management at the plant—the Co-op hat and what he said about saving the fishing industry just now. But would he know of Troy's dealings?

"You know Markus O'Shea?" she says, thinking she might kick up some dirt on the local bayman-turned-billionaire if she has to wait out the rain.

"Everybody knows Markus," he says.

"Is it true he wants to set up a hotel on the fish plant site if it goes under?"

"That's what they say. Eco-friendly and locally outfitted."

"And what do you say?"

"I says there's always some shit trying to shut us down, and Markus O'Shea's just a scavenger waiting for that to happen."

"Can I quote you on that?"

"You a journalist?"

"Of sorts."

He sniffs. "What's in the jar?"

"Your sister."

"Could've left her outside then." He stares hard at the urn. Silent awhile. And she's about to ask after the outhouse. To get this switch done and call Ger back, thinking it was probably Ger on the phone before, saying he'd caught the noon ferry.

But then wouldn't he have found his way here by now? Or called at least?

She takes another searing gulp, feels the burn in her belly, and remembers the baby—or whatever it is at this point. The size of a cherry or plum maybe. She sets down her drink, not sure if it's the rum hitting her or what. Smell of boozy Pepsi, maybe.

Wind whistling in the chimney.

There's another shot of that burned-out rowhouse on the news. The volume on the TV is down low. She can't hear what the reporter is saying now—the woman standing there in front of the smouldering house, a house Teffy thinks she recognizes. She catches a few words of the caption scrolling across the bottom of the screen.

Firebombing in St. John's, it says

"Can you turn that up?"

Daryl does, just as the reporter says something about the RNC believing a rival gang targeted the wrong house in Rabbittown.

She sits forward, feels the knotted ropes creak against her hips. Tries to focus on the burned building. *The stoop*, she thinks, seeing it there in the news shot. Like in that live feed Troy flashed her the night he said he'd abducted Ger. She doesn't hear Daryl or the reporter. She stares at the rusted Folger's tin by the stoop full of Dougie's spent butts. The camera pans down the street and she sees clearly that it's Merrymeeting Road—their street—hers and Ger's.

Her breath catches and she wonders if Ger was in the house when the bomb went off. He'd stayed late. To finish something. Finish what? She hears the reporter say no one was inside and that police don't think the targeted house was a dealer's.

And she thinks, *No, Dougie's the closest thing to a dealer on their street but he only shoplifts Pseudoephedrine that Vinnie sells to a meth cook in Mt. Pearl.* Something Dougie told her once, over a six of beer split in their alley.

But why would a dealer target a no-nothing little skid like Dougie? Unless. . . .

She pulls out her phone. Looks from it to the TV.

Unless Troy is trying to get her attention.

~ 23 ~

THE SHED DOOR BURSTS OPEN and the baby in her fist starts wailing again.

"Will you shush that thing?" Daryl barks.

She clicks off her phone and stares at Mike, who just barged in—Mike swiping rain from his face as he lights into his brother: "Want to explain to me why your fuckin goat's eating the seat off my La-Z-Boy!"

Daryl smiles, but his smile slips when Lisetta and Ellie walk in out of the rain. Turning back to his brother, he says, "Well, did you leave your door open?"

"Markus said he saw it go in."

"Then have that one talk to Markus, b'y." He nods at Ellie

"I just did," Mike snaps. "And you know who's missing?"

"If it's my nanny, I'm sending you the bill."

"Jake Crawley," Mike says.

Daryl sits forward on his couch. "What do you mean Jake's missing?"

"Dorothy called me to ask if I'd seen him."

"Checking snares most likely," Daryl says—and Teffy fists her phone tighter. Shoots Ellie a look, but Ellie is eyeballing Daryl.

Lisetta nods at the urn and says to Teffy, "See you brought Mother with you."

"She was just leaving," Daryl says. "Your mother, I mean."

Mike bangs the door shut. "Even with her dead you still can't get over yourself?"

"My shed, my rules," Daryl says.

"She's your fuckin twin!" Ellie snaps, staring Daryl down as she reaches for the urn in Teffy's hands. Teffy hands it over, wondering if Ellie will notice it lighter than before.

She doesn't seem to.

Just bounces the urn on her fingers and says, "We're taking Stefany here out to the Kid Brothers today."

"There's no graveyard on that rock," Daryl says.

Mike snorts. "See, you weren't born yesterday."

"Scattering human remains is against the law," Daryl says. "Big fisheries lad like yourself should know that . . . amongst other things."

"Markus just gave me a tip that I should keep an eye out for big salmon nets," Mike says, "when I'm out to the islands."

Daryl stiffens at that. "Markus said that?"

"Says he thinks someone's at bringing illegal salmon through the fish plant."

"The shit that comes out of his empty head."

"Shit is it?" Ellie says.

"What else?" says Daryl.

"Is it true?" Mike says.

"Slander is what it is," says Daryl. "Defamation of bloody character." He grabs the remote and flicks the volume up. "Big Money Markus shooting off his fuckin mouth. Trying to undermine a fishery he'd like to see closed so he can build his fancy new hotel." Daryl raises the volume higher, his voice all but drowned out by the reporter.

The baby starts wailing in Teffy's hand again. But she silences it quick and catches a glare from Daryl who is going on about Markus O'Shea being in with the mainland fish merchants, elbow-deep in a bid to gouge the St. Mark's Co-op. He sneers at Ellie. "And that's exactly what your Marky-Mark wants, isn't it?" He wags a finger at his brother. "You knows as well as me that the Union is dead-set on shutting us down because they can't control us. That's why they starts rumors the likes of Markus O'Shea—to turn the last few captains we got against the Co-op—get them to take their hauls to other plants. And who's behind that but Markus?" He flicks a hand at Ellie. "Ask her. She's in bed with him."

Ellie shakes her head. "You're a tissy ol' cunt, Daryl Strickland. Stuck in a past that's not coming back. We came to ask a last time if you wants to see Stefany buried. A chance for you to let something go for once. Now, are you gonna take that chance or sit here pissing into this roundabout wind?"

The room is silent a second and Teffy goes to say something, glancing from her phone to the TV. Something about the bombing. About Ger.

But Mike says, "As for Markus, if a local boy wants to build a hotel designed by local architects, built by local builders, and run by local residents,

I'll back him over your obsolete fishery any month o' the year." He stares down his brother. "Christsakes," he says, "Markus is a saint if he saves us from you and your hillbilly scheming."

Daryl raises his chin to Ellie. "I sees she's got her hooks into you now."

"I can think for myself," Mike says.

Daryl laughs. "'I can wipe myself,' says the arsehole to the hand."

"Fuck off."

"That does seem to be the general message here. But has it slipped your notice, Mikey, that you gots a job because I keeps things going here? Has that occurred to you, ya stunned arse? I break bones to keep us afloat—to keep us in fish!"

"It's crab now," Mike says. "Times change and crooked dealings only spoil what's coming—spoil it for everyone."

Daryl laughs. "Neither you nor Markus has a shred of proof there's anything crooked been done *in* or *through* that plant."

Teffy squeezes her phone. The reason Ger was coming to St. Mark's was because he believed Troy was planning to ship something through that fish plant. More of what she carries now—more of what's in that urn. More and worse. But who was Ger's connection on St. Mark's? Maybe this Jake Crawley. "A lad splitting time between fish plant and ferry," Ger said.

But where's he to now? Teffy wonders. *And who's bombing our place?*

"Either way," Mike is saying, "I'm keeping an eye for illegal salmon nets."

Daryl waves him off and slumps back onto the couch. Grabs the remote and changes the channel, but Teffy yells, "Wait!" And they all look at her. "That's my house!"

"Your house?" Ellie says.

"On the news! That bombing in town. That's my apartment."

Ellie stands up straight, Mike's face softens, and Lisetta spins her mother's urn in her hands. "I'm sorry," Lisetta says—and Teffy looks at her, at the urn in her hands. She has no idea how she's gonna get it back and what it is Ger's been calling to tell her, screaming that baby in her hand.

Does he even know their place got hit?

"I need to call him," she says, tears sudden and choking. She swallows hard against the pain in her throat, feels that wet-cloth panic clamped over her face—*Just breathe, girl, breath!*—and she looks at Ellie: the only one to halfway guess what she's snared in. But even Ellie can't know what she's kicked through to save Ger from Troy. And now Troy is maybe tied to St. Mark's here and the fish plant: to Daryl and that Jake kid who's gone missing.

All this mess, she thinks, *and you might be the reason someone blew off the front of your own house!*

"Who is it you need to call?" Mike says.

"My boyfriend," she says—and the baby screams.

Mike opens the door and says, "There's an outhouse handy to the shed."

The clouds are breaking up overhead and she hears Daryl yell, "And kill that young whelp in your pocket!" as she runs out the door.

~ 24 ~

"GER!" SHE PRESSES THE PHONE to her ear. "Where are you?" Nasal breathing, then static. As if the phone is being wrestled from one hand to another. "Seriously, Ger! Where are you?"

A man's voice crackles on the other end: "How are you, Toffee?"

She swallows, feels Jake's weight on her throat.

Tastes toilet water: sees blood.

"Where's Ger," she says, walking around the side of the shed—hearing Ellie and Mike giving Daryl the gears inside.

"Toffee," Troy says, "any idea why I haven't heard from my guy yet?"

"Where's Ger?" she says again.

Dirty laugh. "And why would I know where Stuckless is?"

"Because this is his phone," she whispers.

"Nothing gets past you, does it?"

"Was he in the house?"

"Did you see something on the news?" He chuckles. "You see, Toffee, I have this guy—loyal guy—who specializes in such PDAs."

"PDAs?"

"Public Displays of Affection, Toffee. That's what that was. My affection for you, for going through with the meeting I set up in North Sydney. And for somehow making it past my pick-up guy on the ferry."

"He's just a kid," she says. "What did he need so bad that he'd listen to you?"

"You probably don't know this, Toffee, given that your dad landed a job when the bottom fell out of the fishery, but some people just don't want to be poor. Being poor is terrifying—wondering month to month if you can keep the heat on, if you'll get thrown out of your shitty little apartment for shorting the landlord on rent. Folks just want to keep the few things they can claim as their own."

"If you care so much about that kid, are you gonna pay him?"

"I pay people who do their jobs, Toffee."

"And Ger?" She blinks. "Did you pick him up because I didn't do my job?"

"You're lucky," Troy says. "You know that?"

"Lucky?"

"Lucky Stuckless is here with me. And not a charred corpse in that house. That's because of my affection for you, Toffee."

"I did what you asked, though. I have the stuff you sent me to pick up. I have it for you. Right here."

"And here is where, Toffee?"

"St. Mark's," she says. "Can you just tell me if Ger's okay?"

"Toffee, do you masturbate with your left or your right hand?" She bites her tongue. Waits. Waits. "That's right," he says at last. "I haven't asked 'cause that's your own fucking business. And how Stuckless is doing right now is *my* business. And it will continue to be my business until I get what I sent you to fetch in North Sydney."

The yelling in the shed quiets down, so Teffy takes a few steps away from the wall, toward the outhouse Mike mentioned. The shed door opens and Mike, Lisetta, and Ellie file out and head toward Mike's place—*to make those sandwiches*, she thinks. Lisetta waves, a worried look on her face. And Ellie stops a second to stare at her. Then she moves on with the others.

"Toffee," Troy says, "why hasn't my guy messaged me?"

"I heard he's gone missing."

"Missing?" Troy says.

"That's right," she says.

"And how do you know that, Toffee? Did you Ike him? Cut his nuts off and stuff him in a trunk? 'Cause, you know, if you did. . . ."

She squeezes her bruised throat so hard her eyes water. "He was alive when I last saw him. On the ferry."

"So you still have it?" Troy says. "What he was supposed to pick up?"

She runs a hand over the satchel, feeling the bulge of ash there—the little sandwich bag of heroin. She says, "I do."

"Then maybe we still have a deal, Toffee."

"Ger's my anchor now, is he?"

"Told you I liked offshore diving, Toffee. Don't make me sink him."

She recalls that underwater pic of the drowning man—Connor Moffet—naked and tied to a bag of beach rocks. "So we still have a deal?" she says.

"That depends on you, Toffee. This is a courtesy call. I'm giving you the courtesy of telling you that you're gonna make the next drop or your Ger shows up facedown offshore. Are you listening, Toffee?"

"But I'm stuck on an island," she says.

"Toffee."

"Even if I—"

"You're on St. Mark's, you said."

"Yes, I—"

"Toffee!" Troy snaps. "Every time you interrupts me, Stuckless here gets it." She hears Ger then, faint in the background, telling Troy to go fuck himself. Static. Then a vicious wallop stings her ear. More static. "You hear that, Toffee?" Troy's winded voice. "Every time you cuts me off or your boy here runs his mouth."

She doesn't say anything as Troy breathes in her ear.

"You there?" he says.

"I'm here."

"I have business on St. Mark's."

She thinks of Ger's lad from the fish plant, the dirt they were going to get on Troy—Daryl's darkened look when he heard Jake Crawley was missing. "What kind of business?"

"Which hand is it, Toffee—seriously?" He waits, but hearing no answer says, "I have business on St. Mark's."

"Okay?"

"I'm gonna call a guy to see."

"To see if you have business?" she says.

"If I do," he says, "then I'll meet you there."

"So I should wait for your call?"

"Unless ya can read my thoughts, Toffee, then, yes, I would wait for my fuckin call."

"Okay."

"And, Toffee?"

"Yeah."

"Don't let that phone die.

She looks at the battery icon drained to a quarter, her own ragged face reflected in the touchscreen. "I won't," she says, hoping Lisetta has a charger with her—knowing she forgot hers back in St. John's. "I won't let it die."

"You said you have the stuff, right?"

She thinks of the urn in Lisetta's hands and the girl's planned trip to the Kid Brothers to scatter her mother's remains—the rest of Troy's scat. "Yes," she says, the word a condom coming up her throat.

"I'll call you back, Toffee."

The line goes dead and she barfs beside the outhouse, staggers toward Daryl's shed, thinking she needs to beg her way onto that boat and answer every one of Ellie's questions. But she hates the thought of being on another boat, and a punt at that—out there on the open water. But she's no choice. Not really. Not if she wants to see Ger again—to make all this worth something.

She's just about to the shed when the door shoves open, and not wanting to talk to Daryl, she ducks under his shed behind the woodpile. Hears Daryl's boots squelch in the mud.

Hears his phone jingle.

"Hello," he barks. "This is Daryl."

She crouches lower, flicking her own phone to vibrate, not wanting her screaming baby to give her away.

"Yeah," he says. "I'll process it."

~ 25 ~

DARYL TROMPS TO THE BACK of the shed, still on the phone, and Teffy creeps further under the outbuilding, crouching lower behind the stack of split wood.

Claws a split piece of spruce for support.

"Yeah, I know," Daryl says into the phone. "I understand these things don't often come around twice. No, I . . . I appreciate the business, yes. Yes, I know Markus O'Shea is after asking you. . . . I'm just surprised you're interested in doing business with us again. . . . Yeah, Markus is your buddy, I get it. Not a problem, I'll take care of it. . . . That'll do. Sure. That shouldn't be a problem either, no. I understand it's your business. . . . Yes, I get it—a favor to Markus. Just let me know when you plans to dock."

Daryl's hand drops to his side, the cell phone mitted in his fist. Teffy can see his knuckles whiten and imagines her own bruised neck in that grip. Imagines this old booze fart coming after her like that kid Jake.

Her phone buzzes in her hand. Ger's number again. Meaning Troy is calling back. But she can't answer without giving away that she's just been eavesdropping on Daryl.

The phone vibrates again, and she sees Daryl turn to the shed, so she tucks her head under her arm like a crow in rain. The phone zizzes and she presses it to her chest. Hears Daryl's heavy breathing as he stoops to fill the crook of his arm with the split wood she's hiding behind.

The phone massages her sternum as Daryl pulls on the split piece of spruce she's using for support. He grunts and tugs again and she lets go of the piece of wood and hunkers down more. The phone goes off again as Daryl picks his last block of firewood. He steps out from under the shed and she feels the phone's whir in her wrist bone, and when Daryl strides into the shed, Teffy clicks the touchscreen—Troy's voice biting her ear: "Toffee!" he yells.

She glances over her shoulder at the shed.

"Was I interrupting something?"

"No, I—"

A sharp slap in her ear, Ger's voice a distant whimper.

Troy breathes heavy. "Did you hear that?"

She cups the phone with both hands. And in that second she wants to be back in St. John's. In her own bed. With Ger. She presses a hand to her stomach. Wants to curl up and cry.

Troy's voice on the other end: "You still there, Toffee?" Static-shuffle, another skin-slap, and she almost hangs up, her fingers numb.

"I'm here," she says.

"Be at the St. Mark's plant tomorrow night."

"What time?"

"Seven."

"Are you bringing Ger?"

"Just make sure you have Ike's stuff."

"Will you—?"

"Will I what, Toffee?"

Her eyes water as she squints to see the far islands, hazy now in the distance. Can she even get there and back in a day? "If I get you your stuff. . . ." She squeezes the baggie in her satchel, thinks of the urn in Lisetta's hands. Shuts her eyes and shivers at a crow's sudden *haa haa haa*. "If I do that, will you let us go?"

"Who's *us*, Toffee?"

"Me and Ger."

A chuckle like a diesel engine turning over, and she almost screams but the line goes dead. When she opens her eyes, she is looking down Mike's boat slip. Sees a crow on the stones below, next to Mike's rocking punt, pecking the spiny husk of a cracked sea urchin.

~ 26 ~

ON THE WATER NOW and passing the breakwater to the open sea, Teffy green and wishing she had more than the taste of puke and Pepsi-splashed rum in her mouth.

Ellie and Lisetta both look leery when she tells them, over the motor's roar, that Ger is fine—"Out to my parents in Placentia," she says, "thank God." And they don't press for more, and she's glad for that. Thankful for the engine-hum quiet as they drive on.

The quiet could also be because Daryl jumped in the boat at the last minute, right before they shoved off. Dropped by the stage and threw a duffel in with the rest of their gear.

"And what do you think you're doing?" Ellie had said.

Daryl shrugged. "Seeing off my dead sister. Like you suggested."

"More like keeping an eye on your salmon nets," Mike said.

"Just shove off, Mikey."

Daryl had hopped into the boat and wedged his butt between Lisetta and Ellie on the center seat, his broad, slickered back to Teffy.

"Come on now," Mike had said to him, "you're corrupting the view."

"Just pull the fuckin cord," Daryl said, and Mike did so, buzzing them slow out of the bay.

On the open water now, Mike nods to the Kid Brothers, miles off yet. "Where St. Mark's folks used to follow the fish," he yells above the motor's roar.

St. Mark's shrinks behind them slowly, and Teffy—in the bow facing back—feels every *woof* and *whomp* as Mike steers them on. Over the engine, Lisetta asks Teffy what her boyfriend said about the bombing, and Teffy shrugs, sees the wind spark tears in Ellie's eyes, and says something about that being the neighborhood and "Thank God no one was hurt."

"Did you call the cops?"

Teffy says, "Yeah," as if that's the only sensible thing to have done. No hint she's been talking to the dealer that set the bomb in the first place. No waver in her voice to signal that she heard Ger on the line—his take-no-shit snap. Heard him smacked for it too. *Christ!* Walloped so hard her teeth ached.

Music pounds her mind, that Skuzzcut-thrash Ger let wail the night she dodged out to meet Troy in his cab—*Bring it on! come on come on!*—distorted as that child's cry, the ringtone on her phone—amplified in her core by the boat's vibrations. The baby buzzing inside her belly. *Busy, sure—and probably a redhead like you*, she thinks, feeling helpless in that moment.

"Almost there," Mike says, pointing beyond her to the approaching islands. He slices them rough through swell after swell, and Teffy wonders what these islands mean to Mike and Daryl, what they mean to Ellie and the show she's crafting, what they mean to the memoir she's trying to finish as part of the show.

She meets Ellie's wind-stung eyes, and though the old artist must suspect something, she smiles at Teffy. A kindly smile. Like a friend who wants to trust you again.

Like Fin.

She feels a sudden ache at the thought of losing Fin, at wanting him back. As close to the bone as what a prayer might be. That frosty morning when she and Ger made love on that roof. Natter of crows that day and this vivid dream of a baby's soft snoring while Ger makes her coffee—the *tink tink tink* of his spoon in her mug.

A cold wind caws off the water and she flicks Ellie another look, but Ellie is fixed now on something beyond her. She follows the old woman's gaze. Feels the temperature drop as they sail into Arctic air, and sees the islands suck out of the sea into storm clouds, dry land lava-lamping between sea and sky in surrealistic blobs, as if siphoned out of this world into another and decanted back again. In that witching moment she recalls Fin, half a bottle deep and with a lit roach in hand, saying that he just wanted to see it the once—"Just the once," he said. "The world within the world."

And she thinks, *This . . . this is what you wanted to see.*

But as soon as she thinks it, the islands slip back into the sea and grow large and real and more solid—bone-white under the darkening sky.

"It's gull shit," Mike hollers, pointing at the white cliffs. He twists the throttle to slow the boat, and they putter into calmer waters amongst the islands. He eases off a bit more and calls up to Teffy to keep an eye out for shoals.

She crouches in the bow and peers into the dark water, glancing up now and again. Spies an old fishing stage built into the nearest cliff and feels Mike shift course in that direction.

Lisetta asks if people still live out here.

"Last one to live out here," Daryl tells her, "was Lemuel Crawley, and he's dead now, what, twenty-two. . . ."

"Twenty-seven years," Ellie says.

"Back when the whale washed up?"

"After that," Ellie says, her face grim as Mike shifts course from the fishing stage north.

"Remember that iceberg I pointed out this morning?" Mike says to Lisetta.

Lisetta is busy snapping pictures with her cell phone. She twists to get a shot of him standing astride his seat. She goes to snap a pic of Daryl too, hunched beside her, but he paws away her phone and points at a lone rock sticking out of the water.

"Virgin Rock," he says, and as they pass it by the rock takes on the shawled shape of the Mother of God, a momentary vision now gone.

"Well," Mike says as he motors past the point and steers east—toward an iceberg near the size of the island next to it. "There it is! When it disappeared after our walk, I figured it blew into these islands."

"Hung up on the rocks," says Daryl.

Lisetta reaches for her bag. "Can you get closer?"

"A bit closer," Mike says, the bob of the boat roughening as they drift in close to the berg's backside, a yellowish submerged basin of polar ice that slopes into a sharp crag ahead of them and breaches like a white whale to their port-side.

Teffy can't fathom the depth of the iceberg's underwater belly, the dip between its hill and peak, or the water's weird yellow wimple, as if lit from below by a deep-sea sun. She almost falls over the edge gazing sickly into that submerged basin, but Ellie grabs her beltline and sits her down.

"Could split right there," Daryl calls to Mike above the idling motor, half turned in his seat and slashing his hand down in front of him.

"That humped bit's what's holding her upright," Mike says—and Teffy looks to where he's pointing.

"Sure," says Daryl, "but if that snaps off we're all of us sunk."

The punt bobs forward, lolling side to side, and Teffy leans over the edge again, sure she's gonna chuck, waves lopping the bow and splashing her face like toilet water.

She bites her lip. And Mike steers the punt so they drift within a stone's throw of the iceberg's steep slope. Teffy closes her eyes against the underwater glare—like the sun on that rooftop not so many days ago. The keel scrapes ice and she goes to yell but Mike revs the boat and Ellie grips her leg as she heaves her guts out overboard—Lisetta barking like a goddamn seal behind her.

Mike buzzes them away from the iceberg, and Teffy pukes again. Wipes her eyes with scabbed knuckles and glances to see a little red shack on the cliff above them. She notices, as Mike steers toward a warped boat slip, that Lisetta is holding her mother's urn now.

Showing her the water? she wonders sickly. And Ellie asks Teffy if she's okay. Teffy spits overboard and looks at the old artist through what she's sure are bloodshot eyes.

"Is this where it happened?" Lisetta says.

Daryl lets the anchor rope slip through his fingers. "Where we all shot the whale?"

Teffy looks to Ellie and Ellie nods. "It's true," she says, then grabs the rickety slip, both her and Teffy missing what Lisetta says to Mike, though Teffy sees Lisetta stashing away her mother's urn again in her backpack.

"Over there." Mike points to a high place on the other side of the inlet.

Ellie grabs one of the slip's poles and brings the boat to a rocking halt.

"I'm gonna check the lobster pots." Mike motions to the painted buoys bopping along the bay's edge. "Take your gear and climb on up."

"I'll come with ya," Daryl says.

And Mike says, "I thought you might."

Teffy stands in the boat. "How long are we staying?"

"Overnight," Mike says. "There's a couple of old houses back of the cliff edge, and a church up the hill."

She gapes at him. "You're serious?"

He looks skyward, and Daryl checks a weather app on his phone. "That's a northerly kicking up," Mike says.

"It'll be full-on in less than an hour," Daryl says, replaying on his phone the orangey-red fog about to wash over them.

"Might chance a run back if it was just me," Mike says. "Or this cunt," and he nods at Daryl. "But there's no telling what a roundabout wind will do."

Fucking hell, she thinks. *Seriously?*

Lisetta asks which building they should bunk in, and Mike says, "That's Burnsy's cabin at the top of the slip. I'll bunk there. Windows are smashed out, though, so the wind might drive ya." He pauses to consider the other options. "Probably the church. They put a new roof on her last summer and she's never locked. Wood's piled under the bridge, and there's a stove inside."

"When will you be back?" Lisetta asks.

"An hour tops," Mike says.

"Less than that," says Daryl, "unless you forgot how to haul traps."

Mike winces a smile. "We'll have a boil-up in Burnsy's place when we get back." And he shoves off, Daryl at the oars already and rowing them round to the first trap.

Ellie and Lisetta climb the slip and head toward the little white church on the hill, Lisetta's backpack slung loose on the girl's shoulder, the urn in it swinging side-to-side.

Tick-tock, tick-tock—that stickman spinning time in Teffy's head. Time she doesn't have. Time she's running out of fast. But here she is. And with a job to do. A job to do and this time—*this time*—Ger's life is actually on the line. Teffy watches Ellie and Lisetta go, thinking tonight she'll make the switch. One way or another.

You've no other choice, she tells herself.

It has to be tonight.

~ 27 ~

THE RAIN IS LASHING AGAINST the windowpanes of Burnsy's place by the time Teffy sees Mike and Daryl tie-on to the slip and scramble up to the cabin. Mike bursts through the door and sweeps back the hood of his slicker, holding out a plastic bag writhing with fresh lobsters.

"Supper!" he says, seeing only Teffy by the window.

Daryl pokes his dripping head in the door. "Where're the girls to?"

"Up at the church," Teffy says. "Still."

"I'll go get 'em," Daryl says.

"Go on," Mike says and shucks off his slicker. Hangs it by the door and heads to the cold stove. "Figured a baygirl would have a fire on and the pot boiled."

"Got distracted," she says.

But the truth is she's stood here silent the whole time, watching the church to see if Lisetta takes off somewhere on the island with Ellie, with that backpack and urn. There's been no movement from the church, though, and the rain's come on hard, running down the cracked panes and pooling on the ledges, *drip-drip-dripping* on the old linoleum.

But no movement from the church. The sanctuary door shut against the weather. Teffy looks out the window and down the slip to the bay. "So," she says, wanting to get the story straight, "the book *Lured to Slaughter* took place right here, did it?"

Crackle of wood in the stove now, and Mike says, "We shot it just the other side of that wall—big fuckin thing. Huge." He shakes his head. "Before that, b'y, I never would've imagined a thing done all the way out here would piss off people in Vancouver and L.A. But Lisetta's dad . . . well, his book sure travelled." Mike scrapes the lid onto the stove, grabs a pot from the shelf, and heads to the door beside her.

She looks out the window as he flings open the door and sets the pot under a spout of rain sluicing off the roof. "I just can't picture Daryl pumping rounds into a whale," she says.

Mike stands silent watching the pot fill.

"Daryl's the one made the papers," he says, hefting the half-full pot back to the stove. "He took the brunt of it and I took off for Toronto."

"Toronto?"

"For a woman," he says.

"I'm guessing she's still there?"

He nods and leans back on the counter. "By the time I came home, Daryl and Ellie had banded people together to form the Co-op and keep the plant open. I just wanted to throw my hat in—be useful, ya know—so I became the fisheries officer. No big deal policing the local operation. But Daryl," he says, shaking his head, "Daryl has done some crooked shit to keep that plant going. And in my position you can only look the other way so often."

The pot lid trembles, and she looks again out the window to the church. No sign of Ellie, Daryl, or Lisetta yet. "What sort of crooked shit?"

Mike lifts the writhing bag. "Planning to write this up for your paper, are ya?"

"It can be off the record if you want."

He nods and says, "Please."

She says, "I'm more interested in anything on Markus O'Shea." And Mike raises his brow at that. She changes bait and asks, "Do you hear of any smuggling on St. Mark's?" tossing out Ger's angle.

"Smuggling?" he says.

"I'm just scratching around," she says. "No agenda. It's just that everyone I talk to seems to be big fans of Markus O'Shea. Everyone except Daryl, that is."

"Well, it was Markus asked Ellie to New York for a weekend, and now they're shacked-up together in town."

"Just gotta wonder if he's as squeaky clean as he seems," she says, and Mike snorts at that. "His persona is like Captain Planet: earth-friendly developments, cash dropped into testing windmills built for Newfoundland gales."

"Our wind's too strong, they say."

She shakes her head. "That's bullshit, apparently. Modern windmills can handle whatever. And O'Shea has these re-enforced designs made for here. I've seen them. And he'd have those up and running, he says, if not for Bill 61."

"Bill 61?"

"Essentially outlaws the development of renewable energy in New-foundland and Labrador. Who has more wind than here and why aren't we using it?"

"You make him sound like he's going against the grain," Mike says. "Maybe he's got some good things in the pike—things we could use."

"I want to like him," she says, and in all honesty she means it. "Everyone else does. Ellie's keen on him obviously. In town they call him St. Markus of St. Mark's."

Mike whistles at that and shakes his head.

"They say his ideas will save outport Newfoundland."

Mike looks at her. "Who says?"

"He does." And they both laugh at that. "Seriously though, what can you tell me about the hotel he wants to build here?"

"It's supposed to be all solar powered," Mike says, "and wood-heated from a managed forest across the tickle." He checks the water in the pot. "If it come down to a vote between Mark's hotel and keeping the fish plant on life-support, I say pull the plug already."

"So you're on O'Shea's side?"

Mike sighs and opens the bag. "Well," he says, drawing out a lobster with only one claw, "you'll not finger him for it now but—and this is defi-nitely off the record—Markus once fronted Daryl cash to bring something like fifty bales of weed through that plant."

She sits up straight. "Weed? When was that?"

"Late eighties," he says, dropping the lobster in the pot.

"Fifty bales?"

The lobster flicks boiling water. "Something like that, yeah."

"And they got away with it?"

"It was the eighties." The next lobster screams when it hits the pot. "That scam got Markus his start in the developing business in town actu-ally—where he belongs, as far as I'm concerned. And it kept the plant from closing when the cod fishery collapsed." He drops in the last two lobsters, checks his watch, and lids the pot.

She looks to the church and sees a light through its lone window. "But now O'Shea wants the plant to close?"

"That's what he's been saying. So he can built his fancy hotel."

"I've seen the rough mock-ups," she says. "They're nice. Everything down to the playing cards in the bedside table all locally made."

"The beds too," he says, "and the quilts on them. Full time employment for Ellie's crew at the church, and at twice the pay that she can offer them with her grant money."

"And you all get checks cut from the profits. Right?"

"Yes," he sucks in the word. "Every islander gets a piece of George Clooney when he comes. That's Markus's big pitch. Haul in the big stars with the deep pockets instead of risking it offshore for what fish the Chinese have left us. A new kind of fiscal fishery, he calls it." Mike spits on the stove and it skittles across the hot top.

"But Daryl wants no part of Markus's big plan?"

Mike checks his watch. "Not after Ellie left him for Markus. They had a famous falling out after that. Daryl told Markus to go fuck himself with his self-sustaining bullshit. That the plant would stay open if he had to freeze-dry Mexican mud to do it."

"Heroin?" she says.

He nods and reaches for a bottle of Lamb's on the shelf and the tin cup next to it. She sees Ellie and Lisetta run out of the church and into the rain, racing each other to the cabin, Daryl sauntering along behind them, hands thrust deep in his pockets. "And do you think he's doing that?" she says. "Smuggling heroin through the plant?"

"Daryl would have to be six degrees south of where I think he is to get involved in something like that. But you honestly never know with him."

"Would he ever take help from Markus?"

The door bursts open and Lisetta shoves in after Ellie, saying, "The island's gonna sink if this keeps up!"

Ellie smears water from her face and eyes Mike by the stove and Teffy by the window. Teffy notes that Lisetta is without her bag, without her mother's urn.

Must've left it in the church.

The pot lid rattles and Mike says, "Supper's boiled," and he raises his cup of rum. "Anyone else care for a drink?"

They all say "yes," save Teffy, who says she's still not over the boat ride but will play bartender for them. So she serves up drinks, offering one to Daryl when he walks wet through the door. They all salute each other and Mike dishes out the lobsters and shows Lisetta how to crack the claws with a hammer.

Lisetta burns her fingers trying to peel the cracked shell away from the crescent of cooked meat, so she smashes the claw again with the hammer and sprays Daryl with hot lobster juice. But Daryl just shrugs and throws more wood on the fire, and Ellie yips and pulls a glug of rum straight from the bottle, then sloshes another sloppy shot into her cup.

They toast each other repeatedly and laugh, Teffy faking interest and trying to sip a mug of water slow, keeping her eye on Lisetta. Hoping the girl gets right buzzed and passes out so she can nip across to the church and get back Troy's heroin.

She tops them all up and they toast again and Mike flips his lobster and points to the third phalange from the tail. "You snaps that off," he says, "like this!" And Daryl burps and Ellie wallops him in the chest and they both laugh. Then Daryl shows them how to thumb the meaty tip out of its shell in one big piece. "Voila!" he says, pinching the shucked tail between his face and Ellie's as Lisetta snaps a pic. Daryl paws away the phone, telling his niece to "Put that friggin thing away."

"You got lobster goo on it," Lisetta pouts, showing her phone drunkenly to Daryl, who leans over and licks the screen, only to get flicked in the forehead by Ellie and told he's disgusting. He just winks at her slyly and raises another toast as Ellie squeezes out her own lobster tail and splashes a bit of rum on it, Lisetta filming them as Daryl slurps the rummy lobster juice dripping off the counter's edge.

Mike pours himself another drink and leans against the slip-side wall. Starts singing a shanty Teffy recognizes, but she can't stay to listen. She knows that.

The rain has let up and now is her window, her only shot since the urn has been left in the church. Lisetta has rooted herself on the cot, happy with the rum bottle in hand, and Ellie is lounging next to Daryl, Mike's throaty voice lilting the story of a young lad gone to the Labrador and not seen again.

I'm going for a walk, she mouths to Ellie.

And they all raise their glasses as she slings her satchel over her shoulder—Mike singing "away away away" and Ellie asking for the bottle of rum, taking it from Lisetta's tattooed hand, the old artist's face blushing as she shrugs off Daryl who's whispering in her ear.

Teffy closes the door on their laughter and heads straight for the church.

~ 28 ~

SHUFFLING INTO THE CHURCH, she stops—thinks she hears someone in the sanctuary. Breathy wind and a creaking floorboard, she tells herself. Just the sound of her own steps.

Echoes in an empty room.

"No one here," she says, testing the silence and crossing herself, dusting fingers into the dry bowl next to a statue of Our Lady.

She genuflects and crosses herself again, like she is a little girl—Kate Byrne's wee redhead—and this a simple Sunday back home. But it isn't. Nothing simple about the mess she's in now. And no one to tell. Not a soul.

None but Ellie, she thinks, *and she only knows the half of it*.

The other half is here in this room, though. In this bag slumped against the wall with the backpack Daryl packed for the trip. She sees spare shirts and blankets. Lifejackets for pillows. All piled together near the woodstove, and the stove warm to the touch still. Lit like the lamp on the wall, and both left burning when they all ran back over to the cabin.

Teffy kneels and pulls the bag to her, back to the pine rail sacristy that separates the spare altar from the bare-board pews. Christ on his cross looks over her shoulder and she shifts to block his view. His body thin as Fin's.

And what would Fin say to this?

Her hands shake as she peers inside the bag. Kisses her palm and presses down on the silver lid—*please, God*. . . .

Come on, girl! she tells herself. *Twist and switch! Hurry it up*.

She lifts the jar and feels. . . .

Nothing.

"No."

She spins the lid off and yanks out the empty plastic bag. Clutches it in her trembling fist. "No. No no no no. . . ."

All of it?

Gone.

Wind in the cracks, the creak of a pew—lamplight flickering.

She trembles and drops the urn at her knees, her vision blurred by hot tears, thinking of Troy's hand hard across Ger's face, her own face in Ike's toilet, scat she's carried alongside this baby. Her baby. The size of the cherry slipped from her mouth to Ger's that morning they watched the sun rise on St. John's, frosty shingles biting her knees.

"What do you want from me?" She turns on the crucifix, fierce tears glowering the lamplight red—*her hair*, she thinks, *my baby's hair!* She fixes on those pierced feet bolted into place—"Jesus!" she screams. "Sweet fucking Christ! What am I gonna do?"

She hears a creak and spins, searches the tear-smudged room, but there's no one there. Not a soul. Only her. Her and the goddamn wind.

"And you!" she turns on Christ. "Why is it that we ask and ask and ask and you do nothing? You do nothing! Not for me or Fin or Ger. Not for any of us! *Who are you!?*" she screams. "Who are you to shuck off being God!"

Her gaze lifts from the wound in Christ's ribs and scurries along his arm to nest in his pierced palm. That hand contorted and clawing. Grasping for something denied it, out of reach.

A small bag of scat and burnt bones. That's all she has.

Not even a knife this time.

She looks to the wax-encrusted rack of empty candleholders against the far wall, the black box of unlit votive tapers hanging from it.

"You've already taken my friend," she whispers. "Is it my child you want now? Or Ger?" She thinks of Teresa and that coded journal: all those women Marjorie has not been able to reach in time. "How many more will die before you move your hand?"

She wipes her nose on her sleeve. Fishes for her last fifty-dollar bill—all the money she snitched from Ger's account before hitching a ride with Ellie across the island—gone now.

Like a match blown out.

She looks a last time at the crucifix, wishing it gone. Then she chooses three tapers from the box and twists them into three of the little clawed holders: wax-skinned infant fists reaching for her—for that part of herself she has never opened to anyone, not even Ger. She angles the candlewicks together, breaking the one taper, its string the only thing holding it upright.

Then she lights them as one. The wicks burn and she grips the lighter, squeezing it till the door bangs open and a gust of wind gutters the flame.

She hears Ellie shriek and laugh on the step, and she dives under the altar, pulling her knees up to her chin, her back to the altar's boat-shaped façade.

"Here," Ellie says—and Teffy hears shuffling, a belt buckle hitting the floor and dragging across wood. "Here," Ellie says again, coyly this time—her voice above Teffy now, the altar shifting, scraping the floor.

"Right . . . here."

Daryl says, "That crazy look gets ya in trouble, woman," and Teffy feels the altar jostle overhead. *No,* she thinks. *No, you can't. It won't hold you.* "You'll go straight to hell for this," Daryl slurs.

"Can't be any worse than half a life with you."

Daryl's knees knock the boat-shaped façade, against which Teffy is leaning to try and keep the altar upright. "Never complained about *this*, did ya?" his rubber boots squeaking the floor.

"Yeah, well, never thought you'd . . . listen."

"Christ, woman, I. . . ."

"Go on then, Strickland. Like Jesus is watching." And they're rocking the altar now, like it's a punt they're trying to sink and plim up. Swell the old caulking and make it float again. Ellie grips the altar's rough edge, her paint-stained hands so close Teffy could lick them.

And Christ stares down at the three of them. Teffy glaring back at his rosy cheeks and thinking, *You're helpless, you are. Utterly fucking helpless.* And she closes her eyes to that pitying look and covers her ears. Turns to see Daryl's rubber boot edging her satchel.

Kicking his dead sister aside.

~ 29 ~

ALONG WHILE AFTER THE LAMP dims, she struggles out from under the altar. Stretches her legs and tries to sneak quietly past Ellie and Daryl now rolled in their blankets and fast asleep.

Looking back at them—faint heat wafting off the woodstove yet—she hopes she and Ger make it to that age, and that they'll surprise themselves, as these two obviously did tonight. She casts a glance at Christ's cast face in the dark. His thorny head tilted helplessly.

A pitying look, she'd thought, wedged under that altar while the senior citizen rage-fuck banged on overhead. *Jesus Murphy, boy, what was that?*

But back here by the door, in the dark, it's not pity she sees, but the look Ger gave her before they climbed down off that frosty rooftop, the last of a cigarette on his lips.

"I love you," he said.

First time he uttered those words and she shushed him, wondering if he'd ever said them before to Teresa. And what if he had? What if he dreamt of her still? What did that matter?

Fin told her the once that the love you give never lessens you.

So why'd she shush him? Gave him the last draw, sure, before they climbed back down to the street, but did he know she was thinking it, kicking that glass bottle all the way home? *I love you, I love you, I love you.* The bottle *tink-tink-tinking* along on concrete. Hand on her belly now and she swears she'll tell him. If she makes it out of this alive, she'll tell him.

She lifts the latch, holds it tight against the wind, and slips out into the wet grass. The torn clouds claw at the moon and the hill on the far side of the bay gleams like a whale's skull.

She can't bear going back to the cabin. Not just yet. She wants this one moment. This one moment of calm before the bloodletting begins.

That's how it'll be. That's how it'll be.

And she has nothing now to keep Troy's hand from slapping Ger's face—nothing to keep Troy from drowning them both offshore. She climbs the hill to quell those thoughts and can see clear across the water to St. Mark's. Can hear waves on the rocks below, the nightwind gusting.

Across the bay, in Burnsy's cabin, a light flickers for her. And over the marshy hollow and up the hill, the church sits steeple-less and small. Human.

She wonders then when Lisetta would have scattered her mother's ashes—what she thought was her mother. Was it while she watched from the cabin?

No, she thinks. *Earlier. It must've been earlier.*

In the boat, then? Or by the iceberg.

When she was sick?

The church door opens and Ellie staggers out and squats to pee in the long grass. Teffy watches the old woman look about, finishing her business. Then Ellie hops up quickly, stares straight up the hill to where Teffy is standing and starts up the hill. Teffy looks down at her cast shadow, realizing the moon must be a bright halo behind her head.

So much for stealth.

It doesn't take long for Ellie to reach her. And together they face the wind a while, saying nothing. Just shivering. Looking out at knobs of shagrock punched up through the sea.

"Do you have any idea what you're carrying in that satchel?" Ellie says, crossing her arms. "How many kids has that passed through to get this far north, and how many of them are drawing breath still?"

"I was blackmailed," Teffy says. "They told me—"

"That they had your boyfriend, I know." Ellie looks at her. "And *do* they have your boyfriend?"

"They didn't," she says. "But they do now."

"So you need to get that back to them?" Ellie nods at the satchel strung across Teffy's chest. "Have they given you a drop place yet, a time?"

Teffy shakes her head.

"Will you give it back to them?"

She says, "I guess," though she has no idea if passing off human ash for heroin will work with the likes of Troy Hopper. What if he tests it? What then? What will happen to Ger?

"You know that stuff will just wind up on the streets," Ellie says. "Dealt to pimps and fed to the kinds of people Marjorie Petty is trying to help. That shit keeps them stuck in that world."

The world within the world, she thinks. "It's not like I chose this, you know."

Ellie nods. "So what about calling the cops?"

"If they didn't have Ger—"

"Your boyfriend?"

"If they didn't have him, I'd call the RCMP right now." She pulls her phone from her pocket and flicks it on. "We even got a signal out here." She clicks the phone off. "But these guys *do* have Ger. I heard him on the phone when they—" and she hears that godawful smack again, Ger's muffled groan, and she closes her eyes to hide the tears.

"Maybe Markus can help you," Ellie says—and Teffy looks at the old woman's spiked gray hair. "He has connections. Knows lawyers. Higher-ups in the RNC. Maybe...."

"Maybe what?"

"Maybe he could just pay off this dealer."

"I don't think this dealer cares about the stash I'm carrying. I mean, not really. He's after revenge. Ger's testimony put him away a while back."

"Oh?"

"Ger and a bunch of his buddies tried to pin a girl's murder on him—a call girl they all knew—but that didn't stick. The only thing that stuck was that Ger had been one of this guy's collectors and had dirt on him. About some deals gone bad. Explosives dropped through letter slots of people who didn't pay. Enough for a couple of years. But even that fell apart."

"And he's out now and has Ger?"

"That's right," Teffy says.

"And this all happened...."

"In the last few days."

"You should talk to Markus," Ellie says again. "Seriously. He might be able to help. I mean, Daryl tells me Markus is gonna help *him* keep the plant going, and I *never* would've seen that coming." She shakes her head. "Never."

"I thought O'Shea wanted the fish plant closed so he could build his hotel."

"Who told you that?"

"Mike."

"Well, Daryl says he's rethinking that, which is the first I've heard of it. But Markus is like that. He's from here and knows what it is to go without, to have little to no recourse. He knows what it's like to be forced into a bad situation, like that Jake kid you met."

"You make it sound like a date that didn't work out."

"I'm just saying, now that Markus has money, and the power that goes with it—the connections—he tries to give folks the leg up they need."

"Even his girlfriend's ex-husband?"

Ellie kicks a rock. "Apparently."

Teffy glances sideways at Ellie, wondering if Markus O'Shea would be as magnanimous to Daryl if he knew what had gone on in that island church down there. They'd been husband and wife once, sure, but however enlightened Markus might be, Teffy can't imagine him being cool with that bucking altar grind.

"Do you know what they call this hill?" Ellie says, and Teffy shrugs. "Baldy."

Teffy kicks a white rock. "Birdshit hill is more like it."

"True," Ellie says, and they stand awhile in silence. Until Ellie says, "You'll think about it, won't you? About asking Markus for help?"

Teffy shrugs again, and that seems to be answer enough for Ellie. The old woman kicks stones on her way down the hill, and with a glance back at Teffy, disappears inside the church—smoke still whisping from the chimney.

Some heat in there yet for you, Teffy thinks, shivering on her lonely hilltop, wondering, as she looks back across the water to St. Mark's, if that bit of heroin she has left will give the ash enough zip to pass it off as cut dope.

Maybe, she thinks.

Maybe not.

All she can do now is peck her way down the hill, scraps of moonlight making the shit-spattered rocks almost bright enough to see by.

~ 30 ~

I T'S A CLEAR MORNING and Teffy wakes to find Mike gone from the
cabin and Lisetta asleep on the cot still. She makes the fire and sets the
kettle to boil and is searching for tea when she hears the boat's motor
coming around the island's head, approaching the rocky inlet.

She steps out to see Mike putter into the bay and sees Daryl standing
at the top of the slip. Mike cuts the motor and floats the punt sidelong to the
slip so Daryl can see his cargo, and Teffy can hear Mike mutter, "Here we go."

"See you hauled up more goddamn rope," Daryl calls down to him.

"There it is," Mike says. "Go sink it again if ya want."

"You'd slap a fine on me if I did."

"Because it's against the law."

"And you're the fisheries officer," Daryl sneers. "And a St. Mark's boy.
Or so I thought. But can ya tell me whose lobster pots we raided last night?
Everybody knows they're Burnsy's, and everyone knows he slips you a few to
keep from fining him."

"Burnsy's got a few dozen pots," Mike says. "He wouldn't make in profit
what the fine would be. So I leaves him alone. But this is for a big salmon net."
He kicks the rope. "How much have you got out of this operation? Enough
to keep Markus off your back another month or more? That's it, isn't it? See,
I knows how you operate."

Daryl snorts. "Do ya now?"

"What about this rope?"

"Could be anyone's."

"It's the whole Co-op I'm talking about, not a length of fuckin rope!
How many jobs are at stake if you get caught processing poached salmon? It's
fifty people out of work if that plant closes."

"I knows how many people work at the plant," Daryl says. "I run the bloody fuckin joint in case ya forgot."

"And you'd risk their jobs for some salmon?"

Teffy can barely hear Daryl's murmur.

"What's that?" Mike snaps. "Can't hear ya with your mouth in your pocket."

"A net like that," Daryl raises his voice, "*might* keep the plant open, *if* there was fish in it, but there'd have to be fish in it."

"So are ya saying there's no fish or more than one net?"

Daryl waves off the question. "The captains are going elsewhere," he says. "Better deals and bigger trucks."

"Thought you had that Co-op loyalty angle."

"Didn't ya hear," Daryl says, "loyalty's gone up in price. Now, if there's no fine—"

"There should be!" Mike snaps.

"But if there isn't a fine," Daryl says, voice calm as he looks away, "I have things to do. Like to get back home and keep a certain plant in operation. If you wants to fuck off to Toronto again, you'll not be missed, I can tell you that."

Mike hammers his fist on the motor. "Just stay out of that racket!"

"Look. I've got a boat coming in at sunset. That's what I'll be doing all day, Mikey. Calling folks up and telling them they have a few hours's work."

"Whose boat?" Mike says.

"Doug Crawley's."

"Thought you pissed him off and he went elsewhere."

"Seems the Alberta Big Hat knows Markus and Markus has convinced him to come back to the Co-op. At least for this load."

Mike's mouth falls open. "And why's Markus helping you?"

"Change of heart, I guess," Daryl says.

"And is that what was going on in the church last night—a change of heart?"

Daryl smiles at that. "That's a conversation for Ellie to have with Markus. As far as I'm concerned, grievances can be put aside if it means keeping that plant open and keeping bread on people's plates."

Teffy watches how Mike takes in that news. He takes a slow breath. "You knows the RCMP might stop by if Crawley's kid brother doesn't show up soon."

"We're all wondering what happened to Jake," Daryl says. "Dorothy has got people out looking for him. It's a big island, but they'll find him, poaching caribou if he's anything like his brother Doug."

"I'm just saying there'll likely be a cop onsite."

"Not without a warrant," Daryl says. "And what about you, Mr. Fisheries Man? Aren't you gonna inspect the boat? You seems a bit off after last night's shed party. Is it a hangover or sugar low?"

"Do me two favors, will ya?" Mike says, looking out to the water.

"And what's that?" Daryl says.

"First, fuck off for once, will ya?"

"And second?"

Mike sighs. "Ask if Del will cover me tonight."

Daryl cracks a full-on smile. "A Mike Day, is it?"

"Fuck off, I said."

"I'll call her," Daryl says, his whole mood shifting. "And you rest easy, Mikey. I can even drive back if you want."

"I said fuck off already. Whatever you gotta do, just do it and keep me out of it." Mike looks out to sea again. "And go see if Ellie and the niece are ready to go, will ya? This place gives me the creeps."

"She's ash, Mike. Ash and gone. That's it."

Mike slumps against the motor, all the fight bled out of him.

Daryl grins, and Teffy thinks he must have gotten what he wanted: for Mike to stay home tonight. Let Del do the inspection. She remembers Del playing cards with Daryl on the ferry.

A special arrangement maybe?

Which makes her think there's more coming in off that boat than crab, and that Troy coming to St. Mark's has more to do with that extra cargo than with her and the stash she's carried from North Sydney.

But can you fish-pack heroin? And how much will be coming in exactly? And how did Ger find out?

She looks at Mike struggling to tie-on the boat. Deep slump in his shoulders like he's carrying on his back the great coil of rope at his feet.

Daryl walks off and her phone screams in her pocket.

A text. From Ger's number.

7 p.m. fish plant.

When she looks up, Ellie is coming down from the church. She feels naked with Ellie knowing what she knows—about the heroin and Ger's abduction. When Ellie sees her leaning in the door of Burnsy's cabin, Teffy turns and disappears inside. To hide. To clean-up and pack her things. Which she does. She wakes Lisetta.

Ellie pops in and hands Lisetta her backpack. With the empty urn inside. She looks like she's about to say something to Teffy, but Teffy turns her back on her and starts rummaging through the cabin's drawers.

She hears Ellie leave, and Lisetta too. A few minutes later, Daryl hollers that it's time to go. And she feels helpless in that moment, unable to find what she's looking for. Helpless as she felt stuck under that bucking altar last night—*And what was that?* she thinks. *Seriously, what was that? Old memories or menopausal hormones? Or just Daryl being a fucking prick?*

"Teffy!" Ellie calls. "We gotta go! Come on, girl!"

"Fine!" she snaps to the empty room. "If it's up to me, then it's up to me." And that's when she finds it. There. In a drawer alongside a set of rusty pliers, a ball of frayed twine, and an old hammer head. She spins it on her thumb and catches it by the handle. Like her Nan taught her. Like she showed Fin that day in his dad's stage. Spin and catch. Spin and catch. *It's not much,* she thinks, testing the slender blade with her thumb.

But she knows how to use it.

~ 31 ~

ON THE BOAT RIDE BACK to St. Mark's, Ellie huddles with Teffy in the bow.

"Have you thought about what I said?" Ellie asks. "About asking Markus for help."

Teffy thinks of the knife in her satchel, tucked alongside the gray ziplock of Stefany Strickland's remains. That one small baggie of heroin she managed to grab, thanks to Markus O'Shea trying to play the cheery bayman. "Yeah, I've thought about it," she says.

And Ellie smiles at that. "I'll text him then and see if he has time to talk today."

"It has to be before 7 p.m.," she says. "I have a meeting then."

"On St. Mark's?"

"Via Zoom," she says.

"I'll tell him," Ellie says, and she sends Markus a text. They're coming in past the breakwater when Ellie's phone dings with O'Shea's reply. *I'll swing by Mike's at 6:30 p.m. She can use the wi-fi at mother's place for her meeting. How were the Kid Brothers?*

"Sounds like a plan," Teffy says.

"You're in good hands."

"I hope so."

But that hope wavers like the threat of rain over the island, through the afternoon and on into the evening. Mike crashes in his goat-chewed La-Z-Boy, and no matter where Teffy is in the house, she can hear him snoring. Lisetta retreats to an upstairs room. "To message some friends," she says, "and set up a few gigs next week. Help pay to get that car back on the road." And Ellie heads out to meet with her church ladies: to tell them of her vandalized show and of the new quilts she'll need to re-stitch the whale's hide.

Ellie's gone a while but comes back to Mike's place a little after 5 p.m., chipper enough to hum as she makes some tea and toast.

"You're happy," Teffy says. She's pulled the prayer card of John the Baptist off the wall and has been trying to focus her thoughts on it. The sprigs of parsley on the tray, half dipped in saint's blood. "Have you seen Markus today?"

"He's been with Daryl most of the afternoon, I think."

"Isn't that a bit weird?" Teffy says.

"Sure. But nice for a change."

"You don't want them fighting over you?"

"I think Stefany coming home has been good for Daryl. Seems to have knocked some prickles loose. He's a spiny old whore's egg, that one." She's silent a moment, lost in thought, then the back door opens and someone scuffs their boots on the plywood floor.

"Ellie," Daryl calls, sticking his head into the kitchen.

"Speak of the devil," she says.

"You up for a little tour on the bike—down the coast past the Blowin Hole?"

"But you got a boat coming in."

"Del has it covered down to the fish plant. We can be out and back in an hour, and I can close things up at the plant. What do you say?"

He smiles at her and she tilts her head. Like she wants to say something but won't because Teffy is there.

If only you two knew, Teffy thinks.

"You'll be alright here?" Ellie says to her.

"I'll be fine." She waves her phone. "A bit of battery and tons to read."

"If Lisetta asks, tell her we'll be back in an hour."

"Or so," Daryl says.

"Go on," Teffy says, and they do. The quad roars to life and takes off in the purple light. And Teffy adds the remaining heroin to the bag containing Stefany Strickland's remains. She shakes the bag to mix it, bile building in the back of her throat.

Then she waits.

Waits and watches John the Baptist's blood pool on that silver platter on the prayer card in her hands. She waits, watching the saint bleed out. Until she can't stand it and slaps the card face down on the table. Then she pulls up the coded journal on her phone. Flicks through pages, trying to recall the song that came to her the last time she scrolled through these figures. *The Jackson 5's "A, B, C"—that was it.*

And she'd thought: *Letters and numbers. A clock. But if it's a clock,* she wonders, *which upright stickman is midnight? The one with hands or without?*

She puzzles this out for a while, breaking off when a vehicle drives by outside, wondering suddenly if Ger might be tied up in it. *Like Jake was going to do to you.*

She's just decided that the stickman with hands must be midnight—the letter A—when O'Shea barmps his horn. 6:45 p.m. by the clock on the wall. Teffy slides the fillet knife back into her satchel, along with the bag of ash and heroin. She stuffs in the gory prayer card, then pockets her phone, pushing the coded journal from her mind.

Mike snores away in the other room, and Lisetta is quiet upstairs. Both of them beat out.

O'Shea barmps again and the stove clock winks 6:47. She stops by the tin of water on the wall and tries to conjure up some image of someone—*anyone*—who might hear the thrashing fear in her mind. Someone to tell her what to do. Nan or Ger. But it's that island crucifix that flashes in her mind. Christ pinned to pine boards. Beat out. Helpless in the face of others's savagery. *Don't let that be you, girl. Don't let that be you.* She dips her fingers in algae water and crosses herself as she walks out the door.

O'Shea reaches across the passenger's seat of his boat-sized Buick to let her in, and they drive into the Gulch, past the big gray house there.

"So this is Doug Crawley's place," she says, trying to make conversation with the millionaire, wondering how much of her situation Ellie has shared.

"It's Doug Crawley's crab boat getting processed tonight," Markus says.

"Ellie says you were talking with Daryl today."

Markus chuckles. "Daryl and I have some history, you might say."

"You're dating his ex-wife."

"Ellie said you were in some trouble and thought I might be able to help you out."

"Did she tell you the trouble?"

They drive on slowly past Hurley's store, the pink neon sign blinking OPEN even though the windows are dark. "She told me a little," he says. "That there's a dealer involved."

"Troy Hopper," she says. "Have you heard of him?"

"A little by reputation," he says quietly. "Went to prison a couple of years ago?"

She grips the satchel tighter. "He's out now," she says, and across the bay lists a big, double boom trawler knotted to the plant's wharf—Crawley's boat.

"So this Troy Hopper is out now and you need some help with him?" Markus says.

"I need to pay out the debt my partner owes him."

He nods thoughtfully, pulling his car between two small trucks in the fish plant parking lot—on the right a red S-10 Chevy with a camper strapped in the bed, and on the left a boxy gray Nissan Frontier with rust-rotted wheel wells. O'Shea cuts the Buick's engine and kills the lights. "From what I hear," he says, "you can never pay these guys enough for them to lay off."

"Sounds like I'm not the first person you've tried to help," she says.

And he smiles. "You could say that."

Teffy can see the two loading docks through the windows of the Chevy: a white cube van backed up to the one dock and a green minivan parked in front of the other. By the lamppost glare, she can see that the windows of the Chevy are all splotched with greasy kid prints, and she thinks of Ger palming their front windows in winter—his prints frosting when the temperature drops. Poor man's stained glass, he calls it. And she wonders if he'll teach that to their kid.

"That's Cliff Burnsy's," Markus says of the truck next door. "He and Mike are thick as thieves. The guy's got grandkids in Halifax. Says the camper saves him on motel costs when he takes the ferry to visit them."

A big blue Dodge Ram with a shiny grill sits across from them.

"Looks like Daryl's truck," she says.

Markus peers at it. "Except that one's new to the island."

"How do you know?"

"I'm up here more often than you'd think."

"Laying plans for your new hotel?"

"Is this a press interview?" he asks. "Or am I helping you?"

A gunshot cracks and Markus smiles at the way she jumped. "That's just the gull-banger," he says. "To scare off the gulls. Does living in town put you on edge like that?"

"Gunshots put me on edge!" she snaps, looking around the parking lot, counting a dozen cars and trucks, and wondering where Troy might've stashed Ger. In which one of these vehicles? That truck maybe?

The dashboard clock reads 7:10 now.

Past due. And no Hopper.

She is just about to open her door to start checking vehicles when she sees Troy Hopper and another guy in rubber overalls, both wheeling dollies stacked with crates. "That's Doug Crawley," Markus points to the guy in the overalls.

"And that's Troy Hopper," she whispers, watching Crawley cradle the top crate on his dolly, a lit cigarette pinched in his fist as he eases the dolly down the cement ramp and pushes it through the gravel to the minivan, Troy close at his heels.

Teffy crouches low as Crawley and Hopper scan the parking lot. Neither seems to have noticed the extra car tucked back between the two trucks, though. Crawley flicks the smoking stub of his cigarette and slides the van door open, turning to reach for the top crate.

Teffy looks to Markus slouched next to her, watching Crawley heft the crate off the dolly. Crawley saying something to Troy as another guy—in work boots and a hooded sweater—wheels a third dolly out the open gate.

Mitt the taxi driver, she thinks, watching the guy round the van to where Crawley and Hopper are loading. Troy grabs a crate from his stack and the van rocks back and forth and a writhing body pitches out onto the ground, kicking up dust.

Ger! she almost yells.

And Troy drops his crate, grabs Ger by his zip-tied hands, and wrestles him back into the van with Mitt's help—Crawley saying, "Who the fuck is that?"

She's about to say something to Markus but he opens his door. No interior light, and she looks to see he's switched it off. He's around back of the car now, opening the trunk. And all Teffy can do is watch Troy and Mitt struggling with Ger as Crawley asks them what the hell's going on—Teffy praying they don't overhear Markus getting whatever it is he's after in the trunk.

Fuckssake! Does he not know who these guys are!

She's about to swivel in her seat, to signal to Markus, but he walks right past her toting a scoped hunting rifle. "Markus!" she tries to hiss, but her window is up and O'Shea is past her now, starting toward the loading docks and yelling for the three men to put their hands in the air.

Troy cocks his head and glares at Markus dusting toward him, the rifle drawn up to O'Shea's shoulder. Troy's one hand is on something in the van, the other half raised and gesturing for Mitt to calm down.

Mitt's back is to O'Shea, and he raises an arm slowly. Follows O'Shea's orders, but keeps his other hand tucked in his sweater's front pocket.

"Both hands!" Markus yells.

"Markus," Crawley says, "the fuck's with the rifle, b'y?"

Teffy watches O'Shea step closer, waving the barrel of the gun from Crawley to Hopper to Mitt and back again to Crawley.

Troy glares at O'Shea, and Teffy thinks he's about to say something to the armed billionaire when the gull-banger goes off. O'Shea fires and Crawley's head snaps back in a spray of blood. Mitt ducks, draws a handgun from his sweater pocket, and swivels in the dirt. O'Shea fires again, and Mitt fires back, winging O'Shea and knocking the rifle from his grip. O'Shea struggles for his tossed gun, but Mitt charges him and kicks the rifle away, hoofing him in the ribs with a steal-toed boot, and then twice in the head.

Teffy opens her door and drops to the ground, looks under the truck to O'Shea sprawled on the ground. He doesn't move.

Mitt spits, "Fuckin pig!" and Teffy slithers back toward the trunk. Thinks to call for help but knows that if they find her snivelling to a dispatcher—without their heroin—that'll be the last anyone hears of her. Gravel bites her palms as she crab-crawls toward the still-open trunk.

Mitt says, "He shot buddy's fuckin face off. Look."

"He shot out a tire," Troy says. "Won't get far on that."

Another thudding kick—"Fucker!" Mitt says—and Teffy is back now by the open trunk, thinking to hide in Markus's Buick while Markus lies shot over there in the dirt.

"Want me to wire a truck?" Mitt says.

"No," Troy says. "Where the fuck's *his* car?"

Teffy glances at the dark hills and sees nowhere to run: nowhere she won't be seen and shot—except in the Buick's trunk.

She hears boots on gravel, footsteps approaching, and the world spins. Find a focus—*there!* That gash in the clouds—those stars and that single one falling, like an ATV's headlamp. She rolls into the trunk, clutches her satchel to her chest, a tarp crinkling under her.

She's about to pull shut the lid when she sees a pair of boots by the gun case.

Black Kevlar-capped boots.

Inches from her face.

Like in the gallery. She blinks. Sees the slash of spray paint livid across the one toe. But Mitt says something nearby and Teffy takes a deep breath and quietly closes the trunk on herself. Click. Mitt's muffled voice nearer now—"Fucker's car is over here," he says—and Troy asks if the keys are in it. "In the ignition," Mitt says and clamps shut the door.

"Then get it over here," Troy says. "Time to load up."

"Thought you said this had all been cleared. That there was an understanding."

"There *was* an understanding."

Their voices recede and Teffy hears them straining as they drag the bodies to the van. More talk as they load their crates but most of their jabber is too low for her to hear.

Except Mitt asking if that young cunt is gonna to show with Ike's scat.

She presses a hand to her belly.

No sound now. So she tries to reach inside the satchel for the knife but the van revs on the far side of the lot, tires crunching gravel as it pulls up behind O'Shea's car. The engine idles, then cuts. She scoots back quickly and bumps the empty rifle case. Wishes the gun was still in the case as she squeezes over it. Swipes the spray-painted boots aside and props the case up on its side. There. She wiggles back another inch behind the rifle case, feels the edge of the tarp, and—as silently as she can—pulls the tarp over her, trying not to breathe.

The latch clicks and she feels a rush of cool air. Hears Troy say, "There's the gun case," close enough she can smell his cigarette.

"Want me to check for extra shells?" Mitt says.

"Come on, b'y"—Troy grunts—"toss him in. They won't take forever in there."

Mitt curses Crawley's dead weight and the car bobs as they roll Crawley and then O'Shea into the trunk—Troy saying, "Shove 'em back," and they mash Teffy into the back of the trunk. The rifle case flattening her nose, her hand stuck in her bag.

She fingers the knife she stole from Burnsy's cabin. Tries to get a grip on it.

"You wants me to finish off Money Bags?" Mitt says—and Teffy thinks they must know who O'Shea is then.

"Let the cunt bleed out," Troy says. "Fancy shirt will sop it up."

"What are we gonna do with the car?"

"Drive it off the wharf," Troy says.

Another crate drops in the trunk. "Got another four that won't fit."

"What's he got jammed back there?" They give everything another hard shoulder-shove and the knife pricks Teffy's palm. She bites her lip.

"We'd have to haul all this out to see," Mitt says.

"Don't bother. Just stack the rest in the car."

"With him?"

She hears Troy smack something fleshy—*Ger's face?*—and she almost yells, nicking her hand again on the knife blade. More scuffling, then something torn away—duct tape from skin—and another harsh slap. "If you yell, b'y, Mitt here ends it."

"You're talkin dirty." Ger clucks his tongue. "My safe word's *fuck you*."

Another slap—and another.

No jokes from Ger now, and Troy says, "Your girlfriend's late, Stuckless."

"She's always late," Ger spits.

"I gives her two minutes," Troy says, "then I stuffs you in the trunk with the bodies."

"There's more than one?"

"Gag him, Mitt."

Scuffling and muffled screams, then Mitt asks how Troy wants it done if the cunt doesn't show—"Knife or rope or what?"

And that's when Teffy starts banging the trunk with her good hand, yelling, "I'm in here! I'm fucking well in here!"

~ 32 ~

THE LATCH POPS AND SHE SWIPES the knife blindly, but Mitt jerseys her and hauls her out by the bra strap, kneeing her in the ribs before she hits the gravel head-first.

She coughs, flails halfway back into Mike's bulky shirt pulled over her head. Tries to stand but gets booted in the side of the knee, feels a snap and yells as she keels over.

Two hands yank her upright, her shirt shucked from her face. She swipes the knife, half an inch from catching Troy's side—but Troy pulls a gun on her. Tells her to drop it, and smiling says, "Toffee, you made it." Then he signals Mitt, who rests a boot on the back of Teffy's bad knee, applying pressure until she drops the knife.

Troy claws her hand that's gripping the satchel. "Is this the stuff?" he says, and cranks her finger back till the joint snaps and she yells and Troy fish-hooks her face sideways to see Ger three feet away—hands zip-tied, mouth duct-taped shut again.

Troy nods at Mitt, who leans on the back of her broken knee again, and Troy forces two fingers down her throat, sidestepping when she spews.

She heaves until her eyes blur, trying to see Ger. Troy yanks the satchel strap from her neck and flips it open. Pulls out the ziplock and scoops up the knife. Says, "I'm impressed, Toffee," and checks the blade with his thumb. "Very impressed."

Then he glares at Mitt to hold her while he yanks open her shirt. He fists the fabric into her mouth and, flicking the knife, says, "Baygirl like you knows how to gut a fish, right?" And he slashes her belly—a shallow cut—and jams her loose shirttail further down her throat. Ger yells through his duct-tape and Troy kicks him in the face. "The both of you, shut it." Then he nods at Mitt, who kicks the back of Teffy's knee again and throws her to the ground.

"That," Troy says, straddling Ger and leaning in to catch Teffy's eye, "that was for being late."

Ger—on his stomach between Troy's legs—cranks his head back into the guy's crotch, and Troy grabs himself, staggers, and kicks Ger's face as he stumbles.

Finds his footing and kicks Ger again.

"That's a bitch-move, Stuckless."

And Teffy moves but Mitt puts a heel to her forehead and thrusts her back, saying, "Stay where you're to," his sweater pocket heavy with that gun.

She sees Ger on the ground and shifts. Tries to keep her weight off her broken knee. "You said"—sharp gasp—"you said you'd let us go."

Troy looks at the blood trickling down her belly. "There was never any *us*, Toffee." He tilts his head. "Just you. Just you who climbed in my cab. Just you I sent to North Sydney. But you knifed my guy so"—he nudges Ger with his boot, and Ger glares at her, at her cut stomach—"thought I might better send my message direct to Stuckless here. So the both you would be sure to get it."

Mitt puts his boot to Ger's forehead and shoves him back—Ger's fingers clawing gravel. "I said stay where you're to."

"Check it." Troy tosses the satchel to Mitt.

She reaches for the strap with her good hand, but Mitt kicks her onto her back where she twists in the dirt to see Mitt peel open the ziplock, take a pinch, and snort it.

"Nothing," he says, "barely a zip."

She looks up at Troy, who shakes his head while Mitt licks a finger and tastes the contents. "It's fuckin ash," he says, tossing the open bag back to Troy.

Troy peers into the ziplock. "What kinda shit are ya trying to pull, Toffee?" She can't read Ger's look, and her knee blazes when she puts weight on it. But she knows she has to say something, so she tells Troy what happened, gasping every few words. Tells him that she switched out Lisetta's mother's burnt remains for the dope on the ferry, fearing what would happen if a cop searched her. "And then—out there," she says, breathing hard and raising her broken finger to the darkened sea, "out there—someplace—she dumped it—Lisetta—all of it. Thinking it was—*ahhh!*—her mother's ashes. It was Lisetta!"

"Who the fuck is Lisetta?" Troy tightens his grip on the knife.

She says, "A girl that I—that I caught a ride with," hair sweat-slicked to her skull. "From the—from the ferry."

"You let a mainlander dump a pound of my good heroin?"

"I didn't let her. I—"

"Then you let Mitt here snort human remains?"

"I tried to say—"

Troy kicks Ger in the spine, Ger's body knotting into a tighter ball. "Don't interrupt me, Toffee." His voice calm now as he spins the knife on his thumb and catches it by its handle. Spin and catch. Spin and catch. "It pisses me off when you interrupts me." He holds up the blade, as if inspecting its honed, bloodied edge. "It's a sick cunt who makes a man eat human ash."

"A sick cunt," Mitt says.

"You thought you were gonna get lucky, didn't you?" He nods at Mitt to grab Teffy's arms and Mitt grips the wrist of her pricked hand and twists it up between her shoulder blades. "You thought you'd get lucky with Stuckless here, because he once had my ear." Mitt raises her wrist an inch, the joint about to suck out of its socket. "You wanted my ear, didn't you, Toffee? You wanted me to listen to you. And I might have. I mean, you kicked through more than I thought you would. More than Stuckless here would've. But. . . ." Troy leans into Ger's face, grips his ear and jerks Ger's head sideways. Says loud enough that Teffy can hear, "But you really fucked this one up, Toffee."

Then he slices off Ger's ear.

She and Ger both scream and Troy punches Ger in the mouth and hooks him across the face with his other fist, knocking him to the ground. Blood smears across Ger's face, pulsing from his severed ear and running into his eyes as he writhes and kicks in the dirt.

She tries to yell but has no voice. Can do nothing with her arm bent back but watch Troy stuff the severed ear in Ger's mouth and clamp a thick hand over his lips, holding his nose until he swallows. Then Troy yanks the gray ziplock over Ger's head and holds it tight around his tattooed neck— Ger kicking and flailing, inhaling human ash.

She yells and Troy rips the plastic bag from Ger's skull. The ash scatters in the wind. And Ger inhales sharply. Spits the sludge from his mouth and coughs. Sucks sweet, sweet air, gasping. Gasping.

But Troy puts a gun to Ger's face. "Six years," he says—and she yells. An engine roars and Mitt pitches her sideways. But she sees Ellie launch the quad onto the parking lot and tear toward them, Daryl hanging on like a scared kid.

Troy cracks his gun across Ger's bloody face, spins toward the oncoming quad, and shoots. Ellie's body snaps right. Blood splashes Daryl's face and he catches Ellie. Cranks the quad into a sideways skid and rolls Ellie off behind the machine as Troy fires at them again. Another shot blasts over Teffy's head as she cradles Ger's bloody face—too stunned to yell or call out. Just rocking back and forth. *Tick-tock tick-tock.*

The midnight stickman falling, falling.

Off the edge of here and gone.

Into the sea.

Car doors clamp shut behind her and an engine revs.

She sees Daryl peek over the quad's seat and the Buick's back tires spin gravel over her. Daryl scrambles to pull out his cell phone. "Mike!" he yells into the device as the Buick races out of the gravel lot and down the road. "They just shot Ellie and took off. What? It's a fuckin island, of course they're headed your way! Yes, ya stunned arse, in Markus's Buick!"

Teffy cranes to see the Buick fishtail at the corner and pick up speed as it zips past the streetlight at Hurley's store and disappears into the Gulch— eclipsed by the Crawley house—its taillights blinking a second later, the driver gassing it out of the village.

Then a flash and distant crack—a rifle's report echoing over the water—and the Buick flies off the embankment into the lamp post by Mike's house, cracking the pole and toppling it onto the hydro lines that spark and black out the light.

~ 33 ~

THE AMBULANCE CAREENS AROUND a corner and Teffy—strapped to the gurney—sees the medic brace herself. Someone up front says, "Just coming through Clarke's Head."

She was dreaming, fading in and out.

Recalling Daryl's voice, asking if she was alive—and then nothing—then flashing red lights—the sudden, sickening weightlessness as she was deadlifted onto a gurney—"Where's Ger? Where is he?" she kept asking, feeling for his bloodied face—that missing ear—the ambulance idling and voices talking about the ferry coming in—"docking soon, docking soon," they kept saying—in and out, in and out—then the rough crossing, world listing—

The medic's voice now: "Can you hear me?"

"Yes," she says.

And her eyes snap open as they hit a pothole—knee flaring like Mitt just stomped on it—"Christ!" she groans. "My knee!"—that instant frozen in her mind: when Ellie's body snapped back—the spray of blood across Daryl's face—and the gravel pelting her as Troy tore away in the Buick—the rifle's report echoing across the water—the streetlight sparking out.

She sees the medic about to administer something through her intravenous line and says, "I'm pregnant," her mouth chalky.

"You're what?" the medic says.

"I'm. . . ." She has to mouth the word, and the medic's eyes widen and she calls up to the driver. "She says she's pregnant!"

"Call ahead and let them know," the driver says.

The needle in her hand pinches as she reaches for her belly, the strip of gauze and new tape there, but the IV tube tugs her skin, and her other hand, pricked by the knife, is bandaged, fingers free. She can almost make a fist.

"Where's Ger?" she manages to say, letting her hand relax—and the medic tells her that the guy she was holding—"Ger, is it?"—is in the ambulance ahead of them, on the way to James Paton Memorial in Gander.

"Was he alive?"

"Oh yes."

The ambulance jostles and jerks and she grinds her teeth, the medic chattering into the radio, updating her status and asking what to do for a sedative. She doesn't hear the answer—barely feels a thing save her pulse in her fingers as the blood pressure cuff inflates.

The medic rattles off her stats. More radio chatter she can't make out. Then the ambulance jolts over another pothole, and she yells, and the medic calls up to the driver, "Hey! Take it easy!"

"What—on this road?"

"I can't give you another sedative," the medic says to her, glaring at the driver's shaved head. "So, it's gonna be a rough ride to Gander."

She tries to grab the medic's wrist but the ambulance bangs through another pothole, sending lighting through Teffy's knee.

"The woman on the bike?" she says, breathless from the pain. "The one . . . shot off the quad. Is she . . . is she alive?"

"She was airlifted to St. John's. Alive."

"And the guy in the trunk, Markus O'Shea . . . is he alive?"

"That was Markus O'Shea?" the medic says, eyes wide. "Seriously?"

"The one shot in the. . . ." she winces. "The one shot in the arm, I think."

"Hey, the guy they pulled from the trunk is Markus O'Shea," the medic says to the driver. "And yes," she says to Teffy, "he's alive and in the helicopter to St. John's."

"And the others?"

"Besides him," the medic says, "I know of two fatalities in the car that ran off the road. Passenger seat and trunk. The arm-shot victim—Markus O'Shea—survived."

"And the driver?"

"Missing."

Hopper, she thinks as she shifts and moans. "So, Ger is alive, then? In the ambulance ahead of us?"

"Is he a friend?" the medic says.

She touches the bandages on her stomach, winces at the wound beneath. "He's the father. Please," she says. "I need to know he's alright."

~ 34 ~

A T LEAST YOU'RE A LITTLE MORE symmetrical," Teffy says as Ger pulls Ellie's red Corolla into a parking space at the Health Sciences Center in St. John's.

"The perk to having your ear sawn off"—Ger checks the bandage in the rear-view mirror—"is that I can ignore people on this side of me." He waves vaguely in her direction with his bandaged hand: cut, he said, in the scramble during his abduction.

"You heard me when I told you how much heroin they recovered."

He fakes deafness—"What's that now?"—and she's about to swat him but he steps out of the Toyota and she struggles to do the same but can't quite dislodge her braced leg from under the dash. Ger comes around and helps her out.

As they start for the hospital doors, Teffy slings her arm through his and says, "Just glad I get to do this again," and gives him a squeeze.

He opens the hospital door for her and asks if she's sure they said they could speak with Ellie this afternoon.

"Once the constabulary has finished questioning her," Teffy says.

"I honestly thought she was dead from that shot. The way her body snapped back. The blood on Daryl's face."

"She was ten inches away from being face-shot like Crawley."

"The boat captain?" Ger says, and Teffy nods. "Have you sorted why Ellie was out with Daryl and why Daryl wasn't running things at the fish plant?"

Teffy hobbles into the elevator and waits for the door to close before saying, "I think Daryl might've been trying to win her back from O'Shea."

First floor, second floor.

Then Ger says, "So it was more than just an island rumfuck?" right as the door dings open. Teffy punches his arm, then latches onto it and they limp out into a hall flashing with police badges. "Ready for more interrogation?" he whispers.

A female constable asks them who they are and who they are here to see. Teffy says, "I'm a friend of Ellie Strickland," and produces her license as ID. The constable holds out a hand for Ger's ID while she reads Teffy's.

"Teffy Byrne," the constable says, glancing down at her braced leg. "You write for that news site . . . what's it called?"

"*The Miscreant*," Ger says.

The constable looks from Ger to his ID and back, then hands him his card. She nods at Teffy. "If she's Broken Leg, then you must be Missing Ear."

"Your Van Gogh jokes can't be any worse than hers," Ger says and soft-elbows Teffy, who smiles back, trying to loosen the tension between them and the cop.

"I'm Melanie Parsons," the constable says. "I'm told you called ahead to speak with Ellie Strickland?"

"And Markus O'Shea," Ger says. "He's on this floor too, right?"

"O'Shea's in with senior officers right now," Parsons says. "But Ellie Strickland is just this way." She ushers them into Ellie's room and the old artist looks up from a left-handed sketch she's doing on a napkin: a whale diving deep, the cross-like tail split into an island on which stands a female figure. Two, Teffy sees. Ellie stares at them, her hospital gown drooped off her bandaged right shoulder.

"Do you know these two?" Parsons says—and Ellie nods, fixing a hard look on Teffy. "I'll be back in ten minutes then," and the constable closes the door. Ellie takes in Teffy's braced leg. Motions with her IV hand to the lone chair by her bed.

"If either of you needs it," she says, her voice croaky with phlegm.

"Your shoulder," Teffy says. "Will you—"

"I should be able to draw again. If it heals right."

Ger nods at the sketch on her bedside tray. "You're pretty good left-handed."

Ellie sips her drink and sets the cup down on the sketched whale. "So are you here to tell me what the Jesus I'm mixed up in? Vandalized show and getting shot in the arm. There are better ways to spend a week, I can tell you that."

"Actually," Teffy says, "one of the things I—we—wanted to talk to you about was the vandalized art show."

"And I wants to talk to you two"—Ellie nods at Ger, who's drumming the end of the bed—"about the heroin and human ash found all over this lad's face at the fish plant."

"I heard they did a DNA test," Teffy says.

"It was Stefany," Ellie says. "But what I don't understand is if *we* scattered Stefany out by that iceberg how did she wind up in *your* bag."

"Have they not shared my statement with you?" Teffy asks.

"They have not."

"The truth—"

"That'd be nice," Ellie says.

And Teffy nods. "The truth is I haven't been completely honest with you from the night of the break-in. At the gallery."

"Oh?"

"I wasn't just walking by and saw the break-in," she says. "I was inside the gallery when the vandal broke in. I was upstairs. Returning something." She swallows and looks down at her braced knee. "The journal I'd been looking through earlier. That dead girl's journal."

"But with good reason," Ger cuts in.

"Oh?" says Ellie.

"Teffy recognized the stickmen in the journal," Ger says. "The drawings. They were like something my old girlfriend used to sketch."

"And your girlfriend was?"

"Teresa," he says.

"Teresa Squires," Teffy adds.

Ger nods and says, "She'd starting using, behind my back, and I think she got in deep with a dealer in town. Mixed up with the guy's prostitution ring."

"Turning tricks?" Ellie says.

Ger nods. "For dope."

"And you knew about this?"

Ger winces at that. "I had my head pretty far up my own arse at the time. So I'm sure there were signs. I just didn't read them. Or didn't want to."

Ellie says, "I'm not seeing the connection to my gallery."

"Teresa was found murdered," Teffy says—and the knuckles of Ger's bandaged hand whiten on the end of Ellie's bed. "She was murdered in much the same way as Marjorie described the death of that girl—the one who handed over that coded journal."

"The journal is gone," Ellie says. "The vandal took it."

Ger smiles. "Well, when Teffy brought it to me, I scanned a copy. So she could return the original. We still have that copy," he says and he pulls out his phone to show her. "We just wanted you to know. To be in the loop."

"And Marjorie," Teffy says. "We wanted Marjorie to know too. I should've just asked you. I should have—"

"Yes, you should have." Ellie looks up from Ger's phone.

"I guess I just thought since I was going to be working with you—to cover the show and its backstories—that I could borrow it and bring it back? That it wouldn't be a big deal, especially if I found some way, through Ger, to decode the thing."

"So, what happened on Peppett Street?" Ellie says.

"Peppett Street?" Ger says.

"Why was there all that blood? And why"—Ellie slaps her tray and points at Ger with her left hand—"why were my sister-in-law's remains smeared across *your* bloody face!"

"Teffy was trying to save me," Ger says quietly.

"I got blackmailed," Teffy says, "and things got outta hand—"

"So what happened on Peppett Street?" Ellie asks again.

"I was blackmailed. To carry some heroin."

"Heroin? That's what we scattered at sea, thinking it was Stefany?" The old woman takes another sip from her plastic cup. An IV alarm dings. "How much heroin did we toss overboard that day?"

"About a pound," Teffy says—and Ellie's eyes blister in shock.

"And this d-dealer," she stammers, "he's missing now?"

"That's right," Ger says.

"He's the one who shot me?" She wiggles the IV needle in the back of her hand. Starts scratching at the tape.

"They're searching the island for him," Ger says. "The whole of St. Mark's. It'll maybe take a couple of days, but they'll find him."

"So when I drove into that firing range," Ellie says, "this dealer, he was giving you hell for trying to pass off my sister-in-law's remains as his heroin—is that right?"

Ger looks at Teffy and drops his head. "Yeah, that's right."

"Well, good," Ellie says. "Then I don't have to." She dips her head to catch Ger's eye. Ger looks up, and Ellie winks at him. Teffy blinks, not sure she saw that right. But Ellie shifts to point at her. "Fucking up your knee, though, that was maybe a step too far. Maybe."

Ger smiles. "You'd have settled for kicking our heads in?"

"That's right," Ellie says. "Now, I want to ask you both a question the cops have been asking me: Why was this dealer running a load of heroin through the St. Mark's fish plant?"

"To get back in business," Ger says. "I've told them that. After six years behind bars, you got to make a statement to your suppliers if you wants back in the game—something big. The question is *why* St. Mark's and who helped him?"

"The cops are already asking those questions," Ellie says.

Teffy looks to Ger, who nods, and she says, "We might have another angle, though. One not on the cops's radar. Yet. We just want to be sure, though, before we kick up more dirt."

"Sure of what?" Ellie says.

"Do you think Markus was involved?" Teffy says. "At St. Mark's."

Ellie blinks. "He got shot trying to stop them. And he almost died in his own trunk, stuffed up against Doug Crawley."

"Who Markus shot in the face," Ger reminds her.

"After one of them shot first!" Ellie snaps.

And Teffy thinks, *It was the gull-banger that set things off.*

Ellie looks from Ger to Teffy, scratching at the taped needle in the back of her hand. "How exactly do you think Markus was involved?"

Teffy sighs, "It's just that the journal—"

"But what does the journal have to do with Markus?"

Teffy looks to Ger and he nods. "We think the journal might connect Markus to Troy Hopper," she says, and Ellie blinks. "Teresa was working for Troy, and if the journal was written by her and if she was trying to tell Marjorie Petty something, then maybe. . . ."

Ellie glares at her. "But *why* do you think the journal is connected to Markus?"

"Because he stole it from your gallery."

~ 35 ~

CONSTABLE PARSONS STICKS HER head back into the room and says, "That's the ten minutes," and a nurse pushes past the constable to check on Ellie's IV.

"Could I have another five with them?" Ellie says—and Teffy gives Ger a hopeful glance. "They're gonna look after my car and place till I'm released."

"We have your address down as Portugal Cove," Parsons says, checking her notes.

"That's Markus O'Shea's address," Ellie says. "My mail goes to Livingstone Street. I have a small place there, near Long's Hill."

Parsons points a pen at Teffy and Ger. "And these two are going to be looking after that for you?"

Ellie raises her chin to Teffy. "Didn't you say your place was bombed?"

"It was a letter bomb, wasn't it?" Ger says, looking to Parsons.

And Parsons steps inside the door, holding it open for the nurse on her way out. She lets the door sweep shut, then says, "A UPS parcel. We think."

"Which Troy used on occasion if his buyers weren't paying up," Ger says. "A debt collector's bomb. Like I said in court. Only Troy liked to deliver them himself. Send a personal message that the debt was past due."

"Would anyone else working for Hopper have known how to make one of these IEDs?"

"IEDs?" Ellie says.

"Improvised Explosive Device," Parsons says.

"Mostly Troy," Ger says. "In my day at least."

Parsons scratches a note. "Did Ben Critch know how to rig one of these IEDs?"

"Maybe," Ger says. "Why?"

"Ben Critch was found murdered in his apartment."

~ 163 ~

"Seriously?"

"He lived just over the hill from us," Teffy says. "On Malta Street."

"We found materials in his apartment." Parsons keeps her eyes fixed on Ger. "Like those used in the IED detonated at *your* house. Do you know of any reason why Ben Critch would be involved in your abduction and bombing your house?"

"Ben and I haven't spoken much since the trial," Ger says.

"But he lives a five minute walk from your house."

"That's St. John's," he says. "But seriously, we haven't hardly talked since the trial. I call him on occasion if I think he might know something in relation to a story I'm working."

"So you do admit to calling him recently?"

Ger looks at Teffy. "The night you stepped out to talk to Troy, I called Ben." Then back to Parsons, "You'll find the record on my phone."

"And what did you talk about?"

"I was asking after Troy, and if he knew anyone still working for the guy. I ended the call shortly after finding out Ben had been more or less running Troy's operations the last six years—enough to keep Troy in business while Troy was locked up. When I found that out I told him to go fuck himself."

"So you weren't at his apartment between the night Teffy disappeared and the night you were abducted?"

"No," Ger says. "Why?"

Parsons checks her phone. "They're going to be issuing a statement soon at a press conference, so this doesn't get posted to social media before that. Understood?"

"Understood," Teffy says.

"Ben Critch was found murdered." Parsons nods at Ger. "And they've put the time of death within six to eight hours of when *you* were abducted. Looks like he made the bomb that blew up your place and was murdered shortly after."

"How did he die?" Ger asks.

"Cause of death was strangulation. But there was also water in his lungs and duct tape residue on his clothes." Parsons peers at Ger. "Does any of that sound familiar?"

"If by familiar," he says, "you mean something I can imagine Troy Hopper doing or ordered done, then yes, it's familiar." He looks at Parsons, and Teffy can see sudden tears in his eyes. "That's why I got out." His voice cracks. "Ben should've done the same."

An awkward silence stiffs the room. Parsons's phone rings and she answers it. Says, "Just a second," cupping the phone's mic. Then to Teffy and Ger: "It's time to go. I'll see you out after this call."

"I just need five more minutes with them," Ellie says.

"Three minutes," Parsons says, and she steps into the hall and the door swishes shut behind her. The three of them wait a second, then Ellie says:

"How do you know Markus stole from my gallery? You were saying that before the constable came in. But how do you know it was him?"

"He walked past where I was hiding," Teffy says. "And I saw a strip of spray paint across his one boot. Red paint. Like the vandal used to tag your wall."

"But why would Markus destroy my whole show?" Ellie says. "My whale? And how do you know those were his boots?"

"Because of the meeting you set up," Teffy says. "For me to talk to him. About Hopper. See if he could help. You were out with Daryl when Markus picked me up in his Buick."

"Yes, but the boots?" Ellie says.

"When Markus grabbed his rifle and started for Troy and Doug Crawley, I climbed in his trunk. And when I did, I saw the same set of boots—slashed with red spray paint—that I saw in the gallery that night. Right there. In Markus's trunk."

"And I'm supposed to believe that after you just admitted to stealing from me?"

"Me seeing the boots doesn't necessarily prove anything," Teffy says. "Only that it might give you reason to want to look into it more. Because if it's true, what does that say about Markus? And will we find anything—?"

"Like what?"

"Anything else," Ger says.

"So, what are you asking?" Ellie says.

"Will you let us look into it more?"

"You need my permission?"

"We need your key to Markus's house," Teffy says.

Ellie's eyes flick from Ger to Teffy and back again. "Markus risked his life to save yours." She nods at Teffy. "He was going to try to help you get out of *your* mess. He told me so. And now you wants me to okay you two digging through his house?"

"We'll be respectful," Ger says.

"There's no respect in what you're asking!" Ellie snaps. "Now I've said you can use the apartment till I gets out the end of the week. Call that my good deed and search *that* place, if you want. But after that, I think we're done."

"But the journal," Teffy says. "And the piece I'm writing on you and Marjorie—your art show and all those women."

"I said, we're done."

~ 36 ~

THE SUN HAS COME OUT by the time they leave the Health Sciences Center, thorny rays spiking over St. John's. Muggy as that rooftop sober-up a week ago. It's so bright on Livingstone that Ellie's house seems cave-like when they walk through the front door.

Ger knocks the brightly painted door and says, "What hateful shade of orange is this?" before closing it behind them.

"Sunkist," Teffy says to him, "and I like it."

"Like a 'cheer-up' bitch-slap, isn't it?"

"Did she give you the password to the wi-fi?"

"Yeah. I'll get set up in here," he says, and ducks into the front room. The hallway runs straight to the back of the house. There's a bedroom on the right. And a bathroom at the back, Ellie had said. Plus a small kitchenette across the hall from the toilet.

She pokes around in the bedroom then heads back to the front room. Leans against the wall to take the weight off her braced leg and considers whether to plop down on the ratty couch against the bedroom wall or in the La-Z-Boy next to the street-facing window. Ger is setting up his laptop—recovered from the Merrymeeting place—at a small writing desk against the far wall. But it's the painted walls that drive thoughts of rest from Teffy's mind.

Starting at the recliner, a mural wraps around onto the far wall: an immersive, almost life-sized version of a submarine dreamscape from Ellie's first show: *The Secret Lives of Whales*. But here the whale's tail—that whale shot on that faraway island so long ago—begins where the window ends. As if birthed out of light itself today. And the way the great fish bends onto the next wall brings it to life so that it swims in the room's shadows—surging halfway across the next wall where the paint streaks out and the whale smokes into a skeletal charcoal sketch that almost reaches the white-washed bedroom wall.

Teffy stares at Ger working away under the arch of the whale's belly. "You not afraid?" She laughs as Ger boots up his laptop.

"Of what?" he says.

"Of the leviathan about to swallow you."

He looks up and rubs a charcoaled line, smudges the black on his fingertips. "I've already been swallowed up," he says. "And spit back out." And she wonders at his seriousness and if he means his childhood on the Brow or his time with Troy. *Or is he talking about Teresa?*

"What did Parsons want on the way out?" she says.

"Said she'd be by with some follow-up questions about Ben Critch. Anything from my time working with him that might give them some leads."

"So Critch's murder is now the priority over the heroin bust?"

"Let them fight for what should be headlined," he says. "We have a house to case. And"—he flourishes a last click—"the internet's working!"

"Are we actually gonna break into Markus O'Shea's mansion?"

"If there's something there to find," he mutters, pulling up his browser, "then that's the only way we're gonna find it. Especially if Ellie's not giving up the key."

"Still can't believe O'Shea survived that wreck," she says.

"Heroin air bags. Expensive but effective."

"And the body of the guy he shot in the face."

"How *that's* gonna go down for him, I don't know," he says distractedly. Ger's phone dings with a text and he pushes back from the desk and laptop and moves quickly past her into the hall.

"What?" she says. "What's wrong?" and he asks if she wants some Mary Brown's. A few days ago deep-fried chicken would have made her gag, but now it's making her salivate. "Can you order taters?" she says, following him toward the kitchenette.

"I did," and he winks over his shoulder.

"You already ordered?"

They turn into the kitchen and she jumps when she sees Dougie sitting on their countertop. "Ger didn't tell ya I was here, did he?" Dougie scratches the crotch of his cut-offs, a greasy bag of Mary Brown's chicken on the counter beside him. He tuts Ger, "Shouldn't do that, yo—scare her like that."

Teffy thumps Ger in the chest. "He's right," she says.

"It's bad for the baby," Dougie says.

"So you told him?" she says to Ger.

"Yeah," Dougie says, "you fuckin tell family this shit. Congratulations by the way," and he offers up a big greasy bag of Mary Brown's chicken.

She takes the bag from him and settles into a chair by the table, careful as she bends her bad knee. "Does this mean you're not still pissed at us?" she says.

"You drove fuckin Troy Hopper into a light post. I can stop being pissed at you for that. Like I said, family."

"And how's your dad?" she says.

"Still bouncing his arse on the ol' stick shift."

"And who's the boss at Skimpy's now that Hopper's gone missing?"

Ger says, "Remember I was gonna hit Dougie up about that new Mt. Pearl dealer?"

"Turns out it's my dad," Dougie says.

"Your dad's dealing again?"

"Check the coleslaw," he says.

She peers in the bag. "Coleslaw crystal?"

"Right!?" he says. "And here I was thinking the old man was cracked. But crystal in the coleslaw, even I couldn't have thought of that."

"I believe that," she says.

Dougie shrugs in his oversized basketball jersey. *I'm with Mr Big*, it reads, the *g* dropped into a dick-shaped arrow pointing at his crotch.

She glances at Ger, on his phone now. "And what are *you* doing?"

Ger taps the screen a last time and pockets it. "Just texted Parsons that we're here now."

"Skid Parsons?" Dougie laughs and pervy-eyes Teffy. "Not for one of them pornos, I hope. Skid's a fuckin kink, ya know."

"*Constable* Parsons," she says.

And Dougie says, "Christ!" and is halfway out the kitchen door—Mary Brown's bag in hand—when Ger stops him.

"You gotta tell her what you told me," he says.

"I don't gotta do shit," Dougie says. "Is this 'cause of the coleslaw?"

Ger nods at Teffy. "I mean *her*—tell her."

"What—with a cop on the way?"

"Talk fast," she says, peeling the skin off a wing. "You can do that."

Dougie, toe-to-toe with Ger, says, "Having your ear hacked off has rattled some of your sense, yo."

"Come on, man. You said you'd help."

"And you said my dad wouldn't get popped."

"You mean shot?" she says.

"Fuck you!" he says. "He almost got strangled the other night. And they just got it out on the radio that fuckin Ben Critch got strangled too. Did you hear that shit?"

Ger says, "Look, just tell her what you heard?"

"About Ben Critch?" she says.

Dougie twists the greasy bag in his fist, like he might punch Ger with it. He doesn't move from the door, but starts in, talking fast and low. "Okay, so a couple of days ago Dad gets the call from this guy who says he knows Ben Critch—"

"Someone working for your dad?" she says.

"Are you wearing a wire?"

"Why would I wear a wire?" she says, reaching for the chicken.

"You got a cop coming to the house, don't you?"

Ger says, "Just tell her about the ride in the trunk, man."

"You were in a trunk?" she says.

"Yeah," he says and pushes Ger back. "Just before *this* fucker got his ass abducted, Dad gets this call from a guy who says he knows Ben Critch."

"Who was the guy?" she says.

"How long till that cop gets here?"

"Tell her about the trunk," Ger says.

"Yeah," she says, "I'm all ears."

"So I'm at Leggy's," Dougie says, "and this girl goes down on this stripper, like right on the edge of the fuckin stage—"

"The trunk, Dougie!"

"That's how I got in the trunk, yo. This girl comes up for air and I gets the wink-and-nod from the stripper and goes to nose in there like a fuckin badger—"

"He's gonna make me sick, Ger."

"Dougie. . . ."

"That's when this bouncer hauls me off her—the fuckin prick—and I—"

"You screamed and ran out of there?" she says.

He shrugs her off and spiffs his shirt. "More or less."

"But you gave him the slip," Ger says.

"And thankfully Dad was by the corner in his cab. Just dropped a guy off and I jumps in and Dad gasses it, but says to me, 'Climb in the trunk 'cause I gotta pick a fella up.' And I says, 'Who?' And he says, 'Ya smell like wet cunt, b'y.' And I says, 'Who the fuck says that to their own son,' right? But he gives me the glare and I climbs through the back seat into the trunk, and he yells for me to keep my fuckin mouth shut or we'll both have our heads bobbin in the bay. And I thinks, sure, like this is fuckin Colombia or something. But I stays quiet and this lad gets in and there's not much for a long while. Just turns and speeding up and slowing down and shit. About to nod off on the carjack when buddy starts into it like. Dad says he can take the fuckin mask off and cut out the Batman talk. But this guy just goes on growling. Says he knows who dropped this girl's body in a fuckin alley, and when Dad says, 'Yeah, and how do you know that?' the fucker says, 'Ben Critch said so.' And then the fuckin car starts rocking—like rocking hard, yo—and Dad barmps the horn, gurgling and shit—"

"Gurgling?"

"Buddy was fuckin strangling him till I kicks in the back seat and the fucker bolts into the woods, up by the fuckin golf course."

Teffy looks from Dougie to Ger. "Do you think he was talking about Teresa—the girl dumped in the alley?"

"Dad had nothing to do with that," Dougie says. "Says the fucker got it wrong and if I hadn't been in the fuckin trunk he'd have wound up dead in his own cab."

"The point," Ger says, "is that whoever got Ben Critch went after Vinnie Coles too."

"And this happened when?" Teffy says.

"The night I was abducted," Ger says.

"And you think this is connected to Teresa?"

Ger blinks. "What if it's O'Shea?"

"Markus? You think he took out Critch and tried to off Vinnie?"

"What if they knew something—something he was tied up in that linked him to Troy—and he wanted to clean the slate? Keep himself in the clear."

"If you'd brought that up with Ellie," Teffy says, "she'd have thrown us out."

"I knows when to keep my mouth shut," Ger says. "Trust me."

"So, what're you gonna do?" Dougie says—and Teffy is about to say they should break into Markus O'Shea's house, but there's a hard knock at the door.

Dougie tears open the coleslaw, scoops out a Mayo-wet baggie, and stuffs it in his mouth, then runs into the bathroom. And Teffy, on her way to the door, sees him scrambling out the big window by the toilet.

"Did he come in that way?" she says—and Ger shrugs, reaching for the doorknob. She puts a hand on his. Whispers, "Lock it, okay—the window?"

And he mouths that he will, then opens the door to Constable Parsons who waves at them as she steps back and calls down the street: "I see you, Dougie Coles!"

Teffy leans out and sees Dougie on the corner of Long and Livingstone. He nods sharply at Parsons—cheeks puffed like a chipmunk—and crosses the street.

She yells, "No one's gonna buy shit you've had in your mouth, b'y!" And he gives her the finger and scurries off, hiking his pants as he goes.

Teffy steps aside so Parsons can walk in.

"So you know about the coleslaw crystal?" Ger says.

Parsons raises an eyebrow. "Well, I'll have to pick him up next time I sees him. Scare some sense into him."

"What else do you have on him?" Ger asks.

And Parsons smiles at him. "How about you and I take a trip up to the station and talk a bit more about Ben Critch?"

~ 37 ~

WHILE GER IS GONE WITH Constable Parsons, Teffy gets to work on trying to decode the journal. She pulls up the scanned copy on Ger's laptop and scrolls through it again, trying to think back to sitting by the woodstove in Mike's place on St. Mark's, back from the Kid Brothers and just before O'Shea showed up in his Buick. Before the fish plant crackdown with Troy.

She remembers humming the Jackson 5 and thinking, *Letters and numbers, letters and numbers . . . and a clock.*

But if it's a clock, she thinks now, *which upright stickman did I say was midnight? The one with hands or without?*

It wouldn't have occurred to her before, but she keeps thinking of Ellie's shot-up shoulder and Ger's ear sawn off. Of her own father's finger, the tip lopped off by a table saw. And Fin's mother's mastectomy, her breasts removed shortly before they found more cancer in her ovaries. *We were in high school,* she thinks, and Fin had been planning to come out to his mother, in hopes she'd soften his father's drunken choke holds. But Fin had put off telling her in the days leading up to her surgery. Then again after the surgery because, as he said, she needed time to recoup. Time to handle one grief before being handed another.

Teffy had tried to convince him that his mother wouldn't—or at least shouldn't—feel any grief in finding out who her son really was. "Who you are is a gift," Teffy had said. "Not a burden. You are not a burden, Fin. Not to me. Not to anyone."

She told him that coming out would make things lighter.

"Rainbow flag bright!" she'd promised.

But Fin had held off. He held off a long time. Too long, she told him. But he kept on waiting. Waiting for just the right time. And then his mother died and Fin started cutting himself. Teffy tried to stop him at first, told him his mom wouldn't want him to carve himself up, leave razor slits to scab under the long sleeves of his Slipknot shirts.

"But what does it matter?" he said when Teffy confronted him, his arms a scabby, infected mess because he'd been using his dad's fillet knife. "What does it matter?" he said. "We're born in one piece. Then all the parts we like get cut away. Like Mom. Like how she'd flake cooked fish from white bones."

The slender bones of Fin's thin arms around her neck, dancing alone on Argentia's abandoned airstrip, back when they were happy. Back before Fin's bleeding wrists, cuts so deep it was like he was trying to nick bone. Or to get up courage to end it.

Test the cliff edge between here and gone.

Yet somehow still alive, she thinks.

And she dreams him now, like she hasn't dreamed him in years—like the beautiful, flamboyantly kitschy Christ above their altar back home. God in exquisite agony. No roughed-up savior, just a beautiful boy. Dying. "Like me," Fin murmured, flaming his cheeks red with his mom's make-up, those long mascara-slick lashes dark as sunspots from staring too long at the writhing sea urchin sun outside, that lone star burning over St. John's like some coming judgement, scorching this shabby town. This town she moved to just to be near him.

But she never visited. Never even called—and why?

Because she couldn't face him. Couldn't face the recurring dream of him on that cross, the beam of his father's stage, the crucifix in their hometown church where they hid on that horrible night. Hearing sirens wailing in the bay, knowing their end had come, that their childhood had choked on its own blood and died gasping at their feet. A knife in its chest. There. Hidden beneath that high altar. Even now she feels she's there. Right there. In that dream. Fin looking down at her helplessly, pulling so hard against nails driven into his infected, razor-slit wrists that he rips himself free of his own greening hands. Blood splashes her face and she blinks and Fin keeps trying to grab her over some boat's edge—the knobby, protruding bones of his lovely arms thrashing her in water, salt water tears, trying to grab her, to save her but with no way of holding on to her, with no way of holding on.

She pushes back from the desk, looking up to see herself submerged under the belly of Ellie's great whalefish. *Gone*, she thinks. *Long gone.*

The journal's stickmen dance on the flickering screen of Ger's laptop. And she thinks, Ger. His tattoo. *The off balance, hand-standing stickman. But without hands. A gift from Teresa. Her name? No. Just her initial. Her first initial—the letter T.*

And as if in a different color, she sees the figures on the page standing straight up. As if rising from some sketched grave. Straight up and in one piece.

The upright stickmen with hands: the first set of twelve.

Her letter *A*. Midnight on the first clock.

~ 38 ~

SHE'S DRAWN OUT TWO CLOCKS in a notebook by Ger's laptop, her alpha at midnight on the first one: the letter A. Then 1 a.m. through to 11 a.m., the letters B, C, D, E, F, G, H, I, J, K, and L. All with hands, each successive figure at a slightly greater tilt than the one before. And on the second clock a repeat of the first but with hands severed. *Something lost*, she thinks. The letter M for noon, then starting at 1 p.m. the letter N, and on and on to W. She's clustered X, Y, and Z by 11 p.m., but thinks the code likely drops X and Z.

And from that she's garbled out half a page of the journal, enough to know it is Teresa's and that Teresa had managed to get a long-term trick through Troy Hopper: a guy in Portugal Cove who paid really, really well apparently. Teffy is working on the line, *I have a driver and a ha—* when she hears something in the back of the house. Someone coming through a window. The bathroom window.

She fists her pen, sharp tip down, splinted finger sticking straight out.

Eases back from the desk and crosses the room as quietly as she can. Peeks in the hallway to see . . . no one. *Ger would come in the front door*, she thinks, *so it must be Dougie back for something*. She's past the bedroom now, dragging her braced leg, and close to the bathroom when she hears the toilet flush.

"Dougie?" she calls.

"Has that shithead been back already?" Ger says—and Teffy looks into the room to see Ger buttoning up his jeans, the window by the toilet open enough for him to have crawled in.

"Are doors a fuckin thing of the past?" she says, showing him the pen in her hand. "I was about to come flying in here and stab you in the neck."

He chuckles and says, "I'd laugh at anyone else, you know."

And she says, "You're laughing now," relief hitting her like a sunny day high after a quick dodge downtown on her scooter. "Do you hate the orange door that much that you're coming and going now by the toilet seat window?"

He laughs and says, "No, I just wanted to see the route Dougie took to get in here. You slip three fences easily and come in off Long's Hill."

"Well," she says, stepping into the room, "I have cracked the code to that journal."

"Oh have you?" he says—and she can't quite read his look. She'd expected more excitement, more . . . something. But he smiles and asks how far she's got with it.

"Only half a page," she says, struggling a bit to jump up onto the washer to rest her leg. Ger helps and asks her what it says.

"What it says?"

"So far, I mean."

"I've got that it's Teresa's journal, for sure. And that she's got a long-term trick in Portugal Cove. I think she's going to name her driver and someone else, but I haven't got that parsed yet."

"That's huge," he says.

"Isn't it though? I mean, seriously—if we get a driver and whoever else's name, they'll have to re-open the case, or at least look back into it. None of this came up in the trial."

"Only that she'd had sex recently." He says this quietly. She reaches her hand for him and he takes it and steps closer. She places his hand on her hip and asks how the conversation with Parsons went. "Oh," he says, chuckling, "just dragging out the same old shit."

"From the trial?"

"Exactly. Basically trying to establish Ben's habits and routines, what he was into, which meant rehashing all I was into."

"But you've served time for your part."

"And I reminded them of that, and that I had nothing to hide, but also nothing much to offer beyond what they already have on record."

"Did they ask for an alibi for the night Critch was killed?"

"They did"—she moves his hand up under her shirt, and he smiles and slips his hand up further—"and I told them I was in the process of being gagged and loaded into a van."

She cups the back of his head and pulls his face closer to hers. Touches the bandage where his ear used to be. "We're so close," she says. "So close to finding out what happened."

"We know what happened," he says and his eyes drop, then he pops the clasp of her bra and looks up with a grin on his face. "We just need to find out who did it. And then. . . ."

"Then we lay this to rest and. . . ."

He kisses her neck. "And then?"

She laughs and pushes him back, gently. Gives him the serious eyes. "I should keep working on that journal."

"And what should I do?" he says, popping a button on her jeans.

"You?" she says. "You should finish casing O'Shea's place online. We're doing that tonight aren't we?"

He presses his mouth to the zipper of her jeans and breathes, and she fists a handful of his hair. Says, "Don't make promises you can't keep, Stuckless."

"I intend to keep this one," he says, breathing each word.

"Oh for God's sakes," she says and pushes him back a bit to shuffle off her jeans. He helps get her good leg free and starts kissing up from her knee, and she finds the back of his head with her bandaged hand and presses hard.

"I gotta breathe," he laughs into her.

"You just gotta . . . yeah. . . ."

"That?" He flicks his tongue.

"Yes, that," and she stares at the silhouette of a tree through the fogged glass of the bathroom window, about to close her eyes and disappear inside this small moment, when she sees someone trying to peer through the fogged glass.

She slaps Ger's head and Ger says, "The fuck?" as she pushes him back and goes to jump off the washer but catches Ger in the face with her brace. "Christ," he says, "you cut my lip!" And she's struggling to get her bad leg over his head so she can hobble-jump to the window, dragging her jeans still hooked in her brace. "What're you doing?" he says, and she grabs a towel from the shower rack—that figure still hovering at their window, knocking now.

She staggers to the toilet as the peeper cracks the window an inch and Dougie says from outside, "Is that cop still here?"

Ger yells, "Shut the fuckin window!"

And Dougie looks past Teffy to Ger nursing his cut lip. Then he spies the towel around Teffy's waist, her jeans on by only one ankle, and says, "You were banging, weren't ya?" letting out a whistle. Teffy slams the window on his snapping fingers and he screams. She lifts the window and he yanks his hand free and she slams it again, hearing him yell on the other side of the glass: "You fucking owe me for the chicken, yo! Fuck, man! My fuckin hand!"

Then something occurs to her and she slides up the windowpane.

"You've broken into my house twice," she says.

"You fucked-up my hand!"

"Close the window!" Ger yells.

"This is fucking assault!" Dougie moans.

And Teffy says, "*You* were breaking-in through *my* bathroom window."

"I need money for that chicken!"

"Do you think you can break in anywhere?" she says.

"I was just coming to get what Ger fuckin owes me."

"I asked if you can break into *any* place," she says.

"No," Ger says, reading her. "Teffy, that's not a good idea." And she mouths, *It's better than both of us getting caught.*

"I just want my money," Dougie says, sucking a knuckle.

"You'll get your money," she says. "And more."

"More?" Ger says.

"More," she says.

And Dougie says, "What do I gotta do to get this 'more'?"

"Help us break into Markus O'Shea's mansion."

"Markus O'Shea?" Dougie says. "And how am I gonna do that?"

"You tell us," she says.

"No way," he says. "There's fuckin alarms and shit for sure. I just fuckin jimmy your windows, la. You're talking Ocean's fuckin Eleven. No way!"

"Come on Dougie," she says. "We need your help."

"No we don't," Ger says.

"Shut up," she says.

Dougie stops shaking his hand and stares at them. "No way, man. I just deliver fried fuckin chicken."

"And meth," she says.

"I don't break into people houses!"

Both Teffy and Ger stare at him through the open window.

"Fuck you," he says.

~ 39 ~

GER LOOKS AT TEFFY in disbelief. "How was I supposed to know the coleslaw comment was gonna get Dougie busted?" She unbuckles instead of answering him. "You shouldn't be the one going in," he says. "I can go."

"Dougie was gonna be the one going in, remember?"

"I can do it," he says.

"Right," she says, "and who's gonna do the recording? The one who has no clue how you record from a phone, or the computer hack in this relationship?"

"It's not that hard," he says.

"And neither is a little break-in around the bay, Ger. And if the door's unlocked it's hardly a break-in, is it?"

"The point is you're pregnant."

"No, Ger, the point is that you're not calling the shots on this. I am. And I'm going in and you're staying here and running that"—she waves a finger at his laptop—"thing."

She looks across the darkened tickle to the few faint lights on Belle Island. "Are you sure whatever it is you're gonna do will work this far away from the house?"

"O'Shea's is just up the hill behind us," he says. "And I could record in town if I wanted. Your phone's gonna call the computer and the computer records what your phone hears."

She sharpens her glare with a raised eyebrow.

"I'm not trying to make you feel stupid," he says. "Geez."

"You're mansplaining."

"Seriously?" he says. "Just go already."

"You know I have no idea what I'm actually looking for."

"Hard-drives, thumb-drives. . . ."

"The file labelled 'Shit I've done with Troy Hopper'?"

"Just scoop up what you can find. And, as you say, we'll be back if we need to. Just remember to plant the phone someplace he won't find it." She tries to step out of the car but Ger grabs her arm. "Put it someplace we can hear him talking."

She twists loose of his grip and gets out of the car. "He won't be talking to himself."

"As I said, if we *don't* find anything, we drop in on him. Tomorrow morning. The battery should last that long. We'll see what he knows, and if it squares with what we discover in that journal. Trust me, there are ways to ask the right questions."

"And how do you ask the right questions, Ger? Tell me that. What did you do to get people to talk when you were collecting for Troy?"

"Easy," he says, a smirk on his face. "It's not my fault Dougie broke off a good time."

"It's that you got Dougie in trouble," she snaps.

"So that explains the mood, does it?"

"There is no mood, Ger."

"Just trust me," he says and goes to touch her hair but she pulls away. "Dougie has been in worse trouble. Parsons is only gonna try to scare him straight. He'll be goofing off again in twenty-four hours."

"I just feel responsible for the little prick."

"Responsible? For Dougie?"

She can't explain it, but there's something of Fin in Dougie. It's there in the eyes, if in no other way. Hyper observant. Jumpy. A kid who's been slapped around. *And more*, she thinks, remembering the bruises on Fin's neck. And it's not so much that she feels responsible for Dougie as she feels she owes him. That somehow looking out for Dougie will make things . . . right. But Ger wouldn't understand that if she told him. *It's just Dougie*, he'd say, *come on.*

"Look," Ger says, "Dougie will be crawling back through the bathroom window by tomorrow, I promise. End of the week at the latest."

"Fine," she says and clamps the door of Ellie's car shut, heading up the hill behind the sea-facing bank of big houses, her eye on the slick red one.

She's given Ger a hard time since Dougie got picked up by the RNC, but she has to admit he's done a decent job casing O'Shea's place. Only took him a few hours, sure, and in that time she was able to get a bit further in the journal, finding out that Teresa's driver was Vinnie Coles—something she didn't tell Dougie—and that Teresa's handler was Ben Critch. Then there were half a dozen dates of times Teresa was blindfolded and driven out to a large house. *The john is rich*, Teresa had written using her stickman alphabet. That was the last line Teffy was able to make out before getting a call from Dougie, who'd gone out for snacks, saying the RNC had picked him up for questioning. "So we can't be at it tonight," Dougie said and hung up. That's when Ger had pulled together everything he'd found online and said they had to try to hit O'Shea's tonight, even if Dougie was out the game.

"Don't worry," Ger had said, "I have a plan. Several." And he did. Thanks to him, she knows there are two doors on this side of the house. An upper one that opens onto a deck, and a lower one that leads into the basement.

Ger even found the floor plans online, showcased on the O'Shea Shoreline Inc. website. "Right there on Google," he said. And he mapped a couple of routes for her from that basement door up to O'Shea's office on the second floor.

"If that door is locked," he told her, "you'll have to climb to the balcony. But in your condition—"

"Fuck off about my condition," she told him.

"The knee," he said.

"I can manage the knee."

"You had a hard time getting off the fuckin washer."

"Because your head was in the way."

"I'm just sayin—"

"Don't."

Edging up beside the door now, she looks through the window at the basement window—sees comfortable brown leather furniture lounged around a driftwood coffee table. Locally made like as not. And books on shelves, paperbacks all. But no TV, and she thinks that's weird because she'd always pegged O'Shea as a TV guy—*golf or some shit.*

She touches the door latch and wonders—Dougie's voice ringing in her head—about alarm systems. But Ger combed everything he could on the construction of the houses in this row—all O'Shea developments.

This one in particular.

He knows for sure that two of the places up the hill installed security systems, but he didn't find any evidence that O'Shea had.

Be the trusting bayman, she thinks, and presses down on the latch and the door swings in and she hears . . . nothing. Pray God it's not a silent alarm.

Could Ger detect that—the going off of a silent alarm?

She closes the door behind her.

There are stairs at the back of the room and she heads for them, nipping past these framed ink sketches on the wall, all of them three feet wide and only six inches high. Full circle panoramas of St. Mark's, she realizes, spying Daryl's shed and Mike's house in that one, the buildings small next to near-endless sea, blue-washed and flat save for the heightened pulse of the Kid Brothers on the horizon.

Ellie's, she thinks, knowing she should move on and find the office upstairs. But she wants to spend the night in this room, looking at this art, reading these books—all Newfoundland authors by the looks of it—Crummey, Moore, and Johnston. Harvey too. And newer ones—those *Eating Habits* stories she liked, and a thick one on Marlowe, and the one that just won the Governor General's—spines candle-bright in the dark.

You're here for info, she tells herself, *not art. Move on, move on.* And she does. Up the stairs and into the kitchen, the whole wall behind her glass and Belle Island's lights peering at her from across the dark water.

Open a bottle of wine from the rack there, she thinks, *and get drunk awhile on that view. O'Shea is in hospital until tomorrow, so you have time.* Ger called in earlier, faking relation, and found out Markus was to be discharged in the morning. *Still,* she thinks, *you could pop a bottle. Some fine stuff stocked here no doubt. But that'd mean pickling the baby and nixing the whole thing. Come on.*

You're here for a reason, remember?

So get on with it.

But as she moves past the big window, those island lights watching her, she can't shake the feeling she's not alone in the house. Maybe it's the wall-sized window or the open concept, this whole floor one room or near enough: treed throughout with these pine-trunk pillars, bark-stripped but un-planed—all kinked and knotted, scarred and interesting.

This one, she thinks, passing a hand over it, like the scar forming on her belly from Troy's knife. If the hotel O'Shea planned to build on St. Mark's is anything like this house, in design and feel, then she's starting to think she wants it built—even if she could only afford to walk through the lobby. *Maybe you could get a* Miscreant *pass, spend a night and do a feature story. Snuggle in the rooftop Jacuzzi with George Clooney himself.*

She touches the couch, sealskin soft, and thinks Ger would like to see her spiffed on that in naught but her starry socks. The pervy things he'd want to be at in this room. Five minutes would give her a selfie to tease him with. Maybe make up for kicking him in the teeth—for that whole Dougie fiasco on the washing machine.

Get to the office first, though, and nose around a bit before lushing-out, plush as this rug. Something tan-like, isn't it—the rug? And she bends to touch it. Elk hide. Shot with his own rifle, she bets. The .308 he used on Doug Crawley. She shivers and crouches to touch the rug, soft as a shorthaired dog, and thinks, *Here under the couch.*

So she pulls out her phone, dials the number Ger keyed-in and sees it ringing silently as she slides it underneath. Then something creaks behind her and she shoots upright.

Sees a silhouette against the sea-facing window and turns to run but big hands claw her back and she thrashes out of their grip, knocking the couch cockeyed. Hears a guy groan and turns to kick at his junk with her good leg, but he sidesteps and lunges at her—catches her by the shoulder—and she claws at his eyes, her bad knee spasming.

She gets her nails on his skin, though, and scratches him deep.

"Ellie!" he hisses, clamping a hand over her mouth, but she bites the hand and stomps his foot. He lets go of her and she sucker-punches his belt buckle, and he drags her to the floor as he falls back over a chair. She manages to get on top of him—knee flaming under her—and twists his wrist when he grabs at her face, punching the heel of her palm against his locked elbow. There's a crack and he roars as she kicks off to stagger upright. Bounces on her good leg. Sees him find his feet too, a knapsack dropping off his buggered arm.

"Ellie!" he hisses. "Jesus woman!"

And she knows that voice, peers at his face in the kitchen's half dark and sees the Co-op ball cap, the cleft chin. "Daryl?" she says.

"You gave me the basement key—who else would it be? And why aren't you in the fuckin hospital, woman!"

"I'm not Ellie," she says.

And Daryl is the one to peer at her now. "Who are you then?"

"No," she says. "*You* tell me why your ex is helping you break into her own house."

"Not breaking in if you're invited," he says.

"Then what's with the camo gear?" She picks up his bag and throws it at him, and he tries to catch it but misses.

He winces with the pain and says, "You're that redhead from the island."

"Did you come to see Ellie again" she says. "Like on the island? Is that why you're here in the dark?" He holds his broken arm with his good hand, but doesn't say anything. "Did Ellie tell you to come here?" He growls trying to hold his arm at the right angle—and she says, "And how are they not after arresting you already? How much dope passed through your plant?"

"Arrest me for what?" he says. "Doug Crawley running drugs through my place of work and me not there?" He takes a couple of short breaths, sizing her up. "Why are *you* here?"

"Yes"—the lights go up and they both wince—"why are you here?"

She hears a round chambered—and Daryl says, "Nice rifle, Markus," sweat beading on his wind-burnt face, damaged arm limp by his side.

Markus says, "Like the one you used when you shot that whale."

"But not like that pump-action you used, hey?"

"That's not so clear in my mind as the likes of this gun in your hands, Daryl, and that whale crying for its mother. Made you the first Newfoundlander to make the *L.A. Times.*"

"Somebody had to be the scapegoat, Markus."

"Mike tells me you're raising goats now."

"Diversifying," Daryl says. "Between boats."

"I could use a local goat cheese supplier for the hotel," Markus says. "But I imagine you're here 'cause of the news, aren't ya, and not to sell me goat's milk?"

"What news?" Teffy says.

Markus smiles. "The fish plant's officially closed and the bank's putting the property up for bid."

"To islanders," Daryl says. "Resident islanders."

Markus says, "Good that I still keeps mother's place there, hey?"

"We'll see how that holds up with council," Daryl says.

"It'll hold up now that you're off the board."

"It was you talked me off council in exchange for you calling Crawley. Didn't tell Ellie, did ya: that your big gesture had a price tag on it?"

Teffy glances at the cockeyed couch. Sees the corner of the cell phone there. "What is it you think might not hold up?" She raises her voice a bit, hoping Ger is getting this somehow.

"He wants to see"—Daryl takes a sharp breath—"if his claim to being an islander holds up." He breathes fast against the pain—swallows hard.

Markus says, "Once a St. Mark's boy, always a St. Mark's boy."

"It's you and Mikey wants to say that," Daryl says, the collar of his camo shirt dark with sweat now. "But it's me who took on every Greenpeacer. Me and Ellie who owned up to shooting the whale 'cause you were afraid to lose that scholarship. And it was me who shoveled your mother out of nine-foot drifts when she had that fall. And Ellie cut her wood the last year, when she hadn't the strength to swing her own axe." A drip of sweat hangs off his nose. "And all that while you were where, Markus? Making those deep-pocket Dalhousie friends—all that old Halifax money."

"New money," Markus says, "new investments, new developments."

"But a couple bad ones, hey? In the eighties. And that's when ya come asking will I help ya bring ashore them fifty bales. A one-time thing, ya said—remember that? 'Cause ya weren't into that racket. But here we are. . . ."

"Fifty bales of what?" Teffy glances at the phone again and back to Daryl, who sways a little—eyes locked on Markus.

"The eighties were hard times," Markus says.

And she's gonna press him but Daryl cuts in: "And what about those summer parties and you sending me home all liquored-up?"

"You never complained about that, as I recall."

"But I didn't know ya were feeling up my wife."

Markus smiles, cheek to the rifle's chamber, the stock against the shoulder of his wounded arm. *If he fires,* Teffy thinks, *he'll feel it for weeks.* "Ellie makes her own decisions," Markus says. "You knows that better than me."

"Did she decide to stay out in the car, then, or did you tell her to stay put?"

"She's still in hospital," Markus says. "Shot in the shoulder, remember? Protecting you. Tell me, did you always ride bitch with her?"

Teffy says, "How'd you know to grab the gun, Markus?"

"A silent alarm," he says. "The app's on my phone."

"So why not call the cops?"

"I was nearly in the bay when the alarm went off. And I keeps the rifle in the garage. And, just to be clear, the police *are* on their way."

He moves toward them with the gun and Teffy steps behind Daryl—who tries to straighten his shoulders to face his old friend. She puts her back to the soft couch and gently heels her phone out of sight.

"What are ya gonna do with that gun?" Daryl says, taking a step toward Markus.

Markus matches him—and now there is barely a foot between them.

"Open your blowhole and you'll find out," says Markus.

"Is that what you told Vinnie Coles?" she says.

Markus looks over Daryl's shoulder at her.

"When you tried to strangle him the other night," she says. A flick of recognition in O'Shea's eyes. But she needs that on tape: needs him to say it—*Say something, Tefs! Use the journal, see if he snaps.* "How do you know Vinnie Coles, Markus? Or Ben Critch? What's your business with them?"

Daryl half glances at her over the shoulder of his broken arm, confusion and pain deepening the crow's feet clawing his eyes.

Markus watches her, and she thinks for a second he's afraid of her—unsure of what she might say next—so she presses on: "Vinnie and Ben know things about you, Markus. Or Ben *did*, before he was murdered. I know the timeframe too. I know you could've got to Critch at his apartment and still made that ferry next day. Did you kill Ben Critch, Markus? Did you?"

He shifts and she can't see his mouth for the rifle's chamber, his finger resting on the trigger. But she can't tell by his eyes if he's smiling slyly or grimacing. "A nice theory," he says, "but I have no idea who the hell you're talking about."

"Are you sure?" Daryl says. "She asks good questions."

"She does," says Markus. "Off base, but good. Intent. And that's why I invited her here." He glances at her leg. "Didn't realize your condition, though, love."

"I have a busted knee," she says. "I'm not cancer-struck."

He sniffs a laugh. Says, "It was you wasn't it, Daryl, who said you gotta face the press, especially if you have nothing to hide."

"The press?" says Daryl.

"*The Miscreant*," says Markus. "Local shit-slinging news site run by the couple who survived the St. Mark's heroin bust. Her and her partner Ger Stuckless are the ones who first put away the now infamous Troy Hopper." He cocks a wink at her now—*Performing*, she thinks. "Didn't know you were famous, did you, Teffy Byrne?"

"You didn't invite me," she says.

"She broke in," Daryl says. "Same as me."

Teffy stares at Daryl's wrinkled neck. Like her dad's, she thinks. A wrinkle for each finger of her mother's hand. And she wonders if Ellie touched Daryl that way after the altar stopped rocking against her back in that island church, both of them trying to catch their breath and laughing. She hopes so. Because in saying he broke in, Daryl is choosing a B & E charge to keep her out of it. Yet she must have let him in. For some reason.

Why else would Daryl have called her Ellie in the dark?

Markus looks at her over Daryl's shoulder again and says, "Is that what you want me to tell the RNC—that you were breaking into my house?"

Daryl turns his head but doesn't look her way. Asks her what she was hoping to find, his good hand shaking as he reaches for his broken arm. "Before we bumped into each other?" he says. "Or do ya not want to say that in front of the man, here?"

"Is it true?" she says, steadying her voice, wondering how far her phone's mic can reach. "Is it true, Markus—that you knew a girl named Teresa?" He blinks. "You'd remember because she was a hooker. You'd have paid her pimp—Troy Hopper."

"Always thought you'd be the kind to have to pay," Daryl says.

"That's quite the accusation," Markus says to her. "And not the kind of thing house guests usually ask, even if they're reporters."

"Is it true?" she says.

He laughs. "First I'm murdering guys I've never heard of, or trying to," he says—gun on Daryl, eyes on her. "Next I'm paying Troy Hopper, a known drug dealer, for prostitutes."

"Her name was Teresa," Teffy says. "Teresa Squires."

"You knew about that Hopper fella working with Doug Crawley," Daryl cuts in. "That's why you got Doug to come back to the Co-op. And why you pulled your rifle on him."

"I saw a gagged and handcuffed man jump out of a van," Markus says. "A van that should *not* have been at the loading gate. A shot was fired and I—"

"You shot Doug Crawley in the face."

"It was an accident!" Markus snaps.

"An accident?"

"Guns were going off! And I was shot too, remember."

"I see that," Daryl says, nodding at Markus's taped-up arm.

"I had no idea Crawley was carrying a load of heroin. He's captain of a *crab* boat, for God's sake, and I happened to still be on speaking terms with him. So I gave him a call. As we discussed. For you. As a favor. Remember?"

"Because you wanted me off council."

"Because Ellie asked me to."

"Oh, it was Ellie, was it? And not you just setting yourself up as the hero? The one who stops the big heroin deal, gets *me* fired, and the plant shut down—and all so you can build your swank hotel!"

"Where's the profit in that, Daryl? Think about it. Just for a second. The hotel creates jobs for people on St. Mark's. Jobs lost when the plant closed because someone—and I won't say who—saw fit to run drugs through it."

"You sent Crawley to me!"

"And how was I to know Crawley was running drugs?"

Daryl says, "You made sure he'd never tell his side of the story."

"It was a fucking accident!" Markus yells. "One I gotta live with for the rest of my life! Do you know what that's like Daryl? Do you?"

"Do you remember that big fuckin whale, Markus?"

"That's gonna be your blubbery badge of honor from here to Judgment, isn't it? You and that fucking whale. Daryl Strickland, defender of St. Mark's."

"Me and Ellie," Daryl says. "While you and Mike fucked off to the mainland."

"At least I made something of myself."

"If you rang Doug Crawley in so you could shut down the Co-op that Ellie and me started—if that's your game, Markus, then all's I can say is—"

"Will you listen to yourself?" Markus snaps, eyes wide. "I just happen to have an idea in the wake of all this, Daryl—a viable business plan. One that'll keep St. Mark's alive and people living there. An idea to fix another one of your fuck-ups."

"Like listening to you?"

"The fish plant is done, Daryl. It's dead. You tried and you failed. But my hotel will fill that gap. And it'll do one better. The hotel profits will pay the hotel workers—all St. Mark's people—and the extra will be paid out equally to *all* island residents."

"Including yourself," Daryl says, "seeing as how you're an island resident."

"You sound sore 'cause I knows your by-laws better than you."

"No," Daryl says, "'cause you gets what you wants, like always."

"I get what I want?" Markus says. "I got shot, remember? Do you think I wanted to get shot? Was that part of my plan?"

"A likely result of having piss-poor aim."

"Do you know what I want, Daryl—do you? Do either of you knows what that is? To save St. Mark's from becoming another resettled outport. To keep jobs on the island. To stop the brain drain to town and the mainland—where I had to go to *fight* my way back. To show the rest of this backwards-run province how to survive without either fish or fossil fuel. That's what I want, Daryl—that's what this hotel will do."

Daryl spits on the polished floor. "Don't make me stand in your shit, Markus. Not with a buggered arm and a gun in my face."

"Is your dream worth it," Teffy says, "if it costs people their lives?"

"I didn't kill Ben Critch," Markus says.

"No," she says. "But you remember his name."

Markus stares at her over Daryl's shaking shoulder. "Yeah, well, do you remember the name Jake Crawley?" He turns to Daryl. "They still haven't found Jake. Dorothy's beside herself, out every day with the search parties."

And Daryl says, "Why're you changing the subject, Markus?"

"Jake went missing off the ferry that first took missus here to St. Mark's."

"You ask Ellie about Jake Crawley," Teffy says, and she feels that windshield scraper pressed to her throat, her own sweat now like Jake's spit in her face.

"Jake's still out there," he says, "and with that dealer of yours still on the loose, too." She's wondered about that: where Jake is off to and if Troy got off the island. Did Jake help him? Was that the plan? She wonders what the RCMP will find in the next couple of days searching St. Mark's and the surrounding shores. Where will they find that blue Chevy van?

Sirens whir faintly in the distance.

"Remember," Markus says, "when the cops ask why you're here, you're my guest, and we were interrupted by Daryl. That is"—and he catches her eye—"unless you wants the same charge coming his way. In which case"—he nudges Daryl's chest with the rifle—"be my guest."

"You'll want to take that offer," Daryl says to her.

Markus says, "He's talking sense, girl."

"I'll be your guest," she says.

"Then take the old man's phone and drop it in the bag there by his feet. Quick now." Markus waves the barrel at her and she slips Daryl's phone out of his pocket, picks up the fallen bag, and drops the phone inside. "Password," Markus says.

"1, 2, 3. . .4," says Daryl.

Markus smiles. "You always were a simple man."

Daryl turns to her now, his back to Markus. Tells her to call Mike. "And tell him I told you to. He'll know."

"See, Mike is someone I can work with," Markus says. "But you'd rather starve our kids of work—keep them on the rum and welfare—taking government money and praying for fish that aren't there."

"Never assume Mike's in your pocket," Daryl says to Markus. And Teffy wonders, looking at the old man's face, why Ellie left him for Markus. And why did she let him in tonight? What's on that phone and in that bag in his hands? Why call Mike?

Markus says, "I'll give you above market price for your place on St. Mark's, Daryl. Top dollar. A peace offering. To help with your lawyer fees."

"If you wants my house," Daryl says, "you'll find me home and this situation reversed."

"We'll see if I finds you home," Markus says.

"And me?" she says.

"You're my guest," he says, "if you kick me that bag."

The sirens are in the drive now, the wide room pulsing red and blue. And she does as she's told. Answers the RNC's questions the way she imagines Markus wants them answered.

Not a missed beat.

"Yes, I broke his arm," she says, "self-defense training. It's just a buggered knee. No, I came in the way he told me to. On the phone when he agreed to an interview. Yes, after he got out of hospital. A guest, that's right. Buddy jumped me in the dark—it was self-defense, like I said. Yes, I was at St. Mark's. No, this is unrelated. I don't know, you'd have to ask Markus."

In and out, around and around. And not once does she glance at the couch. Not until Markus follows the cops out with Daryl in handcuffs, Daryl yelling at them whenever they bump his bad arm. That's when she stoops to retrieve her phone from under the couch.

I hope you got that, Ger. I hope you got that.

~ 40 ~

SAINT TERESA OF AVILA CAN KISS my ass. Teffy goes over the stickmen figures again, testing them against her letter clocks. That's it, though. That's what Teresa wrote under *password*.

"But how's that a password?" she says. "And to what?"

"Let me see," Ger says, and she shows him the phrase.

"Is it self-referential? A joke about herself?"

"Simpler than that," he says, motioning for Teffy's pen. She hands it over and he writes *SToAckma*, hardly glancing at the original phrase.

"What's that?" she says.

"Did they not show you that trick in high school?"

"What trick?"

"Create a password out of a memorable phrase," he says. "One that contains a mix of caps and small caps."

"There's no caps in the code, though."

"Well, no." He scratches the back of his head. "But if there were capitals, it'd be on those letters . . . the S, T, and A. That gives you a stronger password. Better if you have numbers."

"And they teach this in high school?" Ger nods and she says, "Well, I don't remember that fancy trick."

"Well, no," he laughs, "you still use your birthday as a password."

"Shut-up about that."

"I'm just sayin."

"And Saint Teresa?"

"Teresa's namesake," Ger says. "We called her Saint Teresa to piss her off."

"Who's we? You and. . . ."

"Ben Critch," he says. "And Connor Moffet. Mostly Critch."

"But you're sure this is the password?" she says, tapping *SToAckma* in the notebook. And when he nods she says, "But the password to what?"

He shrugs. "Is it not in the journal?"

"No," she says. "That's it. *SToAckma*—the Saint Teresa phrase—is the last thing. She says just before that that she has video, which I assume connects the pieces. That must be why she gives the password. But she gives no clue as to what the password is for." Teffy scans her translation of the journal, which offers little they don't already know, apart from Vinnie Coles's involvement, which they could take to the police. "Did you two ever share a Dropbox?" she asks.

"No," he says, voice hushed.

"An email account maybe?"

"She had a Yahoo account," he says, "and Facebook."

So they try the password on the Yahoo account and her Facebook, as well as on all the other accounts Ger can recall, but they're denied access to all of them.

Teffy says, "Are you sure the password is *SToAckma*?"

"Yes, I'm fucking sure."

Teffy turns in her chair, seeing in Ger's face that this is no abstract puzzle, no Sherlockian mystery game in need of one more clue. He's leaning forward on the couch—elbows on his knees, hands clasped—and she rests a hand on his tattooed arm. "I know—"

He jerks his arm away from her touch and a darkness passes over his face. He's somewhere deep inside himself, she thinks, back in those last days when Teresa was alive.

Teresa and Fin, she thinks. *The twin shadows we never talk about.* "I get what she meant to you, Ger."

He lets out a bitter laugh. "You do, do you?"

The comment pricks like a knife. Like a knife plucking a stitch on her cut stomach. "Teresa was important to you. I get that, Ger. I get what it is to have lost someone you—"

"Really? Were you sleeping with him, Tefs, and was he saying, 'I love you'—buying you ink to needle it into your skin?"

He did say he loved me, she wants to say.

"And what did you do when you found out that money for your tattoo was from her giving blow jobs in toilets downtown—and that's how she got that tooth knocked out—'cause a guy made her lick the toilet seat he'd come on?"

"Ger. . . ."

"Seriously though! How is Fin stabbing his own dad anything like having the person you love betray you—rip your heart out—again and again and again?"

"Like you're doing now?" she whispers—and he jolts from the couch, walks away from her toward the window.

"She was strangled in some dark alley, Tefs. By people she knew, people she grew up with—guys I trusted." He looks back at her, straight through her to whatever it is he's planning to do. *Just tell me, Ger. Just tell me.* "If there's nothing else in that journal," he says, "then I'm gonna go find Vinnie."

"And do what?"

"See if he can fill in some blanks. It's his name in there."

"Ger?" she says as he heads for the door.

He's in the hallway, kicking into his shoes. "What?"

"When you called me in Grand Falls that night, you said you'd got information." He stares at her, a tattooed hand pressed to either side of the living room entrance, leaning in. "You said it took some . . . persuasion." She meets his glare and holds it. "Is that why Ben Critch had water in his lungs?" The thought's been chewing away at the back of her mind. And she feels that whale's weight in the question she's about to ask: that half-sketched humpback on the wall behind her. "What happened to Ben Critch?" she says.

"You don't understand a goddamned thing," he says and slams the orange door behind him. His rustbucket Ford fires up out front and he's gone. And she thinks he'll have to have a lot of nerve to come back. But she knows he has that nerve. *And more.*

He'll come back. Eventually.

But then what? The stitches have been pulled, haven't they? The wound open. How is she to hold it together now?

She'll find out when he shows up. In the meantime, she has a journal that tells her next to nothing about what happened to Teresa and doesn't once mention Markus O'Shea. Maybe Ellie was right. Maybe Markus is okay. Business slick and stupid rich, sure. But . . . okay. She thinks of his plans for his fancy hotel, and how that project will in fact fill the gap left by the closed fish plant. It will make jobs on the island, and if Markus can attract the deep-pocket billionaires and movie stars—the people who can drop a hundred grand on a weekend away on the far-flung edge of flipping nowhere—then maybe St. Mark's will survive to the end of the century. Maybe.

But she also thinks of Daryl in Markus's house. And why was he there? That's the sticking point. Ellie must have sent him. But why? If Markus is okay, then why send in the ex-husband? Ellie didn't buy Teffy's story of the spray-painted boots, and obviously couldn't picture her wealthy boyfriend breaking into her own gallery.

So then why send in Daryl? And what did Daryl find that Markus didn't make him hand over before the RNC showed up? Did he send Mike something? Is that it? Is that why he said to call Mike? "Call Mike," he said. "He'll know."

He'll know what though?

It's nearly an hour later, after trying Mike's number several times, that she gets a call—from Ellie—saying she was just getting discharged and would like to meet Teffy down at her gallery. "No need to break in," Ellie says, "I'll be there to unlock the door."

~ 41 ~

S HE SETS HER SCOOTER BY THE boarded-up window and tries the gallery door. Finds it open and hears voices upstairs. She limps toward the lift, the ache in her knee aggravated by the scooter ride down here. But then she remembers the whale ground in the elevator's gears. The stairs it is, then, each of which is a hammer's claw *thunked* against her braced kneecap.

She's breathless and in eye-throbbing pain when she reaches the landing where she tackled O'Shea that night—before he threw her down the stairs—the word MURDERER still gashed red across the white wall. The whale still mangled in the lift. The room still a trashed disaster zone.

Next to the sea-facing window she sees Ellie, her arm in a sling. And next to Ellie, Mike Strickland. "I've been trying to call you," Teffy says to Mike.

"And I've been getting them," Mike says, scuffing his boots.

"But he's been with me," Ellie says "And given our recent history"—she nods at Teffy—"you'll understand us not being too keen to pick up."

Teffy says, "I'm sorry about Stefany's ashes. I wish—"

"See," Ellie cuts her off. "That's the difference. To you, those were ashes. To me"—and she motions to Mike with her left hand—"to us . . . that was our sister."

"I gets why you might've done it," Mike mutters.

"But that doesn't change things," Ellie snaps—and Teffy looks at them both.

"So, why did you call me?"

Mike glances at Ellie and nods at her purse, and Ellie says, "I heard you went ahead and broke into Markus's house. After I told you we were done."

"Then why'd you send Daryl?" Teffy says.

"Because you got me thinking."

"About the boots?"

"About the boots," Ellie says. "I even asked Constable Parsons to check if the boots were in evidence, along with Markus's Buick. They were."

"And . . .?"

"And they compared the tread with prints found here at the gallery."

"And they were a match?"

Ellie nods and pulls out her phone. "So I asked Daryl to search the house." She unlocks the device and scrolls to find an email attachment. "In addition to finding you," she says, "Daryl also found this," and she turns the phone to Teffy.

On the small iPhone screen, in a message from Daryl to Mike, Teffy sees the familiar stickmen figures, but on a small scrap of paper—lined note paper—and prefaced by a sloppy scrawl in cheap blue ink. Teffy squints to read the line. "What's it say?"

"It says, 'Figure this out and I'll bring friends.'"

Teffy looks from the coded note to Ellie. "Do you know what the rest says?"

"Only that they're the same kind of figures used in that dead girl's journal."

"I can translate what it says," Teffy offers. "I figured out the code."

"I guessed as much," Ellie says, "which is the *only* reason I called you. I want to know Markus's connection to that journal. To that girl."

"May I see the phone?" Teffy says—and Ellie hands over her device. "And do you have a pen? Or something to write with?"

Ellie searches through the table of art supplies and produces a blunt-nosed Sharpie. And when Teffy asks for paper, Ellie points to the wall smeared with the word MURDERER. "Go on," Ellie says. "If you can, tell her story."

The Sharpie squeaks and skitters on the white-washed cinderblock wall as Teffy works quickly through the short note—*i know who you are*—the marker's scent pungent, turning her stomach as she writes.

"Where did Daryl find this?" she asks Mike over her shoulder.

"In a locked drawer in his desk," Mike says. "Daryl always was a hand at locks."

"Sounds like a kid I know," Teffy says—Dougie's punk face flashing through her mind as she finishes the line: *i know who you are m oshea*. "M O'Shea," she says. "She wasn't supposed to know who he was then. That would explain the blindfolding. She wasn't supposed to see him."

"How do you know she was blindfolded?" Ellie says.

"She wrote in the journal that two guys, her handler Ben Critch and her driver Vinnie Coles"—and she wonders if Ger has found Vinnie yet—"they would tie her up and blindfold her, to deliver her to this rich guy's place."

"Are you okay?" Mike says to Ellie, but she waves him off, watching Teffy work her way through the translation: *i have video—message me.*

"The journal gives a password," Teffy says, "but Ger and I couldn't guess what it was for. It didn't work on any email address or Facebook account Ger knew."

"The last part here is an email address," Ellie says, pointing to the @ sign, the only mark not in stick figures—and Teffy works out the Gmail address Teresa left for Markus.

She asks Ellie if she can use the phone to try the journal's password on it, and Ellie nods but says, "I probably don't want to see this video, do I?"

"Probably not," Teffy says.

"I second that," says Mike.

Teffy types in the strange password—*StoAckma*—and the account opens. She quickly scans the received emails, spam as recent as this year, wondering if Teresa would've emailed these videos to herself. She's keying the Gmail address into the search bar when it occurs to her how many times she's tried to send video to Ger for *Miscreant* stories and how the files, if they're over a few minutes in length, are too large to attach and send. "So just drag the files into the Gdrive," Ger told her. "Then share them with me."

"What do you see?" Ellie says.

"Just clicking into her Gdrive."

"Her what-now?" says Mike.

"Here," Teffy says. "She labelled it 'for marjorie petty.' See," and she shows the screen to Ellie, and Ellie taps the video to play it.

The frame is dark and Teffy maxes the volume on Ellie's phone. There's no sound though. But there is movement. A light is flicked on and a young woman comes into the frame and Teffy recognizes her from the photographs presented in Troy's trial. Teresa. *She's beautiful,* Teffy thinks, watching Teresa glance at the camera.

Her cell phone camera.

Then Teresa slips out of the small black dress she's wearing and, in her lacy lingerie, takes a black cloth bag and pulls it over her head. Ties it at her neck. Then sits back on the bed and waits. A long minute ticks by, then the door opens and Ellie says, "That's Markus."

"You don't have to watch this," Mike says. "We can take it to the police."

But Ellie doesn't look away. Teffy watches the old artist's eyes narrow. When she looks back at the screen Markus is naked and spread-eagled. Cock a stickman's flagpole and his back to the bed's headboard. Teresa standing by his knees, bag still on her head, naked herself now, and slipping a belt around her neck—*Practiced,* Teffy thinks as Teresa buckles the belt loosely.

Then Teresa hooks the belt over a solid looking light fixture bolted into a beam, one of six or seven running the length of the fancy room.

"What the fuck's he into?" Mike says.

And Teffy thinks, *Autoerotic asphyxiation.* "He's gonna watch her get off," she says.

"She'll choke like that."

"That's the point," Teffy says.

"So," Mike says, "he's just gonna watch her go at herself, strung up like that?"

Ellie cringes. "He's doing more than just watching."

Mike's eyes go wide. "Jesus," he says. "He's gonna chafe himself—"

"Are you enjoying this?" Ellie snaps.

"Weirded out is more like it," Mike mumbles. "Did you know he was into the kink?"

"There's a world of kink beyond this," Teffy says.

"I don't wanna know," Ellie says.

"No, you don't."

Mike lets off a quick whistle and says, "There she blows," shaking his head, then peering closer at the phone. "What's he at now, b'y? He's . . . oh, say. Do you think? Jesus Murphy . . . he's just gonna eat her out, is he?"

"For the love of God, Mike!"

"Look, she's got her legs right around his head, la."

Ellie swats him away and she and Teffy look back at the phone to see Teresa's body tense, her legs straining, both her hands fisted in Markus's gray hair. Then she slackens and goes limp. Her body sags, its full weight noosed in that belt. Markus falls back from her, his eyes flashing, smiling lips glistening. And he watches her hang there. Ten seconds—his smile slips—fifteen, twenty, half a minute. And he scrambles suddenly to take down Teresa's limp body.

Lets her flop on the bed, pulls off her black hood, and, looking panicked, begins to slap and shake her, holding her nose and forcing air down into her lungs.

"She's not dead, is she?" Ellie says.

"What?" Mike says.

"She posted this video," Teffy says, "so. . . ."

In the video, Teresa kicks. Her arm flails weakly. Fingers quiver and she opens her eyes. She opens her eyes and stares at Markus straddling her. And Markus stares back at her.

That's when she saw his face, Teffy thinks.

On screen, Teresa pulls a blanket over her eyes and waves toward the door, and Markus leaves, and Teresa throws back the blanket, coughing and gagging as she struggles her way back to her phone to end the video.

"So he didn't kill her," Ellie breathes.

"No," Teffy says. "Not this time anyway. The video was for blackmail. Or curiosity. I don't know. But she wasn't supposed to know who he was."

"Hence the bag over the head," Mike says.

"That's right," Teffy says. "Maybe the blackmail occurred to her when she watched the video. Maybe that's when she uploaded it and bought the journal. When she thought the whole thing up. After she was certain of who he was."

"How can anyone be certain of that?" Ellie mutters.

"We know she was hooking for Troy," Teffy says. "From the journal. So this would show Markus with a prostitute. Bad for his reputation, sure. But this, the blackmail note, and the journal don't tell us much else. They don't tell us *how* she wound up dead in an alley." She shakes her head. "She wouldn't have been able to tell that story."

"No," Ellie says as she snatches the phone from Teffy's hands and storms for the stairwell. "But I've seen all I needs to murder the bastard."

~ 42 ~

MIKE JOGS TO KEEP UP WITH Teffy on her scooter, Teffy's braced leg on the board, good leg kicking her on after Ellie. And Ellie is half a block ahead of them, booking it to Atlantic Place where O'Shea keeps his company offices on the third floor.

"Where did you park?" Teffy calls back to Mike.

Mike, sucking wind, says, "The underground lot there," and he waves at the A. P. Parking Garage ahead of them across Clift's-Baird's Cove.

"What do you think she'll do?" Teffy says.

"I don't know," Mike says, "but he'll not want to be himself when she finds him."

They follow Ellie into the underground parking lot and manage to catch the elevator door right before it closes on Ellie's livid face. The doors ding shut once they're all onboard, and Ellie presses the third floor, stands back, and says, "You gonna keep me from killing him?"

"Not if that's . . . what you decide," Mike huffs.

"You gonna show him the video?" Teffy asks.

The door opens on the third floor and Ellie storms out without answering. Teffy clicks along behind on her scooter, Mike still struggling to keep up.

"Where's his office?" Mike calls.

And Ellie flicks a hand at a door she passes. "He's presenting today," she calls over her shoulder, "on the hotel project." Ellie stops at a large conference room.

"It's full in there," Teffy says, peering through the glass. "Are you gonna confront him now or after?"

With her left hand Ellie pushes open the door marked O'Shea Shoreline Inc.

"That's your answer," Mike says—and Teffy leaves her scooter in the hallway as she squeezes with Mike into the room behind other reporters and camera people, politicians and developers, reps from the university she recognizes, as well as architects from here and abroad. A screen descends from the ceiling and the room lights dim as O'Shea's voice comes to hover over them, above the faint sound of a helicopter—"Thank you all for coming today."

"Didn't know this many people cared about the hotel," Mike says to Teffy, his voice hushed, sweat glistening on his face.

The screen lights with a God's eye approach to St. Mark's—O'Shea's own helicopter swooping over the water toward the tiny outport. Ellie scans the back of the room as O'Shea says, "St. Mark's is my home," and Teffy sees Markus step onto the stage as the flight-shot lands to focus on an old saltbox house by the sea. The shot shutter-clips like an old slideshow, the house graying—time cycling backward—grass turning to snow, snow to grass again and again, peeling away years like old wallpaper, until the house disappears, leaving only the land and sea.

"Before the Irish settled St. Mark's," O'Shea says, "it was part of the French Shore and fished by the Basque as far back as the sixteenth century. Most settlers were Irish Catholic, but there were a few English and later a few Irish Protestants."

Ellie tucks herself behind a woman with a shock of pink hair running an NTV camera. Mike and Teffy shift closer to her and Mike says, "I wish he'd skip the history lesson and get to the virtual walk through. I'd like to see it before Ellie does whatever it is she's gonna do."

Ellie taps a cordless mic in a stand next to the sound booth, and asks the tech running the board, "Is this for questions later?" The guy nods, and she says, "Is it on?"

"Just press the button when you want to talk," the tech says.

Markus is calling up old images of the fishery—the fish flakes and boats, old cod jiggers and traditional tackle—the new trawlers going out to sea. Animated charts flicker and show the cod fishery sinking. The '92 moratorium and the new measures—Daryl and Ellie's Co-op in quick, sliding shots, from the late '80s to the police-taped aftermath of the now infamous heroin bust. That green van Ger was tied-up in. The quad Daryl hid behind, cradling Ellie while Troy fired off his final shots before booking it in Markus's Buick—Markus in the trunk with Doug Crawley's faceless corpse.

Shadows on the ground.

Pools of blood.

"Desperation," says O'Shea. "Desperation from a lack of fish, a lack of worth, a lack of purpose. That's poverty, folks. Hard times, like most of you will never know. And with that comes a lack of direction, a lack of vision. But," he says, "not a lack of pride. The people of St. Mark's don't want your government handouts, nor do they want to be tied to provincial purse strings. They want to make their own way. *We*"—he leans hard on the word—"*we* of St. Mark's have always wanted to make our own way. We want our own jobs, our own way of life—our own bit of rock to call home."

He stares out at the shutterfly crowd, the wavering mics, phones outheld, recording his every word. "Desperation," he says, "means change is needed. If we can't process fish or fish ourselves, then what? What do we do?"

"Hunt sea cucumbers!" someone shouts.

"Ask the Mexicans!" says another.

"You mean the cartels," O'Shea says. "Not Mexicans writ large. The *cartels* might offer economic viability, sure—but at a price. Our Constabulary in town and the RCMP in St. Mark's are still calculating that cost—that *human* cost—to our community."

Teffy watches Ellie switch on the cordless mic.

"If you resist change," Markus says, "if you resist *innovation* simply to conserve things as they've always been, then you—unknowingly, and with good intent, always with good intent—can strangle the very things you love. This is what led to the St. Mark's Heroin Bust as we know it. This is what has—sadly—led to the closure of the St. Mark's Co-op and the island's fish plant. Greed," he says. "Sheer stubbornness. Desperation. But"—the image of the bloody parking lot behind him rolls back like a scroll—"*but* we can still hold fast to our culture, *our* way of doing things—our pride—while still grasping a rich future!"

And he stretches out his arms, fists clenched, and then throws his hands open and the screen behind him erupts in a firework, the frame flashing with flankers that hit the rocky ground and begin to sprout virtually—to shoot up into CGI-generated support beams capped with pine board floors, walls clicking together with clapboard siding. All of it self-constructing into something stark and strange, ultramodern.

Nordic and new.

Windows peer at them now, in all shapes: some round, some rectangles, diamonds and crescent moons—"Each window will be custom-framed," Markus says, "each glass will be hand-cut by an islander and installed by islanders—"

"Cleaned by islanders?" calls a man in the middle of the room.

"See, that's the question," Mike mutters.

"Every job," O'Shea says, "from construction to cleaning to cooking, will be done by the islanders of St. Mark's."

Ellie pulls the mic from its stand. "And who designed it?" she says—and Markus scans the room for the person who asked the question—the other person with a mic.

The woman running the NTV camera looks at Ellie, sees the mic and Ellie's arm in a sling, and spins her camera on Ellie, who says, "The hotel, Markus—it's designed by a Norwegian, isn't it?" And O'Shea sees her now.

"Ellie," he says. "When did they discharge you?"

"This morning, Markus."

"This is Ellie Strickland," Markus says, offering her the room's attention. "Whose debut art show this past fall you all remember—*The Secret Lives of Whales.*"

"It's Old Sculpin," someone says.

"Have you found out who vandalized your show?" the woman running the NTV camera asks Ellie.

"We think we've found the person, yes," Ellie says—and Teffy watches O'Shea's face for some telling twitch or wince—a curl of the lip, a downward glance. But Markus keeps his eyes locked on Ellie, betraying nothing—and Teffy thinks, *This isn't the first time you've worn that mask, is it?*

"Any idea why the vandal spray-painted MURDERER on the wall?" a reporter asks.

"That," Ellie says, "is a question for the man who wrote it." She glares at Markus who stares blankly back at her.

"But the show will go on!" Markus says, trying to regain the room's attention.

"Yes, the show will continue," Ellie says. "It will continue because it has to. Because too many women in this town have been kept from telling their stories."

"The new show's about sex workers, isn't it?" another reporter asks.

"Women involved in the sex industry," Ellie says. "Yes."

"And a giant whale?" asks another.

"What happened to your arm?" someone else yells.

"A drug dealer shot me," Ellie says, and a murmur passes through the crowd—a wave that breaks in a sparkle of camera flashes. "A dealer with whom you've done some past business, haven't you, Markus?"

The room fixes on Markus now. "I tried to break up what looked like a shady deal," he says. "I was shot by this dealer too."

"Troy Hopper," Ellie says. "You know the name, Markus. And you must've known that Doug Crawley knew him too."

"That's ridiculous," Markus says. "Why would I know someone like Troy Hopper?"

"Because he did a favor for you once," Teffy calls, projecting her voice over the murmuring crowd.

Ellie looks at her sharply and O'Shea says, "And why in the world would I need a favor from a drug dealer?"

The knuckles of Ellie's left hand whiten around the mic. "Because he cleaned up your mess, Markus."

"I'm sorry, folks," Markus says, clapping his hands, "Ms. Strickland here seems to have something she wants to tell me in private. If you can give us ten minutes, I'll—"

"It was about ten minutes, wasn't it, Markus?" Ellie says.

Markus motions to the door he'd entered by. "We can talk in there," he says.

"How much did you pay for her, Markus? And how much did you have to pay Troy Hopper to make sure she never told anyone she saw your face?"

Markus's face pales—and Teffy sees now how the different threads have been hooked together in Ellie's mind.

"She saw you," Ellie says. "She saw your face—"

"I don't know what you're talking about."

"She saw your face and she wound up strangled, Markus. Her body dumped in an alleyway. That's not a coincidence."

"Whose body was dumped in an alley?" someone shouts.

"Her name was Teresa," Ellie says. "Teresa Squires."

Markus says, "I don't know a Teresa Squires."

"You wouldn't have," Ellie says.

"Then why are you bringing her up?—and in front of all these people? These people have come to hear about the future of St. Mark's: a way to save and sustain outport Newfoundland."

"Your hotel," Ellie says.

"St. Mark's hotel."

"A vision that is what, Markus—five, six years old?" Markus doesn't answer, and Teffy doesn't know where Ellie is going now. "Is the hotel really about trying to change the story about St. Mark's? To say, 'Look, we're more than the whale-killers you've thought us to be? We're innovative and earth-friendly too, leaders in low-impact environmental tourism?' I've lived with you a while now. I've heard *all* the angles. But it's never been about the whale, has it? That's old history anyway, and no one now—except those of us who lived through the aftermath of the whale's death, the short-lived mainland media storm—only we remembers that they called us MURDERERS!" She shouts the last word and O'Shea's mouth clamps shut.

"Only you would know or care that we were once called that, Markus. Only you would spray-paint that on my gallery wall. And to do what? To steal a journal written in the same kind of code as a mysterious note a woman once gave you." Teffy sees it now, sees the pattern emerging from Ellie's sharp mind, clear as the pain and rage in the old artist's face.

Markus tries to laugh. "A note? Can I see this note?"

Ellie clips the microphone back into its stand, then fishes her phone out of her pocket with her free hand and holds it up. "Daryl found it," she says. "And he sent a pic to Mike, who gave it to me." And Teffy can tell by the way O'Shea's face darkens, that he's destroyed the note, and Daryl's phone, and likely the journal too—all burned in his woodstove, no doubt. "She gave you the note, didn't she, Markus? Was it during your last *encounter*, if you can call it that? Did she give it to you then? And you could make neither heads nor tails of it, could you?—which is why you kept it."

"Ellie," Markus says, "you're grasping at threads."

"Don't gaslight me, Markus. I've seen the video she threatened you with."

"What video?" he says. "I was never threatened!"

And he sounds like he means it, Teffy thinks.

"The note," Ellie says. "When you saw the journal in my gallery, you knew it was written by the same woman who gave you that note, didn't you? The woman you hired. That's why you broke into my gallery. Because you realized there was some kind of evidence out there linking her to you. Even if nobody could read it, it was still there. Out of your control. And it wasn't enough that this woman was dead already. No, you had to raze any trace that she ever existed."

"Ellie," he says, "this is embarrassing. Come into my office."

"Don't, Markus."

O'Shea catches sight of Teffy and says, "That reporter—*who broke into my house the other night*—obviously has some kind of vendetta against me and she's been filling your head with—"

"She translated the journal, Markus. And the note." Teffy sees the twitch in his eye as he glares at Ellie. "So we were able to access a video this woman took of the two of you. Together. That's what the note was about. She was warning you, telling you she knew who you were. But you took care of her without even reading the note, didn't you?"

"Where's this video?" the woman behind the NTV camera asks.

"Right here on my phone," Ellie says. "What will all these people think, Markus, when they see how long you let her hang from your bedroom ceiling?"

O'Shea's face palsies and Teffy thinks he might stroke-out.

The crowd seethes and Teffy loses sight of Markus in the swarm of people trying to capture and tweet images of the millionaire—some livestreaming, others calling in, flashes sending up the whole room like a bonfire.

"He's gone!" someone yells.

"He slipped out the side door!"

Teffy whips around to Ellie, but Ellie knocks her into Mike's arms as she blows through the conference room doors and into the hall. Mike tilts Teffy to her feet and rushes after Ellie, and Teffy tries to run in her brace but stumbles in a flash of pain, crashing through the door. She sees Mike disappear down the stairwell and thinks Ellie must be trying to beat Markus to the underground parking lot.

But maybe he's headed out the front door, she thinks, and hops on the elevator. Hits the first floor and thinks she could try to flag Ellie and Mike down where Harbour Drive hits Water Street—*If you can get there in time! Should be able to on the scooter but—*

"Fuck!" she yells.

The scooter is still upstairs, by the conference room door. She slaps the elevator doors in frustration and they ding open. First floor. She pushes through a crowd and out the front doors onto Water Street—sees the distance she'll have to hobble-skip to that corner.

"Fuck!" she yells again and takes another step out from the building to see if O'Shea or Ellie and Mike are already running the light in their vehicles.

You can't even see it from here!

A kid on his scooter goes to dodge her, but she hip-checks him into a ticketed Jeep, grabs his scooter with her good hand, flicks the board under her braced leg, and starts wheeling down the sidewalk—the kid up and yelling that she stole his ride, racing after her on foot.

She clears the Franklin Hotel, makes the corner of Clift's-Baird's Cove, and sees O'Shea a street below her ripping up Harbour Drive in his red pickup. The kid catches her and grabs her jacket but she uses the handlebars to swivel the board and hack his shin.

Then she kicks-off down the hill.

The board wobbles and she crouches to steady it, picking up speed, zipping past the parking garage. Two cars blow by her through the intersection and she leans right and swerves to keep from hitting an SUV going the same direction, her elbow bumping the truck's white panelling. The SUV gasses it to clear her, and she sees Ellie blast Mike's truck out of the parking garage. The SUV clips Ellie's tailgate, spinning her grill in the direction of O'Shea's disappearing truck.

Teffy swerves behind the SUV's taillights, right in front of Ellie, who'd just gassed it but brakes hard and lays on her horn, the bumper of Mike's truck next to Teffy's braced knee. Mike, belted in place, sits white-faced in the passenger seat, hands splayed on the dash.

Teffy flings the scooter to the sidewalk, palms the hood with her hand, and hauls into the passenger seat as Mike squishes into the middle. She hits the dash and says, "Let's go!"

And Ellie peels down Harbour Drive and up Job's Cove, screeching right on Water and gassing it up onto King's Bridge Road, left on New Cove, then the steady stoplight-blowing climb up the north side hills from the harbor—horns blaring over Prince Philip and Newfoundland Drive, Ellie weaving one-handed in and out of vehicles.

"Too stunned to pull over!" Mike yells, flipping off a car they cut off.

"And what if I'd run you down back there?" Ellie yells across Mike's chest.

"You wouldn't hit a preggo," Teffy says.

"You're pregnant?" Mike says.

"But what if I had?" Ellie says, eyes fixed on the blurring road.

They blow past the airport entrance off Portugal Cove Road and Teffy says, "You don't think he's catching a flight? I'd catch a flight."

"I think he's going home," Ellie says.

"Did you see his face," Mike says, "when you asked about missus hanging from his bedroom ceiling?"

They zoom onto a straight stretch and Ellie punches out and past a Prius, Gladneys Arm a blue water blur to their left. In a few short minutes, she's steering them through Windsor Heights. Ellie looks across Mike to Teffy. "Where's that boyfriend of yours?"

"He's missing all the action," says Mike.

"He stepped out," Teffy says.

"Did he say where?" asks Ellie.

"He plays some things close to the chest."

"So he doesn't tell you everything?"

And Mike snorts. "Seems we all know a guy like that."

Rock cut walls whiz by either side of the roaring truck—the bay ahead of them now. "Do you think Markus loves you?" Teffy asks, and once the question is out of her mouth she wishes she'd kept her lips shut.

Ellie grips the wheel one-handed and says, "Hold on," and pulls out to pass a Bronco on the corner. A Smart Car honks in the other lane and Ellie swerves left of the Smart Car and punches it, the driver's side tires on the gravel shoulder fishtailing—and she cuts back quick to her own lane, spraying gravel.

"Jesus!" Mike yells. "Keep your eyes on the fuckin road!"

The Bronco flashes his lights in their rear-view mirror and barmps his horn, but soon disappears in the bend of the road behind them.

"Markus has gotta know you're right behind him," Teffy says.

Ellie squints. The road bends ahead and Teffy can see those suburban-style saltbox mansions on the headland, O'Shea's red truck just pulling into his own driveway. Ellie rips along the asphalt, skidding road-grit and tearing turf as she brakes on Markus's little patch of retainer-walled lawn—the truck's headlights on Markus trying to key-in the code for his front door lock.

Ellie lays on the horn but she doesn't move to open her door.

And Teffy says, "Are you going after him before—"

"Before what?"

Teffy's phone screams: that familiar child wailing in her pocket and Ger's number flashing on her screen. She swipes to answer and looks up to see Markus fling open the door and launch suddenly into flaming air, right off his steps—like a saint ascending—lifting up and up and up in a ball of fire that evaporates, crashing the man through the truck's windshield.

Teffy blinks, glass in her hair—Markus's clothes smoking as he elbows her bandaged stomach, ripping stitches as he falls off the dash onto their laps, his ankle hooked over the steering wheel by Ellie's face.

No windshield now and Teffy looks to see the doorframe of O'Shea's house blasted off, windows blown out—the ruins inside blazing.

Those tree trunk pillars like bent bodies on fire.

And through the ringing in her ears she faintly hears Ger's panicked voice asking if she's alright—"Teffy!" he's yelling. "Are you alright? Is the baby alright? Teffy! TEFFY!"

~ 43 ~

SHE'S PERCHED ON THE DRYER in the bathroom of Ellie's Livingstone place, the window by the toilet long gone dark since she showed Ger the video. His face had grown grim as he watched the whole thing. *Like he's numbing*, she'd thought.

Then, as if switching the whole thing off, he started asking after O'Shea, wanting to know if Markus survived the blast.

"The baby's fine," she says quietly, "in case you were wondering."

He stares at her, the tape on his bandaged ear peeling loose. "I did ask that," he says, "at St Clare's."

"He just fell out of the sky, Ger, straight through the windshield."

"Do they have any idea who would've set it?"

She doesn't answer. Just hops off the dryer and turns the water on in the shower stall. Struggles her stiff arms loose of her torn shirt.

"Aren't we talking here?" Ger says.

She tries to shuck off her jeans but gets the one leg stuck in the brace. So she loosens the brace and shifts out of her jeans and underwear. "Their main concern was pressure damage to O'Shea's lungs," she says. "He was struggling to breathe. Suffocating."

Like Teresa strung up in that video.

"Did they say anything else?" Ger says. "Was the IED anything like the one used on our Merrymeeting place?"

She shifts her weight to her good leg and is about to ask again what happened to Ben Critch—about the water in his lungs—but she slips into the hot shower so Ger doesn't see her shaking. She's hardly flinched since the blast but can't stop trembling now.

She bows under the hot pour to block it all out. All of it. The video of Teresa hanging from O'Shea's bedroom ceiling. The burning house. Markus smoking through the air like a tossed cigarette. Ger has nattered away the last half hour, the sun gone down and her mute on the dryer, trying to listen through the ringing in her ears.

She pulls her head from the water now, breathes deep, and wipes back red hair. "Did you find Vinnie?" she says, hoping the answer is no. For Dougie's sake. If Ben Critch had water in his lungs, what would Ger do to Vinnie?

Ger opens the door, water splashing off her freckled shoulders. "Vinnie's disappeared," he says. "No one has seen him. Not since St. Mark's."

"You asked Dougie?"

"I did."

She peels the loose bandage off Ger's mutilated ear and sees the raw cartilage nub beneath. Touches it and wonders, as she pulls Ger into the shower, how he sees her now, after all this—the shower spraying off her and soaking him through, filling his shoes with water.

"Are you sure you're okay?" he says, smoothing wet hair from her face, a tilt to his head like he thinks she might be crying.

"Why did you walk out on me?" she says.

He cups her face in his hands, and she wants to believe in those hands, in their goodness. She wants to believe in him. Wants to believe that he'd do anything for her. "This whole thing is messing me up," he says. Then he drops his hands. Rubs steam from the shower door to peer into the empty room. "I said some shitty things about Fin—"

A rush of cold, wet wind blows through the room and she hears a voice by the toilet. "Who the fuck is Fin?" Dougie says—and Teffy swears and shifts Ger in front of her.

"Do you ever come in an actual door?" she yells, seeing Dougie's hazy form through the shower stall's mauzy glass.

"That's a cold rain," Ger says, "close the friggin window!"

"I got caught in it," Dougie says. "That's why I dodged in here. You guys are like fuckin rabbits, though—at it every times I comes to the window."

"It's our bathroom!" Teffy says. "Not a drive through."

"I thought it was that artist's place," Dougie says. "Are you leasing it now?"

"The artist let us stay a few days," Ger says. "But she's gonna be back later—"

"To kick us out," Teffy mutters.

"So I wouldn't come through the window again," Ger says.

"Or what?" Dougie says. "What's she gonna do?"

"She'll call the cops on you."

"Then she can join the fuckin party, can't she?" Dougie says. "And fuck you very much, by the way, for telling Ossifer P-dog about the crystal in the coleslaw. How did you know that my favorite thing to do on an afternoon is to get hauled in and fuckin interrogated?"

Ger says, "That crystal's shit, man. You gotta stop passing that out."

"See, Dad was right about you being a bit uppity these days."

"That's 'cause I've seen someone fucked up on meth," Ger says. "You don't want to be part of that. That's all I'm saying."

"Well when *you* start paying my rent, then you can start being my mother. Fuck, I'll suck milk from your goddamn nipples if you pays my rent. But right now I gots a one-room apartment, and a mattress and sandwich maker I found in a dumpster by the university. So if I can upgrade to a fuckin microwave, I'm gonna do it, don't matter the hustle."

Ger sighs. "Just go to the kitchen, Dougie—will you?"

Dougie shuffles off across the hall to the kitchen and Ger sops after him, leaving a trail of puddle-prints behind him. Teffy dries off, cinches the towel tightly around herself, and grabs new clothes from their bag in the bedroom. In the kitchen, Dougie is presiding from his countertop throne, and Ger is grilling him about an open bag on the counter with what looks like a small bottle and a syringe.

"It's just Telazol," Dougie says. "Dog sedative."

Teffy says, "Is this the new hustle?"

"Did your dad ask for that?" Ger says.

"Wait," Teffy says, "you've heard from your dad?" She looks at Ger. "I thought Vinnie was in hiding or something."

"He is," Dougie says. "Ever since that fuckin guy tried to strangle him in his own fuckin cab. But he says he knows who buddy is—the guy I fuckin beat with the back seat of the cab. Fuckin car-trunk Kung-Fu. Telazol's to get the jump on him. Jab Batman in the neck, then start working him over while he's drooling out the side of his mouth."

"So your dad thinks this guy knows who killed Ben Critch?" Teffy says.

"If Dad knows he hasn't told me," Dougie says. "He just said to pick up the dog meds and he'd knock a couple hundred bucks off what I owes him."

"How did you wind up in debt to your own dad?" Teffy asks.

"Point is," Dougie says, "once I'm outta his debt, I'm done. Just so happens the quickest way out is delivering his damn coleslaw."

"Crystal's one thing," Ger says. "But if your dad's planning what I think he is—"

"And what's that?" Teffy says.

"Persuasion," Ger says, and she understands his meaning.

"Dougie," she says, and chokes on his name, panic setting in at the thought of this kid—this dumb, sweet kid—being in a room with his dad and this other guy. This other guy who's tried to strangle Vinnie in his own cab. She thinks of Troy sawing off Ger's ear and Fin with that fillet knife in his hand—Fin staring at her wide-eyed. The crippling shock each time.

"Ger," Dougie says, sly twist to his grin as he looks at Teffy staring at him, "she's giving me the come slither look."

"It's the come hither look, you idiot," Ger says.

But it's not that at all. She stares at Dougie, punk-regal on that countertop, shooting his mouth off because he trusts them. Because he feels safe. Out there he's a dealer's target—a sea urchin to a sharp-eyed gull like Troy. Or his own dad. A dealer would look at Dougie and think he's a kid going nowhere—like Ger, like Teresa—so what does it matter if money's made off his bent back? What's it matter if he's strung up like a piece of meat and left to hang?

And wasn't she going to do the same thing in having Dougie break into Markus's place? Wasn't it Ger who saved him from actually getting locked up by dropping that coleslaw comment to Parsons?

"It's just your dad," she says.

"What about my dad?"

"Please," she murmurs, "just stay clear of whatever he's into." He looks at her strange, and she can't tell if he's understood her or just marked the words coming out of her mouth. "You think I'm going in on this," he says, "with Dad?"

"Aren't you?" Ger says.

"No way, man. That back alley shit's all Dad's. I just wanna get paid. So when I drops this stuff off, I'm out of there. Dad can deal with his own shit. Speaking of which"—Dougie checks his phone for the time—"I gotta get this stuff up to him."

"Up to him?" Teffy says. "Is he back in Rabbittown?"

"Likely in his spot on Harvey Road," Ger says. "Near the Timmies."

Dougie glances from Ger to Teffy. "I didn't fuckin say anything," and he edges off the counter and gathers up his gear. Twists his wet ball cap low on his head. "If you two hops back in the shower, though, send me a selfie."

"You'd post it to Facebook," Teffy says.

"Naw," he says, "fuckin Instagram that shit."

Teffy watches him raise the window by the toilet and leg his way out into the rain. Three steps and he's gone from Ellie's yard. "I'm gonna follow him," Teffy says as she sits on the toilet to click on her brace. "Can you get me my coat and your ball cap?"

"You're just gonna get wet," he says, tapping his way down the hall to get what she asked of him. When he comes back into the bathroom, he says, "Dougie will be halfway up Long's Hill by now," and he hands her a cap and jacket and nods at her braced knee. "And it's not like you'll be chasing anyone down."

She pulls the hat low over her eyes. Halfway out the window, she says, "If Vinnie's not on Harvey Road, is there another place up the hill he parks?"

"And what're you gonna say to him if you finds him?"

"To leave Dougie out of whatever shit he's into."

"The coleslaw crystal?"

"And this strangler," she says.

Ger nods, stretches to crack his neck and says. "Sometimes he waits for calls in the Rooms parking lot or by the Basilica. Sometimes up to the Sobeys. But Harvey Road is his spot."

"'Cause of the Timmies?"

"Everybody loves Timmies."

The rain's spitting now like half-thought insults as she slips the first fence. Then the second. Ger calls from the bathroom window, "Grab one of them big bags of M&Ms!"

She gives him a wave and slips the last fence.

Then starts up that cocksucking hill.

~ 44 ~

S HE'S SOAKED BY THE TIME she reaches the convenience store
near the fire station. Halfway up the hill the rain came on hard, blowing in under the rim of her ball cap like some random dick on Twitter
ducking into her direct messages. She elbows into the store to escape the
berating rain.

The fluorescent lights numb her and she feels exhausted from dragging her bum leg up that hill. And from the thought of having this baby. She
catches a glimpse of herself in the store's corner mirror. If it wasn't for feeling
constantly knackered and nauseous—and that she'd heard the heartbeat in
Gander a week ago—she wouldn't even know she's pregnant.

The baby there but not there—"Anterior," the technician had said.

Witness to everything, but hardly noticed.

Deformed, she fears, from the condom-socked heroin Ike made her
swallow. She grabs a small jar of instant coffee from one shelf and a jumbo
pack of M&Ms from another.

At the counter, the attendant—a young girl with acid-blonde hair and
caked-on mascara—is accepting a stack of newspapers from a brush-cut
delivery person in a brown uniform. The attendant doesn't say anything as
Teffy steps up, the stack of papers still on the counter. Doesn't even make eye
contact. Just takes the coffee and candy from Teffy's hands and scans them,
pausing occasionally to scroll through something she's reading on her phone.

The girl rings in the items and Teffy glances at the phone on the counter. Sees it's a news article and asks, "What's the story?" nodding at the phone
when the girl looks up.

The girl stares at her, hand near her phone.

"I'm just interested," Teffy shrugs.

The girl flicks the screen a couple of times and spins the phone so Teffy can see the headline: *Portugal Cove and Merrymeeting Explosions Linked.* She snatches up the phone and the girl says, "Hey!" but Teffy keeps scrolling quickly through the short article. "I just gotta read this," she says. "I know someone involved."

"Ohhh," the girl says, then nods at the phone in Teffy's hands. "They used the same stuff that that Timothy McVeigh used down in Oklahoma. Did you see that?"

Teffy nods. *Ammonium nitrate,* she reads, connected to a theft of the substance from the Duck Pond Mine in central Newfoundland, near Buchans.

"Did you see the bit about the smart caps?" the girl asks. "Apparently, if you knows what you're at, you can set those off with your phone now."

Teffy scans the rest of the article and sees O'Shea is still in critical condition. Ger will want to know that, but how will that news hit Ellie? What's screeching in her head now?

"Are you done with my phone?" the attendant asks as Teffy slips her purchases into her jacket pockets. Teffy hands over the phone and payment.

"Thanks," she says and heads out the door, the M&Ms rattling in her pocket. She veers downhill in the dark so she can cut up a set of stairs to Harvey Road. An old shortcut. But she regrets that decision halfway up the stairs because her leg seizes. She limps on, though, trudging through the pain—each step like breaking through thigh-deep, crusty snow—because she thinks maybe, just maybe she'll find Vinnie parked somewhere nearby in his Skimpy cab. Waiting on a call. Or figuring how best to stick this strangler with the needle Dougie's brought him.

On the sidewalk above, she scans Harvey Road—up past the Timmies to the fire station—for any sign of Vinnie. But Vinny's pink cab is nowhere in sight. So she stretches her leg as much as she can in the brace, thinking she'll make it as far as the Basilica before heading home out of it.

She scrapes her hand along a chain-link fence that runs to the Presbyterian Kirk, the fence in her mind like the net cast from that boat in Ellie's mural. She thinks of the whale downtown and how Markus hauled it into the rickety lift and crushed it. To make the break-in look like the work of an old-time Greenpeace vandal. Shift the blame so he could grab Teresa's journal and make it disappear.

Teffy carries on past the Kirk, ducked against the drizzle, thinking she'll cut down Garrison Hill and back to the house if she can't find Vinnie by the

Rooms—her leg so stiff in this shit weather she's gimping now, wincing with each step.

She feels gutted at the thought of what Ellie must be going through, all the shit with O'Shea compounded by Teffy's own betrayals. Stealing the journal and switching her sister-in-law's ashes for heroin. She'll be the subject of some dark song when Lisetta decides to compose these last days into a bluesy rock ballad to sing on every stage from here to Vancouver.

And what if Markus O'Shea survives? What becomes of him? Will he, like so many men before him, be able to buy his way out? Likely. He'll disappear for a while, then design some scheme to get what he wants—what he feels entitled to. Like building his earth-friendly hotel. He'll land on his feet. Men like him always do.

But you? she thinks. *They'll cut you wide open. Just like Troy would have had he gotten the chance to finish what he started. You're no more than a Whitechapel girl to them. A young slut from around the bay. What'll she do? they'll whisper. Do you know what she can do with a knife? Have you heard?* Bloody faces spitting at her out of the dark and slanting rain. She shivers. Feels that scraper pressed to her throat again—Jake leaning on it, Ellie's voice overhead, and her phone in her pocket dinging that she's got a text. She pulls it out to see a message from Ellie.

I'll be home at 10 p.m. You can leave the key under the brick by the front door. I'd like you gone when I get there.

10 o'clock and they'll be out in the street or sleeping the night in Ger's rust-bucket Ford. St. John's is easier to love, she thinks, if you have a decent roof over your head. Face eviction or a night on the street though and the place may as well be God's outhouse pit, divine piss raining down on you and all your wretched moaning like a strong wind whistling up some christly arsehole in the uncaring sky—a good wind doing what good intentions can't.

She's about to cross the street to the Basilica, hoping Ger has secured them a hotel room for the night, when she sees a pink Skimpy cab parked illegally on Garrison Hill. She works her way down to it and finds it locked. No one inside. But it's Vinnie's number and she thinks he must be somewhere in this neighborhood.

But where?

No one is on the street save her. And she's seen no sign of anyone in the last half hour who might be Dougie or his dad.

If Vinnie's around, she thinks, *he's indoors somewhere.*

She thinks to knock on some numbers down the street, but it's pissing now, and she's wet through, so she heads downhill for home—Ellie's home—her knee on fire and Troy's last words rank as his cigarette breath in her face: *You really fucked this one up, Toffee.*

~ 45 ~

T HE SKUZZCUTS'S DEBUT ALBUM grinds away inside Ellie's Livingstone place—Ger's ripsaw jam since she dropped Teresa's coded journal in his lap. The last song savages her ears when she opens the door, the screeching finale sharp enough to snap neck muscles. The song severs suddenly with that child's familiar screaming—the ringtone Ger programmed into her phone.

Your future, she thinks, glancing into the darkened front room—Ger's open laptop eerily lighting the skeletal, half-painted whale from below, like the yellowish hue of that iceberg's underwater basin off the Kid Brothers. Into which they poured a pound of heroin, she thinks. All of them imagining that flying dust to be the remains of a woman who'd betrayed their trust.

"Ger?" she calls, raising her voice above the child's wailing. "Ger?" She flicks on the bedroom light and sees the child's voice bleeding red the levels on Ger's smart speaker.

She leaves it playing—the kid wailing purple now.

In pain, she thinks. *Angry.*

And she wonders whose kid it was they used and why it was screaming like that—ratcheting up, losing its mind. *Never thought to ask that of the band, did you, Ger?*

"Ger?"

She heads back into the hallway, the glow of Ger's computer in the front room splaying the ceiling fan's shadow against the hallway wall like a giant spider poised to launch at her.

She turns and heads to the back of the house, the child on the record hiccupping sobs as she checks the kitchen, calls Ger's name again, then heads across the hall to the bathroom.

The window by the toilet is open a crack and she wonders if Dougie came back or if Ger slipped out for one of his rare smokes. Thinking puffs, he calls them. She tells him he's no Sherlock, and he says he can show her his Watson again if she'd like.

That's how it goes with them. Back and forth. A sarcastic give and take. And she loves it, feeds off it, because it reminds her of Fin—the two of them a circle loaf.

Cracked, Fin would say.

She looks through the window for Ger but he's not in the backyard, and neither is Dougie, the child's scream on the record sharper now, barbed and twisting her stomach like that bent tree twitching in the wind, like a street walker fixing on Dougie's meth, craving some of that scat she would've given Troy to get Ger back. The tree shakes like she is now. Violently. Uncontrollably. And she finds herself teary, near crying but not letting herself go—not letting herself go back there—the dark tree alien as her own baby inside her. Some body horror she's only beginning to comprehend.

She imagines it twisting inside her now, the baby, like her own raw need—her need to find a house and keep the paper going, to keep money trickling into their bank account so there's food on the table. All this anxiety palpitating inside and beyond her. Beyond any future she dared reckon before she saw it: her baby, there on the ultrasound screen.

Felt it list inside her the once on their way back to St. John's.

Her child, that tree in the rain. *Helpless*, she thinks. Helpless as Christ in that church where she and Fin hid all those years ago. Helpless as Fin screaming her name over his dad's dead body—Fin yelling: What have you done? What the hell have you done? WHAT HAVE YOU FUCKING WELL DONE!?

And she heads straight for the bedroom to flick off the bloody scream slicing into her. Pulls the cord and all she can hear is Ellie's neighbor's TV—faint through the wall—playing some shoot-'em-up special.

She grabs the pen to scribble down a reminder to track Vinnie down. That is, she thinks, if Vinnie can manage not to get himself killed by this strangler: this St. John's bomber who seems to know as much as she and Ger do about the things that went down all those years ago, things that have come glaringly to light in the last twenty-four hours.

Ben and Markus, she thinks. *Teresa*.

Back in the hall, clicking the pen, she sees the poised spider become the ceiling fan as she approaches it. She's so intent on the fan's crouched shadow, though, that she almost misses the La-Z-Boy's creak.

She pockets the pen.

"Ger?" She pulls the bag of M&Ms from her jacket. Steps into the front room, kicking something across the floor. She stoops to pick it up and sees that it's an empty syringe. Like the one Dougie was showing Ger an hour ago in the kitchen.

She stands and sees Ger in the La-Z-Boy. He's groggy and limp, struggling to stand, to point behind her, as the shadow behind him becomes a man in a black coat.

"Who the—?"

Someone breathes on her neck and hooks a belt over her head. She drops the M&Ms, grabs the belt, and the person behind her knees her in the back. The guy yanks and the cinched belt punches her left hand into her throat, gurgling her scream.

The belt cuts into her hand, her own knuckles crushing her trachea.

She panics, plants a foot, and kicks back off the arm of the couch, crashing her assailant against the wall—the bag of M&Ms kicked into the hallway. The volume goes up on the TV next door and the belt tightens against her caught hand, the knee in her back digging deeper—flashing pain that buckles her.

She plants her heels and pushes back—her bad knee screaming—but her attacker dives to the side, swings her around, and jabs two elbows into her shoulder blades. The belt cuts the side of her palm and the attacker bashes her face against the wall.

She can't breathe, the side of her face mashed against plaster—eyes to Ger, who's trying to struggle upright. But the man behind him pulls Ger's drugged body back into the La-Z-Boy. Puts a knife to Ger's throat. And Ger blinks at her, the knife scaping skin.

"Teffy?" he groans.

She grips the belt but the assailant yanks, the belt cuts deeper, and she cocks her good knee to kick off the wall. Flies back into her attacker—both of them crashing over Ellie's writing desk—the belt loose enough in the tumble for Teffy to roll free. She struggles to her good knee, gasping. Sees Ger try to shift in the chair, the man with the knife pressing the blade harder against Ger's throat. A hand grips her bad leg and yanks, jolting a gasp from her lips. Another fist grabs her shirt and she surges forward, popping snap-clasps and slipping loose of her sleeves.

Her attacker falls back with the empty shirt and lunges at her as she claws for something—*Anything!*—grasping Ger's laptop and planting her braced leg to swing around, cracking the laptop against her attacker's face.

The guy crashes onto the coffee table. And she axes the broken laptop down onto his raised arm—his own fists clenched in dark gloves.

The guy whimpers as he rolls onto his back and kicks her braced knee, shocking her white. Breathless. She bites her lip. Tries to breathe as she raises the laptop for another blow. But her attacker reaches behind him and draws a gun from the back of his pants.

She freezes—laptop by her ear.

The guy on the floor chambers a round, spits blood—and she sees his face now.

"Vinnie?"

She coughs and drops the laptop, reaches for her belt-burned neck and staggers against the doorjamb. Goes to say something but Vinnie levels the gun at her.

"Seven rounds," he says. "Two for him"—he points the gun at Ger, then swings it back to her—"and the rest for you if you makes any sudden move."

Blood trickles down her face from a cut above her eye, drips off her chin onto the carpet. She blinks. Vinnie waves her toward the couch, and as she shifts, the streetlight through the pulled curtain catches the face of the man holding the knife to Ger's throat.

"Troy?"

"Toffee," he says. "You made it."

Teffy's phone starts ringing somewhere in the room. She sees it by the overturned writing desk, the whale on the wall arching over its glow. From where she stands she can see Ellie's name flashing on the screen.

"Sure they'll call back," says Troy.

"But will I be here?" she mutters, wondering how the hell Troy got off the island. She remembers the diver's mask between them in Mitt's taxi. But there's no way anybody would be able to swim that distance, she thinks. That's miles of open sea between St. Mark's and the mainland.

"I figured you'd still be out looking for me," Vinnie says to her.

"Who told you that?" she says—and Vinnie nods at Ger in the La-Z-Boy.

"Stuckless here is full of information," Troy says. "Pump him full of dog tranquilizer and he'll tell you just about anything." He knocks Ger's head with his free hand. "Won't you?"

Ger holds up a finger, trying to say something, but Troy tells him to stay still, and Teffy watches as Vinnie steps to the side of the La-Z-Boy, next to the curtained window, casting Troy's face in shadow. Vinnie's back is to Ger and

Troy, and Ger is fighting to look at her now, blinking against the sedative in his system—Troy's knife scraping his neck like a straight razor.

"Does Dougie know where you are?" she says to Vinnie.

"He's a good kid," Vinnie says. "Can't tell cherry pits from sheep shit but he does what he's told. Mostly. Probably chasing tail. Or up to the Sobeys bumming smokes."

Troy says, "Vinnie tells me his kid was in the trunk of his cab when Stuckless here—"

"When he tried to strangle me," Vinnie cuts in.

"*You* tried to kill Vinnie?" Teffy fixes on Ger.

"It's nnnnnot what you thhhink?" Ger slurs.

"Oh, it is," Vinnie says. "But don't worry. Stuckless here was just trying to protect you. After all, murdering your buddies, that kinda stuff you don't tell the family."

"It can be upsetting," Troy says, "when they learns what fish you actually split for a living. Isn't that right, Stuckless?"

Ger tries to swallow against the knife blade pressed to his throat and Teffy gapes at him as he struggles to speak. "You seriously tried to kill Dougie's dad with Dougie in the fucking trunk?"

Vinnie laughs and spits again. "You know, that might've been the one time my kid's ever done something halfway useful."

Teffy turns on Vinnie. "He runs your fucking meth!" she snaps and Vinnie's eyes widen in amusement. "And he nicks you tranquilizers to go after the only two people who actually care what happens to him."

"You seems to have a sweet spot for him," Vinnie says. "Kinda young for you, isn't he? Or maybe you likes 'em young and well hung."

"Go fuck yourself!" she says. "And you!" She turns on Ger, Troy's knuckles at his chin. "You tried to kill Dougie's dad, *then* you let Dougie bring you *chicken*? Let him crawl through our window and sit on our kitchen counter?"

Troy clears his throat. "Seems you have some explaining to do, Stuckless." He grabs a fistful of Ger's hair. "Probably a lot he hasn't told you, Toffee. Like half the shit he did on my payroll. I'll tell you this, though: what he tossed the court to convict me—to set my business back six years—that was surface-level bullshit." He yanks Ger's hair, draws a nick of blood with the knife. "Isn't that right, Stuckless?"

She stares at Ger as he tries to push his doped body up in the La-Z-Boy to ease the knife's pressure on his neck. "Teffy," he says. "I—"

"Did you think for one second about Dougie?" she snaps.

Vinnie kicks Ger's knee and Troy says, "Trying to repeat your date with Critch, hey Stuckless?" He glances down at Ger, then raises his eyes to Teffy standing shirtless by the couch across the room. "Your boy here got in good with me, Toffee." He gives Ger's hair a sharp yank. "But it was Vinnie who taught him the ropes."

Vinnie smiles. "Taught Stuckless *and* Critchy how to move product."

"Like your coleslaw crystal," Teffy says.

Troy cuts Vinnie a sharp look. "You're what now?"

Vinnie just laughs it off. Says, "Fuckin loudmouth kid," and pulls a black cylinder from his back pocket. Weighs it in his left hand, the gun in his right.

Teffy nods at the cylinder. "And what else did you teach them?"

Vinnie grins and twists the black cylinder onto the muzzle of his handgun. *A silencer*, she thinks—and Vinnie aims the silenced gun at Ger's crotch. Says, "I taught them how to get information. How and where to hit so as not to leave any bruises."

"And did you practice on Dougie?"

Vinnie nudges Ger's limp leg. "Likes 'em scrappy, don't ya, Stuckless?"

Teffy takes a step toward him but Vinnie flicks the gun's safety off and holds up his other hand. Raises a finger and nods to the couch behind her. "Quietly," he says and she steps back and he flicks the safety back on.

Troy pulls Ger's head back so he can stare Ger in the face. Teffy expects to see anger in Troy's eyes, snarling hate. But his straight lips betray nothing. "When you went against me," he says, "I knew it'd be a fight. And I knew you knew some of my . . . weaknesses, we'll say. But I play the long game. You never understood that. Always wanted it yesterday. But I've learned to wait. To plan. That's how I got out, you know. Out of the shithole I was born into. Same as you. I watched. Watched and knew exactly what people wanted. Once you know that, Stuckless, you own them. Remember me telling you that? You supply their demand. Taxis and pills. Girls, or whatever they're into. My old man liked little boys, you see. Thought I wouldn't say anything. But the thought of me saying something chewed him out from underneath. Made him . . . pliable. And I made him pay. You always gotta make 'em pay. I taught you that, Stuckless."

"We don't owe you anything," Teffy says. "Ger served his time."

"Sure. But somebody has to pay for St. Mark's, Toffee."

"And Vinnie?" Teffy says. "What does he owe you? Why's he here?"

"Vinnie's taking over my townie operations."

"And where're you going?"

"I get on a ship tonight and go on. New town, new gig. A gift really. That's how I'm seeing it. You gave me a gift, Toffee. A chance to get off this fucking island."

"If you have a ship waiting," she says, "why'd you stop here?"

"To make sure you two aren't gonna come after me. Because that's something I can imagine Stuckless here doing. That or fucking with Vinnie's business. We both have a vested interest in . . . resolving past grievances."

Ger swallows against the knife. "You're finished," he chokes, voice dry as rasping leaves. "You put everything on St. Mark's." He stares up at Troy's hardened face. "You're so fucked you don't even know it." He cracks a stoned grin. "That's why—"

"That's why you're here, isn't it?" Teffy cuts in. "You got nothing except taking it out on us. The whole island is looking for you—"

"They're looking for me on St. Mark's," Troy says. "Not here."

"How did you get off the island then?"

"Your man Jake. He owed me after letting you slip by."

"Then you're free and clear," she says. "Why'd you come here?" She nods at Ger. "Is taking him out worth the risk?" Ellie comes to mind suddenly, and Teffy realizes the old artist is due to evict them soon. But the key's still in her pocket. Not under the brick by the front door. "A cop's comin by," she lies. "Tonight. Wants to question us. She'll find you—"

"She'll find Stuckless." Troy doesn't look at Teffy. Just keeps staring at Ger, like a surgeon deciding where to start the first incision. He lifts the knife and presses the tip against Ger's clenched teeth. Clicks the tip against a yellowed incisor. "Open up, Stuckless."

Ger shivers his head *no*.

Troy taps again and Vinnie clicks the safety off, gun still trained on Ger's crotch. "Either open your mouth," Troy says, "and swallow what I feeds you, or Vinnie does to you what your girlfriend did to Ike Battersea. You remember Ike—our North Sydney guy?"

Ger twists his head to see Teffy, teeth still clenched against Troy's knife.

Troy looks at her now, at her bra and the scabbed cut he left on her stomach. "You haven't told him yet, have you, Toffee?" The barest hint of a smile on his stubbled face. Then to Ger he says, "Your girlfriend cut off Ike Battersea's balls. That's right. In his own house. Then she took a pound of my heroin—"

"He force-fed it to me!" Teffy hisses, her skin crawling with Troy's eyes on her, muscles tense trying not to cover up or clench her hands. Trying to keep her hands open, arms ready, like her Wing Chun instructor taught her.

Be ready, now. Be ready.

Troy taps Ger's teeth with the knife. Says, "If you don't open your mouth, Stuckless, Vinnie's gonna un-man you. See if you can handle it better than Battersea."

"Ger," Teffy whispers, her own jaw clentched. "Don't—"

But Ger opens his mouth.

"You remember this game, don't you?" Troy says as he slips the knife slowly between Ger's teeth. Scrapes it over Ger's back molars and slices out slowly—carefully—until Ger's left cheek tents against the blade. "This is how we gets what we want."

Blood dribbles from the corner of Ger's mouth.

"You wanted to make this personal," Troy says. "So I'm supplying your demand, Stuckless. We finish our business tonight. Then I go on. And you— you're a dog that needs putting down." He leans closer to Ger's face. "A little Brow-born bitch."

Vinnie smiles. "Like your Saint Teresa."

"She indicted you in a journal she left," Teffy says, trying to think of anything to stall that knife slicing through Ger's cheek. "Didn't know that, did you, Vinnie?" She tries to catch Troy's eye too, but he's fixed on his knife in Ger's mouth. She remembers how Troy sawed off Ger's ear. He'll do it here she thinks. He'll cut Ger's smile to his cheekbone. *Say something!* "Teresa gave the journal to someone she trusted. Before you killed her—you and Ben Critch."

Vinnie clucks his tongue. Laughs and flicks the safety on. Then off. "Teresa ever tell ya, Stuckless, that she was sucking off Critch for nickel rocks? In back of my cab on our way out to O'Shea's." He kicks Ger's limp leg. Did you not know that, Stuckless?"

Teffy hears the safety click, clocks it, and says, "Did you know it was O'Shea seven years ago, when you were driving Teresa out to Portugal Cove?"

"Sure," Vinnie says, "but he was paying Hopper there serious hush money."

"You got your cut," Troy says.

"Given what you gave me," Vinnie says, "O'Shea musta been paying you hand over fist, 'cause I knows you didn't give me the tenth you said you did."

Troy stares Vinnie down. "You got yours."

Vinnie smirks and says, "I was supposed to get a cut of what came through St. Mark's too, remember?"

Troy nods at Teffy. "She's half the reason the deal fell through. You want to stay in business in this town—take over running my show—you don't want a loose end like her. Or Stuckless." He eases his grip and slides the knife out of Ger's mouth. Teffy lets her held breath whistle through her teeth.

So he's not going to cut Ger open. What then?

Vinnie looks from Troy to Teffy, silencer still trained on Ger's crotch. Smirking at Teffy, he says to Troy, "So ... him first, right? Then her?" He flicks the safety off.

"Make it look like he turned the gun on himself," Troy says.

"Okay," Vinnie says.

Then he raises the gun and shoots.

Teffy blinks.

No flash. No gunshot crack. But she knows Vinnie fired. Because Troy was there one minute, behind Ger's La-Z-Boy. Knife in hand. Then the gun kicked Vinnie's fist and Troy's head snapped sideways and his body slumped out of sight behind the La-Z-Boy, the blood splash on the wall the only sign he'd been there at all.

"So this is gonna be a little trickier," Vinnie says. "But I think Ger offing himself in the end is still the best bet. Fuck knows why, but let the RNC figure it out, hey?" He nudges Ger's knee and Ger slumps a little lower in the La-Z-Boy, fighting to keep his eyes open, arms slack at his sides. Vinnie turns to Teffy, his back to Ger—and Teffy, still in shock from seeing a man shot in the face, glances from the gore-smeared wall to Ger's bloodshot eyes. His eyes open now. Now that Vinnie's back is to him.

Okay, Stuckless, she thinks, *now what?*

A nod from Ger and she tries to think of what to say. But she just saw a man blown away. *What to say? What to say?*

Just keep Vinnie's eyes on you.

"Do you know"—she starts—"do you know what O'Shea had her doing in that house?" That's right, she thinks, keep him talking till Ellie shows up. *Sure, and then what?* "Did she tell you what she was at in there?"

"No," Vinnie says. "Critch and I speculated, sure. But she was the ATM. Don't need to know how an ATM works. Just as long as it spits out bills. She didn't say, we didn't ask. We were professional like that."

"With Teresa?"

"That's right."

"And that included strangling her?" Teffy sees Ger lick the blood at the corner of his mouth. Sees him blink. *Or is it a wink?* She takes a half-step toward Vinnie and says, "Did professional include dumping her body?" She wants Vinnie close to her so she can knock him back into Ger—into the belt Ger's slowly drawing loose of his jeans.

Keep him talking, she thinks and takes another step.

Vinnie raises the gun to her face. "No closer," he says, the silencer close enough she can smell it. She backs off and Ger pulls the belt free of the last loop. Lays it across his lap.

"The one fact you're missing," Vinnie says, flicking the safety on, then off, "and I don't think even Stuckless knows this, is that I didn't kill Teresa. Neither did Ben."

"So it was Markus?"

"That's what Critch and I thought at first, when we showed up to collect her and O'Shea was fuckin crying in his garage. Kept asking us what he should do—'What should I do? What should I do?'—saying he'd pay us if we helped him."

"What did he do to her?" Teffy says.

"That's the thing," Vinnie says. "*He* didn't do anything. She'd brought pills with her and convinced him to do some before they got into it."

To get him strung out, Teffy thinks *So she could set her camera up again. Get another sex tape to blackmail him with.*

Vinnie sniffs. "O'Shea said he passed out watching her get ready. Apparently he liked to watch her get off while she—"

"While she choked herself."

Vinnie cocks his head. "How do you know that?"

"How do *you* know that?" she fires back.

"The kinky fucker spilled the whole thing asking us to help him."

Teffy sees Ger pull the belt tight between his fists. Says, "She took a video and was set to use it against O'Shea." Teffy keeps her eyes on Vinnie's face. "Did you know that?" She can see that's news to him. "Teresa had video. Even coded the journal, afraid one of you lot would find it and rat her out to. . . ." She stares at Troy's blood on the wall. Spattered like paint. Like Ellie's paint. Ellie. Ellie will be here any moment and she'll—

What? She'll do what?

Ger wraps the ends of the belt around each fist. Nods her back to Vinnie. *Focus, girl, focus.*

"Well," Vinnie chuckles, "all I knows is me and Critch came into the room and found her blue on the bed. O'Shea said that when he came to he started freaking out 'cause she was hanging over him. Shit down her legs. Probably so fucked up on pills she just started into whatever their routine was but choked herself out." Vinnie drops the gun slightly, flicks the safety on, then off. On, then off. "Nobody killed her," he says. "Dumb bitch killed herself."

"Who gave her the pills, though?"

"Critch. On the drive over."

"For a blow job?"

"I don't think you bounce backwards on someone's lap for a blowjob," he says.

"And Markus paid you to get rid of her body?" She sees Ger tighten the belt behind Vinnie's back, looping it one last time around each fist.

Vinnie says, "He paid Troy to keep us quiet. But a favor like that puts you permanently in the pocket of someone like Hopper. Trust me, I know. If I hadn't shot the straight-lipped fucker, I'd still owe him, right?"

"So when Troy needed back into business—"

"He called O'Shea, and O'Shea helped call in favors to get a shipment ashore. A big one." Vinnie flicks the safety on. Wipes his nose with his gun hand. Sniffs. "Big. Fuckin. Shipment." He clips each word. "And we all knows how that played out, don't we, Stuckless?" Vinnie goes to look over his shoulder at Ger, but Teffy says:

"You'd be dead now if not for Dougie. You know that, right?"

Vinnie ogles her chest, his head half turned toward Ger. Wobbles the gun as if considering the point. Or the view. "You know Troy was surprised when I showed him this gun. Every one and their uncle has a rifle on this island, sure. But a Smith and Wesson .22 compact, suppressor-ready?" He whistles. "That impressed him. So, he made it part of the plan tonight. Walked me through what we were gonna do, step by step."

"And what about that last step?" She glances at the blood-splashed wall, at Ger giving her the *ready-now* nod. "Was that part of the plan?"

"Like he said. Some dogs need putting down."

"And where'll this put you?"

Vinnie sops his face with the back of his gun-hand, his fist trembling slightly.

See that—he's jittered. Shook up more than he's letting on.

"Ha," he says, "I just—"

And the doorbell rings. It rings again and Teffy hears Ellie's voice outside the curtained window—"Teffy!" Ellie calls. "Teffy Byrne? You in there? It's pissing out here and you have my friggin keys!"

Vinnie raises a cut hand and mouths, *Don't move.*

Three sharp knocks.

Mike's voice this time: "Teffy? Come on, girl—it's wet out here!"

She sees Ger grip the belt, pulling the leather taught around his fists. She shakes her head. Vinnie takes two steps toward her, the gun's silencer three fingers from her face now.

"I'll shoot if I have to," he whispers.

"I doubt it."

He flicks the safety off to show he's serious. Goes to look over his shoulder at Ger, but Teffy presses her left eye against the silencer and spits, "You're a fuckin coward, Vinnie Coles."

Vinnie blinks. She can feel his fist shaking the gun against her eye.

What the fuck are you doing? He's going to—

The doorbell rings and Ger stands—Mike and Ellie knocking hard, banging their fists against the door and calling out to them. Vinnie straightens, steps back—and Ger hooks his belt over Vinnie's head and yanks it tight to his throat as Teffy pushes the gun up.

The gun goes off, blasting the ceiling. Ger crosses his hands over his head, spins his back to Vinnie's, choking the belt tight as Vinnie fires off three wild rounds. Ger yells and lifts his feet, the belt leather cutting into his hands, his full weight on Vinnie's neck and Vinnie straining forward, trying to toss Ger over his shoulder—firing again at Teffy's face. But Teffy rolls off the couch into the hall, landing on the M&Ms and bursting the bag.

The candies explode across the floor.

Ellie bangs on the door. "What's going on in there? I can hear you banging around!" she yells as Vinnie bulls toward Teffy—Ger on Vinnie's broad back yelling now and fisting the belt tighter. Vinnie gurgles and skids on the scattered M & Ms, crashes to one knee in the doorway—fires again—the bullet whizzing into the wall by Teffy's face as she reaches for the deadbolt.

She grabs the gun's silencer with her other hand, bends it down the hall as Vinnie pulls the trigger. It goes off and Vinnie backhands her across the face with it, gouging deeper the cut at the corner of her eye.

Ger finds his feet, Vinnie gasps, and Ger yanks the belt tight again. Vinnie strains against it, trying to haul Ger onto his back—toss him over his shoulder to relieve the pressure.

Vinnie presses the gun to Teffy's eye again.

"Ger!" she yells and—

Click.

Ger plants his feet and lunges forward—and Vinnie tries to throw himself back but Teffy hooks her arm under the belt and yanks Vinnie's head to hers, bracing her feet either side of the living room doorway.

Ger strains, Vinnie's eyes bugged red as Teffy feels him shiver and flail. She holds him there. Holds him and flicks the pen from her pocket. Fists and clicks it. Aims for that bulged artery in Vinnie's neck—the mark she missed on Ike—and she stabs him. Shocks his eyes wide. Vinnie boxes her ears and grabs a fistful of her hair.

She grits her teeth. Reaches for the pen again, her other arm still hooked behind Vinnie's head, holding the guy's purple face to hers, but Ger yanks on the belt and Vinnie chomps at her reaching hand, trying to catch her fist in his teeth.

Mike boots the door, then throws his body against it. "Open the door!" Ellie yells. "Come on! Open the door!" she screams as sirens rip down Long's Hill—and Teffy thinks, *The cops! She's called the cops!* as Mike boots the latch again.

"Use this brick!" Ellie yells—and Mike breaks the door's latch with the brick under which Teffy was supposed to have left the key. He shoulders through the door, smashing it into Teffy's side. She groans and Mike sees a beefy guy with a pen in his neck clawing Teffy in the hallway—Ger trying to strangle the guy from behind.

"The fuck?" he says—but Ellie just grabs the brick from his hand and heaves it at Vinnie's skull, knocking him limp.

Ger scrambles to disentangle himself from Vinnie's slumped body, from the belt cut into both his hands. And together with Mike and Ellie they haul Vinnie off Teffy, their wet boots pinballing bloody M&Ms down the hallway as the cops arrive.

~ 46 ~

I T'S INTO MAY NOW, four months into a new year, and winter still
clings to St. John's in desiccated snow drifts, clumps of skin melting off
old road bones.

Teffy is returning from a walk around Quidi Vidi Lake after visiting Ger
at the penitentiary, Anna, their daughter, asleep in a harness salted with road
grit. Teffy turns the corner onto Livingstone and sees a woman in a beige
Carhartt construction coat by the entrance to her place, the woman kicking
snow off her boots against Teffy's sunny orange door. Teffy slushes toward
the woman, about to ask if she can help when she sees it's Ellie Strickland.

"Is this a landlord visit?" she says.

Ellie eyes her crossing the street: Teffy soaked from the knees down
and splashed with street muck from passing cars, her hand on her baby's
head shawled in a newly knitted toque and warm blanket. "See it's still winter
in town," Ellie says.

"And on St. Mark's?" Teffy glances from the bright orange door to the
spot on the street where Ger used to park his rust-bucket Ford, a sudden
ache catching in her throat.

"Might surprise you," Ellie says, "but moving back to a small island
in the North Atlantic in the middle of November isn't in fact my worst life
decision."

"And Daryl"—Teffy smiles—"how's he doing?"

"Prickly as an old whore's egg. So, normal. For him."

"Must be glad you're back home, though," Teffy says. She recalls the
shift and grind of that altar overhead in that drafty island church, Daryl's boot
kicking aside the final fistful of his dead sister in Teffy's satchel.

"I can tell you," Ellie says, "living separately has made being together a hell of lot easier." She puffs out the oversized coat with hands thrust deep in her pockets, and Teffy sees by the coat's size that it must be Daryl's.

Teffy nods. "You have your art and he—"

"He has *Hockey Night in Canada.*"

They both laugh as Teffy pulls her keys from her pocket and asks why Ellie didn't use the key under the brick. "You could be in where it's warm." Teffy pushes in the orange door and the house's rare warmth rushes past her into the street. It's a drafty house and wet as late winter snow, but warm enough, she thinks. If you're huddled on the couch under a thick blanket. "I know I've said it before"—she heels her boots off inside the door and motions for Ellie to come in—"but thank you for renting me this place. Really. It's a godsend."

"Well, you, me, and God'll have to discuss a monthly rate," Ellie says. "After you're done editing the memoir, that is."

"Sure," Teffy says, as Ellie closes the door behind herself. Teffy has known the monthly rate is coming. That's why she's stretched out the editing of Ellie's memoir this long.

"So have you got it done?" Ellie asks. "The book? I was in town and thought I'd drop by to see how it's coming along."

"What're you in town for?" Teffy stalls, glancing down at Anna who shifts and turns her wee head the other way against Teffy's chest. "Shhh," Teffy soothes, "shhh."

Ellie says, "I'm in town doing a couple of days of sensitivity training. With the RNC."

"You and Marjorie Petty?"

Ellie nods, placing a paint-spattered hand on the wall near a salt circle left by Teffy's hand, from all the times this winter she's leaned in that same spot to kick off her boots, her other hand cupping Anna's head as she's doing now.

"I can send you the file end of the week," Teffy says.

"You said that last week too."

Teffy stays in the hallway as Ellie wanders into the living room. The old artist takes in the handiwork of her unfinished mural, the whale diving beneath the bobbing punt, smudged out in streaks of slush-gray charcoal. "There's a part of the book," Teffy says. "A scene near the beginning that keeps hooking me back."

Ellie glances her way. "What scene?"

"When you were a girl, watching caribou cross the bay." Teffy imagines her front stoop view, between houses, of the gray harbour below. She thinks of that scene early on in Ellie's book. A herd of winter-lean caribou crossing St. Mark's harbour to avoid the village, skittishly sliding across the thin ice on a sunless winter's dawn, picking their way slowly so as to avoid scars of open water.

"You mean where the calf goes through the ice?"

"Yeah," Teffy says, shivering in her wet coat. "I keeps coming back to the description of her knuckling her way back onto the ice. Alone. Trying to get purchase with knee-joint and hoof. The rest of the herd just watching her struggle."

"So, what do you want me to do with it?" Ellie asks.

"I think you can hook back into that moment—that image—in the final chapter, when you describe life since . . . well, since the—"

"Since the explosion?"

Teffy can still see Markus' body smoking through the air. She blinks against the shattering of the windshield in her mind, against the shock she felt the day she heard that Markus had died in hospital. "Anyhow," she says, "I think you should weave that image back in at the end."

"So I'm the one gone through the ice, is that it?"

"The one pulling yourself up. Alone."

"And Marjorie Petty?"

"Maybe her too," Teffy says, though that's been a sore point for her since Ellie and Marjorie cut her out of the art show project because of what she did with Stefany Strickland's ashes. That and they got a reporter from the *Telegram* to write the story about the NEXT program. Editing the memoir in exchange for a few month's rent is a pity project, Teffy knows. A way for Ellie to keep her at arm's length while still offering a helping hand. A grudging Good Samaritan act. Teffy licks her lip and tastes road salt. Pictures that young calf flailing in the frigid sea, snorting slush. She knows what it is to slip beneath the slob ice of everyone's general concern.

After some thought, Ellie says, "I think Marjorie will go for it."

"I'll work it in, then," Teffy says, shushing Anna, who's begun to wake. She steps into the living room behind Ellie. Sees through the front window her own wet mood and wants to say to Ellie that she admires her. The work she does, advocating in workshops, art, and on stage for better treatment of people in the sex trade. She admires the old woman's persistence. The straight line of Ellie's lips that can curl into a wry smile or break open in sudden, teary-eyed laughter. Lips just as quick to praise as to tell you to fuck off. She hopes one day for Ellie's praise.

She wishes Ellie was her friend.

Anna stirs on Teffy's chest as she follows—over Ellie's shoulder—the unfinished arc of that half-painted whale on the living room wall, thinking that losing the NEXT story and betraying Ellie's trust ranks up there with her biggest regrets.

Right behind failing to visit Fin in prison.

She asks Ellie if she can help loosen the harness, and as Ellie unclicks the buckle on her back, Teffy holds Anna to her chest and slips the carrier from her shoulders.

"She sleeps like the dead," Ellie says—and Teffy can see in the sudden wrinkle of Ellie's brow that she regrets the choice of words.

Anna bobs her head, trying to wake, but Teffy bounces her gently, shushing her by singing, "Ladybird, Ladybird, fly away home, your house is on fire and your children are gone. All except one, and her name is Anna, and she doused the fire with a rotten banana." Ellie's face softens and Teffy feels Anna fall back to sleep in her arms. She rocks from foot to foot, still favoring that bad knee, taking in Ellie's spiked white hair and the artist's unfinished whale on the wall, the great beast swimming into a half-sketched future behind the ratty couch.

Ellie looks at her and Teffy says, "I can't remember, is white the absence or the presence of all colors?"

"The absence," Ellie says. "You can't mix any colors to make it." She takes a deep breath. "I like the revised lullaby, by the way. Anna, rotten banana. I like it."

"The older version ends with the Ladybird's children burning in a fire," she says and sees Ellie wince, wondering if she too is thinking of Markus's house on fire, Ger's distant voice screaming through her cellphone, asking if the baby's alright.

"I can see why you wanted to change the words," Ellie says.

The song's original fiery ending is often on the tip of Teffy's tongue, though. It's the truer version, she thinks—the more likely way of things. "Ashes to ashes, we all fall down," she mutters.

"So you sunny-up the song for your girl?"

Teffy nods. Yes, she sunnies it up for Anna. Sure. Paints it Sunkist orange against the endless dead of winter in this miserable place. She sings in her head, *Bounce-bounce, bounce-bounce the baby.* "Gotta be happy, don't I?"

She says this more to Anna than to Ellie, but sees Ellie shift and, sensing her discomfort, says, "Perky at least. Halfway hopeful."

"A lot of responsibility being a mom," Ellie says. "I wouldn't know myself, of course. Always thought Stefany and me would suffer it together."

Teffy sniffs the top of her daughter's head. Road salt and new skin. Realizes that's the first time Ellie's brought up Stefany without trying to blame her for what was done to her sister-in-law's remains. It's the first time Teffy hasn't felt helpless in the face of Ellie's anger.

Almost as if she's been forgiven.

Almost.

She angles her head and says of the whale, "I like how it resembles a woman swimming when I looks at it like this."

Ellie tilts her head too and says, "Blur your eyes, though, and it's a chalked body print at a crime scene."

Teffy squints and sees the court photos of the alley in which Teresa was found. And who was responsible for that death? she thinks. Who took the first shot? Was it Ben Critch giving her those pills in exchange for that last ride? She looks at the back of Ellie's tilted head. Or was it Markus using Teresa, repeatedly, and being so stupid as to knock himself into a drugged sleep while she asphyxiated above him?

Or was it her choice?

That's what Teffy can't fathom.

"She was cunning, though," Ellie says. "Teresa, I mean. Smart enough to blackmail Markus and create that stickman code."

"And separate the password from the Gmail account."

"But she gave the journal to Marjorie," Ellie says. "And she knew who Marjorie was. What does that say about her—about what she wanted?"

"I don't know," Teffy says, shutting up the very questions she often finds herself asking. Like, did Teresa just want to screw more money out of Markus? Or did she want out of Troy's shallow world altogether, the storm-surge thrill gone out of it? "Ger said she had a head for math."

Ellie looks back at her. "For math—really?"

"Said she could skim off Troy's cut and fix the books so he didn't know."

"Handy skill, I guess, in that line of work."

"I keeps wondering what she could have done with it, though."

"But did she *want* to do something with it?"

Teffy doesn't answer. Simply stares at the wall. At that big stretch of unknowable whiteness. All that possibility—gone. Punched through with bullet holes from Vinnie's gun. Eventually she says, "What do you think Marjorie would say?"

"Marjorie says her work is simply to help people in the trade regain control of their lives if they've lost control."

"Or if control has been taken from them."

"That's right," Ellie says.

"So what did Teresa want?"

"We can't know, can we?"

"If she'd known the way she'd die—?"

"She didn't know the way she'd die."

Teffy thinks of that St. Mark's whale following the fish in that freak storm surge. Following the fish or some primordial instinct to climb up out of the waters it was born into. Ellie wrote in the memoir of how prehistoric whales used to crawl up onto beaches to breed and give birth. She wrote that maybe there was this memory deep in that slaughtered whale's instinct that drove it to try and climb that rock shelf to get away from Daryl's speedboat.

To escape.

Teffy knows from her group home story that Troy offered escapes to kids as young as fourteen. All they needed to do was run his errands all over town. Ben Critch had been one of those kids. And Ger. Teresa and Vinnie too.

And Vinnie's after getting Dougie into it.

"Not everyone is a fighter like you," Fin told her once.

She shivers, realizing she's still wet from her walk home, the baby carrier still belted around her waste and hanging down her front like a soaked apron. "Can't believe it's May and still the dead of winter," she says.

Ellie laughs. "You're a Newfoundlander and you're just realizing that now?"

"I gotta get into something dry," Teffy says. "Can I make you a cup of tea before you go?" She recalls the *tink tink tink* of Fin's spoon against her favorite mug. Bootlegged brew, he called it. Strong enough to stand a spoon up in it.

"Tempting," Ellie says. "But I have to be up to the police station soon."

"Two bags a cup," Teffy offers teasingly. "And a shot of something besides, if you needs it." It's a down home offer, and she sees Ellie appreciates it. But the truth is, they've chased up everything they could possibly talk about. Fired off what thoughts they're willing to share with each other. And that's it.

So Teffy steps back to let Ellie cross into the hallway, and they exchange some niceties, and then Ellie is gone, the door shut tight behind her.

Teffy cups Anna's head in her hand, wondering suddenly if she and Ger will find each other again, like Ellie and Daryl did in that island church. Desecrate the altar of everyone's expectations. She wonders if that's even possible now: them staying together through Ger's sentence which has yet to be set. Could be another lifetime before she sees him this side of that razor-wired wall. *Are you sure you want that?*

I do, she thinks. And she does. She wants Ger back. Wants him fiercely. Stupidly even. And, remarkably, in a way that now feels different from how she's long wanted back her friendship with Fin. But maybe that's because Fin is stopping by today.

Soon, in fact, she thinks as she gently rests Anna in the middle of the bed. She strips out of her wet things and pulls on track pants and a hoodie. *Warm up first,* she tells herself, *then change before he gets here.* It's hard to believe Fin's actually coming. The first time in almost ten years that they'll see each other.

"I'll even bring my husband," he said over the phone.

"You're married?" she said, smiling.

"I've moved on," he said.

"And you're happy?"

She wasn't sure if it was static or a chuckle. But then he said, "I'll see you at three." And it's almost twenty to three now. Teffy glances at Anna asleep on the bed, still bundled in her winter clothes. The dummy slips from the girl's lips, and Teffy heads down the hall to the kitchen to make that tea. Maybe top it off with a shot of tequila.

As she pours water into the kettle, she thinks of how she's not touched Ger's side of the bed in a month, save to change the sheets. She hasn't really touched anything of his since his arrest in June, the same night Vinnie was rushed to Emergency Care and they found Troy was still breathing behind the La-Z-Boy.

She turns off the faucet, shaking her head at Vinnie not being the crackshot he thought he was. Even at point-blank range. *Fucker.* The bullet apparently caught the outside edge of Troy's left eye socket. Knocked him out cold, Parsons said. But aside from losing the eye, he recovered and is in maximum security somewhere on the mainland.

Vinnie, on the other hand, is in Her Majesty's by the lake. With Ger.

She sets the kettle to boil, thinking on why the cops showed up that night—*to arrest Ger.* Ellie hadn't called them. They were already on their way. Because they'd found Ger's fingerprint on Ben Critch's eyelid.

She leans against the counter and finds herself, as she often does in this part of the house, imagining Ben's apartment, moments after Ben slumped dead against Ger's chest. She watches Ger through Ben's dead eyes as Ger scours the apartment. Watches him stop at the door on his way out and turn back to her—to Ben. He crosses the room and crouches by the body of his friend. Then, slowly, he thumbs open an eyelid.

To see what, though?

In all her visits to Her Majesty's, Ger hasn't said why he touched Ben after he'd scrubbed the rest of the apartment down with Ajax. They don't talk about Vinnie Coles or Ben Critch. Or Connor Moffet, whose body has not yet been found. They don't talk about those things because their talk is always "Anna this and Anna that." Nothing of the world outside the small fire that is their baby girl's life. Not even when it hit the news that Markus O'Shea had died in his sleep, and that his entire estate had been left to the islanders of St. Mark's.

She knows that Ger wanted Markus to suffer.

"He did suffer," she says to the empty room. He did. For months he hung on, breathing through a ventilator. Wheezing to stay alive. And there's part of Teffy that thinks at least some of that pain was deserved. Not because he hired Teresa for sex. And not that Markus hid being a john from everyone, including Ellie.

Ellie is allowed to be livid at him for that, she thinks.

No, the knife's sharp edge for Teffy is that Markus treated Teresa like human garbage and disposed of her body to protect his good reputation. For that, he deserved to have his house blown up in his face. How do you just decide to do something like that anyway? she wonders. Just throw a life away? As if Teresa had no family to mourn her.

As if no one would miss her.

But Ger missed her. Terribly. Enough to kill those responsible for dumping her body. Or try to. Teffy thinks of Ger's actions—the murders he committed or tried to commit—as a way of screaming that Teresa's life mattered. That no matter who she was or what she was into or what she chose to do with her body, she was not trash. Her life meant something.

Of course, as with almost everything else, Ger hasn't talked with Teffy about his role in all this, but she thinks he must've known Teresa's Gmail account and that he'd translated the journal long before she did. If that's what led him to Ben Critch's apartment, then he would've known the journal's contents by the time he called her in Grand Falls.

Was he in Ben's apartment, though, when he made that call? Had he already water-boarded the St. Mark's connection out of Ben Critch? And was Critch coughing up a lung in some other room while Ger talked cheerily about seeing her soon on St. Mark's—the murder yet to come?

He had sounded elated that night.

Thrilled with himself.

But they got his fingerprint on Ben's eyelid. And then, once in custody, they scrubbed his hands and found traces of ammonium nitrate, which linked him to Critch's apartment and to the bomb at O'Shea's place. That and witnesses remembered seeing his rust-bucket Ford in Portugal Cove shortly before the blast that blew Markus through the windshield of Mike's truck.

Right into Teffy's lap, Markus's singed head next to her pregnant belly.

And how're you gonna explain all this to Anna?

The kettle whistles and she realizes they haven't talked about any of this. Not a word. And she's been to see him every week since his incarceration.

Every week, she thinks, testing the edge of her mug with her tongue. Every week, except two weeks ago. Two weeks ago, she showed up for a visit and got told Gerard Stuckless wasn't seeing anyone. Like Ger would rather sleep than visit with his newborn daughter. She told the guard that was bullshit but he just shrugged. Nodded at the exit and said nothing of the fact that Ger had been pulled into the inmates's chapel and beaten until his eyes puffed shut.

There's been no investigation yet. And from what she's heard of Her Majesty's, she doubts there will be one. The tea burns her tongue but she takes another gulp, feeling it sear all the way down. Vinnie is doing fine inside. Just fine. Though the voice on him now is like driftwood dragged through beach rocks. But he's alive. Incarcerated, like Ger, but very much alive. And not a mark on him, she's heard—save for the scar she left on his neck with her pen.

Her phone vibrates in her back pocket and she sets down her cup and steps into the bathroom so she can close the door and answer the call from Ger's lawyer.

"Tim," she says, "what did you find out about the guys who jumped Ger?"

"The guards saw nothing apparently."

"Nothing?"

"And the camera in there had a towel thrown over it."

"It's Vinnie Coles," she says.

"Or half a dozen guys Ger screwed when he went against Troy."

"Somebody saw something, Tim. His face was a plum today. Couldn't hardly open his mouth or see me through the glass."

"I know," he says.

"Oh," she says, "were you into see him today, Tim?"

"Well, no. . . ."

"Then you don't know!" she hisses into the phone, wanting to yell at the useless tit but not wanting to wake Anna in the other room.

"Look, the Warden said this sort of thing happens. Especially with high profile inmates like Ger. It's kind of a hazing ritual."

"Are you serious?"

"It's to be expected, the warden said."

"Expected?" she says.

"Within reason."

"And what's reasonable, Tim? They've locked him up with Vinnie Coles. They'll kill him in there! He needs to be quarantined."

"They don't have the space with the over-crowding—"

"Then put him in solitary confinement! Just do something!" She ends the call and checks her phone for messages she might've missed and sees one from Fin's Corner Brook number.

Call me, it says.

It's quarter past three by her phone. Fin and his husband Theo should be pulling up any minute. Maybe they're wanting to ask if they should bring anything. No, she thinks, anticipating the question. Just bring yourselves.

She calls Fin's number and waits . . . waits . . . waits. . . .

"Hello?" Fin answers the call, his voice a slice of sunshine after months of winter's cold wet gloom.

"I saw your message," she says. "I was out with the baby." She can't tell if it's a laugh or a crackle she hears. "I'm sorry," she says. "I think we have a bad connection."

"You were out to the penitentiary," he says.

And her mouth snaps shut. "Did you—"

"I recognized you, Teffy."

"You recognized me?"

"We were at the Sobeys, in the parking lot," he says. "Theo went in to get some cheese and a bottle of wine. I told him to get a bottle of tequila too. For old times." He lets that hang. "I was having a smoke by the car when I saw you go by. Could tell it was you by your hair, even under that floppy toque."

You always obsessed about my hair, she wants to say.

"Do you visit him often?" Fin asks. "The guy you're with."

"I do," she says.

"I see."

And she hears the drop in his voice. A knife clattering on a wood floor. "It's different," she says. "I'm different now. I wouldn't do that to you again."

"Wouldn't do what again?" he says. "Would you not visit me again if I was in that same prison? Is that it?" He takes a deep breath and she can hear it whistling through his teeth. "Or would you not stab my father again with his own knife?"

"I. . . ." She tries to breathe. "I only remember you yelling at me."

"Because you killed him, Teffy. You stabbed him how many times? And on the floor of his own fishing stage. As if that would make things better."

"I wanted to make things better," she whispers.

"You killed him. In cold blood."

"He was killing you."

"Mom's death was killing me."

"I just . . . I . . . ."

"Do you not find yourself back there?"

"I'm constantly there," she says. "With you. In your dad's stage. In the church, under that altar. I remember holding you—you holding me—the both of us wrapped in your scarf."

"It's done, Teffy."

"What?"

"I said, it's done."

"So you're not—"

He laughs, and his laugh is like vinegar on an open wound. Like sour wine on the tongue. "No," he says. "Theo and I are not gonna stop by today. I wanted to. I really did."

"Because I went to see Ger? He's my baby's father, Fin."

"And I sat in a jail cell for you, Teffy. For three years. Because you were my friend. My only friend. The only person who knew everything about me. How else was I supposed to say I still loved you after what you did?"

"That's why," she whispers. "That's why I couldn't visit you. I couldn't face that."

"You mean me?"

She blinks and inhales her "Yes."

"Then you understand," he says, and ends the call.

She stares at her phone and swallows hard, a knot in her throat the size of her baby's fist. She looks in on Anna and sees her still sleeping, thank God. She's so tired suddenly, too tired to cry. Somewhere beyond tears—somewhere close to the edge of here and gone. And she doesn't know what to do. So she crosses to the kitchen and boils the kettle again.

Adds a shot of tequila to her cooling cup.

As the kettle mounts to a boil she thinks to grab a spare blanket from the bedroom, one of the original quilts salvaged from the show Markus trashed. She'll mummy herself in that ratty blanket and drop dead on the couch for an hour . . . or as long as Anna naps.

She pads softly down the hallway. Peeks in the bedroom again. Anna is still sleeping soundly, snug in her winter gear. Teffy taps the doorframe, then hears the kettle go.

"Go on! Scald some life into you," Ger would say. But what was it he said today? What did he slur through that wired jaw?

He said, "You're not helpless, maid. Go on."

But what did he mean by that? Back in the kitchen, she tops up her tequila tea with water from the kettle. Was he telling her to move on and not to wait for him, like Fin waited for her? Is that what's best for their girl—for Anna?

She walks into the front room where Ellie's half-finished mural still swims, and she sees the tiny boat there, in the corner where the street-facing wall bends into the far wall, where the whale begins to swim out of its realistic waters and into an abstracted yet-to-come. Black lines on a white gessoed wall. And on the edge of where the paint streaks out floats that solitary boat.

On the edge of here and gone.

You're not helpless, Ger said. *Go on.*

She cups her mug and feels its warmth. Then she sneaks again into the bedroom, sets the steaming cup on the bedside stand, next to her new pen, and she slips under the covers and curls around Anna. She tries to focus on her daughter, on her baby's breathing—those soft snores.

She doesn't dream, but wakes to Anna stirring. Reaches behind her to feel her mug. Some heat in it yet, so she hasn't slept long. But it's cold in here—even under the blankets. She slips out of bed and hugs herself against the damp chill.

Colder than it was in that icy visitor's room with Ger.

She rubs her arms on her way down the hall to check the thermostat. Steps into the kitchen and feels a sudden gust of wind and the bathroom door slams shut behind her.

The window by the toilet, she thinks. *But who's in the house?*

She hasn't seen Dougie in months. Not since Old Christmas Day when she spied him downtown, hitching his jeans and jogging in the opposite direction. She pulls a butcher knife from the cutting block and steps into the hall. Sidles up next to the door. Knowing only that she needs to put herself between whoever has opened that window and her baby fussing now down the hall.

She turns the knob, feels wet wind on her feet, and thrusts the door open, clanking it against the dryer. No movement in the dark. Not by the shower, hot water tank, or toilet.

She flicks on the light. Scans the room again.

But sees nothing.

Only the window wide-open, and a mauzy wind gusting through it.

She sprints to the bedroom, knife in hand, and flicks on the lights. Checks behind the door and in the closet and under the bed. But sees nothing—only Anna kicking and crying now in her snowsuit. Teffy whips around the corner into the front room. Nobody by the desk under the whale or in the window-side chair.

No one by the lamp in the corner where Vinnie jumped her that night.

They're gone, she tells herself. *Whoever it was, they're gone—*

The blanket on the couch moves.

Someone groans.

And she whips off the blanket, raises the knife above her head and hears Dougie groan, "The fuck is it?" He grabs sleepily at the blanket in her hand, until he sees the knife. "Jesus!" he screeches. "I was just crashing on your couch!"

"Dougie!" She drops the knife and takes a deep breath, hand to her throat.

"You were gonna stab me?" he says.

"'Cause you were sleeping on my couch!"

"I just needed a fuckin place—"

"But you came through the back window."

"'Cause you fuckin lock your front door."

"Which means I don't want people in my house!"

"I'm not fuckin *people*!" he spits.

"I've been jumped in this room, Dougie!"

"Yeah, by my fucking dad," he says. "I know!"

"He had a belt around my neck."

"I know!" he yells.

"So I'm just a little on edge about strange people in my house who sneak in through the back window while I'm sleeping!"

They stare at each other. In the yelling, Dougie has edged up the back of the couch and sits there. Hair grease-spiked, like he's been pulling at it. And she can smell him now. Days-old funk and he's still wearing his grimy shoes, salt and muck marking the couch.

"Why did you break in?" she says. "I have a baby sleeping in the next room."

He shrugs. Like he doesn't understand the question. "I didn't fuckin break in."

"You came through the window."

"And who else comes in that way?"

"It's still breaking in—"

"And if you climbed in your parents's window?"

"They're my family, Dougie."

"And who do you think you are to me?"

She stares at him, his face pale and streaked. "Have you been crying?"

"Fuck you!" He drags a sleeve across his face. "If not here, then where do I go?"

"Why don't you go home?"

"What home?"

"Your apartment."

"Landlord locked me out beginning of last week. Used to be I'd go to Dad's and crash a while till I got another place. Or Ger would set me up. But he's arrested for trying to kill Dad and Dad's arrested for trying to kill him and fuckin Troy Hopper—and what the fuck am I supposed to do with all that?" He looks at the knife on the floor. "You're the only person I trust."

"Dougie, I . . . ."

"You know what," he slaps his knees. "Fuck you." He steps off the couch and into the hall, bare feet squelching in wet shoes. "I don't need this," and he turns on her. "I don't need you!" The baby wails louder in the other room and he points down the hall. "And I don't need *that* either!"

"Dougie—"

He slams a fist into the wall by the door. Shakes it out and she sees plaster dust on his roughed-up knuckles. His face red and streaked and staring at her.

She looks to the knife on the floor, Anna crying louder now, and she takes a step toward him. Sees by the flinch in his shoulders that he's fighting not to back away from her. Then he just starts crying. Big sobs shaking his thin body.

She puts her arms around him. A tight squeeze and three pats on the back. Because anything else just seems weird. *It's Dougie, not—*

Not what? She rests a hand on his scruffy face. He sniffs and says he'll fuck off then. And she says, "Just text the next time, okay?"

He stops, hand on the new latch, door unlocked—and she sees his fist print in the wall. Circled by the salt of her own hand.

"Imma bring you some chicken," he mumbles, then pulls the door open and steps out into the night, wet wind clanking the door against the wall and Anna wailing in the other room.

She closes the door. Waits a sec.

Then bolts it.

In the bedroom, she picks up Anna and starts rocking her, humming "Ladybird, ladybird, fly away home" as she walks back to the bathroom, intent on a hot shower. She turns it scalding and begins undressing herself and her baby. Once the room has begun to steam she reaches in and cools the temperature a little.

"A bath to warm us both up, okay?"

She holds Anna to her chest, the baby's hands cold on her clammy skin, and she's about to step into the shower stall when she thinks of the window by the toilet.

Shut now, but did she lock it?

She steps over to peer at the latch. An old copper latch like a half moon or a boat on water. That punt in Ellie's mural. She flicks it locked, overturning the boat.

She holds her daughter tightly, thinking of how she held Fin under that high altar, trying to tell him it was necessary and that it would be okay, not knowing he would take the blame—that he would overturn her intent and say, "I killed him. I killed my dad. Teffy only found me there. Crying." And because of that he sat three years in a cell. Alone. For her.

And what has she done with that love?

Seriously, what have you done? What are you gonna do?

She cups her child's head. Feels her baby's skin on her skin, Anna's tongue dabbing her collarbone, where Ger used to kiss her, tasting the world of her body. Steam fogging the window now, condensing on the hand-printed glass—Dougie's prints—dripping down around the latch.

She looks through her fogged reflection and sees a dark figure in her backyard. Her breath snags in her throat and she grips Anna, thinking of the knife on the floor in the front room.

But she can't move, can't breathe.

All she can do is peer at the figure—what feels like a huge hand gripping her face, an arm around her neck choking her out—and she squints to see the figure's raised hands. Like she's pointing a knife at it now. That bent tree, she thinks, backlit by a light up the hill. Twisted in the smudged light. Crooked as Fin's father before she stabbed him.

The tree seems alive through the wet window, and she wants to run. She wants to run but feels herself bolted to the floor. *You're not helpless,* Ger said. *You're not helpless.* But she still can't move, thinking the smart thing to do is to leave it be, the latch. Keep it locked. Raze the dead and move on. Let Dougie find his own way.

"That's what we should do," she whispers to Anna. "That's what we should do."

But she flicks the latch and rights the boat. Blinks.

And she leaves it that way.

Acknowledgments

I STARTED THIS NOVEL IN 2012 while serving as Writer in Residence at the Bridge Studio in Deep Bay, Newfoundland and Labrador. I'd like to thank the residents of Deep Bay for their hospitality and trust; the people of Fogo Island Arts for the enriching experience; the folks of Tilting for launching my book in Foley's shed; the Kindergarteners for letting me swap stories with them; and Norm Foley for the boil-up at Cape Cove, the "styling" iceberg, and for letting me write at his kitchen table and punk his rhubarb jam.

Though some might be tempted to blame the Book of Jonah, the idea for the whale actually came from Roger Strickland, who (I think permanently) loaned me Farley Mowat's book about killing the whale. Fishery details came from notes on conversations in a Tilting shed. I won't hold anyone but myself responsible for mistakes, exaggerations, or bald-faced lies parsed out of those chicken scratches. The joke about the strong wind up the poop-hole of a cliff-side outhouse is sadly not original. I overheard it in a repurposed church outside Joe Batt's Arm. Though I managed to write it down, I never did make the teller's aquaintance. Adam Young's art, also found in that church, served as inspiration for Ellie Strickland's early work in the novel. And Paddy Barry once said I could make him into a woman in my next story if I gave him pink hair, so I made Lisetta Barry in his honor.

To the wary reader, a note: the ferry to Fogo Island is far, far safer than I make such boat rides sound in this novel. In all my times crossing, I've never had any mishaps with windshield scrapers. And no, St. Mark's is not Fogo Island. St. Mark's is a made-up place populated by made up people.

Thanks to my Iowa friends and colleagues who discussed many drafts over nearly as many drinks. Joel Westerholm, Don Wacome, and Mike Kugler, I owe you three or four. Ann Lundberg taught me that fighting to save someone, even if you fail, is worth the risk. Such risks forge lifelong friendships. Thank you, Ann. My friends at the Institute for Advanced Catholic Studies—Jenny Shank, Lisa Ampleman, Dave Griffith, Brian Volk, Gary Adler, and Kathleen Witkowska Tarr—all read early-draft chapters and offered needed encouragement. Thanks, gang. And Larry Matthews suggested I make Teffy the main character. Sound advice, as always.

In writing this book, I consulted *Rock, Paper, Sex: The Oldest Profession in Canada's Oldest City* by Kerri Cull for insight into the lives of sex workers in St. John's. Marvin McMurray filled me in on some details about blasting techniques at the Duck Pond Mine. And Janice and Javier Ortiz put me up for a month while writing.

Writing this novel has been a long, rough journey. When I started writing, Samantha and I had no children. Just a black lab named Vader. Now we have four wild kids and, sadly, no dog. Each of our kids, though, have marked this book's making in a particular way. Liam learned to walk while I finished draft one, the two of us circling that small apartment in Sioux City, figuring each other out and hiding in the laundry room when the tornado sirens sounded. Micah left sticky, mulberry fingerprints on the pages of my writing journal to remind me of sweet summer days at Whippoorwill Cottage. As Charlotte dozed in my arms, swaddled for a nap, I remember daydreaming about who'd she'd someday become. One of those daydreams turned into the little girl on the Port aux Basques ferry who said she wanted to be Thor, "because he smashes *everything*." If anyone is set to smash the patriarchy, it's Charlotte. Emberly, our wily youngest, was born January 6, 2021, in the hours when insurrectionists stormed the U.S. Capitol, and has since overseen the reconstruction of the novel's final draft.

This book has passed through many hands in its making, including a stint on Joe Durepos's editorial cutting board. But I am glad this story finally found a home at Slant Books and that I got a chance to work again with Gregory and Suzanne Wolfe.

Finally, my biggest *thank you* goes to Samantha, who knows every high and low, every twist and turn in this journey. You've always made space for me and my "book world," and you've never stopped believing in me, no matter what. I know now what it means to grow strong on one person's belief. I know that no matter what comes our way, we'll make it. Together.

Samuel Martin (Iowa, April 2021)

This book was set in Arno Pro, designed by the American typographer,
Robert Slimbach, for Adobe Systems. Named for the river that runs through
Florence, Italy, Arno Pro is a contemporary adaptation of type styles
that flourished at the height of the Renaissance Humanist movement.

~

This book was designed by Shannon Carter, Ian Creeger, and Gregory Wolfe.
It was published in hardcover, paperback, and electronic formats
by Slant Books, Seattle, Washington.

CPSIA information can be obtained
at www.ICGtesting.com
Printed in the USA
BVHW032012020322
630389BV00001B/61

9 781639 820665